test of
TIME

BLOSSOM PEAK SERIES

Book Cover by Abigail Davies

Edited by Jenny Ayers (Swift Red Pen)

Proof Read by Emma Cook

9798991541954

Contents

To anyone who found the strength to leave *what* or *who* no longer
served you.
Sometimes strength is quiet.
But that doesn't make it less important.

Faith is a muscle.

You won't know how strong it is until it's tested.

Unknown

Prologue

Rhonan

Shots Fired

My eyes lock on the fucker pointing a gun at my daughter and the woman I love, and something inside me snaps.

I refuse to watch two more people be ripped away from me—especially after what I've been through to get to this point.

With my gun raised, I approach the back door of the cabin and slowly turn the knob, finding it unlocked.

There's yelling inside, but I won't be distracted. My focus is on getting to Ellis and Vienna before this motherfucker snaps.

I slip into a mudroom where there's a washer and dryer, coats hanging on a rack, and a water heater tucked in the corner. Then I hear a loud crash deeper inside, so I move into the hallway.

Peering around the wall, I try to pinpoint the source of the sound through a narrow view of the living room. Another man holding a gun is standing over someone on the floor, and I can see the top of Ellis's head as she crawls across the couch toward Vienna, who is now lying on the ground.

Fuck this guy.

More yelling.

Vienna sits back up on the couch.

And then noise from out front pulls the man's attention. He moves toward the front door, so I take this as my opportunity to make my move.

But I'm not slick enough.

Not fast enough.

Shots are fired.

Screaming rings out.

And I fear that yet again, fate has stepped in, hell-bent on testing my strength and proving that no matter how hard I fight, I can't stop the people I love from being taken from me in the most catastrophic ways.

Chapter 1

Rhonan

Two and a Half Months Earlier

Bad Dreams and a Threat of Penis Mutilation

"She's gone, Rhonan."

Three simple words alter my brain chemistry as I sit in the hospital chair, desperately trying to blink myself back to reality. I heard what Laney said, but it still doesn't seem real. None of this does.

This wasn't how this day was supposed to go at all.

"I'm sorry," my sister continues as tears fall down her cheeks. "But I wanted to be the one to tell you."

"Who's gone?" I need clarification because there are two people in that room I care about now, and even though losing either of them is going to kill me, I need to know which grief to brace for.

"Sarah," Laney says on a shaky breath. "She—she didn't make it."

My lungs fight to pull in air as my body launches itself from the bed. I scan my room next, focusing on my surroundings because it usually helps me snap out of the dream faster.

"Jesus," I mutter as I drag my hand down my face and swing my legs over the side of my bed, resting my elbows on my knees and my head in my hands.

It's been months since I've had that dream—the one where I'm back in the hospital the day that my daughter was born. The same day my wife died giving birth to her. But just like every other time the dream reappears, I take it as a sign to be prepared.

Something is going to happen today, so I need to be on high alert.

"Daddy!"

Ellis barrels into my room, slamming the door into the wall before launching herself into my arms.

I kiss the top of her head as I breathe her in, cherishing the feel of her locked in my embrace, especially after where my mind just took me. "Hey, sweetie."

"You didn't come kiss me goodnight like you said you would." She leans back with a pout on her lips that she's damn near perfected at the tender age of five.

"Yes, I did. You just don't remember because you were sleeping."

One of her eyebrows arches. "Are you sure?"

"Positive, Ellis. Besides, you know I wouldn't lie to you." *Not about the important things, at least.*

"You promise?" Holding out her pinky to me, she waits as I hook mine around hers.

"Pinky promise." I shake our intertwined hands up and down and then release her. "Now, it's time to get ready for school."

"Are you taking me this morning?"

"Yes, ma'am."

Jumping up and down, she bounces out of my arms and out of my room screaming, "Yay!"

And just like that, my world is back to normal.

I rake a hand through my thick hair and stand from the bed, walking over to my dresser while studying my appearance in the mirror. Scratching through my chest hair, I move my hand down to the scar on my arm that looks angrier and darker than normal today.

Seems my body is trying to remind me of multiple injuries from my past all at once.

"Did I hear that right? You're taking Ellis to school today?" Joanne, my live-in nanny, rests her hip on the door jamb and crosses her arms over her chest as I open my dresser and pull out a clean shirt.

"Yeah. I'm supposed to hit the gym with Elliot this morning anyway, so I might as well."

Joanne nods. "Okay, just wanted to make sure. That girl is great at telling stories these days, you know?"

A soft chuckle shakes my chest. "Oh, I'm completely aware."

"How was your shift?"

"Uneventful, thank God. Just a few traffic tickets for people speeding on the highway leading in and out of town. The usual."

"Glad to hear it. The moment you come home from a shift and tell me there was some actual crime committed here in Blossom Peak is the day I might just have to move back to Charlotte."

"Oh, where crime is non-existent?" I ask sarcastically. Joanne rolls her eyes before tucking her shoulder-length gray hair behind her ears. "Besides, those threats don't mean much anymore. I know you'd miss Ellis and me too much."

She snickers before pushing herself off of the door jamb. "There you go getting that big head of yours again."

"Love you too, Joanne." All I see is her back as she waves me off and retreats to the main part of the house, but I know there's a smile on her face as she does. When you live with someone for five years, you get to know them pretty well.

I like to joke that Joanne was my angel sent to earth after I lost Sarah, but I honestly believe it. I was a new dad, a widower, and a sheriff who had to report back to work at some point, with shifts that varied between nights and days. I needed help, and that's when my father and his friends—Henry, Anthony, and Brian—started asking around town for someone who could help me.

Luckily, when Henry's sister-in-law, Joanne Collins, heard my story, she instantly volunteered for the job. It was supposed to be temporary, but she stayed. She's part of our family now, and I couldn't raise my daughter or hold my life together without her.

Still, I know she'll leave me eventually.

Most women in my life do.

After a few more moments of self-contemplation, I dress in my gym clothes, mix up a protein shake, and grab my keys.

The drive to Blossom Peak Elementary is short and filled with Ellis's chatter from the back seat.

"Today is Mrs. Allen's last day," Ellis informs me for the fourteenth time since we left the house, our hands clasped together as I walk her toward the front gate of the school.

"I know, sweetie."

"I'm going to miss her. What if our new teacher isn't as nice as she is?"

"I'm sure she will be."

"But what if she's not?" Her voice wobbles and her grip tightens on my hand.

I pull Ellis to the side and crouch down until we're eye level, smoothing her hair away from her face. "Listen, I know you love Mrs. Allen. She's an amazing teacher, but she's going to have a baby, and her baby is gonna need her to be home with it."

"Him, Daddy. He's not an *it*."

I fight the urge to laugh. "Noted. But as I was saying, I'm sure they've found someone just as amazing as Mrs. Allen to spend the last few months of the school year with your class. Besides, next week is spring break. We're going to have so much fun that when you come back to school, you're going to be so excited to meet your new teacher."

"She'd better be nice. If she isn't, then I can't be nice back."

"Oh, really?"

Ellis nods confidently. "Yeah, it's the Golden Rule, Daddy. I'm sure you've heard of it."

Shaking my head, I stand upright and lead Ellis down the sidewalk again. "You know what, Ellis? I think I have." As soon as we arrive at the gate, I bend down to kiss my daughter's cheek and squeeze her tightly. "Have a good day, baby."

"I'm not a baby, Daddy. I'm five."

"You'll always be my baby girl."

"Not if you have another baby." Her eyes light up. "You should have another baby, Daddy! Like Mrs. Allen."

"That's...uh..."

Luckily, the bell rings before I can come up with a response.

Literally saved by the bell.

"Have a good day, sweetie."

"Bye, Daddy!" Ellis waves at me as she skips through the gate and runs to catch up with a few of her friends.

I blow out the breath I'd been holding.

I swear, nothing can prepare you for parenthood. There's no guide or instruction manual that tells you how to talk to them about tough topics. And of course my daughter has to be extra inquisitive. I fear for what the rest of her childhood is going to be like, especially when I can't dodge the tough questions any longer.

My phone vibrates in my pocket and as I pull it out, I see Elliot's name flash across the screen.

"What's up?"

"You still coming?" His voice carries over the noise of weights being racked on bars. He must already be at the gym.

"Yeah, just dropped off Ellis. Be there in five."

"Good. And when you get here, I need to ask you for a favor."

"I don't know. The last time I did a favor for you, you took me ring shopping for your ex-fiancée."

"Well, it's not to buy a fucking ring, that's for damn sure," he grates out. "Just hurry up."

"Calm down, Emperor Eeyore." I laugh to myself as I use one of the many names that Dilynne, Henley's younger sister, has given Elliot since his fiancé left him at the altar.

"If you want to insult me, I prefer Grumpzilla. And also...fuck you."

I bark out a laugh as I shove my phone in my pocket and head back to my truck, already bracing myself for whatever Elliot's about to drag me into.

***

"I'm sorry. You want to go *where* for *what*?" I lower the weights to my sides, gripping them in my hands between sets as I attempt to comprehend what just came out of Elliot's mouth.

"You heard me." He completes his last rep of chest flies and drops the weights to the ground, planting his hands on his hips.

"You fucking hate The Charming Bull."

"Yeah, well, I figured maybe going someplace I normally wouldn't might help me get back on the horse...or, *bull*, in this case." His pleased smirk makes me roll my eyes.

I bring the weights back to my shoulders and press them above my head, talking through my next set slightly breathless. "Look, I understand your logic, but why do I need to go with you?"

He just blinks at me for a beat. "Am I supposed to ask Fletcher? Or Henley? Everyone else is engaged or playing house. That leaves you and me, Rhonan. I need a wingman."

"You know I hated that shit when we were younger, and even more so now."

He clears his throat. "Remind me, how long has it been since you've gotten laid?"

"That's none of your damn business," I grate out as I push the weights above my head for my final rep.

"You already know how long it's been for me."

"You got left at the altar, Elliot. Nobody expects you to bounce back overnight."

"And your wife died. I think yours trumps mine, Rhonan."

The mention of Sarah brings me right back to the dream from this morning. I shake off the melancholy wave that threatens to overtake me and drop the weights to the ground.

"This isn't a fucking contest."

Elliot plants his hands on his hips. "I know. This is one friend asking another friend for a favor." He takes a few steps toward me and then drops his voice. "You and I both know that I haven't been able to...*seal the deal*," he says, flicking his eyes around us before continuing. "And it hasn't been for a lack of trying. But at this point, man, I'm starting to think Little Elliot is broken and might shrivel up and fall off."

"You call your dick Little Elliot?"

He snaps his fingers in front of my face. "Focus. That's not the point."

"Then why bring it up?" Wanting to tease him a bit more, I continue, "Exactly how little are we talking?"

His eyes narrow. "You're an ass. But just so we're clear, there's nothing fucking little about my dick, all right?"

"Then why—"

"Rhonan, I fucking need you, man."

"To go to a bar and watch women gyrate on a mechanical bull?"

"Without going into detail, yeah. It's an experiment. I figure, if I can get hard watching those girls, then at least I know I'm not broken."

I lean closer to him. "You haven't been able to get a fucking hard-on? At all?"

He avoids my eyes, gazing off to the side of the gym. Everyone around us is wearing headphones, thank God. Otherwise, they'd probably be just as disturbed by this conversation as I'm becoming.

"I have, but not *with* a woman."

I wince. "Jesus, man." Clearing my throat, I continue, "I'm becoming entirely too knowledgeable about your dick, even if you are one of my best friends."

"So I shouldn't tell you about the piercing I'm thinking of getting?"

Holding up my hand in front of his face, I fight to keep my protein shake down. "Please, for the sake of our friendship, don't."

He pushes my hand away. "Then come with me to The Charming Bull, or I'm going to make you go with me to get my dick pierced instead."

"Charming Bull it is," I say without hesitation—because I'll be damned if I bear witness to Elliot getting a needle shoved through his penis. That would make *my* dick shrivel up and fall off, for sure.

He slaps me on the shoulder. "I thought so."

"Are you not actually planning on getting your dick pierced, then? Did I just get manipulated with the threat of penis mutilation?"

He shrugs. "I mean, the thought has crossed my mind, actually. New penis, new me."

"Your dick will still be the same."

"No, he'll be bejeweled."

"For the love of God, please stop."

Elliot tosses back his head with laughter before picking up his weights again. "Let's finish this fucking workout, then decide who's driving tonight."

"I really hate you, man. You're making me spend my one night off watching women dramatize riding a fucking fake bull."

"No, I want you to show up for me like all of you fuckers have been preaching."

That lands. The past nine months have been trying for all of us, not just Elliot.

Fletcher came home for Elliot's wedding that never happened, and I found out he's been in love with my sister since we were teenagers. Now they're getting married in just a few months. While still processing that, we also learned something about Fletcher and his father that he hid from all of us. The truth sort of blew up our friendship.

For a group of friends always preaching how close we are, it became glaringly obvious that we haven't all been completely honest about personal shit we've been dealing with or leaning on each other when it matters.

Then Henley, the other fourth of our brotherhood, found out he had a kid with a woman he slept with once, and she left the baby with him and took off. He hired a nanny and ended up falling for her, but had to face some bullshit from his childhood before he could actually admit how he felt about Elodie. Now, he's so fucking lovesick it makes the rest of us wonder if he's been possessed because he's definitely not the same fucking person.

But while this has all been going on, Fletcher, Henley, and I have been keeping an eye on Elliot, trying to help him navigate his life after the woman he thought he was going to spend his life with left him. Honestly, I wasn't a fan of Tori and neither were the boys, but we tried to be supportive. We've sort of taken turns helping Elliot through the healing process, which mostly involved copious amounts of alcohol, at least for him. But over the past few months, he seems to finally be coming out of his haze, and now he's asking me to show up for him in a different way—a way that will help his dick, apparently.

I guess if that's the support he needs right now, so be it.

"Fine. All right. You've laid the guilt on thick. Just promise me that we won't stay out all night. If I do, Ellis will wake up at five in the morning, man. It never fails."

He holds out his hand for me to shake. "Deal. And hopefully, I won't have to ride home with you either since I'll be getting my own ride in some woman's hotel room or car."

Shaking his hand, I say, "For both of our sakes, I hope so too."

Chapter 2

Rhonan

The Wrong Dick Wakes Up

"This place is a fucking madhouse." I can barely hear myself think as I yell over the music and chatter of people packed all around us. Bars have never been my scene, and right now, I feel especially validated in that opinion.

Elliot leans toward me. "Your age is showing, Rhonan."

"I sure fucking hope so. This place is for people who can drink all night and still function the next day. After thirty, that ship sails."

Maybe watching him get his dick pierced wouldn't be as bad as this.

"You sound like Ross from *Friends* when he, Chandler, and Joey realize they're old after trying to hang out with their buddy from college."

"I haven't *just* realized it, Elliot...I fucking know it. I'm almost thirty-three and have a five-year-old. Peace and quiet is a luxury that I don't take for granted."

Elliot slaps me on the back before leading me over to the bar. I know I'm going to need at least one drink to take the edge off if I'm going to survive until the bull riding contest at the end of the night.

"Quit bitching and remember why we're here."

"I'm here so I don't have to watch you shove a needle through your dick willingly."

He chuckles. "Understood, but in case I haven't said so, I really do appreciate you being here." The smirk on his lips disappears as he watches a leggy brunette stroll past us and sighs. "I need to fucking move on, Rho."

"I know." I catch the bartender's eye and order us both a drink. "So, what do you need me to do? It's not like you've forgotten how to pick up women. You were practically a professional before Tori."

His eyes drop to the floor and his brows pinch together. "That's what I thought too, but something has shifted."

"What do you mean?"

Before Elliot can reply, a scream rings out behind us. Without a second thought, I rush toward the sound, reaching for a weapon I'm not carrying. As I weave through the crowd, I prepare myself for the usual bar bullshit.

Nothing surprises me more than finding a blonde face-down on the hardwood...laughing.

People around her are just staring, and I don't blame them. Her denim shorts barely cover her ass, and her entire back is exposed between two very thin strings holding her silver top together.

Since she's laughing, I'm assuming she's not seriously hurt.

Too bad she didn't land on her back because her ass definitely would have cushioned her fall.

Fucking hell.

I bend toward her just as her head pops up. Light green eyes meet mine—so green they don't look real.

Clearing my throat, I find my voice. "Ma'am? Are you all right?"

Her giggle is soft and feminine, but it's the spread of her lips in a mile-wide smile that catches my attention now. "That depends," she replies, her voice raspy in a way that makes my dick twitch. "Are you asking about my pride or my body?"

I hold out my hand to her. "How about both?"

Still laughing, she takes my hand and I help her stand, but she loses her balance and collides with my chest.

And *fuck*.

The press of her warm curves against me causes an electric current to race through my limbs, reminding me of how long it's been since a woman has been this close to me.

Her hands land on my shoulders, and she looks up at me through thick, dark lashes. Her gaze holds mine until I have to force myself to look away.

"I think my pride will be just fine, but my body might have a bruise or two." She lifts the side of her flimsy excuse for a top and rubs a red spot on her skin right at the bottom of her ribcage. I catch a glimpse of the curve of her breast before I drag my attention back to her face.

I can safely say this woman isn't wearing a bra.

"Do you know what happened?" I ask.

"I tripped on something. Someone's foot, probably. This place is packed."

I dart my gaze around the room. "Yeah, that's what I said to my friend after he convinced me to come here against my will."

Her hand drops from my shoulder and she takes a step back. "Oh, well...I'd better let you get back to your friend, then."

Twisting my head toward the bar, my eyes land on Elliot talking to a woman, but he looks uncomfortable.

"Yeah, probably a good idea," I tell her.

"Thank you again for your help..."

"Rhonan," I finish for her, reaching out my hand to shake hers, and when her hand lands in mine once more, something about it feels unexpectedly comfortable. I try not to fixate on that too much.

"Rhonan," she repeats. "I'm Vienna. Thank you for being my knight in shining armor tonight."

"No knight, I assure you." Nodding curtly, I add, "But happy to help."

The corner of her mouth lifts. "Oh, I don't know about that. Women still wish for that sort of fairytale, especially if all they've ever experienced is the evil prince." Vienna leans in closer to me and presses her lips to my cheek, her scent overwhelming me as I breathe her in. She smells like a mixture of flowers and fruit that I can't name, and for one split second, I want to fucking bathe in that smell.

"You must be one of the good ones, Rhonan," she says, taking a step back and tipping her chin to me, walking away before I can say another word.

My feet feel like cement are weighing them down because I can't move. In fact, I'm not even sure how long I stand there staring at her back until Elliot comes up to me and hands me my beer. "You all right?"

I blink myself out of my trance as an uneasiness settles in my gut. "Uh, yeah."

He tips his beer bottle in the direction that Vienna just walked.

Vienna, I repeat to myself.

"What happened to that woman?"

"She tripped, apparently." Lifting my beer to my lips, I take a long pull. "But everyone just stood around staring instead of helping her."

He slaps me on the shoulder. "Always the man stepping in to save anyone in need."

I know his comment isn't meant to cause me inner turmoil, but something about his words makes that familiar dark cloud gather around me.

You don't save everyone, though, Rhonan. That's the problem.

I swallow past the lump in my throat and steer the conversation back to him. "Who was the woman *you* were talking to?"

"Oh, she just reached for my drink instead of hers."

"Maybe it was a move. You weren't interested?"

He shakes his head. "I thought so, but...nothing." He gestures toward his crotch.

"Jesus," I mutter. "How long until this contest begins?"

"About an hour. Why?"

"I'm just wondering how much longer I'll have to listen to you talk about your junk."

Elliot glares at me before heading toward the bull ring, trying to get us a good seat. Luckily, we're able to snag a high-top table only a few rows back from the ropes, offering a prime view for my friend and his little experiment.

"Excuse me." A soft voice pulls my attention as a short blonde taps my shoulder.

"Yeah?"

She tucks a strand of her hair behind her ear as she brings her drink to her lips. "This might sound strange, but are you friends with Henley Clark?"

Elliot and I glance at each other before I nod. "I am."

The woman smiles. "I thought so. I'm actually friends with his girlfriend." She extends her hand to me. "I'm Lennon."

The name clicks instantly. "Oh, yeah. Elodie's friend from back home in Garnet Valley."

"That's me. Sorry if this is awkward, but I recognized you two from pictures she's posted and just thought I'd say hello."

"We're glad you did," Elliot interjects. "Although I'm sorry to say, Elodie isn't here with us tonight."

Lennon rolls her eyes. "Oh, trust me. I'm aware. Since she shacked up with Henley, I can barely get the girl to answer her phone."

Elliot huffs out a laugh. "Henley is the same way."

A man in a cowboy hat rushes up to Lennon and spins her around to face him. "Lennon..."

Lennon pulls back from the guy. "Leave me alone, Easton."

I take a step closer before I realize I'm doing it. "Is everything okay here?"

Easton locks eyes with me. "If Lennon would just talk to me, it would be."

Lennon glares at him. "I told you, I don't have anything to say to you."

"Well, that would be a first."

The two of them stare at one another before Lennon lets out a sigh and turns back to us. "Tell Elodie I said hello, will you?"

Elliot nods. "Of course."

"And maybe I'll see you guys soon. I think a trip to Blossom Peak could help me clear my head," she says while still glaring at Easton, and then slides away from us toward the other side of the bar.

"Fucking pain in my ass," Easton grumbles as he chases after her, leaving me and Elliot confused.

I shake off the tension-filled interaction as my mind drifts back to the pain-in-my-ass friend sitting right in front of me. "I thought of how you can pay me back for this, by the way," I say as I take another drag from my beer, my eyes casting over the crowd, assessing the room once more. Even though my ass is planted firmly in my seat, being aware of my surroundings is a habit I've picked up between my years in the Marines and law enforcement. It's so instinctual for me now that I barely notice I'm doing it until someone brings it to my attention.

"This isn't a tit for tat situation, Rho."

"It wasn't, but now it is."

Elliot groans. "Fine. What's up?"

"I need you to come to Career Day at Ellis's school next week."

"Aw, fuck. Why do I need to go when Henley and Fletcher are going? You and I know damn well that all anyone is going to care about is Fletcher, the football star."

"Doesn't matter. You're going for Ellis."

"Fine," he grumbles before bringing his beer to his mouth. "But only because I love that little girl. Not for you."

I nod in acceptance. "I can handle that."

"Speaking of handling things, how are you feeling about Fletcher and Laney's wedding coming up? I bet you can guess how I'm feeling about it," he says sarcastically.

"Look, I know you got burned, but this is one of our best friends and my sister. Does it still weird me out that they're together? Sometimes," I admit, but mostly because I just don't like thinking of my sister with anyone, let alone one of my friends. "But the truth is, I've never seen either of them happier. We don't have to like it, but we need to accept it."

Elliot sighs. "I know. It's sick, really. The way they look at each other." He grimaces, shaking his head.

Leaning in, I say, "Newsflash. You were the same way."

"God, I was so fucking stupid," he says, draining the rest of his beer.

"No, you were just hopeful." The sad thing is, I remember when I felt that way too. "I just hope it stays that way for them."

You think when you find someone that you want to spend the rest of your life with, that that's it. You'll get married and live your lives together.

No one talks about what happens when that plan doesn't work out, or how quickly your entire life can change. No one warns you what losing the love of your life will do to you, especially when you won't really have time to grieve because you have another human to care for.

My eyes drift toward a group of women standing around each other, laughing—but none of them are Vienna. The fact that I even notice makes me feel uneasy, so I focus back on the conversation. "It's easy to be optimistic until life throws some shit at you."

"You think you'll ever get married again?" Elliot asks. Given how my marriage ended and the heartache I went through, it's a question I have answered before. It's just been a while since I've had to think about my answer.

I shrug. "I honestly don't know. You know Ellis is my top priority. That little girl deserves all of me. There's not much room left for anyone else."

"Sometimes I wonder if being alone is just easier," Elliot says. "I mean, I never wanted a relationship until Tori, and look what fucking happened. I mean, hell, she even had me thinking about kids..."

I huff out a laugh. "You don't have to explain that to me, man. I get it. But for future reference, if you find yourself having to change who you are or what you want in order to be with someone, they're probably not the right person for you."

He snorts. "I know damn well those words didn't come from you. So what motivational speaker did you steal them from?"

Grief slices right through the center of my chest again. "My mom."

Elliot's grin fades. "Fuck, man. I'm—"

I hold my hand up to stop him. "Don't. No pity."

He shoves my shoulder. "You know the last fucking thing I'd give you is pity. You know how I feel about that shit."

Nodding, I continue, "I know. But honestly, it freaks me out sometimes the things I remember about her and then how I can't recall other stuff." My beer bottle meets my lips as I take a swig. "Jesus, maybe I did need to get out. Maybe Laney and Fletcher's wedding has got me all up in my head more than I thought."

Elliot leans forward. "See? That's why I needed you here tonight, Rhonan. You fucking understand where my head is at more than Fletcher or Henley. You get what it's like to experience an endless spiral of thoughts that make you doubt yourself."

"I might, but it doesn't mean they don't want to see you move past this either, man. We all do."

Before I can say more, the DJ comes over the speakers, announcing the start of the bull riding contest. My eyes land back on Elliot. "I thought you said we had an hour."

"I guess not." Elliot rubs his hands together. "Fuck. Here we go," he continues, dropping his eyes to his crotch. "Don't let me down, fucker."

"Jesus Christ," I mutter to myself.

I only have to be here for a little while longer and then I can go home to my life—the one I've created that leaves the least room for disappointment.

***

"Anything?" My voice is hopeful as I glance over at my friend.

Sighing, he drags a hand down his face in defeat. "Nothing."

"Not even a twitch?"

"Nope."

"Fuck."

"Our next contestant is ready! Can we give her some encouragement, folks?" The crowd cheers in response to the DJ's announcement.

Elliot and I turn back to the mechanical bull—and freeze.

"Is that..."

"Fuck my life," Elliot grumbles.

"Let's do this, bitches!" Dilynne, Henley's younger sister and Elliot's nemesis, screams over the chaos just as the mechanical bull lurches to life. "Yee-fucking-haw!"

"What are the chances?" I ask.

"Yup. It's official. Someone upstairs fucking hates me," Elliot mutters, but he doesn't move from his seat, his eyes locked on Dilynne as she rolls her hips with the bull. I glance over at my friend, his jaw locked tight and his eyes narrowed, and for the life of me, I can't understand why he's still sitting here.

My attention moves back to Dilynne tossing her head back, shouting over the music. I take out my phone and snap a picture of her, just in case I need it for blackmail someday. Only a few seconds later, she gets whipped off the bull in a quick jolt. The crowd rings out with cheers and applause, and as I look over at Elliot, I watch him stand and adjust his junk before slamming down the rest of his beer and walking toward the bar.

Wait. Did he just...

"Let's hear it for Dilynne, everyone!" the DJ shouts, cutting through my thoughts.

Before I think better of it, I pull out my phone and open my text thread with my sister.

Me: *Do you know where your best friend is right now?*

Her response is instant.

Laney: *Oh God. Why? Is she in jail?*

Me: *No, and I'm not on duty, FYI. She's riding a bull at The Charming Bull.*

Laney: *WHAT? How do you know that?*

Me: *Because I'm here and witnessing it with my own eyes.*

Laney: *Pics or it didn't happen.*

I exit out of our text exchange and attach the picture of Dilynne.

Laney: *See? This is what happens when I get engaged and can't supervise her anymore.*

Me: *You're not her babysitter.*

Laney: *I know. But wait. What are YOU doing at The Charming Bull?*

Me: *I'm here with Elliot for emotional support. He thinks his dick is broken.*

Laney: *What???*

Me: *Long story.*

Cheering interrupts my focus as Dilynne hops up from the ground, hands raised in the air. Then I see who's up next.

Vienna.

Me: *Gotta go.*

Laney: *What? You're just going to leave me hanging like that? What about Elliot's dick?*

Me: *That's what she said.*

I envision her eye roll.

Laney: *You're so immature.*

Me: *You love me.*

Laney: *I do. See you soon! Hope you both score!*

I don't give my sister's last text much thought because now I'm focused on the blonde smiling as she listens to the employee explain the procedures for mounting the bull. If I didn't know any better, I'd say she looks nervous. But given how far I am from her, it's hard to tell.

The DJ announces Vienna as she swings her legs over the bull. "Our next rider is ready! Give it up for Vienna!"

Vienna adjusts her grip on the rope and then the horn buzzes, signaling the start of her ride. She laughs as the bull starts out slow, and within seconds, she's being whipped and spun around. It's tortuous to watch as her hips swivel with the motion of the bull, but when it turns too quickly to the right, Vienna loses her grip and goes flying off, landing on her back on the cushioned mat below.

At least she didn't land face-down this time.

The crowd is a mixture of applause and boos, but Vienna pops up from the mat with a smile on her face while struggling to walk across the ring to the exit. When she finally makes it out, she twists around as if she's looking for someone, and then suddenly, she disappears.

I pop up from my stool instantly. "What the..."

The same screech I heard earlier rings out, and I'm headed in her direction again, finding her laughing on the ground for a second time this evening, but this time flat on her back, gripping her stomach with her eyes closed as she giggles.

Fighting the quirk in my lips, I stare down at her. "You know, I'm beginning to think you like being on the ground."

Her eyes open and lock onto mine, but she's still fucking smiling.

The lift of her lips sparks my own.

"And I'm beginning to think that my shoes are the reason I can't stay standing tonight." She takes my hand when I offer it, and I help pull her up. She brushes her hair from her face as our gazes remain locked. But as soon as she attempts to take a step forward, she winces. Bending forward, she lifts her foot from the ground, rolling it around. "God, that fall hurt my ankle."

My brows draw together. "Can you walk?"

"Yeah, it's just tender."

"You should probably take your shoe off and see if it's swelling."

A wince passes over her face. "It's fine."

"Is that your ankle talking," I ask, "or your ego?"

Her glare makes me want to smirk again, but I keep my composure. "Maybe." She hisses. "God, it really hurts." Before I realize what I'm doing, I'm hoisting this woman into my arms and carrying her across the bar back to our table. "What the...Rhonan!"

Ignoring her, I carefully set her down on a stool.

"That wasn't necessary," she says, folding her arms across her chest.

"Well, it's done. So what are you going to do about it?"

Her eyes narrow, but she doesn't argue. After a beat, she actually surprises me when she says, "I guess I should say thank you, but forgive me for being taken aback by that little display."

"You're welcome. Now, shall we take off your boots to prevent any other injuries tonight?"

After a beat of contemplation, she sticks her foot out toward me. I take a seat next to her, prop her foot in my lap, and make careful work of removing her boot.

"Fine. Although, I've gotta say, I didn't think this is how my night would end up."

"And how is that?" I ask her.

"With a handsome stranger tending to me," she says, a playful grin on her lips.

I try not to focus on the comment about my looks, and instead, slide her sock down her foot to examine her ankle. Her skin is silky and soft, carrying that same floral scent I noticed earlier. Must be a lotion or something because I'd expect her foot to smell like...well, a foot.

"My instinct is to help someone when they've fallen. Most people would do the same, but apparently they aren't in this bar tonight." Lifting my eyes to hers, I continue, "But are you sure that booze wasn't also a factor?"

"Why?"

"I'm just wondering how much liquid courage you have to ingest in order to do that." I motion toward the bull.

She plants her hand on her hip. "I'll have you know I've only had one drink tonight—a vodka soda."

"So, if I gave you a breathalyzer test, you'd pass?"

"Do you have one in your pocket or something?"

"If I had my uniform on, I would."

Her eyes widen in understanding and she snaps her fingers. "Oh..." she says, drawing out the word. "You're a cop. Now the hero complex makes sense."

"I don't have a hero complex," I say a little too defensively. "I just...react when people need help. It's hard to turn that off."

"As I've experienced for myself twice tonight."

My hands start rubbing over her ankle instinctually, and then her eyes close as she lets out a little moan that makes my dick stiffen in my jeans.

What the fuck are you doing, Rhonan? Has the one beer gone straight to your head?

"Oh, that feels good." Her voice takes on a sultry note that has more blood rushing to my cock.

Nope. Everything about this woman is going straight to my dick.

But tonight wasn't supposed to be about *my* dick.

I definitely didn't see that coming.

"So, why didn't the friends you're here with come to your rescue?" I ask.

"Because I'm not here with anyone."

My shoulders tense up as my hands freeze. "Wait. You're here all by yourself?"

"Yup."

I arch a brow. "Some might call that dangerous."

She purses her lips, but there's a teasing lift to them. "You say dangerous, I say liberating."

"Liberating..." I repeat, narrowing my eyes at her, fighting to understand what the hell is going on in this woman's mind.

And that's a first for me because I can't remember the last time I actually wanted to know what a woman was thinking.

She leans in closer to me, resting her elbow on the table. "Yup. And freeing, therapeutic..." Her eyes dip down to my mouth for a beat. "Maybe overdue as well."

My gaze drops to her lips. "Overdue, huh?"

Her smile falters, but she recovers quickly as our gazes return to one another. "Let's just say I'm trying something new when it comes to living my life, and I'm still trying to find my footing—both literally and figuratively," she jokes, pointing to her shoes.

Our eyes remain locked for so long, it takes me a moment to realize that Elliot has walked up beside me. I turn my attention to him and find him watching us, irritation written across his face. His eyes drop pointedly to Vienna's foot in my lap, and I carefully lower it, handing Vienna her shoe. "No swelling. Just...take it easy."

She winks at me as she shoves her boot back on. "Thanks, Doctor."

Elliot arches a brow at me. "Did I miss something?"

"This is Vienna," I tell him, reaching for my beer bottle, only to find it empty. I don't even remember finishing it, but that explains why I'm feeling out of sorts.

Elliot eyes me curiously before turning to Vienna. "Nice to meet you."

"Likewise." She flashes him the same smile she's given me multiple times this evening, but for some reason, I don't like him being on the receiving end of it.

"Where'd you wander off to earlier?" I ask Elliot.

"Decided I needed something stronger after watching Dilynne ride that fucking bull." His comment makes me pause, but he shakes his head and responds before I can speak. "Just...don't worry about it."

"Well, the contest isn't over. Not all hope is lost, right?"

Nodding, he clears his throat. "Yeah. I'm gonna go up to the ropes so I can see better. You good here?" He darts his eyes over to Vienna and then back to me, arching a brow.

I glance back at her just as she licks her lips and pulls her bottom lip between her teeth. The move sends a surge of adrenaline racing through me, centering between my legs. God, it's been so long since my body has reacted to a woman like this that I'm having trouble processing it. "Yeah, I'm, uh...good, man."

"If you say so." Chuckling, he leaves us alone, and I slide my eyes back to Vienna.

"You can go with him if you want. I'll be fine on my own," she says.

"I'm not sure about that. If you fall again, who will be there to pick you up?"

The corner of her mouth lifts as she shrugs. "Well, there's no time like the present to figure out how to do that on my own."

Silence rests between us as I consider her words. I'm getting the sense that this woman is far out of her comfort zone tonight, but she seems to be embracing it.

And fuck... It's sexy. Admirable. Interesting.

Maybe I can learn something from her in that respect, too.

"So, what were we talking about again?" I lift my water to my lips and empty the glass as cheers ring out for the next woman who just mounted the mechanical bull.

"Me trying not to fall on my ass while doing things way out of my comfort zone."

"Is that what the bull riding was about?"

She laughs softly. "Kind of. I've always wanted to try it, so when I saw the flyer at a gas station, I took it as a sign. Sometimes it's the little opportunities that end up meaning the most, you know? I just felt like I couldn't pass this one up."

A flyer at a gas station, huh? "Are you from around here, then?"

She huffs out a laugh. "Not at all."

"Where's home?"

Her head tilts to the side. "Far from here. What about you? You a local who comes to every bull riding contest?"

I push a hand through my hair and adjust my flannel on my shoulders. "Ha. That would be a no. I live about thirty minutes from here. I just came tonight for my buddy," I say, gesturing toward the direction that Elliot went. "He's had a rough year, so I'm supposed to be his wingman."

"The Maverick to his Goose?"

"Something like that."

"I love *Top Gun*," Vienna says wistfully. "And the second movie they made? *Top Gun: Maverick*? Even better than the first, in my opinion."

"I haven't seen it yet."

Her mouth drops open. "What? Oh, you need to change that immediately."

My chest shakes with silent laughter. "You seem to feel very strongly about that."

"I insist." Her smile is ever present. "Miles Teller *and* Glen Powell in one movie?" She starts to fan herself dramatically. "That's a why-choose situation I wouldn't mind finding myself in."

"Not sure those are selling points to get *me* to watch it," I say, teasing her, feeling my smile grow the longer we go back and forth.

Her energy is so vibrant and so honest.

It's addictive, to the point that I feel like I could sit here and talk to her for hours.

When's the last time that happened, Rhonan?

The night I met Sarah.

"Well, Jennifer Connelly is also in it," she says, pulling me back to the conversation.

I shrug. "She's fine. I'm just not really into celebrities."

Seems I'm far more interested in sassy blondes at the moment.

She sighs, resting her chin in her hand, elbow poised on the table. "Maybe flying a fighter plane will be my next liberating experience."

My eyes drop to her mouth. "That might be a little trickier to cross off your list than riding a mechanical bull."

She leans in closer to me. "Maybe...but the adrenaline rush?" She licks her lips. "I bet there's nothing like it."

My heart is pounding in my chest, and my dick is painfully aware of how close she is to me right now. All I'd have to do is lean over just a few more inches and our mouths would connect.

Casual sex has never been my thing. It's been almost a year since I've had sex, and there have only been two women since Sarah. *Two.*

The guilt still eats at me sometimes.

But there's something about Vienna that is drawing me to her. She's bubbly, quick-witted, and fucking gorgeous. Her smile is infectious, and her energy is contagious. Plus, she's clearly strong. It takes guts to go somewhere new, all alone, and participate in something without fear of what others will think of you.

I fucking like that.

A lot.

And the way she keeps licking her lips is making me wonder just what those lips would taste like against my own.

I lower my voice so only the two of us can hear. "There's other things you could do to chase that adrenaline, you know?"

Her eyes light up. "Like what?"

"Like sitting here, talking to a complete stranger for a while."

She wrinkles her nose, but there's a playful smile pulling at her lips. "Not sure I can classify you as a stranger anymore. I mean, I know your name, and you've rubbed my ankle. I feel like we're way past the stranger danger."

"Funny. I was thinking you're the dangerous one."

Her brows knit together. "How so?"

Without thinking, I reach out and tuck a strand of her hair behind her ear, dragging my index finger down her cheek before pulling away. "Just a feeling."

"Huh." Her tongue darts out to lick her lips again. "I don't think that's a bad thing."

"You don't?"

She shakes her head. "No. I'm more about looking forward these days. You can't do that if you're still looking back, you know? Sometimes that requires us to do things we wouldn't normally do."

Fuck. Her words resonate with me harder than they should. "I understand that more than you can imagine."

She brings her water to her mouth, biting the straw between her teeth. "Of course, it's easy for me to say that, but living it is something different entirely."

"Good at dishing out advice, but not taking it?"

She shakes her head. "Actually, I'm not good at either. Lately, I feel like I've made so many mistakes, I don't even know if I'm learning from them anymore."

I open my mouth to respond, but the sudden roar of cheering from the bull riding pen drowns out our conversation. When the noise subsides, our eyes meet again.

She has a look on her face like she wants to say something, but she's holding back. Instead, she moves to stand, as if to leave.

My gut screams at me not to let her.

I reach out quickly, placing my hand on her arm.

Her eyes lift to mine.

"Can I buy you another drink?" I ask, leaning closer so she can hear me.

"I actually didn't plan on drinking any more tonight."

"Great," I say. "Me neither."

She laughs. "What? Then why did you..."

"Soda is a drink, right?"

"It is."

"We could get some soda, play some pool..." I toss my head in the direction of the pool tables on the other side of the bar.

Her spine straightens as she studies me. "Pool?"

"Yeah. You know, billiards."

She chuckles. "Billiards?"

I pinch the bridge of my nose, feeling myself grow antsy. "Fuck. Sorry, I don't know why I said that..."

My attempt at spending a few more minutes with this woman is the furthest thing from smooth, and the longer this silence stretches between us, the more I feel like a fucking fool.

I'm rusty in this department. Flirting? Bantering with women?

The last time I did that was when I met my late wife.

"Rhonan..." she says, waiting for me to meet her gaze before she speaks again.

I lift my head, lock my eyes with hers, and then that smile of hers reappears. "Vienna..."

Reaching out, she cups the side of my face. "I would love to have soda and play pool with you."

***

Vienna smacks her lips playfully after taking a drink from her soda. "Man, those bubbles are gonna go straight to my head."

A laugh slips out of me. "Be careful. I have no problem rescuing you a third time tonight, if need be. But I'd like to avoid any more incidents."

She shoves me playfully. "Be nice."

"I am. By letting you take another shot after you missed your first one."

"That's because my stick didn't even connect with the ball."

After Vienna agreed to play pool with me, she went to the restroom while I ordered us two Cokes and secured a pool table in the corner of The Charming Bull, far enough away from the bull riding that we could actually hear each other talk, but not so far that I couldn't keep an eye on Elliot standing along the ropes, still hoping that his dick might react to a woman tonight.

Once Vienna found me, I racked the balls and started the game, only to learn that Vienna has never played pool.

"I still can't believe you've never played before."

"Why is that?"

"You just seem like someone who would pretend not to know how to play and then end up kicking my ass."

She leans forward over the edge of the table, giving me the perfect view of her cleavage as she lines up her stick to the cue ball, draws it back, and slams it forward, knocking her first ball into the corner pocket flawlessly.

Her brow arches. "Who? Me?"

My eyes narrow as I watch her stand back up and rest her hip against the table. "So you *do* know how to play."

"I played a bit in college. I'm no professional, but I can definitely hold my own." Lifting her soda to her lips, she smirks around the straw.

And there goes my dick getting excited again.

"Anything else I should know you're good at?"

"Nothing I want to reveal just yet."

Nodding, I scour the table and find Vienna's next logical shot. To my surprise, she attempts a different one and sinks that ball into the side pocket. "But come on," she adds, glancing at me over her shoulder. "There's got to be something you're good at that you like to keep tucked close to the vest."

"Actually, there is."

"Care to share since you know mine now?"

I watch her set up for her next shot, but this one bounces a little too far to the right of the pocket, making it my turn finally. "Blackjack."

"So you're a gambler?"

"I mean, not really. My best friends and I learned how to play in high school, so now that's our thing when we get together. Some buddies play golf or poker... We play blackjack."

"I love that. It's different."

"My buddy's sister calls us The Blackjack Brotherhood." Shaking my head, I mutter, "I hate it."

"Oh, come on. That's prime T-shirt material. Can you imagine the looks and questions you'd get if you all wore that out in public? I'm sure women would be foaming at the mouth to know why you call yourselves that." There's a teasing lilt to her voice.

"Not sure women are looking for that, but to each their own. At least it's not golf. I never understood that hobby. It takes way too fucking long to play anyway, and I don't like being away from my daughter for that long."

Her eyes widen. "You—you have a daughter?"

My pulse spikes as I realize I just shared that with her, a person I barely know and yet, feel like I know very well.

"Yeah, I do."

"How old is she?"

"Five."

Her smile is instant. "Such a fun age."

"It really is. Although, some days I feel like she's five going on fifteen. She's extremely observant and never forgets anything you say."

Vienna laughs. "I bet she's headstrong too."

"What makes you say that?"

Her eyes move up and down my body. "I just get the sense that you wouldn't let her grow up unaware of what she does and does not deserve." The compliment catches me off guard, especially since I'm not sure where her conclusion came from. But then she continues. "She's probably just as bossy as you too."

"Oh, you have no idea how bossy I can be." The words flow out of me freely, and I don't miss the way Vienna's eyes darken as she absorbs them.

"Pretty sure I got a glimpse earlier." She kicks her foot out at me. "Remember?"

"That was just me taking the proper precautions."

"Well, it's a good thing you did. Otherwise, we wouldn't be here, huh?" Our eyes remain locked until Vienna breaks our stare and gestures toward the pool table. "Your turn."

Shaking off the tension building between us, I step forward and line up my next shot. The ball drops cleanly into the pocket. "So what is it that you do, Vienna?"

"For work?"

I nod.

"I'm actually moving for a new job...switching careers, you could say."

"By choice or..."

She huffs out a laugh. "Definitely by choice."

"So, what's the new job?"

"Teaching," she replies.

"I can see that," I say as I stand tall after missing my next shot. Vienna moves around the table to line up her next attempt.

"Really?"

"Yeah, I think it definitely fits your personality."

Vienna smiles as she tucks her hair behind her ear, almost shy about receiving the compliment. "Thank you. I've been working toward this for a long time, so to say I'm excited is an understatement."

"Is this another thing you're doing that's related to trying things you never have before?"

The corner of her mouth lifts. "You could say that." She rests her hip against the pool table. "You know, earlier I didn't get the chance to ask you what would *you* do to chase some adrenaline, Rhonan?"

As I round the table to stand within a few inches of her, she stares up at me. My eyes linger on her mouth for far too long before I lean in closer and line my lips up to her ear, letting the lust racing through my body fuel my actions for a change. "I'm not really the adrenaline-chasing type of guy anymore, Vienna."

She clears her throat, pursing her lips as I lean back. "Anymore?"

I nod. "I used to be. Now that I'm a father, the last thing I would do is intentionally participate in risky behavior."

Vienna's head bobs up and down while my heart races. It's rare I would divulge something so honest to a stranger, but I guess she was right—we're not exactly strangers anymore.

"Makes sense."

Without thinking about what I'm doing, I reach out and tuck the other side of Vienna's hair behind her ear before dragging my finger down her jaw and back up, studying the lines in her face—how warm her skin is, how soft and feminine her entire demeanor is, and how her skin pebbles under my touch with each pass of my fingers.

Seems I'm not the only one affected here.

"When you have a kid, life is no longer about what *you* want. My priority is looking out for her."

"She's lucky to have someone putting her first like that."

Our eyes bounce back and forth between one another.

"It makes times like this even more difficult."

Her throat bobs as she swallows. "Times like this?"

I cup her chin and drag my thumb over her bottom lip. "Yeah. When life tests your priorities, sending you temptation to abandon your carefully curated rules."

Her eyes move down to my mouth. "I—I know the feeling."

I watch her tongue dart out to wet her lips before I lift my gaze back to hers. "Vienna..."

"Yeah?"

My body starts leaning forward, slowly, while fantasizing about what this woman's lips would feel like against mine. Her lashes start to flutter close, as if she's anticipating the kiss. My pulse starts to pound in my ears. And when I'm less than an inch from her mouth, so close to finally tasting temptation, a metaphorical bucket of water is dropped on our moment, dousing the flames burning between us.

"You ready to leave?" Elliot's voice penetrates through the haze clouding my rational thoughts.

Vienna practically jumps from her spot against the pool table, brushing her hair out from behind her ears. "I, uh...need to use the restroom," she announces before taking off in that direction.

I scowl at my friend. "Jesus, Elliot."

He holds both hands up in the air. "Sorry. Was I interrupting something?"

"Did it fucking look like it?" I snap.

He arches a brow. "Easy, Rho. I didn't realize you were intent on taking the night further with that one."

"I..."

Was that my intention?

Hell, I know for a fact that I wouldn't have let things get too far. But a kiss? The feel and taste of Vienna's lips on mine?

Yeah, I definitely wanted that.

"I wasn't. But there was *something* there, and you just fucking barged over here—"

"My bad," he says, cutting me off. "Fine. I can order another drink if you have some unfinished business..."

My eyes dart over to the bathroom, waiting for Vienna to reappear while I war with my decision.

Casual hookups aren't my thing, but I'm intrigued by this woman like I haven't experienced in years.

Getting her phone number wouldn't hurt anything, right?

I just know that if I don't, I'm always going to wonder 'what if.'

"I'll meet you over at the bar," I mutter, jerking my head in that direction.

"Don't take forever," he grumbles as he saunters off.

That's the funny thing about time, though. Sometimes it passes in a blur, other times it stretches on endlessly—especially when you're waiting for someone who never returns.

Chapter 3

Rhonan

One Week Later

Chasing Dogs & The Shock of My Life

"Good morning." Joanne's voice carries through the house as I walk past her into the kitchen, desperately in search of coffee. I didn't get home from work until after one in the morning, but I still have to look alive for Ellis's career day today.

My only response is a grunt as I take a mug from the cupboard and pour in the sweet nectar of life.

"Is something wrong?" Joanne asks, her voice closer now than it was before.

When I peer up over my mug, I find her standing on the other side of the kitchen counter, brow furrowed.

"Just tired."

"Are you sure that's all it is?"

"What are you trying to ask me, Joanne?" I don't mean to sound irritated, but lately, that's just how I feel.

Her look of concern morphs into one of annoyance. "Forgive me for wanting to know what died and crawled up your behind this past week."

I've been asking myself the same thing, but I'm not sure I'm ready to face reality. "What do you want from me?"

"Well, for starters, more than a grunt when I greet you in the morning."

Sighing, I set my mug on the counter. "Look, I'm just...in a funk. I can't explain it."

Can't, or don't want to, Rhonan?

"Well, your daughter has picked up on it, so you need to snap out of it."

Fuck.

I try really hard not to project my emotions onto my kid. Everything I've read about parenting suggests being honest about your feelings with your child, but Ellis is also five. She doesn't need to feel like her world is off balance because I feel that way, and there's only so much I can share with her that is age appropriate.

Truth be told, I've been off balance since Sarah died, and I'm not sure if that will ever change, but this past week has been a little more overwhelming than normal, to say the least.

"What did she say?" I ask.

"She asked if you've been hanging out with Uncle Elliot. Said you started acting grumpy like him."

"And what did you tell her?"

"That you're probably just tired from work and our trip to Charlotte last week."

After my night out, I slipped into dad mode for a few days while Ellis was on spring break from school and made sure to get some quality time with her. We made a trip to Charlotte to visit the science center and zoo. Fletcher and Laney joined us, since he still owns a house there that he uses during the NFL season, and Joanne took advantage of the trip to visit with her daughter. But four days was all I got before I had to report back to work.

Being a sheriff in a small town like Blossom Peak isn't very eventful, which is ideal, but it also means that our staff is small. The station has six deputies total, and only three of us on shift at any given time. So that means we all have to take turns taking time off, and certainly for long stretches of days all at once.

"I'm sorry. I don't know why I'm in this funk, all right? But I'll try to keep it in check."

Joanne nods. "That's all I ask. Now that that's settled, I've been meaning to ask—have you met our new neighbor?"

I've been in such a daze that I completely forgot the house next door has a new tenant. "Not yet. Have you?"

"Well, she just moved in yesterday. I caught her while she was unloading a few things from her car. Seems nice. Definitely not from around here."

"How can you tell?"

"Her car."

"What about it?"

"Let's just say she's entirely unprepared for the snow we get with the Mercedes she's driving."

"Ah, so high maintenance. Anything else I should know?" I ask, picking my mug back up from the counter.

"She has a dog."

"Okay..."

"Doesn't seem to be trained."

"How do you figure?"

Joanne chuckles. "It looked like the dog was taking her for a walk instead of the other way around."

"Daddy?"

My daughter's sweet voice pulls my attention to the hallway where she stands, still rubbing the sleep from her eyes while clutching her blanket.

"Good morning, sweetie."

She walks toward me, slowly. "Are you mad today, Daddy?"

My eyes meet Joanne's as she arches a brow at me, knowingly.

Crouching down to her level, I beckon my daughter toward me. "No, baby. Come here." When she finally lands in my arms, I give her a squeeze, letting the guilt plaguing me melt away from her warmth. "I'm sorry Daddy has been grumpy lately."

"You've been acting like Uncle Elliot."

"I know. But you didn't do anything wrong, okay? Daddy is just tired."

"You're always tired." She leans back and studies my face. "Auntie Laney has cream you can use to make your face look better. You should get some from her."

Joanne snorts and then heads toward the sink to deposit her mug while I mentally make a note to talk to my sister about what she discusses with my five-year-old.

"Thank you, but I'll be okay. Are you excited for today?"

Ellis's eyes light up when she remembers what today is. "It's Career Day!"

"Right. Everyone will be there, just like you asked."

"Even Uncle Fletcher?"

"Yup. And he's bringing Carolina Thunder stickers for everyone."

"Yay!" She bounces right out of my arms. "I can't wait! I'm gonna get dressed!"

"What do you want for breakfast, Ellis?" Joanne asks before she runs to her room.

"Can I have pancakes with rainbow sprinkles today?" The look of desperation she gives me with pouty lips and batting eyelashes feels like a warning of what the teenage years will be like.

"Since it's a special day, I think that's all right," I reply.

Joanne nods before pulling dishes from the cabinet.

When my daughter is out of earshot, I ask my nanny, "Does she give you that look every morning?"

"Nope. She knows better than to try that if you're not around."

"So, you're telling me that my daughter knows I'm a pushover?"

Joanne smiles as she heads toward the pantry. "Yup and just wait until she gets older and *really* wants something."

"Great," I mutter as I bring my mug to my lips again and move into the living room, intent on enjoying my coffee in front of the bay window while making a mental list of the tasks I need to get done in the front yard this week. My truck needs a wash, the grass is ready to be mowed, and I promised Ellis that we'd repaint the mailbox together.

As I glance out the front window, movement next door catches my eye. A woman with blonde hair in a red dress briskly walks to her car, tossing a few bags in the passenger seat. When she heads back toward the house, my eyes land on her face and my stomach drops.

It can't be.

My head whips between the kitchen where Joanne and Ellis are chatting and back in the direction of my new neighbor's house, wondering if my eyes are playing tricks on me.

She hustles back down the driveway and dips inside of her car, cranking the engine and barely waiting for it to start before backing out onto the street. I try to catch another glimpse of her face through her window, but she speeds out of her driveway before I can, taking off like someone's chasing her.

I rub my eyes because I have to be seeing things. There's no way that the woman I've been thinking about all week is now my new neighbor.

Right?

***

I'm in my bathroom, getting ready to put gel in my hair, the glob resting in my palm, when a scratch from outside makes me freeze.

"What the fuck was that?"

It happens again, this time followed by a whine.

Like lightning, I race out of my room, down the hallway, and out to the backyard deck, searching the yard for the source of the noise.

And then I see it.

A German Shepherd puppy is digging up one of the rose bushes on the side of my house.

"Hey, you little shit!" As soon as the dog hears me, its head pops up, tongue lolling and a nose covered in dirt. "Get out of here!"

It doesn't budge. Our eyes stay locked, each waiting for the other to make the first move.

I'm supposed to leave for Ellis's career day in five minutes. Joanne took her to school this morning so I could take care of a few things around the house before heading for the school. I don't have time for this shit. If I'm late because of this dog, and my daughter thinks I'm not going to show up for her, I'll never hear the end of it.

"Come here, puppy," I say sweetly, slowly walking toward the dog. Once I'm within five feet of it, it takes off.

"Oh no you don't!" I run after it, darting around the patio table as the dog weaves between the chairs. I chase it through the flower beds, kicking up more dirt in the process. And once I think I have it cornered beneath Ellis's playset, it fakes me out and slips through my hands as it darts right between my legs. The dog races to the waist-high fence before sliding through the hole it must have dug to get here, straight into my new neighbor's backyard.

The same neighbor who might be the woman I wanted to kiss last week, but I don't trust my eyes when I'm this fucking exhausted.

Apparently, Joanne was right about the dog. It's definitely a menace.

I grab a few bricks from a pile in the corner of the yard that I've been saving for a project and toss them in the hole, hoping they'll prevent the dog from returning to my yard for now, and then run into the house. I grab my keys and scrub my hands clean of hair gel, dirt, and dog fur. Then I rush to my truck, hoping I don't make a scene when I inevitably show up to my daughter's school later than planned.

***

I jog through the doors of the cafeteria, barely catching my breath before I hear Ellis's voice.

"Daddy!" She wiggles out of Fletcher's arms and runs across the room to me.

My entire friend group is already here for my daughter's first career day, and I'm the one who's late.

Stupid fucking dog.

Fletcher and Henley are mid-conversation with Laney and Elodie, and Elliot and Dilynne are standing off to the side, not arguing for once. But Ellis has her hands on my face, forcing me to lock eyes on her. "You made it, Daddy! I thought you weren't coming."

"I told you I would be here, sweetie. I just had a little trouble getting out of the house."

"How come? Did you lock yourself inside?"

Sweet girl. I momentarily debate educating her on how that's not possible, but I quickly decide this is not the time. "No, Ellis. There was a dog in our yard."

Her eyes light up. "A dog? Can we keep it?"

"No, sweetie. It actually belongs to our new neighbor."

"Was it a boy or a girl?"

"I don't know."

"Well, we need to find out," she declares as we reach my friends.

"Maybe later," I tell her before blowing out a breath and locking eyes with my sister. "I didn't think I was gonna make it." Setting Ellis down on the ground, I readjust my uniform and belt while still trying to regulate my blood pressure.

"You look like you just ran a marathon," my sister says to me, eyeing me up and down.

"Actually, I was running after a damn dog."

"You said a bad word, Daddy," Ellis scolds.

"Sorry, sweetie."

"I didn't know that was in your job description," Elliot says with a smirk.

"It's not." I force a hand through my hair, trying to tame it since I never got to style it. "It's my new neighbor's dog, and it happens to be a bit of an escape artist."

"Wait. You have a new neighbor? Someone is renting that house now?" Laney asks.

"Yeah, and it's..." My voice trails off as my eyes lock onto the beautiful blonde in a red dress at the front of the cafeteria picking up a microphone before her voice drowns everyone out.

My stomach drops.

You've got to be fucking kidding me.

"Good morning, everyone," Vienna says brightly to the crowd. "If you could all take your seats, please, we will begin Career Day in just a few minutes."

The teachers guide the students to sit in their class groups.

Others begin to follow, but I'm frozen in place as everything around me grows fuzzy and my pulse roars in my ears.

Henley lays his hand on my shoulder, his brows drawn together. "Dude. You okay?"

"Fuck. My. Life."

"What's going on?" Fletcher asks.

"That's Ms. Lewis!" Ellis shouts, tugging on my hand. "That's my new teacher, Daddy."

"She's—*she's* your substitute?" I stutter, blinking myself out of my trance and dropping my eyes to my daughter.

"Yes. She's so nice and pretty. Isn't she pretty, Daddy?"

My eyes land back on Vienna as Henley, Elliot, and Fletcher are all staring at me.

Henley clears his throat. "Uh, Rhonan?"

"Go take your seat, Ellis," I say to my daughter. Luckily, she runs off before I close my eyes, blow out a breath and mutter, "No fucking way."

"Care to fill us in?" Henley adds.

"That's the woman I..." I trail off because how do I explain who she is?

She's not a one-night stand. Hell, we didn't even kiss. No, she's just the first woman who's intrigued me since my wife died, then she ghosted me in a bar.

How the fuck do I explain that without admitting it fucking sucked?

"Wait. She's the one from The Charming Bull, isn't she?" Elliot interjects. "Didn't she go to the bathroom and never come back?"

"Thank you for that," I grate out, glaring at my friend while cursing my fucking luck.

"Shit. She ghosted you?" Fletcher asks.

Sighing, I nod. "Yeah. And apparently, she also happens to be my new neighbor."

"Fuuuck," Fletcher says, shoving his hands in his pockets. "But wait. How is she..."

Gesturing toward the front of the cafeteria, I say, "Well apparently, she's *also* Ellis's teacher for the next three months," I finish as the events from the past week and this morning all come together, leaving me to wonder how the hell the rest of the school year is going to pan out given that I've almost kissed my daughter's teacher...and she rejected me.

Henley lets out a low whistle. "I'm still trying to process the fact that *you* almost hooked up with someone."

I push a hand through my hair again, not even worried about what it looks like anymore, since this entire day just turned into a shit show of epic proportions.

"He was supposed to be there to support *me*, and then he ends up being the one to hit it off with someone," Elliot says.

My eyes find his. "Hey, I *was* there for you. It's not my fault that your dick is broken and mine's not. But again... We didn't even kiss. She left when we almost did."

"Maybe your breath smelled bad," Henley offers.

I shove his shoulder. "Fuck you. That wasn't it."

But the truth needles at me anyway. Hell, it's been over a week and I'm still wondering what happened. I thought we were on the same page. But apparently, I've been out of the dating game for so long I can't even read the signals anymore. And after I got home, that familiar guilt from wanting someone else crept up like it always does.

Elliot glares at me. "My dick is *not* broken, and would you mind shutting the fuck up about it?"

Fletcher and Henley look toward one another. "What the hell did we miss?" Fletcher asks.

I sigh, pinching the bridge of my nose. "Look, this isn't the time or the place to have this conversation, so can we all just take a seat and get through this day, please?"

"Fine. But you're telling us more during blackjack tonight," Fletcher says, nudging Henley's arm with his shoulder. "This is what happens now that we're in relationships. Elliot is having problems with his dick, Rhonan's actually talking to women, and we know nothing about it."

"I haven't had enough coffee or sleep to handle the three of you this morning." Before they can say anything else, I head toward the row where Laney, Dilynne, and Henley's girlfriend, Elodie, are seated.

But when I turn to take my seat, I lock eyes with Vienna.

That's when I see the same stunned disbelief I've been dealing with written all over her face. Those green orbs of hers grow so wide, you'd think she just saw a ghost. Her hand lands on the center of her chest and her mouth falls open, but she doesn't move.

We're both frozen.

Yeah, sweetheart.

Good luck running away this time.

Chapter 4

Vienna

One Choice Can Come Back to Haunt You

"Are you all right?" Stacey, one of the other kindergarten teachers, comes over to me while I'm still staring across the cafeteria at Rhonan.

Once I pick my jaw up off the floor, swallow the drool in my mouth from seeing him in his uniform, and clear my throat, I'm able to finally form some words. "Oh, yeah! Just great!"

"You sure? You looked surprised. Did you see someone you know or something?"

Well, it isn't the person I would be most shocked to see here, but Rhonan is a close second. "Yeah. Turns out I know one of the speakers."

Stacey laughs. "Oh, honey. That's what happens when you move to a small town. Everyone knows everyone. We're all connected somehow. Don't be surprised if this person is the first of a long list of people you didn't realize you had a connection with."

My smile is forced when I look at her. "Oh joy."

Laughing, she flips through the papers on the podium in front of me. "Now, you sure you're up for announcing our speakers? I can take over if you want."

I brush my hair from my face and find my strength. "No, I'm fine. This will be a good way to make it look like I know what I'm doing, you know?"

"Oh, honey. Those kids are going to need a lot more proof than that if you're going to keep them under control until summer." She pats my shoulder and then takes her seat by her class on the left side of the cafeteria.

The kids are seated on the floor, staring up at me, waiting for the event to begin. When Sandra, the principal of the elementary school, called me about this job, I thought she was joking. I applied for it on a whim. I was intent on settling in a town on the coast like Carrington Cove and renting a beach house for a few months while I regrouped. But when I saw the posting, I thought working in a school would be the perfect way to start this new chapter of my life and figure out if teaching is something I still want to do.

I never got to teach like I planned. All that schooling, all that work was for nothing after college. The degree hung on a wall in a fourteen-karat gold frame, but the price I paid for my decisions leading up to that were far more expensive.

"Welcome, everyone, to Career Day at Blossom Peak Elementary School!" I turn on the voice I was raised to perfect and slip into the role of someone who knows what they're doing, even though I feel the complete opposite right now. "I'm Ms. Lewis, the teacher who has taken over for Mrs. Allen while she's on maternity leave, and I'm so honored to be here at this school for this event. I wish they had something like this when I was a kid."

A few laughs trickle out from the audience, so I call that a win. "Anyway, we have many amazing speakers lined up, so let's get started. Each speaker will introduce themselves and tell us a little about what they do. Afterward, students will take a short recess to burn off some energy, then they'll come back inside and get three tickets to visit the speakers of the careers they are most interested in. Sound good?"

The kids collectively convey their understanding.

"Perfect. Well, first up is Dilynne Clark, the owner of Clark Customs & Automotive Repair. Let's give a hand for Dilynne."

Applause rings out as a woman who looks like she could have been transported from the 1950s struts to the front of the cafeteria—pin-up styled hair, bright red lips, oil-stained coveralls, and a wrench held casually in her hand. She looks like Rosie the Riveter's doppelganger, and I'm instantly obsessed.

I take my seat next to my class, and Ellis, one of the least shy kids in the group, slides across the tile floor toward me. "That's my Aunt Dilynne," she whispers proudly. "She loves cars and says I can be anything I want when I grow up."

I glance back up at Dilynne as she speaks with such confidence that I want to be like her too. "Well, she's absolutely right. Now let's listen." I bring my finger to my lips, giving her the universal sign to be silent, and she mimics me, making me chuckle behind my hand.

When Dilynne finishes, I announce Fletcher Adams. I didn't know little kids could scream as loud as they did when he approached the stage.

As I glance down the list before returning to my seat and see the name of the next speaker, my stomach tightens.

Rhonan Hart. Deputy Sheriff for the Blossom Peak Sheriff's Department.

Well, at least he wasn't lying about being in law enforcement.

"Wait... Hart?" I mutter to myself.

My eyes drift to Ellis, who's listening intently to Fletcher, Blossom Peak's own celebrity NFL player, who is also Ellis's uncle, apparently. Each time someone new approaches the stage, she echoes a similar sentiment. I swear, at this point, I'm curious if this little girl is related to everyone here.

And then my mind catches up.

Ellis Hart.

Of course she's related to the man whose fingers I can still feel on my face. The same man I walked away from without explanation. Must be another one of her uncles.

I don't have time to process what this means before Fletcher finishes speaking. The applause swells as he leaves the stage, and I head back to the podium, ready to announce Rhonan to the room while fighting the nerves racing through me.

I grip the edge of the podium, steadying myself before I speak. "Thank you, Mr. Adams. Up next, we have Rhonan Hart, a deputy sheriff with the Blossom Peak Sheriff's Department. Come on up, Mr. Hart."

I watch him stand from his seat, swallowing roughly while adjusting his belt on his waist, and then he's heading toward me in long, purposeful strides.

God, he's just as attractive as I remember, which is both a relief and a problem because I've tried to convince myself I was making that night out to be more than it was.

But as my eyes trace the curve of his biceps peeking out under the hem of his short-sleeved, olive-green button-down and the rugged lines of his jaw framing those lips I remember wanting to kiss more than I wanted my next breath, and my gaze dips lower to the impressive bulge in his pants, I can confidently say I didn't imagine any of it.

That night was supposed to be fun—a chance to let loose and feel liberated, just like I told him. It was me taking back control of my life and experiencing something new and completely out of my comfort zone.

Turns out the joke is on me because the last thing I anticipated was seeing this man again after I ran away from him at that bar, which doesn't bode well for my character.

But the truth is, Rhonan scared me. Our connection was so instant, so easy. And when he leaned in to kiss me, I wanted him to.

But then I realized that kissing another man would go against everything I wanted in this new life—primarily, my independence. The last thing I should be doing is getting involved with anyone in any capacity.

When Rhonan reaches the front of the room, just a few feet away from me, he stares directly into my eyes, his jaw tight, and then with a curt nod, twists to face the audience.

I slowly back away from the podium and find my seat again while he speaks.

"Good morning, everyone."

"Good morning," the kids echo back to him, making him smile.

Seeing that familiar lift of his lips allows my shoulders to fall with a small sliver of relief.

"I'm a sheriff, which means it's my job to protect our town from people who break the law, or anyone that might otherwise cause problems." His eyes drift over to me, and suddenly, my heart is racing again.

Wait. Does he think I came here on purpose? Like I knew that he lived here, or something? And that I'm a stalker?

Oh, hell no.

His eyes drift back to the audience. "Now, we all know that Blossom Peak is a safe place, but that's because there are rules in place to make sure it stays that way. When people don't obey the law, that's when they get in trouble and have to ride in my cruiser down to the sheriff's station."

The kids are leaning forward as he continues to speak, and I don't blame them. He commands their attention, much like he did mine that night.

Don't think about it, Vienna.

My gaze moves to his hands as he talks more, and my skin breaks out in goosebumps, like it's still carrying the memory of his touch.

I had never been touched like that—reverent yet commanding, sensual yet desperate, soft yet hard.

I felt his physique through his clothes when I fell into him, and even more when he lifted me from the ground and carried me across the bar.

That man is hard everywhere.

"Ms. Lewis," Ellis says, pulling on the bottom of my dress to grab my attention. I'm very grateful that she can't hear or see inside of my head right now as my thoughts drift to the man standing at the front of the room and how I know what he must look like without a shirt.

"Yes, Ellis."

"That's my daddy! Isn't he big and strong?"

Oh, honey...you have no idea.

But then I process all of her words.

"Wait. That's your dad?"

So much for just another uncle.

"Yes! He fights bad guys. That's why he's so strong."

My throat starts to close up. "Oh, well that's a good thing since his job is to keep everyone safe."

"He does. I always feel safe with him."

Yeah, so did I.

And now everything that he said about his daughter that night makes so much more sense.

"You're very lucky," I whisper to her, then point back up to where her dad is finishing his introduction.

"So, if you want to know more about my job and how I help keep Blossom Peak a safe place for everyone, then come see me later. Thank you." He lifts a hand in farewell and walks back to his seat as applause fills the room.

I introduce the final few speakers, and once everyone has spoken, the teachers take the kids out for their fifteen-minute recess before the question groups begin.

While I'm out on the playground supervising, I keep going over that night with Rhonan in my mind, wondering if he ever mentioned that he lived here. I had only found out about the job a few days before I drove through Asheville and saw that flyer for the bull riding contest that I didn't even stick around long enough to find out if I won. Honestly, I forgot all about the contest because I was far more preoccupied with Rhonan, which was better than any inconsequential prize I could have won.

Besides, I did it for Lydia. And for myself.

Fifteen minutes pass in a blur and then I'm leading twenty-five kindergarteners back into the cafeteria. Each child gets three tickets for the speakers they want to hear more from, and the teachers move around the room helping keep order.

My eyes keep finding Rhonan no matter where I'm standing, but he's focused on speaking with the kids. He's thoughtful, takes his time with each one, and hands out sheriff's badge stickers to every child that comes to see him. Fletcher Adams' line is the longest of all, but that comes as no surprise to anyone. Apparently, since he got engaged to

Laney Hart—who I found out is also Ellis's aunt—his popularity has only grown.

I'm busy watching Fletcher help a boy try to hold a football with his too-small hands when a voice beside me makes me jump.

"So, seems like we're in a bit of a pickle here."

Rhonan.

I look up at him to my left, finding him looking right back at me. "Dill, sweet, or butter?"

He frowns in confusion. "What?"

"The kind of pickle. Personally, I'm a dill gal, but I can go for a sweet pickle on a pulled pork sandwich."

His smile falls. "Vienna, this is serious."

Sighing, I turn away from him calmly and fix my attention on the kids, even though my stomach is tying itself in knots that are going to be a bitch to untangle later. "Look, I didn't know."

"I didn't think you did."

"Really? Because the look you gave me earlier felt pretty accusatory."

He clears his throat. "It wasn't meant to be. I just...don't know how to feel, seeing you here."

"I—I'm sorry, Rhonan," I say on a shaky breath because, even though he might not believe me, it's the truth. The second I left that night, I regretted my decision. But there was no way for me to explain why I did without giving away too much.

There's too much at stake.

"You left without saying goodbye."

"I know."

He clears his throat. "I thought..." Shaking his head, he says, "You know what? It doesn't matter what I thought because now..."

"Now I'm your daughter's teacher," I finish for him.

"And the last thing we need is gossip."

"Agreed."

He straightens his spine. "Good. And by the way, your dog is a menace."

My head whips back in his direction. "My dog? How do you know about—"

"Daddy!"

Ellis runs up to us, cutting me off, and I'm left wondering how he could know about my puppy, Roscoe.

Rhonan reaches down and scoops her up, securing her in his arms as the scowl on his face transforms into a smile. And unfortunately, seeing him with his daughter just makes him that much more attractive.

"Hey, sweetie. Are you having fun?"

She shrugs. "Not really."

His brows knit. "How come?"

"Because I already know what I want to be when I grow up," she answers matter-of-factly.

Rhonan chuckles and turns to me. "Oh yes, Ellis is going to be a princess."

Ellis shakes her head. "I used to want to be a princess, but now I want to be a queen."

Rhonan draws his eyebrows together. "A queen, huh? Since when?"

"Since Elsa is a queen with ice powers, and Auntie Dilynne told me that queens have *more* power."

I stifle my laugh behind my hand as Rhonan replies, "She did, did she?"

"Yup." Then Ellis turns to me. "Or I wanna be a teacher like you, Ms. Lewis."

My hand falls to the center of my chest as I try not to get emotional. I've only known this little girl for three days, but I can already tell she's going to steal my heart. "Aw, that's so sweet, Ellis. Thank you."

"What has Ms. Lewis taught you about being a teacher?" Rhonan asks, drifting his gaze over to me for a second before focusing back on his daughter. I try not to take that look too personally, but for some reason it feels that way.

I may have only been here for three days, but certainly I've made some kind of impact on these kids.

Ellis ponders her answers and then shrugs. "She gets to be the boss of the class, *and* she's really pretty. I like to be the boss too."

My shoulders fall slightly, but I'm also amused. "That's really sweet, Ellis. Being in charge is fun, but it's also a lot of responsibility. And you should remember that pretty isn't a character trait."

Rhonan and Ellis both stare at me at the same time. "What does that mean?" she asks.

I take a second to consider how to explain this to a five-year-old, because I wish this were something I had learned at a much younger age. "Being pretty is not nearly as important as being kind, inclusive, and hardworking. Being beautiful doesn't automatically make you a nice person. I hope that when you're with me, you feel that I'm kind more than anything else."

I can feel Rhonan watching me, but I keep my focus on Ellis. I don't think my heart could handle seeing his reaction to words that speak to every woman's insecurities, including my own.

"You are really nice, Ms. Lewis." Ellis wiggles out of Rhonan's arms, and wraps her arms around my legs. When she peers up and meets my eyes, she continues, "But you're really pretty too." Glancing back at her dad, she asks, "Isn't she pretty, Daddy?"

I don't dare lift my eyes still, but the sound of his voice affects me far more, I fear. "Yes, she is."

"Ellis! We're getting ready to leave!" Dilynne shouts across the room, standing next to Laney and Fletcher, and two other men I introduced today that I'm having a hard time remembering the names of.

I let that be the moment I meet Rhonan's eyes. "I'll let you go."

"Come on, Daddy. I want to say goodbye."

Rhonan keeps his eyes on me but doesn't say anything. He simply follows his daughter's lead until he finally breaks our gaze and joins his friends, leaving me standing there, wondering how I'm going to survive the next two and a half months of Rhonan Hart run-ins.

***

By the time I pull into my driveway and turn off the ignition, I can barely remember the drive home. One thing I was woefully unprepared for when I signed up for this job was how overstimulating it would be. The kids are so sweet and for the most part, well-behaved, but there's never a quiet moment. Questions fly from their mouths at record speed, someone always needs something, and the social dynamics of five-year-olds could rival some soap operas that have been on air for decades.

Needless to say, I'm deeply grateful there's a bottle of wine in my fridge to help take the edge off and help me process the past twenty-four hours.

"Roscoe!" I call out once I unlock the front door to my rental house and set my purse on the kitchen table. "Mommy's home!"

Usually, he's eager to greet me on the other side of the sliding glass door, or already darting through the doggy door that leads to the backyard. But the glass pane is empty except for the streaks from his nose and tongue.

Getting a puppy wasn't in the cards, at least not so soon in this new life of mine. But last week, while I was standing at a gas station staring at the community board, right between a flyer for a mechanical bull riding contest and an ad for piano lessons, I saw one for German Shepherd puppies at a local rescue. I always wanted a dog but was never allowed to have one, so I took it as a sign.

Lydia would have said it was a sign too.

It's at that moment, as I head for the backyard to find my dog, that I wonder what she would say about my predicament with Rhonan. Oh, I'm sure she'd be pressuring me to do something about it, like asking him on a date in the name of moving on like I should be. But thinking about how we were always so different is making the sadness from the past few months reappear.

That familiar wave of grief brushes the edges of my heart as I head to the backyard in search of Roscoe.

"Roscoe? Roscoe?" My voice is loud enough that he should hear me, but I don't see him anywhere, and there's not too many places to hide. The yard is bare except for the wild grass that grows all over the ground here, and there are only two spindly trees that wouldn't hide a squirrel, let alone a puppy.

"Damn dog!" A voice comes from over the fence to my right, sharp and irritated.

Roscoe's bark rings out, igniting urgency within me as I race to the fence. But when I look over it, I can almost hear Lydia's laugh in my head.

You've got to be kidding me.

Rhonan is chasing around my puppy while Ellis laughs on their deck.

"Daddy! He just wants to play!"

"He needs to play in *his* yard," Rhonan says, lunging for Roscoe as he darts to the right and races up the deck steps, skidding to a stop when he reaches Ellis.

"Sit, puppy." Ellis points to the deck below her, and much to my and Rhonan's surprise, Roscoe obeys. "Good boy," she says proudly, scratching his head.

Rhonan's hands land on his hips as he stares up at his daughter from the yard. "How did you get him to listen?"

Ellis pets Roscoe's head as he tries to lick her hand. She giggles.

"The dog would probably stop running around if you'd stop chasing it." Joanne says dryly from the porch, behind Ellis.

Wait. I thought that was *her* house. What are Rhonan and Ellis doing there?

I seriously hope Joanne is just another relative they're visiting.

"How the hell am I supposed to get it to go back home, then?" He pushes a hand through his hair, the same hair that I itched to bury my fingers in last week.

God, that night feels like another life at this point, and certainly one that can't be mine.

There's no way the man I had the most natural and liberating night of my life with turns out to be the father of one of my students *and* my new neighbor.

Would you expect anything less at this point, Vienna? Perhaps Lydia is pulling some strings up there to force you to live recklessly?

For a second, I debate how much longer I'm supposed to let this go on before I say something, but Ellis spots me first and her face lights up.

"Ms. Lewis?"

Joanne and Rhonan's heads twist in my direction, meeting my eyes as I stand frozen in place. I wave timidly. "Hi, Ellis."

Rhonan pinches the bridge of his nose, sighing before walking in my direction. When he arrives at the fence, I can see the frustration on his face. "Your dog—"

"Got out of my yard," I finish for him. "But there's no way that this is..." My words trail off as I gesture helplessly to his side of the fence.

"My yard?" he finishes for me, a displeased arch in his brow. "Oh, it absolutely is."

Shit. I don't even know why I'm surprised at this point.

"Okay... So, *now* I understand how you knew about my dog," I say, trying to make light of the situation.

Rhonan looks less than amused. "He dug under the fence this morning and already got my heart rate up. I put bricks in the hole, but he won't be outsmarted because he just dug another hole and returned this evening."

"I'm sorry."

"Yeah, well, you owe me a new rose bush since he dug up one of mine." He motions to the far side of his yard where a pile of dirt is resting on the ground with a bare rose bush right next to it.

"Of course. But he's just a puppy. I'm working on training him." My eyes drift over to Ellis and the dog where they're playing on the deck. Roscoe is following her around and sitting every time she commands him to. "Although Ellis appears to be much better at it than I am. I haven't been able to get him to sit for me once."

"You move to a new town *and* get a new puppy?" Rhonan asks, clearly confused by my choice. But he doesn't need to understand the decisions I'm making for *my* life.

"Yes," I say, lifting my chin slightly. "And apparently not only am I your daughter's new teacher, but also your new neighbor. As if this could get any more complicated."

He closes his eyes and exhales slowly. "Trust me, I'm well aware of how complicated this is. But right now, I'm more concerned about keeping your destructive dog out of my yard. I'm going to move a boulder into this hole for now, but maybe you should keep him inside while you're at work." This man is far more irritable than the man I chatted with last week.

"He has a doggy door so he doesn't have to be cooped up all day in the pen I have installed around the door. You want me to lock him inside where he'll pee and poop everywhere instead? Or tear up the house? No thank you."

His hands fly up in the air. "Not my problem. Figure it out."

Irritation grows in my chest. "Wow, thank you for the sage advice."

"Daddy! Can we keep the puppy?" Ellis comes racing across the yard next to her dad, Roscoe hot on her heels.

"No, Ellis. We've already discussed this. The dog belongs to Ms. Lewis." Rhonan gestures to my side of the fence.

"Ms. Lewis, what are you doing in that yard?"

"This is my house, Ellis."

Her eyes grow big as saucers, and her smile follows. "Really?"

"Yep. And your dad is right. That's my puppy, but you can play with him whenever you want."

She claps her hands. "Yes! Can I play with him right now?"

I glance back at Rhonan, whose annoyance is palpable. "Just for a few more minutes while I talk to your dad, and then I have to take Roscoe home, okay?"

Ellis nods. "Okay. Come on, Roscoe!" She takes off toward her playset, beckoning the puppy to follow her up the steps and down the slide. Her laughter is so precious, and I'm so consumed with watching them, that I momentarily forget Rhonan is still standing there.

Once I blink myself out of my trance, I meet Rhonan's eyes. "Look, I'm sorry for how things turned out."

"Why? Because the woman who ghosted me turned out to be my neighbor and my kid's teacher?" he quips.

I clear my throat. "Well, yes."

"Maybe it's a lesson," he says, brow lifting. "About treating others the way you'd want to be treated."

I cross my arms over my chest. "I said I was sorry. I can move forward and act like an adult. Can you?"

"I'm working on it," he says through gritted teeth. "But this is my life, Vienna. My town. My daughter. I don't normally—"

"Hit on random women in bars and almost kiss them?" I finish for him.

The narrowing of his gaze tells me he doesn't like that I hit the nail on the head. Much to my surprise though, he simply nods, averting his eyes from mine as he does.

"Well, I guess I can't fault you for that. I was into our conversation too. But rest assured, I had no idea who you were."

"I believe you," he says, his voice slightly calmer than before. I can't decide whether he's always wound this tight or if our prior connection is getting to him. "Can I assume you're only here temporarily?"

"That was the plan until I figure out my next move, but staying isn't completely out of the realm of possibility yet," I reply honestly.

"Understood. Let's just pretend like nothing happened and be friends then, okay?" His eyes meet mine and in that second, my heart says *no*.

How can I pretend like our night didn't happen? How can I push down the feelings he gave me of safety and comfort? How can I pretend that I don't remember how hard he made my heart beat? How desperate he made me, and how willing I was to see where the night would have led us if my conscience wouldn't have gotten in the way.

"Your puppy is so cute, Ms. Lewis!" Ellis shouts from the yard, still running around while Roscoe chases her.

That's how, Vienna. You're his daughter's teacher. You don't really have an option now.

"Thank you, Ellis. Now, it's time that I take him home." Bending down to the hole beneath the fence, I call for him. "Roscoe! Come here, baby. Want a treat?"

Despite his resistance to other commands and words, my dog has definitely learned that one. With a leap, he crosses the yard in record time and crawls right back under the fence, jumping up on my legs until I pick him up, accepting his affection as he licks my face. "I missed you too, buddy."

I glance back up at Rhonan only to find him staring at my lips. "Friends it is, Rhonan." His gaze lifts and meets mine as I continue. "Sorry about Roscoe. I'll see what I can do to keep him in my yard."

Clearing his throat, he nods. "Thank you. Have a good evening, Ms. Lewis."

"See you tomorrow at school, Ms. Lewis!" Ellis shouts, waving at me as she runs to the deck and stomps up the steps.

"See you then, Ellis!" I call after her before I turn back to her father. "Have a good night, Mr. Hart."

I turn around and walk to my house, craning my neck back to stare up at the sky as I say, "God, Lydia. I sincerely hope you're enjoying every second of my life right now, because this is something you couldn't have planned better if you tried."

A wind whips past me as I think about the bottle of wine I need to pop open even more now. And as I close in on my house, I can still feel

Rhonan's eyes trailing me. And just before I walk inside, I glance back to find him right where I left him—eyes locked on me, and the flame that burned between us that night far from extinguished.

Chapter 5

Rhonan

Which Cards Do I Play?

"Why does this room smell like wet dog?" Fletcher deals the cards, nose scrunched up as he sniffs the air.

Elliot shrugs. "Beats the hell out of me. I just cleaned in here."

Henley leans closer to me and sniffs a few times. "I think it's our friend, Rhonan, gentlemen. Also known as the dog chaser. Remember?"

My friends laugh under their breath, and I flip them all off as I reach for my beer, draining the rest of it before tossing the empty bottle into the recycling can right next to me.

As planned before my day took an unexpected turn, my best friends and I are having blackjack night at Elliot's house. He's the only one of us who lives alone, so it just made sense to have it here. Besides, right now, I'm grateful for the distance from my house, especially after seeing Vienna over the fence. The confirmation that she's my neighbor made this all the more real. Space feels like the safest option.

"Earth to Rhonan." Henley waves his hand in front of my face. "You thinking about what Ellis's teacher looks like naked?"

"Fuck off," I grumble while picking up my hand to find I have shit. A nine and a three only makes twelve, which is a shit hand to get dealt in blackjack.

"I think you *almost* getting fucked is why we're all here tonight." Fletcher chuckles as the boys slide their bets to the center of the table. "Fill me and Henley in since we weren't invited to the night where you made sure Elliot's dick is still working."

Elliot flips Fletcher off while shaking his head. "Forgive me for not extending an invitation when you and Henley are both taken men now. You and I both know neither of you would have come anyway."

Shoving my hand through my hair, I say, "Look, like I already told you, we didn't hook up. Fuck, we didn't even kiss." *Even though I desperately wanted to.* "We just talked."

"Did you two use protection?" Henley quips.

Fletcher barks a laugh.

Holding my middle finger up to Henley's face, I keep my eyes fixed on Fletcher while I continue. "Details aside, I'm fucking out of my element, you guys." I drift my eyes between my three best friends before taking my hand out of Henley's face. "There's no way I imagined Vienna would end up in Blossom Peak as Ellis's teacher, let alone my new neighbor. How the fuck do I handle this?" I blow out a frustrated breath.

"I don't get what the big deal is," Henley says.

Fletcher chuckles. "Come on. The woman took off and never said anything. Any man would take that as a hit to their ego."

"She didn't bruise my ego..."

Elliot scoffs. "Yes, she fucking did. You pouted all the way home." I shoot Elliot a glare, but he continues. "And I don't blame you, but

I'm sure you never expected her to reappear in your life." Then he points a finger across the table. "And that's what the fucking problem is, Henley. All right?"

Henley tilts his head side to side. "Okay, that's fair."

"Well, what did she say when you spoke to her earlier today?" Fletcher asks.

I think back to our conversation at the school and our talk over the fence as I toy with my cards. "She assured me it was all coincidental. But fuck. Really? The *one* woman I've been genuinely intrigued by since Sarah turns out to be my daughter's teacher *and* my neighbor?" I dart my eyes over to Elliot and toss my chin in his direction. "This is all your fault."

"Me?" He points a finger to the center of his chest. "You should be thanking me. Even though nothing happened, at least you didn't leave worried whether your dick still works. If nothing else, think of the night as reassurance that your equipment is in working order."

My dick twitches from the memory of Vienna licking her lips and seeing that sliver of her breast beneath her top, but I keep that detail to myself. "If I had known that this turn of events would be the fallout, I would have said no thank you. And besides, the night was supposed to be about you and *your* dick, not me and mine."

"My dick is fine. Thankfully back in full working order. Which means this conversation is officially about you and *your* dick, so stop trying to deflect."

Henley clears his throat. "Can you two please stop with the dick talk?"

I glare in his direction. "Look, I just need some advice. I've never been ghosted, and I've gotta say, I'm not a fan."

"Pretty sure no one is," Henley says.

"Yeah, well, I'm pretty sure most people don't end up living next to the person who rejected them either." There's a pleading lilt to my voice that I'm not proud of, but right now I'm fucking desperate.

Fletcher and Elliot both look in Henley's direction. "What?" he says, holding his hands out to the side.

Fletcher scoffs. "I think out of all of us, you're the one with the most casual dating experiences."

Henley points across the table at Elliot. "That's not fair. Elliot used to get plenty of action too."

"Not like you, my friend," Elliot says while reaching for a handful of pretzels.

Henley snorts. "Yeah, well, I usually did the ghosting. The only time I ever had to face a one-night stand again was when Meghan got pregnant. Honestly, Rhonan, here's my advice." He sits up straight in his chair and looks me in the eye. "Ask her out on a date."

My mouth falls open because that was the last thing I expected to come out of his mouth. "I'm sorry—what?"

Fletcher and Elliot are laughing, but I don't find this funny at all.

"Ask her out," Henley repeats.

My brows are drawn so tightly together that it's starting to give me a headache. "Why on earth would I do that?"

The smirk on Henley's face makes me want to punch him. "Because if the way you're freaking out about this is any indication, I'd say you're still into this woman and want to know if that connection was real or all in your head."

Leaning back in my chair, I blink through my confusion as I consider his words, landing on an indisputable fact as my response. "She's Ellis's teacher."

Henley shrugs. "And I slept with my nanny. Look how that worked out for me," he says, a smug smile on his lips. "If not, at least act like a fucking adult and keep things civil. Because you can't change the fact that she's here. So, decide what you're going to do about it, and fucking commit to the decision. Stop floundering."

I cross my arms over my chest. "I'm not floundering."

Fletcher huffs out a laugh. "Uh, yeah, you are. It's really simple, Rhonan. If you like the woman, then just admit it. All this back and forth about why her reappearance has your panties in a bunch is just going to drive you nuts. I mean, when I realized I wanted your sister once and for all, there was no stopping me from making that happen."

My glare grows deeper. "No need to remind me of how that all went down, thank you. I think the two of you getting married is reminder enough."

Elliot snaps his fingers. "Which reminds me, have we settled on a bachelor party plan yet?"

Fletcher turns to him. "I told Rhonan I didn't want anything crazy, but since a bunch of guys from the team are going, we decided to have it in Charlotte."

Grateful for the change in topic, I nod in agreement. "The plans are in the works. I've got it covered."

Since the four of us have been best friends since high school, we agreed that when it came time to make the decision about who would be the best man for each of our weddings, we would take turns.

Fletcher was Elliot's for his wedding that never happened, Elliot would be Henley's, which we never thought would be a possibility but he's very serious about Elodie now, so it wouldn't surprise me if they're engaged soon. Henley was mine when I married Sarah, and that leaves me to be Fletcher's. I just never thought the fucker would be marrying my little sister, but I can't stay mad about it forever, I guess.

Elliot studies me. "You sure your neighbor isn't going to distract you too much?"

I glare at him as I lean back in my chair. "I'll be fine. And just so y'all know, I'm not asking her out."

Henley shrugs. "Suit yourself. But stop acting like this is the end of the world."

Even though I want to argue, I refrain. It feels impossible to handle right now, just because the shock hasn't worn off. That's it. Once a little bit of time has passed, I'll forget all about that night and things will just slip right back into the routine.

Vienna may be next door and my daughter's teacher now, but she's just like anyone else in town. Yes, she infiltrated my mind the night we met with her wit, clumsiness, and heart buried beneath the sliver of fear I recognized in her gaze. But maybe I'm building all of it up in my head because it has been so long since I've felt that comfortable with anyone.

Yeah, that's it.

Enticements during a dry spell will do that to you, ignite that need all over again until you shove it back down and leave it dormant again for a while.

I can only hope that happens soon because having the temptation of her right next door might make forgetting damn near impossible.

***

"Have a good day at school, sweetie." I bend to kiss Ellis on the forehead as we near the school's front gate.

"I will. We're gonna have pizza for dinner tonight, right, Daddy?"

"Yes, Ellis. I told you we would."

She holds her pinky out to me, poised and ready to seal the deal. "Promise?"

I hook my pinky with hers. "Promise."

With glee, she drops her hand from mine and I watch her walk toward the building. She waves at me as she looks over her shoulder. "Bye, Daddy! Be safe!"

Ever since Ellis found out about my job and the fact that I'm supposed to arrest bad guys—her words, not mine—she's told me to be safe each time I leave for work. Fortunately for both of us, Blossom Peak doesn't see much action that could put me in harm's way, but I appreciate the sentiment, nonetheless.

I lift my phone to check the time, and when I glance back up, I meet a pair of bright green eyes I can't seem to get out of my head, even though I'm desperately trying.

Vienna offers me a soft smile accompanied by a wave.

My instinct is to return both, but I don't. It's not that I'm trying to be rude, it's that I don't want to invite any sort of relationship between the two of us that could be misconstrued. Henley was right—I need to quit wavering when it comes to Vienna.

Just because she's Ellis's teacher and my neighbor doesn't mean we need to be friends. I can be *friendly* with her but still keep a respectable distance.

Because distance is the only thing you can control, right, Rhonan?

I simply nod, then turn around and walk away as fast as I can. After all, I can't be late for work.

***

Once I arrive at the station, the familiar stench of burnt coffee greets me the second I walk through the doors. It's just after nine in the morning, which means the night shift must have left their pot on the burner, and I need to make a fresh one stat.

"Hart. Good morning." Chief Deputy Banks greets me as I make my way toward my desk.

"Morning, Chief."

He nods in the direction of the debriefing room. "We're gonna have a quick meeting before the night guys take off."

As soon as I enter the room, I find Jake, Daniel, Brody, and Jordan waiting for me. "What's up, fellas?"

Jake tips his chin in greeting. "Morning, Hart. How was Career Day yesterday? Did you recruit any future sheriffs at the elementary school?"

"For your information, I had the second longest line."

Daniel taps his chin in mock contemplation. "And let me guess who had the first... It wouldn't happen to be Blossom Peak's most famous football player and your sister's fiancé, would it?"

Chief clears his throat before I can reply. "Gentlemen, I'd like to head home and get some sleep if that's okay with you, so I'd appreciate you all saving the bullshit for later."

Daniel's shoulders shake with silent laughter as I take a seat toward the back, listening with intention so my boss isn't tempted to fire any of us. But I still wad up a piece of paper and throw it at the back of Daniel's head.

William Banks has been the chief deputy here for over twenty years. I remember when he used to be the one who showed up to Career Day, back when I was still a student at Blossom Peak Elementary. His hair is much grayer than it was then, and he's definitely put on a few pounds—thanks in part to the regular donut deliveries from Bites & Bliss Bakery—but there's a comfort in his presence. Like with age comes wisdom, and I know he's about to impart some on all of us.

"All right," he says. "Warmer weather's coming, which means more tourists than we see in the winter. Be alert. Use your senses. If anything doesn't seem right, trust your gut." He slaps his protruding stomach for emphasis. "You know I don't like to say things have been slow, but that's the reality right now. Anytime it gets too quiet around here, there's usually something right under our noses that we don't see until it's too late."

Brody raises his hand like one of the kindergarteners I was dealing with yesterday.

"Yes, Brody."

"Sir, with all due respect, I think the trash panda we caught that was terrorizing the dumpsters in the alley behind the general store is not the type of crime that we should be losing sleep over."

A few of us chuckle, but Chief isn't amused. "I believe you mean raccoon, and tell that to Mrs. Higgins. That woman was traumatized and her business suffered thousands of dollars in damage. Being a sheriff in a town like Blossom Peak may mean far less commotion than some other places, and sometimes our problems might look different than those you're used to." He hoists his pants up on his hips. "But if you can't take this town and its needs seriously, then perhaps you need to find a new station. I'd be happy to put in for a transfer for you."

Brody's smug grin falls as he launches himself upright in his seat. "Won't happen again, sir."

"Good," Chief says. Then his tone shifts. "And don't forget, it's not like this town hasn't seen its share of tragedy."

We all grow quiet, thinking about the summer ten years ago when a little girl about Ellis's age went missing. I was in the Marines at the time, so I wasn't home to see the way Blossom Peak unraveled. It was only about a year after my mother died too, and since she was a prominent figure in our town, having founded my family's winery and all, the two incidents rattled the foundation of this little town—a place most people here have called home their entire lives.

"Hayley Zachmann was the one case that we dropped the ball on, and I'll be damned if we ever do that again." Chief pounds his fist on the table in front of him. "You all might think this job is a fucking joke, but there's nothing funny about telling a parent their child isn't coming home. Show some damn respect while you're wearing the badge. Got it?"

We all nod, the amusement in the room fading quickly, replaced by a sense of purpose and duty.

I knew when I left the Marines that serving my community in a different way was the only logical choice for me, but that's because I *have* experienced what the chief is talking about. I *have* had to come home and tell a mother that her son wasn't coming home. Because I'm the one he asked to do it.

Loss and I are old friends.

Truth be told, I used to run from it. But eventually, it became this familiar ghost that follows me around. Now, I'm not sure what my life might be like without its presence always lurking around every corner.

It's why I keep my circle small. It's why I vow to protect anyone I care about.

And it's why anything new makes my life feel off-balance.

Anything, or anyone, *Rhonan?*

I decide not to answer that.

Chapter 6

Rhonan

Wedding Plans & A Run-In

"Daddy! Can I play Candy Land?" We've barely walked through the doors of Hart Winery, and Ellis is already asking to play her favorite game. Normally, I wouldn't hesitate, but right now? I just need a second to sit.

Joanne clears her throat. "We can absolutely play, Ellis. Come on, let's go find a table."

I catch Joanne's eye and mouth, "Thank you."

Nodding, she leads my daughter into the main tasting room and straight to the little game area my mother insisted on including when she and my father opened the place.

This room holds more of my memories than almost anywhere else.

I can still hear my mother's voice sometimes, explaining the flavor notes of our wine to customers as they swirled their glasses. I can still see Laney and me chasing each other around the tables, hiding behind the large wine barrels topped with thick wooden slabs.

And I can still see the night I walked in with Sarah on my arm and told my dad we were engaged.

It's that memory that chooses to haunt me at this moment.

A slap on my back pulls me from my thoughts almost immediately. "You look like shit," Fletcher says as he hangs his arm around my neck and walks with me over to the bar that spans the entire length of the main wall in the room.

"Nice to see you too, Fletch," I grumble as I take a seat at the bar and Fletcher follows my lead.

My sister comes up behind him, wrapping her arms around his shoulders and kissing his cheek before turning to me. "You okay, Rhonan?"

"Just exhausted," I breathe out. "The past two shifts have been insane, so let's just say I'm thankful for a few days off."

Laney lifts her eyebrows. "Well, if you want some help getting rid of those bags under your eyes, I have this new eye cream you should definitely try."

"Speaking of which, please don't talk about that shit in front of Ellis, all right? I don't need my daughter getting a complex about her face at five."

Laney eyes me curiously. "She brought that up?"

"Yeah, for the same reason you just did. Apparently, my eye bags are noticeable even to my daughter."

"Well, she must have overheard me talking about it to Dilynne because I certainly wouldn't have said anything like that directly to her." She sounds offended. "But I'm telling you, this stuff is amazing. I'm selling out of it at the salon, and I can't wait to see our wedding photos because I know for certain these bags will be virtually non-existent," she says, pointing to her face. "Can't you already see a difference?"

"No, Laney. I don't study your eye bags."

She rolls her eyes. "Whatever. Dilynne agrees with me."

"What do I agree with?" Dilynne asks as she comes up to us, glass of wine already in hand.

"I was telling Rhonan about the eye cream we've been using..."

Her eyes light up. "Oh shit. Yes, Rhonan..." She pauses, tilting her head side to side as she assesses my face. "You could definitely use some of this stuff."

I turn my attention to Fletcher. "Please talk to me about anything besides eye cream."

"We could talk about the wedding," he says. "Since that is the reason why we're all here."

Dilynne raises her glass to her lips. "Yes, please. I have some thoughts."

Laney inhales deeply. "Why am I not surprised?"

When my sister scheduled this meeting with me, Dilynne—her best friend and maid of honor—and Fletcher, I anticipated being given a list of responsibilities for the big day.

I did not count on being ridiculed for the bags under my eyes.

But then Henley, Elodie, and Elliot all walk through the entrance to the tasting room and suddenly, I realize the entire wedding party is here.

"Sorry we're a bit late. It was hard leaving Remy with Carol and Nick," Elodie says, hugging Dilynne and then Laney before reaching back for Henley's hand.

"Aw, how is my little niece doing?" Dilynne asks.

Elodie smiles just like she does anytime anyone brings up Henley's daughter, who is quickly becoming her own at this point. "She's great. Crawling and picking herself up, and so close to walking. But she's also in this clingy stage right now and screams if she notices you leave the room. Henley and I had to sneak out of the house."

I nod, smiling at the memories of my own daughter at that age. "I remember when Ellis did that. Joanne and I had a system down pat."

Henley squeezes my shoulder. "It sucks, but we're here."

I remember the night Henley walked into this same room with a baby carrier and a diaper bag, revealing to all of us that he had a child he had known nothing about. I also remember going home with him that night and walking him through his first night with his daughter.

My dad did that with me when I left the hospital with Ellis.

I never thought I'd have to be that person for one of my friends, but when the time came, I was grateful I could be.

Now, I look at the man he's become—a loving, confident father who's devoted to the woman he loves. A version of him I wondered if he would ever figure out.

I'm happy for him, but sometimes watching him in this new life and role makes me yearn for the life that was robbed from me.

Turning to Fletcher and Laney, Henley asks, "What did we miss?"

"You haven't missed anything yet," Laney replies. "But we do need to move over to a larger table so we can all sit together."

That's when my father appears from the back of the winery. "Well, look who's here!" He veers straight to my sister, pulling her into his arms and kissing the top of her head, before reaching out to shake Fletcher's hand. "Are the bride and groom ready to talk wedding details?"

Laney scoffs. "Dad, I have seen and helped with countless weddings at this place over the years. I know how this works."

"Yes, but you're the bride now, which means you're not working your own wedding. Let Anabelle do her job," he says, referring to the wedding planner who's been working at the winery for over a decade now.

"You're telling Laney not to act like the control freak that she is," I interject, reaching for my glass of wine that Tom set by me earlier. "I think we can all agree that isn't going to happen," I add, taking down the cabernet like it's the lifeline I need right now.

Spoiler alert: it is—especially if I'm going to get through this evening.

My eyes drift over to Ellis and Joanne playing Candy Land, making sure they're both still there. That they're safe.

Old habits and fears never die.

Fletcher stands up from his stool and pulls my sister into his side. "Hey, that's my fiancée that you're talking about."

Rolling my eyes, I stand as well. "Oh, trust me, I haven't forgotten." Henley laughs, and I shoot him a look. "You still think this is funny, huh?"

He shrugs. "I mean, none of us saw this coming, but I think it's hilarious that it still bothers you."

I shake my head, lifting my glass toward Elliot. "Bet you wouldn't find it funny if you found out Elliot and Dilynne were seeing each other behind your back."

Dilynne chokes on her wine and Elliot looks like someone just told him dinosaurs are still alive.

"Jesus, warn a person before you insinuate something that vile," Dilynne says once she's regained her composure.

"You've lost your goddamn mind if you think that would ever happen," Elliot adds.

Dilynne's razor-sharp gaze lands on Elliot. "You could do a hell of a lot worse, Grumpzilla. Oh wait! You have," she says, clearly referring to his ex-fiancée.

Fletcher covers his mouth with his hand, hiding his smile while Elliot looks like smoke might start pouring out of his ears.

"Trust me, Dil. You'd have to be the last woman on earth left for me to even think about making you mine."

"That's comforting," she says sweetly. "Since I'd never belong to a man, nor would I let him call me *his*." Her placating smile is so sharp it could cut glass.

Laney slices her hand through the space between them. "I think I speak for everyone here when I say please let this go so we can focus on the wedding."

Elliot and Dilynne are locked in a stare-down, but Dilynne breaks first. "Fine."

Elliot runs a hand through his hair. "George? You got any whiskey around here?"

My dad meets Elliot's gaze, chuckling. "Whiskey isn't going to solve your problem, son."

"What problem?"

"The one you refuse to see." My dad shakes his head just as Ellis comes running up to him.

"Papa!"

He lifts her into his arms and rubs their noses together. "Ellis, girl. I've missed you. Did you grow?"

"I don't think so," my daughter replies, but my father glances over at me.

I shrug. "I still can't believe she's five."

He nods. "Oh, I remember vividly how fast it goes." Turning his attention back to Ellis, he says, "Are you done with your game of Candy Land?"

Ellis nods. "Yup. And I won!"

Joanne comes up to us. "She did. Beat me good."

My dad bops Ellis on the nose. "Nice. Well, do you want to come with me and help me in my office? I have some papers that I need organized."

"Yes! I love orgamazation!"

"It's or-gan-i-za-tion." My dad's attempt to correct her is feeble as he walks off and she keeps saying the word incorrectly.

Everyone starts moving over to the bigger table, conversation re-forming in pieces. I let myself breathe again, watching Ellis disappear with my dad. She's safe.

"Do you want me to stay?" Joanne asks me before I take my seat at the table.

I place my hand on her shoulder. "No, I think we'll be good. My dad will keep her preoccupied, and when I'm done with the wedding shit, I'm gonna take Ellis to the playground."

Joanne nods, hoisting her purse up higher on her shoulder. "Sounds good. See you at home."

She heads for the exit, and I turn back to the table, where my sister is addressing everyone.

"All right, we need to talk about a few things since the wedding is only two months away," Laney says as I take a seat beside Fletcher. He, Laney, and Dilynne are all on the same side as me, and Henley, Elodie, and Elliot are facing us.

"The most pressing events coming up are the bachelor and bachelorette parties. And before anyone gets any ideas, there will be no strip clubs or exotic dancers in any capacity." Laney looks pointedly at Dilynne and then me. "Do you hear me, you two?"

I hold my hand up. "Heard and understood. Trust me, there are far better things for us to do in Charlotte than watch women take their clothes off."

Fletcher holds a finger up. "I whole-heartedly agree."

Elliot scoffs. "Speak for yourself."

Dilynne clears her throat. "I have to agree with Elliot on this one. I would very much like to watch an incredibly ripped man thrust his junk in my face. That sounds like an amazing night."

Henley's eyes bounce between Dilynne and Elliot. "Everyone go look outside. I think pigs are flying because Elliot and Dilynne just agreed on something."

Elodie giggles while Dilynne rolls her eyes. "It's not that big of a deal. I'm just saying, my best friend is only getting married once and not letting me provide her with visually stimulating entertainment is bullshit."

Laney pats Dilynne on her shoulder. "You'll just have to think of something else that will be appealing to my eyes. Because the only man I ever want stripping for me is Fletcher."

Fletcher yanks her toward him and lines his lips up to her ear to whisper something, and unfortunately for me, I'm able to hear it. "If that's something you want, I can definitely make that happen, angel."

"Her brother is sitting right here!" I bark out.

He turns to face me. "Then plug your ears."

Laney rolls her eyes before whispering something back to Fletcher. Whatever it is earns a low growl from him.

Jesus Christ.

"Can we please move this conversation on to something else?"

Elliot glances over his shoulder, and then back at me. "How about we focus on Ellis's new teacher and your new neighbor?"

I glare at him. "That wasn't what I had in mind."

"Well, I think it's a great topic since she just walked in."

All eyes move to the door of the tasting room, where sure enough, Vienna is standing, surveying the room.

And she looks fucking gorgeous.

The outfit she was wearing the night we met left little to the imagination, but right now she has on a green sweater that hugs her curves and dark blue denim practically painted onto her legs. Her feet are covered by brown boots, and her hair is down around her face, just like it was that night at The Charming Bull.

"You should go say hello," Laney suggests.

I finally divert my eyes from Vienna. "Yeah, I don't think so."

My sister studies me curiously. "Why not? She's Ellis's teacher, and she's new to town. I'm sure she could use a friend. I mean, it's not like you met her before, had an amazing connection, got ghosted, and now have to see her all the time. Right?"

I turn toward Fletcher. "You fucking told her?"

Fletcher shrugs. "She's my fiancée."

"And I'm one of your best friends."

"Fiancée trumps friend, dude. Sorry. That detail was just too good to keep to myself."

Closing my eyes, I pinch the bridge of my nose. "Jesus Christ."

Elodie reaches across the table and puts her hand on my arm. "If it helps, Rhonan, Henley told me too."

I lift my head and glare at Henley. "That actually doesn't, Elodie. But glad to know I can't trust my friends to keep their fucking mouths shut."

Dilynne takes a sip of wine from her glass. "Well, Laney is the one who told me, not Elliot. So at least one of the guys didn't spill the beans."

Elliot looks at Dilynne, confused. "Thank you, I guess."

She tips her chin at him. "You're welcome."

Henley glances at the two of them. "Be careful, you two. That's twice tonight that you've actually been sort of nice to each other."

Elliot and Dilynne both flip him off simultaneously.

"Vienna!" my sister shouts, calling Vienna's attention to us before I realize what's happening.

"Laney, what the fuck?"

She glances down at me and then back up at my neighbor who is slowly walking in this direction. "Oh calm down."

When Vienna reaches the table, she looks over at me as if asking permission, but my sister steps in quickly.

"Hi there," Laney says, flashing a smile that dares anyone to make this weird. "Not sure if you remember me, but I'm Ellis's aunt, Laney Hart."

"Uh, hi." Vienna's nerves are visible—hands clasped, shoulders tight. "Yes, I remember you from Career Day."

"How are you liking Blossom Peak so far?" The table goes quiet, every set of eyes on Vienna.

"Oh. Well, I'm really liking it a lot. The kids at the school are very sweet, but kindergarteners are exhausting," she says through a laugh. "Hence the wine. This felt like the obvious stop after a full week of tiny humans."

Laney nods. "You definitely came to the right place. Our family owns this winery, actually. Isn't that right, Rhonan?" She pokes at me from the other side of Fletcher.

I straighten, every instinct screaming retreat. Instead, I force myself to finally meet Vienna's eyes.

Fuck, she really is stunning.

"Yes," I answer flatly.

Vienna's mouth quirks. "I kind of figured, given your last name."

My sister pipes up again. "This place was my mom's idea, and my dad made it happen. Sadly, she passed away a little over twelve years ago, but Rhonan and I have helped keep this place running with our dad in her honor."

"I'm sorry for your loss," Vienna says, glancing from Laney back to me.

I clear my throat. "Thank you."

"Do you want to join us?" Laney asks. "We have room for one more."

Vienna holds her hand up. "Oh, it's okay. I wouldn't want to impose on—"

"You're not." Laney cuts her off. "I'm offering. We can make room for Vienna, right everyone?" Her eyes move between our group while she nods forcefully.

"Absolutely." Henley slides closer to Elodie, leaving room for Vienna to sit next to him—and straight across from me. "Here you go."

"No, really. I just wanted to grab a bottle or two and head home. My pajamas are calling my name."

Dilynne raises her glass toward her. "I feel that, girl. At the end of a long day, I can't wait to take my bra off and put on the grungiest clothes I own."

Elliot's eyes drop to Dilynne's chest, but I'm pretty sure I'm the only one that caught it.

"You know... Dilynne, Elodie, and I have girls' nights like that all the time. You should join us sometime," my sister says.

I look over at her, narrowing my eyes. "Laney..." I warn, but she ignores me.

Elodie nods enthusiastically. "Yes! You definitely should. I know what it's like to be new in a small town. I just moved here last year."

"Really? Where are you from?" Vienna asks.

"Well, I was in California before I came here, but home is Garnet Valley, Tennessee, which is another small town. Have you heard of it?"

Vienna lets out a small gasp. "I have, actually. I have a friend who grew up there. I visited her hometown with her once. It was such a quaint, rustic little place, and absolutely beautiful."

"What a small world!" Elodie says.

Vienna blows out a breath. "Yeah, I'm beginning to realize that."

Dilynne snaps her fingers. "Wait... I saw you at The Charming Bull a couple weeks ago, didn't I?"

All of my friends' eyes land on Dilynne, but I'm looking up at Vienna as her eyes widen. "Oh my gosh, yes! You were in the bull riding contest too, right?"

Henley looks at his sister. "Hold on. You did what?"

"You act like that's surprising," Dilynne counters. "I came in second, by the way. The woman who won took her top off, and there was no competing with that."

Vienna laughs. "Yeah, I guess not. I didn't even know who won because I..." Her words trail off as she glances at me but doesn't finish her thought.

Luckily, my sister interjects before anyone can insinuate anything. "Well, if you need wine recommendations, Rhonan knows our wines better than anyone."

Vienna glances back at me. "I appreciate that, but I'm going to just stick with what I know and let you all get back to your evening." She waves before heading to the bar. "It was nice to see you all again."

"Vienna!" I call out to her, not liking how this entire conversation went down.

She looks back over her shoulder. "It's okay, Rhonan. Enjoy your night with your friends."

My eyes trail her as she gets further away from us, but my sister shoves my shoulder. "God, you're stupid."

"What? What the fuck did I do?"

"The woman is new to town, and instead of trying to be kind, you're acting like she has a contagious disease or something."

"No, I'm not. I just don't want any lines to get blurred."

Dilynne laughs. "Sounds like those lines were blurred two weeks ago, Rhonan. And not that I need to say this out loud, but that woman is hot."

Trust me, I fucking know it.

"She's Ellis's teacher."

"Yeah, but only for a little while," Elodie chimes in. "And sorry to point this out, but you could cut the sexual tension between you two with a knife."

Henley taps the table in front of him. "I told him to ask her out on a date."

"I'm not asking her out on a date."

"Why not?" my sister asks. "You clearly liked her enough to spend all night talking to her before she left—"

"That's enough," I say, cutting her off. Standing from the table, I rest my palms on the wood and flash my strongest glare among my friends. "Look, I don't need a group vote on my love life. I'm a fucking adult who can make my own decisions, thank you very much. Now, can we get back to the reason we're all here, the wedding? Otherwise, I'm going home."

Everyone shares a look before Laney finally nods. "Fine." She glares at me every now and again as we discuss dresses and tux fittings, speeches, and other details for the day my sister becomes Mrs. Fletcher Adams.

I nod along where I'm supposed to, but inside, I'm fuming while also trying to remember that my sister doesn't mean any harm.

But not everyone gets a happy ending, including her older brother, a fact I'm becoming more aware of as the people around me fall into theirs.

She's going to have to accept it.

So am I.

Chapter 7

Vienna

Fence Conversations & A Shower Attack

All I can hear is the sound of crickets chirping and the slight breeze moving through the trees as I sit on my back patio, savoring the cabernet I picked up at Hart Winery last night. Roscoe is prancing around the backyard chasing fireflies, and for the first time in years, I feel grounded, even though there are definitely details of this new version of my life I wasn't anticipating.

My eyes drift over to my neighbor's backyard, and suddenly my heart rate picks up speed. I knew after this past week that seeing Rhonan wouldn't be easy and that avoiding him wouldn't be possible, but I didn't expect our interactions to be so cold.

When he dropped off Ellis at school, his face remained so stoic that it was hard to read. And then last night, when I walked into the tasting room at Hart Winery and saw him with his friends and family, I could tell he didn't want me there.

I wish I could go back to that fateful night and choose differently.

No, you don't, Vienna. Don't lie to yourself.

Sighing, I relent to my subconscious thoughts. I don't regret that night, not one bit. I just wish the aftermath of it had turned out differently. I let my fear win, and now I'm dealing with the consequences of my actions.

Scratching from the wooden fence catches my attention. Roscoe's digging in the dirt, trying to get to the other side.

"Roscoe! No!"

He looks back at me, we make eye contact, and then he turns right back to his task.

I stand from my chair on the back patio and hurry toward him. "Roscoe!" But then a loud bang on the other side of the fence startles us both.

Rhonan's head pops up on the other side, locking eyes with me as he kicks the fence again. Roscoe jumps back, peers up at Rhonan, and begins to bark.

"What are you doing?" I call over the fence.

"Trying to traumatize your dog so he stops digging under my fence," Rhonan says flatly.

A spike of irritation cuts through my surprise. "Excuse me?"

"It's better than getting electrical wire that will shock him," he retorts, crossing his arms over his chest.

My stomach drops. "You would do that?"

"I'd prefer not to," he says, unbothered. "But I don't want him thinking he can just go between our yards."

"I'll add that to the list of things to include in his training." We stand there, staring at each other before I relent and give in to the need to get away from him. "Come on, Roscoe." Snapping my fingers, I get Roscoe's attention and prepare to leave, but Rhonan's voice stops me.

"How's the wine?"

Pausing, I glance down at my glass and then back to him. "It's wonderful."

"Is that the cabernet?"

"Yes."

"Good. That's usually where I steer people if they want a red that's not too heavy."

"I like it all, actually. I used to go wine tasting all the time with..." Suddenly, it becomes very clear that I'm sharing too much, especially with this man who's made it very clear that we are not friends.

"Was there an end to that sentence?"

I sigh. "Look, you've made it pretty clear you want nothing to do with me, so we don't need to do this." I turn back toward the house.

"I was just asking about the wine," he says.

"Why?" I twist back to face him.

"Because it's from my family's winery. I've helped harvest those grapes and run events on those grounds. I take pride in that place, Vienna."

"Oh." Hearing him speak about his family's legacy hits me square in the chest, and seeing the sincerity in his eyes just makes me want to know more about this man.

There's a pain lurking in his eyes too, though. A pain you don't recognize unless you've carried something similar.

Rhonan brushes his hand through his hair. "Look, I'm sorry about last night. Seeing you at the winery just caught me off guard, and my sister—"

"You know, *she's* the one who called me over to your table. She seems nice."

"My sister is one of the best people on the planet, but she doesn't know how to keep her nose out of other people's business."

"You're lucky to have her. Trust me."

"Only child?" he asks.

"Yes."

"Do you ever feel like you missed out on something because it was only you?"

His question catches me by surprise, but I answer it. "Sometimes… But my friends felt like the siblings I never had."

Until they weren't there anymore.

"Why do you ask?" My question slips out before I can stop it.

He smirks. "I thought we weren't going to interact."

I roll my eyes at him. "Then don't ask me questions."

He exhales slowly. "I worry about Ellis," he says, making my stomach twist. "She wants a sibling, but…" His voice trails off. He straightens, shoulders pulling tight. "Look, if you want any more wine recommendations, you know where to find me."

"I'll keep that in mind, thank you."

"And just so you know, in a few weeks, our spring events will start back up at the winery too if you're looking for something to do around town."

"That sounds nice."

Rhonan huffs out a laugh. "It's something my mom started, and just like Laney said, the two of us along with our dad have kept the traditions alive. We have concerts, movie nights, poker tournaments, cooking classes, and yoga." He rolls his eyes. "I still haven't done that one."

"What? Why?"

"Yoga is *not* exercise."

I cross my arms over my chest as I study him. "Have you ever tried it?"

"Nope, and I don't plan to."

"Then, respectfully, your opinion means nothing. I can confirm it's tough."

"You do yoga?" he asks, dipping his eyes up and down my body in a slow pass that reminds me that he's seen me wearing a lot less clothing.

My skin breaks out in goosebumps, but I try to focus on our conversation. "I do. And I lift weights."

"Weightlifting is exercise. That I'll agree with."

"Yoga is important for flexibility, posture, and circulation. It may not be the vigorous type of exercise most people think of, but I assure you, it definitely challenges your body."

He shrugs. "I'll take your word for it, but just know that you won't ever find me at yoga night."

Laughing, I lift my wine glass to my lips. "Stubborn man."

Rhonan takes a step back from the fence, but keeps his gaze locked on mine. "Enjoy the rest of your evening."

"You too."

For a second, neither of us moves. The air feels oddly charged, like something unfinished humming between us. Then Roscoe lets out an impatient huff behind me, reminding me he's waiting for me to go inside.

"Come on, Roscoe."

I head back into my house, ready for a shower and to get some rest. But I'm left with an ever-growing desire to know more about the man who lives next door.

***

Standing in the bathroom, waiting for the shower to warm up, I take a moment to look at my body in the mirror. My hand falls over my stomach, the emptiness still present even after all these years. Part of me wants to believe that everything happens for a reason, but another part of me wonders why some things happen to certain people and not others.

Eager to change my thoughts, I turn back to the shower and stick my hand inside, testing the temperature of the water. Once I deem it hot enough to almost burn me, I step inside and let the scalding water cascade down my body.

But then a loud clank makes me jolt.

When I turn around to see if I can find the source of the noise, water is spewing from a hole in the wall where the showerhead used to be.

"Oh my God!" My voice ricochets off the tiled shower walls as chaos erupts, water spraying in every direction. I try to find an angle where the water can't reach me, but it's no use. The force is so strong, it feels like a belt lashing at my skin.

"Help!" I shout to no one, panic overtaking.

Reaching down for the handle to turn the shower off, I try with all of my might to turn it back to its original position, but it won't budge. "Oh my God! It won't stop!" Holding my hands in front of my face in an attempt to block the water so I can see, I lean down and pick up the showerhead, wondering if I should try to shove it back in the hole in the wall. But I can't open my eyes enough to tell and the piece of metal slips from my grasp, falling to the floor with a loud bang, sparking Roscoe to bark from outside. "Oh my God! This can't be happening!"

With my eyes still closed, I reach for the handle on the shower door, desperate to figure this out before my house floods. But as I step onto the bathmat, I collide with a brick wall—or, at least that's what it feels like.

"Fuck."

"Ahhhh!" I scream, panic flaring again as I start swinging blindly. I will not die like this. I will not be murdered in the nude in my bathroom with a shower that has been possessed by demons with my dog left to wonder what happened to me.

"Vienna!" A familiar voice cuts through the noise of the water and my screams. "Vienna, it's Rhonan."

I crack one eye open, and when I reach up to wipe the water from my face, I'm finally able to make out Rhonan standing in my bathroom, his white T-shirt now completely soaked and plastered to his chest.

"What the hell?" I choke out.

His eyes are dancing all over my body. "What happened?"

"What are you doing here?" I ask instead, frozen even though chaos is still going on around me. The shower door is still open, so now the water is flowing freely onto the floor, flooding the small room. My hair is matted against my face and shoulders, and water is continuing to drip into my eyes.

It's at that moment that I realize I'm still completely naked.

"Oh my God!" My hands instantly fall to my body, attempting to cover up the important parts, but Rhonan is apparently intent on just standing there. "Get out!"

"I heard you screaming and then there was a loud bang, so..."

"So you broke into my house?" I shout, hunched over as I try to hide my nakedness. I flick my chin toward the counter. "Can you at least hand me my towel, please?"

Something must have finally registered for him because his eyes quickly leave my body and he grabs my towel, handing it to me before turning around. "Sorry, but your back door was unlocked and I just...when I hear someone screaming, my instincts kick in to help, I guess."

"I appreciate the knight-in-shining-armor routine yet again, but I'm not dying. My shower just exploded."

He glances at me over his shoulder to make sure I'm covered up, and then directs his eyes back to the shower, sliding the door closed to help prevent more water from coming out. "I can see that now."

I wrap my towel tighter around my body. "I tried to turn it off with the handle, but it's stuck."

Rhonan just nods and walks out of the room.

"Wait. Where are you going?"

"To turn the water off from the main line." He disappears down my hallway, and after a few moments, the water shuts completely off. Breathing heavily, I take a minute to gather my composure, surveying the room that is now covered in water on many surfaces, before walking out to the main part of the house.

My rental house isn't large by any means. There are only two bedrooms, one bathroom, a living area, and kitchen. It's perfect for one person, but right now I'm realizing that my bathroom is out of commission, and I have no other options to finish my shower.

Rhonan returns to the living area, finding me standing there still wrapped in my towel, but much calmer than before.

"Thank you," I say, still clutching onto the towel like a lifeline while trying not to focus on the fact that I probably look like a wet dog.

"You're welcome, but you won't be able to turn your water back on until that's fixed."

A sigh of defeat leaves my lips. "Just great."

Rhonan's eyes dip down my body again, and even though I'm covered, he already knows what's underneath this towel now.

"Did you get to finish your shower, or..."

"Nope. I had barely gotten started."

He lets out a low growl of sorts as he thinks, closing his eyes before pinching the bridge of his nose. "Well, if you want, you can finish showering over at my place."

My heart instantly races. "What?"

"It's the neighborly thing to do, Vienna," he says with a shrug.

"Oh, so now we're being neighborly?"

"Uh, I ran over here when I thought you were being murdered. I think that earns me some good neighbor points."

"Rhonan…"

"Vienna," he fires back, crossing his arms over his chest. "Just come over and take a shower at my house, and then tomorrow, I can take a better look at *your* shower and see if it's an easy fix, or if we need to call a professional."

"You would do that?"

He tilts his head to the side, studying me, as if he's confused by my question. But then he stands up tall, drops his arms, and crosses the room to close the space between us, tipping my chin up with his fingers. When he speaks, his voice is low but steady, forcing me to give him my attention, even though he already had it the second I saw him. "I know this thing between us is complicated, but I am not about to let you go without running water when I could potentially solve that problem. I know I can seem like an ass, but I don't let others go without. You're my neighbor, and you need help. Let's leave it at that, all right?"

I nod, unsure of any words I could say in response because the command he just delivered in combination with his touch is making me clench my thighs together to fight off the burn between my legs. "Okay."

His eyes dip down to the towel around my chest and then slowly make their way back up to my eyes. "And just so we're clear, you should never be shy about what's beneath this towel, Vienna Lewis. Trust me, I'll never forget what you look like underneath." His thumb toys with my bottom lip before he releases my chin.

With an arch of his brow, he turns on his feet and heads for the door. "Grab your stuff and come over. Ellis is still up, and I'm sure she'll be happy to see you." And then he opens my front door and leaves me standing there, not sure if the dripping sound around me is from the water leaving my hair, or the flood this man just caused between my legs.

Chapter 8

Vienna

Showers & Sprinkles

"I can't believe I'm doing this," I mutter to myself while standing on Rhonan's front porch, holding my bag of necessities so I can shower. I managed to soak up most of the water on the floor of the bathroom with the few towels I have in the house, dried myself off, slipped on some comfortable clothes, and then packed up my things to take Rhonan up on his offer.

But now I'm wondering if this is the smartest thing to do.

The front door opens before I can knock or run away, Rhonan revealing himself on the other side of the screen door still secured to the door jamb. "How long were you planning to stand there before you knocked?"

"Just a few more seconds, actually."

He shakes his head. "Sure, whatever you say." Opening the screen, he waves me inside and I cross the threshold nervously.

"Ms. Lewis!" Ellis comes running over to me in her *Frozen*-themed pajamas, bouncing up and down.

"Hi, Ellis."

"Daddy said you were coming over, but you're really here!"

"I am," I say, smiling down at her because her excitement is impossible not to match.

"He said you needed to take a shower because yours broke."

"It did," I say with a laugh while mentally revisiting the ordeal—her father seeing me naked is just another catastrophe to add to the ever-growing list.

"Hi there, Vienna." Joanne comes into the room from around the corner, drying her hands on a dish towel. "Heard you had a bit of an ordeal with your shower." Her eyes drift over to Rhonan and then back to me, her lips curling into a knowing grin.

"Oh yes, it was *quite* the ordeal."

"Well, it's a good thing Rhonan was there to help you, isn't it?"

I tuck my wet hair behind my ear. "Uh, yeah. I guess you could call that lucky..."

"It's been a long time since I've seen that man dart out the front door that fast," she continues, her grin growing wider.

Meanwhile, Rhonan's glaring at her.

"I was making sure she was all right. She screamed like there was an intruder," he says, his tone clipped.

Ellis pulls on my hand. "My daddy would have protected you, Ms. Lewis. He knows how to catch bad guys."

"I know, and I appreciate him making sure I was okay. Unfortunately, my shower isn't working now and it's going to be a few days until I can get it fixed."

Rhonan crosses his arms over his chest, widening his stance. And God, the way his shoulders are highlighted under his white shirt reminds me of what they felt like under my hands the night we met and he picked me up from the floor. "Only if I can't fix it once the stores open up tomorrow."

"Well, you can use my shower," Ellis interjects. "I even have blueberry bubble bath you can use if you want. Daddy says we should share, and I would share that with you."

I smile down at this sweet child. "That's so nice of you, Ellis, but I brought my own soap."

Her eyes widen. "What does it smell like?"

"Cherry blossom and peaches," I reply.

"Can I smell it?" Ellis pleads with her hands clasped together.

Unable to say no to that face, I pull my body wash from my bag and open the cap, bringing it to her nose. She inhales deeply and then hums in approval. "Oh my gosh, I want to eat that."

I laugh. "I know. It's amazing, right?"

She nods. "Yes." Turning to Rhonan, who's been standing there watching our interaction, she says, "You gotta smell it, Daddy. It smells so good."

My eyes lock with his. "I'm okay, Ellis," he says with a tick in his jaw.

She pulls on his shirt from below. "Please, Daddy."

Relenting with a sigh, he reaches for the bottle. I hand it over and then watch him inhale, closing his eyes as the scent hits his nostrils. For a moment, he stands there with his eyes closed, inhaling again. His eyes open, and I swear those blue orbs have grown darker. He clears his throat before handing me the bottle back. "You're right, Ellis. It smells unforgettable."

A zing of adrenaline races through me, but I turn my attention back to Ellis before I let it take over. "Maybe you can get some of this when your blueberry bubble bath runs out."

"I don't know. This bottle doesn't have Bluey on it, and mine does." Shrugging, she takes me by the hand and begins swinging it back and forth. "Did you bring your puppy?"

"No, sweetie. Roscoe is at my house."

She juts out her bottom lip. "Aw, I wanted to play with him. He's funny and fluffy."

"I know, but I won't be here for very long, so I left him snuggled in his bed."

Rhonan clears his throat, interrupting our conversation. "Ellis, let's let Ms. Lewis take her shower, okay?"

She drops my hand. "Fine."

I try to stifle my laugh, but it's no use. The one thing I've enjoyed most about being around my students, including Ellis, is discovering what things are important to them at the tender age of five. Now, at twenty-eight, it's hard for me to even remember a time when life was that simple and black and white. I've been living under gray clouds for years, but these kids are helping the hues of a rainbow break through.

Always look for the rainbows, Vienna.

"Let me show you to the bathroom," Rhonan says, nodding down the hall.

"Don't leave without saying goodbye!" Ellis calls after me as I follow her dad down a long hallway.

"I promise I won't."

Ellis runs up to me and holds out her pinky. "Pinky promise?"

Glancing over at Rhonan, I ask for guidance with my eyes. "What do I do?"

"You've never heard of a pinky promise?"

"Uh, can't say that I have."

He gently grabs my hand and brings it to Ellis's, intertwining our pinkies. "Lock them together like this and then shake your hands up and down."

"Like this." Ellis guides me as our hands remain connected, laughing. "Good. Now you can't break the promise, or I get to break your pinky."

Rhonan groans. "We talked about that, Ellis. You can't break people's pinkies."

"But that's what Johnny said you have to do if someone breaks a pinky promise."

Ellis mentioning one of the other kids from her class makes me think. "Oh, Johnny said that, did he?"

"Yeah, Johnny likes to say all kinds of shit," Rhonan replies.

"Daddy, you said a bad word."

"You're right. I'm sorry, Ellis. Stuff—Johnny says all kinds of *stuff*."

"You know better, Daddy," Ellis says with an arch of her brow before running back to the living room.

A snort leaves me before I can stop it. "Oh my gosh, your daughter is something else."

Rhonan shakes his head. "Trust me, I know." We arrive at a door, and Rhonan twists the knob open, revealing a beautiful bathroom with pale blue walls and purple décor. "As you can tell, this is Ellis's bathroom, but I promise you, the showerhead won't fall off the wall."

"Thank you, Rhonan. I really appreciate this."

He shrugs. "Again, it's the neighborly thing to do." He moves to walk back down the hall but pauses just as he passes behind me. Lowering his voice, he leans toward me. "By the way, glad to know what body wash you use."

"Why is that?" I ask almost breathlessly.

I can feel the heat of him as he moves closer, his lips just near the shell of my ear. "Because that night, I couldn't pinpoint what the scent you had on was. Now I know. And I wasn't lying, it is unforgettable."

Before I can reply, he walks away. Now I'm even more confused because for a man who told me he wants us to keep our distance, he keeps finding ways to get closer to me, and I can't deny that I don't want him to stop.

***

After I'm finally clean and dressed, I gather my things and step out of the bathroom, only to find Ellis sitting on the couch, apparently waiting for me to reappear. As soon as our eyes meet, she jumps from the couch and races toward me.

"Ms. Lewis! Do you like ice cream?"

"I do," I tell her, laughing at her urgency.

"Do you want some? Daddy said you can have some with us if you want."

When I reach the living room and see Rhonan standing in the kitchen area with his arms crossed over his chest, his face is unreadable. Seems like that's his signature look.

"Is that so?" I turn to look at Rhonan. "What kind of ice cream is it?"

"Vanilla. We keep things simple around here."

"Any toppings?"

Rhonan arches a brow at me. "Chocolate syrup and sprinkles. Will those suffice?"

I turn back to Ellis. "Sprinkles are my favorite."

Her eyes light up. "Mine too, especially rainbow ones! Come on!" She pulls me into the kitchen, but I break away just for a second to set my bag down by the couch before meeting her at the kitchen counter.

"Is Joanne joining us?" I ask as I climb onto a stool.

Rhonan pulls the tub of ice cream closer to him, digging into it with a metal scoop. "No. She's turned in for the night."

"Joanne doesn't like ice cream," Ellis says, shaking her head as she hops onto a stool next to me. Her little legs start swinging while she watches her father. "I loooove ice cream."

"What kind of person doesn't like ice cream?" I wince as I realize my words may have come off a bit rude. "Sorry..."

Rhonan chuckles. "No need to apologize. I thought the same thing, but it turns out when you're lactose intolerant, it's not so much about not liking it as not being able to have it."

"She has to eat a special kind of ice cream," Ellis adds solemnly. "It doesn't taste good."

I nod in understanding. "I don't think I could live without ice cream."

Rhonan slides two bowls across the counter to us. Ellis launches forward, reaching for the jar of sprinkles, but I steady her so she doesn't fall. "Easy, kiddo. Do you need some help?"

"No, I've got it." With the sprinkles in hand, she sits back down and shakes the container up and down until you can barely see the ice cream underneath.

"That's enough, Ellis," Rhonan declares, but Ellis keeps shaking the sprinkles out. "Ellis."

Her eyes lift to find her dad glaring at her, so she slowly sets the container down. "There's no such thing as too many sprinkles, Daddy. Auntie Laney said so."

"Yeah, well, Auntie Laney isn't the one who has to argue with you about brushing your teeth at night, so her word isn't gospel."

"What does that mean?" Ellis asks around a mouthful of ice cream.

I giggle and then begin shaking the sprinkle container over my bowl, opting for far fewer sprinkles than Ellis, but still enough to add some color to the plain treat.

"That's not a lot of sprinkles," Ellis mumbles while assessing my bowl.

"I don't want to overdo it," I explain. "Then I won't be able to fully appreciate the ice cream underneath. Sometimes, less is more." I look up to find Rhonan staring at me. "What?"

"Nothing." He takes the chocolate syrup and drizzles it over his bowl. "I agree. You don't want to overpower the ice cream."

"Wow. Did we just agree on something?"

He narrows his eyes at me. "I don't think that's the first time we have, Vienna."

"It's Ms. Lewis, Daddy," Ellis interrupts.

"Sorry. Ms. Lewis," he repeats my name per his daughter's correction.

"It's okay. But Ellis, you were right about the sprinkles." I take a bite of the ice cream and moan dramatically. "Sprinkles make everything better."

She nods, fixated on the ice cream in front of her. "Yup."

Rhonan and I share a laugh and then in a matter of minutes, the ice cream is gone, and Ellis lets out a yawn.

"It's time for bed, sweetie," Rhonan says to her.

"But I'm not tired." Standing there rubbing her eyes sort of contradicts her words, but I'm not getting involved with their father-daughter dynamic.

"Ms. Lewis is going home too, so you're not going to miss any-thing." His eyes lift to mine, seeking help.

"That's right. I need to get home to Roscoe."

"Can I play with him tomorrow?" she asks, pleading with the most beautiful blue eyes that match her father's. Her hair is much darker than his, though, which makes me think she must have gotten that characteristic from her mother.

Speaking of which, where is Ellis's mom?

"I'm sure Ms. Lewis has things to do," Rhonan answers for me.

"I do, but if there's time, I'll ask your dad if it's okay. How does that sound?"

Ellis nods enthusiastically. "Okay!"

"Now, go brush your teeth so you don't get any cavities." I urge her toward the hall.

"I eat all of the cavities," she mumbles, letting out another yawn.

I turn to Rhonan. "Did she just say she *eats* cavities?"

"Yeah. I made the mistake of telling her that any type of sugar is called cavities, so now that's what she calls candy, cake...pretty much anything sweet."

"That's really adorable."

He shrugs. "Some parenting mistakes work out okay."

"Not sure that's classified as a mistake, Rhonan."

"Well, it's definitely not as big as other ones I've made."

Silence rests between us. "I hope I'm not out of line for asking, but...where is Ellis's mom?"

His smile falls. "I figured you would have already heard that story."

"How so?"

He shrugs. "Small town."

"Yes, but it's not like I've been going around asking about you."

He stares at me, debating his reply, and I'm not sure if his lack of words is annoyance or not. "Ellis's mom isn't with us anymore," he starts. "She, uh...died giving birth to her."

My hand flies to my chest. "Oh my God. I'm so—"

He holds a hand up, stopping me. "We've done okay."

"I know, but—"

"Seriously, Vienna. Don't." I'm not sure if he meant to sound that harsh, but I close my lips like he asked.

An awkward silence rests between us again, but ironically, it's filled with emotions—pain, grief, sadness, and anger—most of which are wafting off the man in front of me.

Not wanting to push him on a topic he clearly doesn't want to speak about, I tuck my hair behind my ear. "Well, I'd best be going. Thank you again for the shower and the ice cream." Reaching for my bag, I hoist it up over my shoulder just as Ellis reappears. "Good night, Ellis. Thank you for sharing your ice cream with me."

"Good night, Ms. Lewis." She runs up to me, hugging my legs tightly until her little arms give out.

Glancing back at the man who is making me more confused by the minute, I wave. "Good night, Rhonan."

"Good night, Ms. Lewis."

As I walk back to my house and step inside, finding Roscoe still in his kennel where I left him, it dawns on me why that look in Rhonan's eyes is so familiar.

It's grief. Pain from loss.

Turns out we have more in common than I thought.

***

"I can't even remember the last time I saw you laugh with him, Vienna."

Lydia holds her wine glass in her hand while resting her arm against the side of my couch. My eyes drift over her sunken face and the scarf wrapped around her head as dread fills my chest. But I can't deny that I'm having trouble recalling an instance to placate her. "The fact that you're still trying to come up with an example is telling."

"We've just...both been busy. Work is stressful for him, and—"

She cuts me off. "Why is it always about him? When's the last time you got to choose what you wanted to do, like your job? Why does your job have to be about what he wants?"

"We agreed it's what's best for us right now."

Lydia shakes her head. "No, Vienna. It's what he thought was best. God, I—" Her frustration is growing and I know I'm about to get hit with a hard dose of reality from my best friend. But maybe that's what I need. She leans forward in her seat. "Look, you know I love you. You're my ride or die, but I've been holding my tongue for far too long because I didn't want to be that friend, the one who criticizes your decisions and tells you how to live your life. But guess what? I won't be around to look out for you..."

Emotion clogs my throat. "Lydia..."

She drains the rest of the wine and sets the empty glass on the coffee table before leaning forward and reaching for my hand, pulling me closer to her. "I'm done acting like your marriage is okay. Cole is a shitty husband."

"Wow. Okay, tell me how you really feel."

"I am. And since you married him, you've become a shell of the woman I've called my best friend for fifteen years." Her words sting as my eyes fill with tears, but I don't say anything. "That man has slowly shown you his true colors, and I'm not sure if you're just oblivious to them, or you're choosing to keep on your rose-colored glasses."

"Lydia..."

"I know you made vows. I know you've been with him for almost ten years, but a part of you has slowly slipped away since you two got married, and given that you haven't been able to..."

"Marriage isn't easy."

She releases my hand and sits upright again. "You're right. It's not, and I don't have the firsthand experience to relate. But I also know that it shouldn't be like what you're living in right now." She lowers her voice. "You used to think that he was just overprotective, but now I see it more as jealousy and a desire to control you."

"What do you mean?"

"Jealousy feels a lot like love until you experience trust, Vienna."

I want to argue with her, but something stops me. Maybe it's the fact that her words are so powerful, they've rendered me speechless. Or maybe it's the way she looks as if she's gearing up to tell me more.

"Look, I didn't want to do this tonight, but there's something I need to tell you."

"Is it about your scan?"

She inhales deeply. "Yes."

"No..." My eyebrows draw closer and my eyes start to sting. "Lydia?"

"I'm not getting better, Vienna." She inhales deeply and then says, "And I'm not sure how much time I have left."

Chapter 9

Rhonan

Plumbing, Piercing Talk, and a Car Wash

"Hold that still." I motion for Elliot to keep the new showerhead stable on the connector from the wall while I grab my wrench.

"I can't believe you called me over here on a Sunday to fix a fucking showerhead for your neighbor."

I wrap the wrench around the pipe and start turning. "Was I just supposed to let Vienna go without a shower?"

"No. But why didn't she just call the landlord?" He arches a brow at me.

"It's an easy fix. No need to bother him, and then one of the two plumbers we have in town when I can get it done in a few hours. It would take twice as long."

Elliot shakes his head at me. "Nah, I think there's more to it than that. I think that since you're fixing her pipes, you're hoping she'll return the favor."

I glare at him as I turn the wrench one last time. "Fuck you."

He barks out a laugh. "So, I'm right?"

Standing tall again, I wipe the sweat from my forehead. "No, you're not. I am simply helping her out. There's no ulterior motive here."

Elliot drops his hands from the showerhead and reaches for a rag, wiping them off. "You know, you might crack a tooth from how hard you're clenching your jaw right now, trying to pretend that you don't want her."

"I'm not...I don't..."

Elliot rolls his eyes. "Rhonan, I hate to tell you this, but you're a horrible liar." He sighs heavily. "Looks like I'm losing another friend to a woman."

"You're not losing Fletcher and Henley, Elliot. And don't worry about me. I don't plan on dating anytime soon."

"So, would you still be willing to go with me to get my dick pierced then?"

I hold a hand up. "Uh, I was never willing to do that."

"Come on, Rho. I need someone else there."

"Why? No one wants to see you get a needle shoved through your penis, man...respectfully."

"Uh... I guess this was not the best conversation to walk in on." Vienna's voice comes from the door. She's standing there with her hair piled up on her head, wearing a green tank top and a pair of denim shorts that are covering far more of her than the last pair I saw her wearing.

"Vienna, let me ask you a question," Elliot starts.

"Okay..."

"If you wanted to, let's say, get your nipples pierced... Would you want a friend to go with you?"

She darts her eyes over to me, but I hope she can't see the thoughts going through my head before she focuses back on Elliot. Vienna has perfect-sized breasts, and the idea of a barbell going through her perfect nipples is making my dick swell in record time. I don't think I'd ever be able to stop playing with her nipples if they were pierced.

You don't want to play with them though, right, Rhonan?

Luckily, Vienna clears her throat while cautiously responding, pulling me from my thoughts. "Well, I don't have any desire to do that. However, I did go with one of my friends to get her nipples pierced because she was afraid of going by herself. So, I can see your side of things."

Elliot holds a hand out to me. "See?"

"Nipples are much different than your dick," I fire back.

Vienna laughs behind her hand. "And yeah, sorry, Elliot, but I have to agree with Rhonan on this one. If she had asked me to go with her to get her clit pierced, I don't think I would have gone."

I arch a brow at her, surprised. "Thank you."

"Of course. Besides, it doesn't look like you're done fixing my shower yet, so I'd better not piss you off or rub you the wrong way before you're finished."

Fuck, I'd let you rub me any way you want, woman.

I groan as that thought swirls in my brain and then turn my back to her and Elliot so they can't see my dick start to swell again in my shorts. "We should only be about another ten minutes. The hard part of installing the new connector and sealing it with tape is done, so now I just need to put on the new head."

"I'm glad it was an easy fix. I can't thank you enough, Rhonan."

I glance at her over my shoulder. "Again, it's not a big deal. Elliot and I will be out there in a little bit. Is Roscoe still with Ellis in the backyard?"

Vienna nods. "Your backyard, yes. Joanne's watching them while I came in here to check on you two."

"Then we'll meet you back over there."

She doesn't say another word before leaving. I reach for the new showerhead and hand the detachable part to Elliot while I search for my other wrench. Elliot remains quiet, but I can feel him staring at me. "What?"

"I'm just trying to decide how long it takes for you to sleep with her."

"You're out of your mind. I already told you guys, I'm just trying to keep things simple here."

"So, you wouldn't mind if I asked her out then?"

I drop the wrench from my hands, the loud clang of it hitting the shower floor ringing out, but my eyes are laser-focused on my friend. "Don't fuck with me, Elliot."

There's a smirk on his lips, but he doesn't flinch. "I'm not. I mean, she's hot, man. I can see why—"

Before I know what's happening, my hands are fisted in his shirt and I have him pressed up against the shower wall. He's fucking smiling at me, knowing what he just did. He dangled a carrot right in front of my face, and I fucking took the bait. But I don't fucking care. The thought of Elliot and Vienna makes me want to pry his hands off of his body so he can't touch her.

"Don't. Fucking. Think. About. It," I grind out, punctuating every word.

Elliot's grin is so irritating right now, I contemplate punching him just because. But I think I've made myself clear.

"Then *you* do something about it, Rhonan."

"I told you—"

He cuts me off. "Yeah, I know what you said. But I call bullshit. I think the reason you're so on edge right now is because your body is telling you one thing, but your head is telling you another."

I deepen my glare. "Funny, I could say the same thing about you."

His smile falls. "What the fuck are you talking about?"

"Tell me why you walked away when Dilynne was riding the bull at the bar," I demand.

His hands wrap around mine where they're still fisted in his shirt. "I needed a fucking drink."

"You sure? Or did your little experiment work and—"

He shoves me off of him, both of our chests heaving. "You don't know what you're talking about."

I huff out a laugh. "Yeah, that's what I thought." Turning back to the showerhead, I pick up the new piece and start to attach it. "Just take this as a warning not to come for me if you're not willing to face your own fucking truth, man."

Elliot stays quiet for a moment, but when he speaks, it's not what I expected him to say. "Will we ever move on, Rhonan?" The words almost come out as a whisper, but they're filled with much more uncertainty than I wanted to hear from him—because he sounds like me.

My thoughts race while trying to find an answer. "I—I honestly don't know, Elliot."

I can pinpoint several instances in my life that have turned me into this man, but the idea of moving forward means letting go of the past—and the only thing I'm certain of is that I have no idea how to do that.

***

"Look at me, Daddy!" Ellis shouts as she cruises past me on her bike, pride radiating from her smile.

"Nice, Ellis! Keep going!" Standing on the sidewalk and watching my daughter ride her bike without training wheels is a feeling I can't quite explain. After last year when this task felt unattainable, she and I are both beyond proud of how far she's come.

"I'm the fastest bike rider ever!" She turns around slowly at the end of our street and pedals as fast as her small legs will allow. I bet if I clocked her with the radar gun, she's barely breaking five miles per hour, but to a five-year-old, I bet it feels like sixty.

Chuckling, I humor her. "Definitely the fastest one I've ever seen."

Reaching down to pick up the hose again, I turn the nozzle on and spray the stream of water over my truck. I meant to wash it last weekend, but I spent that time fixing Vienna's showerhead instead. Now, it's Thursday and I'm working all weekend, so I won't have time to get it done. And I hate having a dirty vehicle, on the inside and out.

Ellis cruises back onto the driveway just as a car slowly comes down the street. It only takes me a few seconds to recognize the silver Mercedes, which means my neighbor is home.

Vienna pulls into her driveway, shuts off her car, and then slowly stands from her driver's side door, smiling over at me and my daughter, waving as well. "Hi there, Ellis. I love your bike."

"Thank you, Ms. Lewis. Uncle Fletcher got it for me." She rings the bell on the handle bar. "It even has a bell and a basket for my dolls." Lifting one of her Barbies from the basket, she waves it around.

"That's really special."

Ellis nods, then takes off back down the driveway and out onto the street.

"I didn't see you look both ways!" I shout after her, but she doesn't even glance back.

Vienna's laugh rings out as she shuts her car door, slinging her bag over her shoulder. "She either didn't hear you or is already great at ignoring you."

"I think it's a little bit of both," I say as I watch her walk toward me, crossing the grass in her heels and navy dress, and doing so almost flawlessly.

Fuck, I've forgotten how sexy she is in the few days since we've crossed paths.

No, you haven't, Rhonan, but keep lying to yourself.

Sadly, my subconscious is right. There has been no shortage of this woman running through my mind, and since I can't seem to shut it off, it's just making me more irritated.

But those legs, that ass, and that fucking twinkle in her eye when she smiles at me—she's got me interested in her, and that's a big fucking problem.

I don't date. And I bet if I hadn't already met her, hadn't already felt that pull, she wouldn't be affecting me this much.

Vienna licks her lips as she arrives just a few feet away from me, teasing me with what I can't have even more. "Well, if it makes you feel any better, she's excellent at listening when she's at school. In fact, she's the one who makes sure the other kids are paying attention."

I can't hold back my smirk. "Yeah, sounds about right."

"She wasn't lying about liking to be the boss, either. But it actually works in my favor because I can count on her to be responsible and help me with passing out papers and things like that."

"Glad you're putting her strengths to good use, but if she ever takes it too far, just let me know and I'll talk to her about it."

"I appreciate that, but I don't think it'll be a problem." Vienna places her hand on my upper arm, making my bicep tense. She catches it, dipping her eyes to my arm and then back up to my face, clearing her throat but not releasing me from her grasp. Feeling her hands on me now is just reminding me of what they felt like as she clung to me while she rested in my arms.

Fuck. I'm gonna need a cold shower after this fucking interaction.

"She's a good kid, Rhonan. You should be proud."

Something tight in my chest loosens. "Thank you. I am."

"Daddy!" Ellis shouts as she returns to our driveway, skidding to a stop right in front of me and Vienna. "Can I help you wash your truck?"

"Yes, sweetie."

Ellis nods while letting her bike fall to the ground and reaching up to unbuckle her helmet. "Yay! I wanna play with the bubbles."

Vienna giggles, and fuck, it reminds me of how that giggle made my chest twist the first night we met. "The bubbles are fun to play with."

Ellis turns to Vienna. "Do you want to help us, Ms. Lewis?" She bounces up and down at the idea.

"Oh, uh..."

I step in so Vienna doesn't have to come up with an excuse. "I'm sure Ms. Lewis has things to do. She just got home."

Vienna nods. "Yeah... I haven't eaten dinner yet."

"You can come back out when you're done!" Ellis pushes more, and I know if I don't put an end to this, my daughter will come up with even more reasons for Vienna to hang out with us.

"Not tonight, Ellis." My tone is firm, and just as I anticipate, my daughter shoots me a glare I know will only get worse as she gets older.

"Fine." She starts to walk toward the garage with her helmet in her hand, but I stop her.

"Ellis?"

"What, Daddy?"

"You forgot your bike. We don't leave it in the middle of the driveway."

Stomping back to where she left her bike, Vienna and I both watch her pick it up and roll it inside the garage. She hangs her helmet on the hook on the wall and then she's going inside to change her shoes because I always make her wear sandals when we wash the truck so her tennis shoes don't get wet.

I glance back over at Vienna. "You were saying my daughter is so well-behaved, right?"

Vienna laughs. "She's just headstrong, Rhonan. Trust me. There are worse things for her to be."

I push a hand through my hair. "Somedays, I'm not so sure."

"Don't worry. She'll be better off for it. She won't let people take advantage of her. She won't stay in a situation that feels wrong, or worse, change who she is for anyone."

Vienna is staring off in the distance, but my gaze is locked on her. The tone of her words right now doesn't sound like she's just spouting something to appease my concerns.

No, she sounds as if she's speaking from experience.

Shrugging, she readjusts her bag and takes a step back, forcing a smile. "Anyway, I'll let you get back to washing your truck."

"Yeah. Okay."

She gives me a soft wave and then heads back to her house. "Have a good night, Rhonan."

"You too."

I stand there watching her walk away for so long that Ellis's voice startles me from behind. "Daddy?"

"Yeah, Ellis?" I turn to face her, expecting to find her waiting for instructions. But to my surprise, she's holding the hose and then unleashes the water on me, spraying every inch of my body until there's not a single dry spot left on me.

"Ellis Seraphina!" I shout at her as her laughter rings out. A dog bark breaks through the noise, and that's when I glance back to see Roscoe poking his nose between two slats of the fence. When I turn back to my daughter, she sprays me again.

"Got you, Daddy!" Her screams filter through her laughter as I lunge for her. She drops the hose and takes off, but instead of racing after her and risking me slipping and breaking something, I pick up the hose and return the favor.

"What are you two doing?" Joanne calls out from the front porch.

I lift my soaking wet shirt from my body and toss it toward her. "My daughter has forgotten who's the adult around here."

Joanne picks up my shirt and starts ringing it out as I blast the water at my little girl.

"Daddy! No!" Ellis is laughing so hard that it's triggering my own laughter, but she keeps running away from me, yet not far enough where the water can't reach her.

"Looks like you both won't need a shower after all tonight."

"Can I take a bath outside?" Ellis calls out to Joanne.

"We're supposed to be washing my truck, Ellis," I tell her. "You started this. Are you ready to surrender?"

She holds up her hands. "Yes, Daddy. I give up."

"Good." Dropping the hose to the ground, we both stand there catching our breath.

"You're running out of daylight," Joanne says from the front porch, reaching for the door handle. "And you have an audience, so you might want to put another shirt on." She motions to the house next door, and that's when my eyes land on Vienna, still standing on her front doorstep, watching my water fight with my daughter unfold.

But her eyes are locked on me, and even though she's fairly far away, I can still make out the movement of her tongue darting out to lick her lips.

I arch a brow at her and then flex my pecs.

Fuck, really, Rhonan? Some might call that flirting, which is a far cry from trying to ignore the woman like you planned on.

"Daddy?" Ellis calls from a few feet away, but I'm still staring at my neighbor, a problem that's getting worse with each passing day.

"Yes, Ellis?"

The hose turns on again and hits me square in the face. "I will never surrender!" she screams as her laughter rings out again.

And even though I'm back to fighting for my life, I can't stop thinking about the way Vienna was looking at me.

How the hell is that supposed to help me keep the distance between us when I'm the one who insisted on it in the first place?

Chapter 10

Vienna

Memories, Gossip, & Rocks

"Ms. Lewis!" Kara, one of the girls in my class, comes running up to me on the playground. "Johnny won't stop chasing me."

I look over at the blacktop where Johnny is waiting for Kara to return. From what I've seen, he seems to love pushing the other kids' buttons. Focusing back on Kara, I crouch down so we're at eye level. "Maybe you should try *not* running from him."

She looks at me quizzically. "Why?"

"Because if you don't run, then he can't chase you."

Her head tilts to the side as she ponders my advice and then she shakes her head. "No, that sounds boring." Before I can reply, she takes off and races right past Johnny, leading him to chase her again.

Stacey—the only person I'd consider a friend that I've made in this town so far, mostly because we see each other every day at work—walks up to me, playing with the lanyard around her neck. "Was Kara telling on Johnny for chasing her?"

"Yeah, how'd you know?"

"Oh, it's their routine. I'm surprised you haven't gotten a glimpse of it sooner."

I think back to the past few weeks, but much of it has become a blur. Between teaching, trying to train Roscoe, and attempting to ignore Rhonan but failing miserably, I'm running on fumes. "Well, now that you mention it, I do think I remember a similar exchange last week."

"I'm telling you, she'll come up to you again at least one more time before the week is over complaining about him chasing her, only to go right back to running around with him." Stacey shakes her head. "Some girls get sucked into patterns at a young age, I guess."

Part of me wants to snap back at Stacey for her judgment, but that would mean opening up about my own toxic patterns and how hard I've fought to overcome them. Instead, I shrug. "They're only kids."

"Yeah, you're probably right. But I just think about how many times I was told as a kid that if a boy is mean to me, that means he likes me. If I only knew what a crock of shit that was back then, it could have saved me a few bouts of heartache, you know what I mean?"

Sighing, I nod. "Yeah. I really do."

Ellis walks up to me now, holding several rocks in her hands. "Ms. Lewis?"

"Yes, Ellis?"

"Can I put these in my backpack, please?"

"Um, you still have about seven minutes left of recess, sweetie."

The rocks tumble from her hands and onto the blacktop beneath her. "Can I leave them here with you, then?"

"Why do you need all of these rocks, Ellis?"

She smiles up at me. "They're for my daddy."

"Your dad likes rocks?"

"He likes the ones I give him."

Her candor makes me chuckle. "Okay, well..."

"Can you please watch them, Ms. Lewis? I don't want anyone to steal them."

My eyes scour the pile at my feet. They look like ordinary rocks to me, but what do I know? Besides, I had a fixation like that once upon a time as well. "Sure, Ellis. I'll watch them."

She lunges for my legs, wrapping her arms around them. "Thank you! You're the best teacher ever!" And then she takes off, running back to the group of girls I've seen her play with numerous times.

"Rocks, huh?" Stacey asks.

I shrug. "Every kid has their thing. Mine was pine cones."

Stacey nods. "My brother collected bugs and didn't tell anyone that he brought them into his room, so one day my mom went in to clean it and noticed the floor was moving. You can imagine the horror of having to exterminate the entire space."

Covering my mouth with my hand, I stifle my sound of disgust. "I would die."

Stacey looks over my shoulder toward the outside of the school. "Is it just me, or has that woman been standing around for a little too long out there?"

Spinning to look in that direction, my eyes land on a woman that can't be much older than me. "I honestly don't know. I didn't notice her."

"She's been there as long as the kids have been outside." Stacey peers down at her watch on her wrist, waving me off with her other hand. "I wonder if she's waiting for someone, or if she's someone's aunt or grandma, or something? It happens quite a bit in our small town."

Awareness creeps up my spine, but I attempt to push it away. Paranoia isn't a friend of mine, but I'm sure this woman is there for a reason. Just as I tell myself that in my head, she leans up against the fence, gripping the metal poles and pushing her head close to the structure, like she's attempting to see something better. If I didn't know any better, I'd say she looks familiar.

"Should I go over there and say something?"

Stacey shakes her head, squinting in the woman's direction again. "You know what? That's Sally's aunt. She's harmless. Walks by the school every once in a while and waves to the kids."

As I'm about to look away, the woman waves in my direction, but it's a small wave. Honestly, if I wasn't looking right at her, I would have missed it. I arch a brow and then twist my head around to see if there's anyone else she might be waving to, but no one is looking in her direction.

I turn back toward the playground, ready to let it go, when that unsettled feeling lingers anyway—prickling along my spine for no real reason I can name.

Why is this woman's presence making me feel curious? And why does she look like someone I used to know?

"You know what, Stacey... I'm gonna go talk to her."

Both of her brows lift. "Are you sure?"

"Yeah. Watch the kids. I'll—I'll be right back."

She nods and I head toward the fence. When I get closer to the woman, her features become clearer, and that's when it hits me—*she looks like Lydia.*

"Ma'am? Can I help you?"

Her eyes connect with mine in an instant before she releases the iron bars and takes a step back. "Oh. No. I was just...watching the kids play."

"You sure? Visitors are supposed to check into the office. My colleague said you are Sally's aunt."

Tears fill her eyes. "Yes. I'm—I'm sorry if I caused any alarm. I just wanted to watch the kids play."

"Are...are you all right?"

A laugh filters through her tears. "God, I'm sorry. This is...this is embarrassing."

"Why is that?"

Clasping her hands over the center of her chest, she says, "I just...I wasn't ever able to have kids, so sometimes I come down to the school and watch them play..."

She keeps talking, but her words hit me harder than they should. Reaching through the fence, I grasp her hand as her eyes dip down to the sight. "I get it."

When she lifts her head, there's a hint of hope lurking in her gaze. "You do?"

I nod. "Yes, but I'm going to warn you, this sort of thing could be received the wrong way."

We share a laugh. "God, I'm sorry. Usually, I just go to the park and sit on a bench and watch the moms chase their kids around to torture myself, but..."

My heart twists in my chest. "It's all right." But before I can say another word, the hair on the back of my neck stands up as the energy around us shifts. Dropping her hand, I take a step back from the fence. "Are you going to be okay?"

"Yes. Thank you for being so kind."

"Of course. We never know what demons someone else is battling on a daily basis." I dart my eyes across the street, searching for the source of this uneasiness building in my gut, but then turn my attention back to the woman. "I hope you find some peace."

"Thank you."

The bell rings, signaling the end of recess and forcing me to put my teacher cap back on so I can gather my class and head back inside. But in the back of my mind, I'm wondering what happened while I was standing there to make my sixth sense perk up.

Luckily, Ellis runs over to me, crouching down to pick up the pile of rocks she collected that I forgot I was supposed to be looking after, bringing me back to the present. "My rocks are still here!"

"I told you I would look out for them."

"Thank you, Ms. Lewis. You're the best." With her arms full, she steps in line and I lead my class back inside, checking over my shoulder to see if the woman is still standing there.

She's gone.

You must just be imagining things, Vienna. Besides, it's not like anyone knows that you're here or would bother showing up if they did.

Well, maybe just one person would.

Once the kids and I are back in the classroom, Ellis walks over to her backpack and deposits her collection of rocks inside.

"What are you doing with those rocks?" Caleb, one of the little boys in the class, asks Ellis.

"I'm putting them away so I can give them to my dad when I get home."

"You give your dad rocks?"

Ellis nods. "Yup." She zips up her backpack and then leads Caleb over to the carpet for story time, plopping down cross-legged in her usual spot.

I settle into my chair and open the book in my lap. "Okay, class. Now, we're going to jump back into our book we started yesterday."

Ellis's hand shoots up.

"Yes, Ellis?"

"Ms. Lewis, when we get home today, do you wanna come over and see my dad's rock collection?"

Johnny snickers from his spot in the back of the carpet. "Ms. Lewis can't go to your house, Ellis. She's the teacher."

Ellis turns around to face him, a look of annoyance on her face. "Yes, she can, Johnny."

"No, she can't. She has her own house."

Ellis sits up taller. "I know that. Her house is next to mine."

Caleb nearly shrieks. "You live next to Ms. Lewis? Lucky!"

Rosalie chimes in. "Does she live in a castle?"

"No, but she has a puppy named Roscoe and I get to play with him."

Chatter breaks out among the kids. "Okay, everyone. Look, we need to finish the story. Eyes on me!" But my words fall on deaf ears.

"And my daddy fixed her shower when it broke, and she ate ice cream with us," Ellis continues.

Henry comes up to me, pulling on my skirt. "Can you come over to my house and eat ice cream?"

"I have a puppy that your puppy can play with!" Jayden's little voice cries out.

I finally lift my whistle from around my neck and blow it, not too loud since we are inside, but loud enough that it cuts through the chaos.

The kids reach up and cover their ears with their hands, but Ellis just sits on the carpet, pleased with herself.

"Okay. Look, I know everyone is very excited. Yes, I live next to Ellis, but I am still her teacher. And right now, my job is to read the rest of this story to you. So, can we all stay quiet long enough for me to do that?" The little heads all bob up and down in unison. "Great. Now, where did we leave off?"

Ellis blurts, "We left off where the cricket was talking to the bumblebee."

Johnny whispers under his breath. "Teacher's pet." A few of the other boys giggle.

Ellis turns back to look at them, but when she faces forward again, she visibly deflates. The confidence she had just a few moments ago has almost disappeared, and I hate that she's suddenly quiet.

I catch her eye and give her a small smile, just for her. "Thank you, Ellis."

I turn to where we left off in *The Very Quiet Cricket* and continue reading.

As I flip through the pages, the story of the cricket begins to resonate with me a bit more. He encounters a flurry of other insects and creatures that all make a sound, but when he tries to rub his own wings together to chirp, nothing happens. Each attempt is feeble, until he finally crosses paths with another cricket—and then he's able to make a sound.

And then something so silly hits me, but it's more powerful than I realize—I wonder if I'll ever find my cricket who lets me be heard.

***

"Daddy, look at how high I can swing!" I've barely walked into my backyard, and I can already hear the precious little girl on the other side of the fence.

"Be careful or you're going to swing to the moon, and I'll never see you again!" Rhonan's deep voice rings out as well, and since it's been a few days since I've heard it, my heart starts to beat a bit faster at the sound.

"I don't want to go to space." I hear the faint sound of wood chips being kicked up followed by the pitter-patter of tiny footsteps.

It's about an hour before the sun sets, and I planned on sitting on the patio and cracking open the latest hockey romance release from my favorite romance author to unwind after an eventful day, but as soon as I heard Ellis's voice, it dawned on me that I should probably speak to Rhonan about what happened today in class.

Now, if only I can manage that conversation without imagining him with his shirt off again.

Last week when his attempt to wash his truck turned into a water fight with his daughter, I tried to look away. My shoulder was crumbling under the weight of my bag and my feet were aching from the heels I now know not to wear when teaching kindergarteners, but I couldn't stop watching the two of them. The sound of their laughter was the epitome of joy. Their smiles fueled the spread of my own.

But when Rhonan took his shirt off? That sight fueled a different sort of response in my body, one that centered right between my legs where a dull ache has resided ever since that night together.

The man is a walking wet dream—sculpted arms and torso, a chiseled jaw and striking blue eyes, and he wears a uniform, for crying out loud. How on earth is any woman supposed to resist that?

And more importantly, how is he still single?

Not only is he insanely attractive, but he's a good man—steadfast, brave, loves his daughter but doesn't let her walk all over him, and he cares about people. After all, he took the time to help me with my shower when I'm sure he had a hundred other things he needed to do with his day off.

I can't remember the last time a man did something like that for me, and that says something, given the status of my last relationship.

I'm so pissed at myself for all the time I wasted getting here, but at least I'm not wasting any more.

I'm making moves, Lydia. I hope you're proud of me.

"Roscoe!" Ellis's voice cuts through my thoughts, and then there's a knock on the fence. "Roscoe?"

My sweet puppy, who is getting better trained by the day, runs over to the fence and scratches at it, eager to get to the sweet girl on the other side.

"Ellis..." Rhonan warns.

"Roscoe wants to come play, Daddy. Can he come over? Pleeeease?"

Knowing I can't avoid him forever, I walk over to the fence and pop my head over the wooden slats. I'm met with those blue eyes that I remember dancing all over my body during the shower incident. "Hey there, neighbor."

The corner of Rhonan's mouth lifts, but it's back to flat in a flash. "Hey. Ellis wants—"

"I know. I heard, and I'm fine with it if you are. I sort of needed to talk to you about something anyway, so that will be a good distraction for her."

His brows draw together. "Is everything okay?"

"Yeah, it's probably nothing. Just something weird that happened at school today."

"Daddy, can Roscoe come over now?"

Rhonan turns to look down at Ellis, whom I can't see over the fence, but can hear. "Yeah, sweetie. Actually, Ms. Lewis is gonna come over too so I can talk to her."

Ellis claps. "Yay!"

Rhonan swings his head toward the gate at the front of his property. "Why don't you two come through there?"

"All right. Come on, Roscoe." I snap my fingers and my sweet puppy follows obediently. He really is doing better with his training, even if it's only been a few weeks.

I've only been in Blossom Peak for a little over three weeks, but somehow it feels much longer. Maybe because this place is really starting to feel like home, or at least somewhere I could see myself living for a while. Or maybe it's because I have connections forming that I wasn't expecting, like the one with my neighbor.

Roscoe waits at the gate, scratching at the wood. Rhonan opens it and Roscoe barrels through, running right into Ellis's outstretched arms, licking her in the face. Her laughter is truly one of the best sounds in the world.

"I'm impressed."

"With what?" My eyes lift to find Rhonan watching my dog and his daughter.

"The dog. He hasn't been digging under the fence."

"Guess the threat of electrocution worked."

Rhonan shrugs. "If he understands English, then yes, that was probably it." With a wave, he motions for me to follow him. "So, is this a conversation that requires us to sit?"

"I mean, sure."

Rhonan heads up the steps to the deck where I see a beautiful wrought-iron patio set over to the right near the sliding door that leads inside the house. To the left is a covered grill and potted plants frame the space.

"This is a nice little setup you have here," I say as I take a seat in one of the chairs, thankful for the cushion to create a barrier between me and the iron.

"Thanks. So, what happened today? Did Ellis try to take over the class?"

My laughter is soft. "No, nothing like that. Honestly, Rhonan, she's one of the most well-behaved kids in my class. And I'm not just saying that."

He meets my eyes as he takes a seat next to me. "I appreciate that."

"But, where do I start? I guess it started with the rocks."

Rhonan shakes his head. "This kid and her damn rocks."

"Yeah, care to explain?"

He pushes a hand through his hair as his eyes trail Ellis and Roscoe around the yard. "I didn't think much of it when it started. Ellis was just collecting rocks she liked, but then she kept telling me that we needed to keep them just in case."

"Just in case of what?"

He shrugs. "She never said and before I knew it, I had a basket of rocks in my house." Our eyes meet again. "I have indoor rocks, Vienna."

Laughing, I nod. "Well, she had me look after her latest find today out on the playground, and when she brought them back inside, she put them in her backpack. But during story time, she raised her hand and asked if I wanted to come over tonight to see all of the rocks she saves for you, which led to her telling the entire class that we live next to each other."

He stares at me curiously. "Okay..."

"The kids started asking a bunch of questions, and at one point, Johnny called her a teacher's pet." Rhonan's jaw ticks. "She instantly deflated but didn't seem to let it bother her too much. I...I guess I just wanted to let you know that these kids might go home and tell their parents that we're neighbors, and I..."

Rhonan leans forward in his chair, resting his forearms on his knees. "Vienna, you realize people probably already know that. This is a small town, remember? If you want to keep anything a secret around here, you don't say a word and you have to be sneaky."

"I know, I just remember you saying you didn't want people talking..."

He sits upright again, blows out a breath, and darts his eyes back to Ellis. "I was an ass for making you think that was something we could control. I'm sorry."

"Wow. It takes a lot of guts to admit when you've acted out of character."

He arches a brow at me, but there's a hint of a smile on his lips. "I'm not perfect, and Lord knows I haven't handled this well. It's just...a lot."

"What is?"

His silence makes me uneasy, almost as if his contemplation is so loud, we can both hear it. "Fuck..." he mutters, right as Ellis races up the steps.

"Daddy?"

His scowl disappears as his daughter stops right in front of him, reaching for his hands. "Yes, Ellis?"

"Can I show Ms. Lewis our rock collection? I told her about it at school."

Rhonan turns to me. "Want to see my indoor rocks?"

I momentarily debate making a joke about his question, but I refrain. "Sure."

Ellis reaches for my hand next, pulling me up from my seat. "Come on."

As we step inside, I see Joanne standing in the kitchen, scrolling on her phone, which she puts down the second she sees me. "Well, hello again, Vienna."

"Hi, Joanne."

"I'm showing her my rocks," Ellis declares, still leading me by the hand.

Joanne chuckles. "Oh boy. Things are getting serious then."

Rhonan scowls at his nanny but doesn't say anything. Ellis stops in the living room right next to a wicker basket that could easily hold ten basketballs, and it's halfway full of rocks.

"Oh my." My hand flies to my mouth to cover my smile. "That's a lot of rocks."

Ellis's proud grin is just too precious. "I know! Now we have lots in case we need them."

"And what might you need them for?" I ask, knowing that Rhonan wants to know the answer to this question too.

"To throw at people." Her response is so forthcoming and automatic that I think it shocks all three adults in the room.

Rhonan takes a step forward. "Why would you need to throw rocks at people, Ellis?"

"If they're mean," she replies, then turns to look up at him. "And in case your gun stops working, you can throw rocks at bad guys, Daddy." Oh, my heart. The way this child thinks is both adorable and disheartening. "I just want you to be safe."

Rhonan crouches down so he's at eye level with his daughter. "I promise that I'm safe. Okay?" She nods but doesn't say anything. "I don't think I'll need any more rocks, though, sweetie."

She shrugs. "Better to be safe than sorry, right?"

He nods. "I guess so."

An idea sparks in my mind. "Ellis, I have an idea for what we could do with some of these rocks."

Her bright blue eyes lift to mine. "What?"

"We could paint them and put them all over your yard as decorations. That way, you still have them, but they're not just sitting in this basket."

Those blue eyes widen so big, I'm afraid they might fall out of her head. "Yes! Let's do that! Can we do it right now?"

I laugh, but Rhonan beats me to a response. "Not tonight, Ellis. It's almost time for a bath and bed."

"Aw, man."

"I promise that we will, though," I add.

Ellis steps up to me with her pinky outstretched. "Pinky promise?"

I lean down and intertwine my pinky with hers. "Pinky promise."

Roscoe scratches at the patio door, reminding us that he's still out there. "Can I play with Roscoe some more?" Ellis drops her hand from mine.

"Just for a little bit," Rhonan says.

"Okay, Daddy." She moves toward the door but then stops and rushes back to her dad. "We can't paint your special rock, though, Daddy."

Rhonan nods while I wonder what she's referring to. "I know. That one stays with me."

Nodding, she moves back to the patio door and slides outside once more, running away from Roscoe as he chases her.

"You have a special rock?" I ask.

He arches a brow at me. "Do you think that's out of line given the context of this conversation?" Waving his hand toward the basket, I smile as he continues. "There was one rock that Ellis insisted I keep on me at all times. She said it was a special protection rock." Reaching into his pocket, he takes out a small, dark gray river rock that is smooth all over and barely the size of a marble. "I don't go anywhere without it."

Emotion threatens to overtake me for the love this man has for his kid.

Cole never would have been a father like that. I know that now, deep in my bones.

This is how a dad is supposed to be.

I cover the rock in his hand with my own. "This is the sweetest freaking thing." Rhonan drops his eyes to our hands. "Seriously, Rhonan. I—I think I might cry."

He reaches for my face with his other hand, drawing his brows together and cupping my jaw. "Don't do that. It's just a rock."

We stand there with our eyes locked for so long, my heart hammering wildly and oxygen depleting from my lungs, that I've completely forgotten that Joanne is in the room until she clears her throat. "So, am I buying paint, or are you?" she asks me.

Rhonan and I release each other from our grasps like we're teenagers that have just been caught making out. I tuck my hair behind my ear nervously. "Um, I can."

"I think we have some paint around here somewhere too," she continues. "But just so you're aware, that kid is not going to forget about this." Joanne points to the backyard where Ellis and Roscoe are still playing.

"Oh, I won't either," I reply. "Besides, I did pinky promise, right?"

Rhonan studies me but doesn't say anything.

"You did. Just let me know when you want to schedule a playdate to paint," Joanne says before heading toward her room.

"Will do!" I call after her.

Rhonan takes a step closer to me. "If you come over and paint rocks with my kid, people might talk about it."

The corner of my mouth lifts. "Well, you said they probably already are talking about us, so what's it matter?"

"You don't have to do this, Vienna."

"Do what?"

"Do extra things with Ellis. You're her teacher, and that can be the extent of it."

"Do you want me to tell her I changed my mind? After I pinky promised?"

He glares at me, but it's not harsh. Almost as if he knows I can't exactly go back on my word, but he wishes I could. "No."

"Then it's settled." I head toward the patio door. "Your daughter is precious, and despite what anyone might say, I truly enjoy spending time with her." I drop my eyes up and down his body and then continue, "And you too, surprisingly."

His mouth opens like he wants to say something, then closes again.

Before he can flip the switch on me like he usually does, I head back outside and call for Roscoe, ready to put some space between Rhonan and me. I'm already more invested than I should be in this little family. I don't need to further complicate things by exploring whatever this is between us as well.

Chapter 11

Vienna

Hair Confessions & A Wedding Invitation

"Hi, there. I have a five o'clock appointment with Laney."

The receptionist clicks around on the computer and then smiles. "Perfect. You're all checked in. Take a seat and Laney will come get you when she's ready."

"Thank you." I take a seat in one of the olive green chairs in the waiting area of Blossom Beauty, scouring the salon and taking in all of the details while I wait—olive green chairs at each station gleaming in the small amount of sunlight coming through the tall front windows, white walls that make the space bright and open, black-framed mirrors hung in front of each stylist's station, and smooth gray floors pulling it all together.

Past the stations on both sides of the room are three separate spaces—one for nail technicians, one for massage services, and one for facials and skin care. This place really is a full-service salon and strikingly beautiful. I bet business is great too, with the number of tourists that come through this town.

"Vienna?" Laney's voice pulls me from my observations.

Standing from my chair, I close the distance between us. "Hey there."

"I was wondering if this appointment was with you or someone else with the same name," she says with a laugh.

"Well, the name isn't too common, but you never know, I guess."

"True. Either way, it's great to see you again." She waves for me to follow her to her station. I hang my purse on a hook on the wall by the mirror and take a seat in the chair as she drapes a towel and black cape securely around my neck. "Are you sure you want to trust me with your hair?"

"Should I not?"

Laney winks. "On the contrary, I'm very good at what I do. I just thought after our little run-in at the winery, you might want to steer clear of me."

"Oh. That. Actually, seeing you there just reminded me that it's been too long since I've had my hair done. And I remembered from Career Day that you own this place, so really, I was grateful."

She blows out a breath dramatically. "Phew. Good. So, what are we doing with your hair today?" Her fingers comb through it as our eyes meet in the mirror.

"Well, I know I need a trim. But I was wondering what you think about the color... I kind of wanted it to be a bit lighter, but I'm not sure."

She lifts a few strands up to the light. "You definitely have some growth. We could touch up your roots and add a few more strands of blonde and light brown in here to give you some depth."

"That sounds great. I trust you."

She laughs. "Most people have nerves about someone new touching their hair."

"Well, you're the expert, so I know I'm better off in your hands than my own. Box dye and I have never met and don't plan to."

"Smart choice. Let me mix up your color and then I'll be back."

"Okay."

Laney is gone for about five minutes before she comes back over with two bowls and brushes. Setting them on her rolling tray, she pumps the lever on the chair, raising me up, and then stretches on a pair of latex gloves. "So, now that you've been in Blossom Peak for a few weeks, what do you think about it?"

"Honestly, I thought little towns like this only existed in the movies or books. It's really special, and so beautiful. The cherry blossom trees especially."

Laney starts parting my hair into sections, separating it with clips. "You're lucky you're here right now when they're just starting to bloom. One morning, the buds are barely there, and the next day, everywhere you look is pink."

"I love it. The weather hasn't been too bad either, which I appreciate. And the wine from your family's winery is amazing."

"Glad you enjoyed it. There's plenty more if you need it." She winks. "So tell me more about where you're from?"

Part of me tenses up at the thought of talking too much about my past, but I don't feel like I have to worry about Laney. Besides, Washington, D.C., is a massive city. "Um, I was living in D.C. before this"

"Wow. That's definitely a different vibe than Blossom Peak."

"I wanted to try something new... Moving on from things that no longer served me."

Our eyes meet in the mirror. "I love that. It takes guts to make a change. Trust me, I know," she says with a laugh.

"Speaking from experience?"

"If you had moved here last summer, the version of me you would have met was clinging to anger and resentment out of comfort. It took Fletcher coming back and not letting me run from him to finally let go of the past and embrace change." Her eyes practically have hearts in them as she talks about her fiancé. "I've discovered so much about life since I finally relented to what I always knew."

"Which was?"

"That the heart knows more than the mind ever will."

Her words strike a chord within me. Sighing, I say, "I guess I'm just finally starting to learn that lesson."

"It takes some people longer than others. Like my brother, for instance," she says with a lilt to her voice, but nerves race through me at the mention of Rhonan. Honestly, though, I'm surprised it's taken this long for him to be brought up. "He's the king of holding on to the past."

"I can see that, I guess." Lord knows the man has been through loss with his mom, and then Ellis's mom. You can't exactly blame him for having a chip on his shoulder after that.

"Has he been a decent neighbor at least? Between his scowls and grunts?"

I chuckle. "He's very good at those things, that's for sure. But he's actually turned out to be the best neighbor I've ever had."

"Oh? Do tell." Laney begins painting the color onto chunks of my hair while meeting my eyes in the mirror.

"You haven't heard?"

"Heard what?"

"About my showerhead falling off the wall and your brother running over to my house because he heard my screams and thought I was being attacked?"

Laney freezes as her lips spread into a grin. "You're joking..."

"Trust me, I wish I were, especially because I was completely naked."

She bites her bottom lip to hide her smile. "What did he do?"

"Turned off the main water line and offered to let me finish my shower at his house."

Laney's eyes widen at that.

"What?"

"I, uh..." Stumbling, she focuses back on her task, but now I'm curious about her reaction. "Nothing. So, did you take him up on that?"

"I mean, I kind of had to. I ended up having ice cream with him and Ellis that night too. That little girl is very persuasive."

"Oh, I know. My niece gets her way around here, trust me. There are plenty of adults in her life that have fallen victim to that smile and pout."

"She's such a sweetheart, though. And my puppy loves her. She asks to play with him all the time."

"And Rhonan lets her?"

"Yeah. Is that surprising?"

Laney shrugs. "Honestly, he's not one to make friends."

I laugh. "Well, he made it clear we aren't friends. But apparently, he's forgotten all about that because he and Elliot fixed my shower the day after mine broke, and I'm supposed to paint rocks with Ellis sometime this week." Sighing, I mutter under my breath, "Confusing man."

Laney shakes her head in disbelief. "Wow."

I arch a brow at her. "Why do I get the feeling there's something more you want to say?"

"There is. I just…"

I hold a hand up. "It's fine. You don't have to."

She shakes her head. "No. I think it's important that you know." Inhaling deeply, she continues. "My brother is pretty closed off, which makes the fact that he's voluntarily helping you and letting you spend time with Ellis sort of…hopeful?" She lifts her shoulders as hope blossoms in my chest, even though I know that it shouldn't for multiple reasons. "I'm just saying, he doesn't do stuff like that for just anyone."

"Oh."

"I love my brother, but I also know that sometimes he needs to be pushed a bit to see things clearly."

"What do you mean?"

Our eyes meet in the mirror. "I heard about the night you met."

My pulse spikes. "I see."

"Yeah. And I'm sure you had your reasons for walking away, but my brother was definitely in a mood after that."

"I've apologized, but I honestly never thought I'd see him again. He just…took me by surprise."

She holds up a hand to stop me. "Trust me, I get it. I hid from my feelings for Fletcher for years and wasted so much time when deep down, I knew what I wanted."

But do you even know what you want, Vienna? And does that involve Rhonan? Or should you just lay low like you planned when you moved here?

Laney taps her chin in thought while my mind is spiraling. "You know, I just remembered that we have room for another guest at the wedding," she says, a knowing smirk on her lips. "So perhaps you'd like a free meal and booze on June 1st?"

"Wait. You're inviting me to your wedding?" I practically shriek, but then glance around the salon to make sure I wasn't too loud.

She laughs. "I mean, you are my brother's neighbor and my niece's teacher. You're practically family now."

Shaking my head, I reply, "That's so sweet, Laney, but you don't have to do that."

"I know I don't, but I want to. And while I'm thinking about it, do you like yoga by any chance?" she asks rapidly, throwing me off kilter.

"Uh, I do actually."

"Perfect. We're having a yoga night at the winery in two weeks. You should come. And invite my brother."

"Oh, we've already had a discussion about yoga. He's not too fond of the exercise."

Laney bounces her eyebrows up and down. "Oh, I'm aware. But I have a feeling that if he knows you'll be there, he might be more likely to participate."

"Should I be scared that you want me to manipulate him into this?" The question is meant to be a joke, but part of me is a bit concerned.

Laney grins. "No. I mean no harm. Honestly, I just want you to feel welcome here. The fact that you have a thing going on with my brother just makes it more fun."

"There's no 'thing,' Laney. We agreed to just be neighborly."

"That's perfect. Neighbors can be friends too."

Oh, God. I should never have said anything about Rhonan to Laney. What if she goes and tells him that I was talking about him. Or...

Laney taps the brush on the edge of one of the bowls. "Hey, I've got to go mix up a bit more color. Your hair is soaking it up. I'll be right back, okay?"

"Okay." My eyes trail her as she walks away, but I'm still nervous about our conversation. I don't have much time to stew on it, though, because my phone vibrates in my purse. I lean forward to pull it out, and when I do, my stomach drops.

A number I recognize flashes on the screen, like a car accident I can't seem to turn my gaze from even though I should.

I don't press ignore. I just let it ring until finally the phone screen tells me I have a missed call.

I'm frozen for a moment until my rational brain kicks in again, and that's when I turn to my settings and make sure that my location is turned off.

You're safe, Vienna. You're fine.

No one knows you're here.

Let's just hope it stays that way.

***

"Vienna! I'm so surprised to see you out here tonight!" Harriet Thompson kisses both of my cheeks before releasing me from her grasp. Her makeup is caked on so thick that it looks like frosting. Although, after I saw myself in the mirror tonight, I shouldn't really judge.

Forcing a smile, I say, "Well, I couldn't hide away forever." Even though I seriously want to, I think to myself.

A cold hand grasps my waist, making my entire body tense up. "This woman could never hide from me," Cole interjects from my right, plastering on the smile I've cursed myself for falling for in the first place. His grip on me tightens as he continues. "In fact, I have a feeling you'll be seeing a lot more of her from now on."

Harriet nods in my direction. "Well, that would be lovely."

"She told me she wants to get more involved in the foundations now, so that when we have children, she'll feel okay stepping away knowing she's contributed to my career in some capacity."

Harriet reaches for my hand as the skin around her eyes crinkles. "We can always use more help with the foundations."

Clenching my teeth together, my smile mirrors Cole's. "Just...glad I can be of use."

When Harriet releases me, another woman calls for her across the ballroom. "I've got to run, but I'll be in touch this week so we can start collaborating."

"Sounds great."

Cole waits for Harriet to get far enough away before the entire tone in his voice changes. "I told you to stay near me."

I straighten my spine while keeping my perfected smile intact. "She came up to me. What was I supposed to do? Run away from her and across the room to you?"

He lifts his scotch to his lips, taking a sip. "You knew that the whole point of you being here was to show everyone that—"

"I know. Appearances are everything," I finish for him, echoing the same sentence that he's used so many times in our relationship to get me to see his perspective that I've lost count.

The problem is, the past few months have given me some perspective of my own. Too bad that it took my best friend dying for me to finally see reason.

"Exactly. So, like I said, stay close. I'd hate to have to go looking for you again."

"And what if I don't?" I challenge, peering up at him.

His dark brown eyes bore into mine. "Just know that I'll always find you, Vienna. You're mine and always will be."

Chapter 12

Rhonan

Spaghetti Confessions & Rock Painting

"I've gotta say, Laney...you've downright perfected your mother's spaghetti recipe." My dad wipes his chin with his napkin before leaning back in his chair, patting his stomach.

Fletcher lifts his water glass toward his mouth before taking a sip. "I agree, George. Every time she makes it, I feel like a teenager all over again."

Ellis pulls on my shirt sleeve. "When will I be a teenager?"

"Not for a very long time," I reply.

My dad chuckles. "It will happen before you know it, son. Trust me. You and your sister grew up way too fast for my liking." He glances over at my sister. "And now my baby girl is getting married."

Laney tilts her head at him. "Oh, Dad. Don't start getting emotional already."

Our father clears his throat. "I just wish your mother was here to see this. She'd be so happy for you and Fletcher."

Fletcher kisses my sister's temple. "That means a lot, George. And I know Elizabeth will be there the day of."

"But Nana is an angel," Ellis chimes in.

Laney leans closer to her from her chair. "She is, just like your mom. Angels can go anywhere, though. That's how we know they're always with us."

Ellis furrows her brow. "Does that mean my mom can go to school with me?"

I decide to shut down this conversation before I get calls from the school, or better yet, Vienna has to talk to me about another incident in Ellis's class. "No, baby. Angels just show up for the important stuff, like birthdays, holidays, and weddings."

Ellis's shoulders drop. "Oh. Okay. Can I go play now?"

I glance around the table and notice that we've all finished eating, so I give her permission to leave. "Sure." Ellis races toward the living room as I meet my sister's gaze. "Let's cool it with the angel talk, shall we?"

"What? Do you not want Ellis to believe that her mom is always with her? She's way more perceptive than you think."

"She's five, Laney. She's not old enough to understand the complexity of what you're telling her."

My sister props her chin in her hand. "Maybe, but she *is* old enough to notice that you smile when your neighbor is around."

Her words make my pulse spike. "What?"

She lifts her wine glass to her mouth now, taking a sip. "Yeah. While she was helping me make dinner, she told me all about Vienna and how she makes you smile."

Fletcher chuckles, his arm still wrapped around my sister's waist from his seat. "That little girl is aware of more than you think and doesn't forget things easily."

I glare in his direction. "Trust me, she still tells me she wants to be a stripper when she grows up. Thanks again for that."

My father hums. "What are you talking about? A stripper?"

Fletcher pushes a hand through his hair. "It's a long story."

Laney pats him on the shoulder. "Why don't you go tell him about it while you two clean up the kitchen, so I can talk to my brother in private?"

"Yes ma'am," Fletcher says, kissing my sister chastely before standing. "Come on, George. Let me tell you why I'm not allowed to talk to Ellis by myself anymore."

Laney watches the two of them walk toward the kitchen before she turns back to me, arching a brow.

"What?"

"You're grumpier than normal."

"Your point?"

"It wouldn't have anything to do with Vienna, would it?"

I lean back in my chair, crossing my arms over my chest. "What are you trying to ask me, Laney?"

"How are things going with you two? Any exciting incidents I should know about?"

I eye her skeptically. "No…"

"Nothing that involves fixing a showerhead? Or seeing her naked?" There's a curl to her lips that tells me she is leading me into a trap, but I'm not in the mood to play this game.

"I think that's an inappropriate question to ask your brother."

"I don't, especially because I'm only trying to help you here."

"I don't need your help, Laney."

Her face softens and then she reaches out, curling her hand around my forearm. "Rhonan. It's just me. Tell me what's going through that head of yours."

Clenching my teeth together, I attempt to stay strong. "Why?"

"Because fixing your neighbor's shower and letting Ellis play with her dog isn't staying away from the woman you had a connection with at a bar before she ghosted you. It actually sounds a lot like the opposite of that."

My face falls flat. "How'd you know..."

Laney releases my arm and leans back in her chair, grabbing her wine glass again. "Vienna came into the salon this week for a haircut and color, and I sort of pulled it out of her."

I sigh. "You know, I'm just trying to be polite."

"You sure that's all it is?" She tilts her head at me again.

"What do you want me to say, Laney?"

"How about that you're still attracted to this woman, for starters?"

I toss my hands in the air. "Fine. I am! You happy?"

"Somewhat. Now, what's going through your head?"

I blow out a breath and pinch the bridge of my nose. "I hate this entire situation."

"Why?"

"Because I let myself get caught up in a woman, and now it's like my choice came back to bite me in the ass."

My sister laughs. "Wow. Ever the pessimist, aren't you?"

"And how am I supposed to be an optimist in this predicament?"

She reaches for my hand, and I let her, her thumb rubbing over the top of it slowly. "Did you ever stop to think that maybe this all happened for a reason?"

"You know I don't believe in that shit."

When you lose your mom and your wife, it's kind of hard to think that those things were meant to happen. Why on earth should any human have to go through that kind of loss so early in life? Why should any young girl have to grow up without her mother? Why did my mother have to die way too fucking young?

"I know you can be jaded about certain things, Rhonan. Trust me, I've had my moments of feeling like that too. But I want to see you move on and stop wasting your life."

"I'm fine. You have your own things to worry about, so stop meddling in mine."

"Forgive me for wanting you to be happy."

"I am happy."

"Could have fooled me with all the joy spewing from your pores right now." I roll my eyes, but my sister continues. "Don't you want someone to share your life with, Rhonan?"

"I had that, Laney...and lost it."

My sister grows quiet, but she finally says something I didn't want to hear, but probably needed to. "I think it's unrealistic to think you wouldn't develop feelings for someone new at some point, Rhonan. Sarah would have wanted you to move on. She wouldn't want you and Ellis to be alone forever."

I swallow down the lump forming in my throat the longer this conversation goes on. "We're not alone. We have Joanne. We have you, and dad."

She squints at me. "You know what I mean."

A heavy sigh leaves my lips, and then I'm burying my head in my hands. "Fuck."

"Talk to me, Rhonan." She rubs my shoulder as I stay hunched over. "It's me. I'm not here to judge. I truly just want what's best for you."

"I'm fucking scared, Laney," I say, my voice low.

"Good."

My head pops up. "Good?"

"Yes. At least you're feeling something."

"Trust me, I wish I wasn't."

"Do you know how scared I was to get hurt again with Fletcher? So scared that I wasted ten years hating the man so he'd keep his distance."

"That's different."

"No, it's not. It's still fear, and right now, you're letting it run the show. Besides, if it makes you feel any better, I'm pretty sure Vienna is just as conflicted as you."

That makes me sit upright again. "What makes you say that?"

My sister shrugs. "She kept trying to assure me that you two are just neighbors, but I could see something in her eyes when she spoke about you...and Ellis."

"Ellis really loves her."

"And don't you think that's a good sign? You and I both know you wouldn't date someone without thinking of Ellis first."

"I never have."

She points a finger at me. "Exactly. You haven't dated anyone since Sarah. I'm not saying marry Vienna tomorrow, Rhonan. But she's the first woman who has elicited a reaction from you since you lost Sarah, and I think you owe it to yourself to at least explore that."

Hearing my sister tell me something I already know doesn't help this war I'm fighting within. My attraction toward Vienna is overwhelming, but is that all it is? Or is Laney right, and I'm just too fucking scared to figure out if there's more between us?

"Daddy?" Ellis comes over to me, rubbing her eyes. "Can I watch a movie?"

Checking the time on my watch, I notice it's already after seven o'clock. "It's too late, Ellis. We're gonna leave soon."

"No," she whines. "I want to stay."

"You can come over and watch a movie with me and Uncle Fletcher soon, okay?" my sister chimes in.

Ellis's eyes widen. "Can we eat lots of cavities?"

Laney bops her on the nose. "Yes. And we can have you practice throwing the flower petals for the wedding."

My daughter bounces up and down, her exhaustion from before melting away. "Yes!"

Laney glances up at me. "By the way, I invited Vienna to the wedding."

"What?" I bark out, but Ellis squeals, clapping her hands.

"Ms. Lewis is coming to the wedding?"

"That's right," Laney says with a grin.

"She'll get to see me in my princess dress then!"

"She will, which means we have to practice a lot so everything is perfect." My sister's eyes meet mine. "You *might* even have to spend the night. That way, your dad can hang out with a *friend* if he wants." Her tone is so suggestive that I'm surprised she was able to say those words with a straight face.

"Subtle," I mutter.

Laney arches a brow at me. "I try."

Yeah, her suggestion was the opposite of subtle, but I can't deny that she's got me thinking—not that I haven't already been doing that. There are only a few things that occupy my mind most days—my daughter, my job, my family, and now my sexy neighbor.

Vienna has slowly slipped her way into my world, and I can't deny that a part of me likes it.

Once my dad and Fletcher have finished the dishes, Laney and Fletcher head home since she has an early morning tomorrow, leaving me with my father. He grabs us two beers, and we drift outside so that Ellis can practice riding her bike in the driveway.

My parents' house sits on the back of the property that Hart Winery is on, with the vineyards that grow most of our grapes just off to the right, climbing up the side of the mountains behind it. I remember running through those fields as a kid, helping pick the grapes and listening to my dad talk to me about how much care is involved in growing the perfect grape for the best wine. This winery was my mother's dream, but sometimes I think he took more pride in what they built together than she did.

"You seem like you have a lot on your mind," my father says, cutting through my thoughts as I watch Ellis circle the U-shaped driveway in front of the house, the lights on the house shining brightly so I can see her.

"As opposed to any other day?"

My father shrugs. "Your conversation with your sister seemed intense."

I glance over at him with an arch in my brow as I bring my beer to my lips. "Are you trying to tell me you were eavesdropping?"

"No, but Fletcher mentioned that I should probably try to get you to talk to me. Why do you think that is?"

"Because now that he and Laney are getting married, he thinks he needs to meddle in my life too."

"Fletcher is just trying to look out for you...like you boys promised each other you would."

Back in June of last year when shit hit the fan between my friend group, the boys and I sat down and hashed out some shit that had happened over the years. The result of that conversation—with the help of my dad and his friends—was that we would agree to lean on each other instead of keeping shit inside.

Let's just say that some of us are doing better with that than others.

My eyes trail Ellis as she continues to stride along on her bike, belting out the lyrics to "Let It Go" from *Frozen*, her own personal theme song at this point.

When I finally feel ready to speak, I glance over at my dad. "Why didn't you ever move on after Mom died?"

The look of surprise on his face tells me that I caught him off guard. "Well, I never met another woman who made me feel that it was worth the risk of loving again."

I direct my gaze back to my daughter. "Never?"

"What are you trying to ask me, son?"

"How do you know?" I cut in. "How do you know if another woman is worth that risk?"

My father sighs, taking a long swig from his beer before replying. "I guess I would wait for the same feeling I got when I met your mom...even though I'm afraid that I never may feel the same way about another woman like I felt for her."

"Yeah, I get that." I take another drink. "But what did you feel?"

My father chuckles. "She made me feel lighter, Rhonan. I—I don't know how else to explain it. But when I was with her, I never wanted to stop listening to her talk. I felt like being with her made me see the world differently. And with her by my side, I felt like we could accomplish anything." He swallows roughly. "She was my best friend, and I miss her every fucking day."

It's rare that my father cusses. "I miss Mom and Sarah too, Dad."

"But this conversation isn't about them, is it?"

"No." Lifting my beer bottle to my lips, I keep my gaze on my daughter.

"The only thing you can do, son, is listen to your gut. I've found that it never truly steers me wrong."

If only my gut was louder than my fear.

***

"I'm going to make this one into a watermelon." Ellis dabs her paint-brush into the bright pink paint, swishing it around a few times before moving the dripping brush to the rock in front of her. She leans as close to the rock as she can, her focus fucking adorable. But if she gets any closer, she's going to end up with pink paint on her nose.

"That's a great idea, Ellis," Vienna says, dipping her brush into the red paint next. "I think I'm going to make mine into a rose."

"Oh, I wanna do a rose too!"

"You can do that next. We have tons of rocks that we can paint, sweetie."

"We need to paint them all," my daughter declares, but my eyes move to the basket, knowing damn well that it could take months for that to happen.

"You won't be able to paint them all tonight, Ellis," I say.

"Why not?"

"Because there's way too many, sweetie."

My daughter looks up at me as if I've sprouted another head, but Vienna chimes in quickly. "That just means that we can do this again sometime, Ellis."

My daughter turns to her, a bright smile on her face. "Okay!" And then she goes back to painting.

It's a Wednesday night and, as planned, Vienna came over about an hour ago to paint rocks with my daughter. Joanne made a pasta dish for dinner that we all ate together, and then she left for the Sip & Smut night at the winery that my sister hosts. I try not to think about the things they discuss at those meetings, but that means I'm alone with my daughter and neighbor, watching the two of them together while I fight the physical reactions happening in my body.

First of all, Vienna is wearing an olive-green shirt that shows just the right amount of cleavage, hinting at the perfection lying underneath that fabric. Then, she's wearing black spandex leggings that put every single one of her curves on display but still allow me to appreciate the jiggle of her ass as she walks.

However, the thing that's truly captivating me right now is how she's interacting with my daughter. Melancholy is resting in my chest because all I keep thinking is how this is something Sarah should have been doing with our daughter—and yet again, I'm making myself feel guilty for the other things I'm feeling for the woman sitting in front of me.

It's not the guilt from wanting to sleep with someone else that is eating at me. It's the fact that I can't stop thinking about her in every capacity. It's the fact that I want to know more about this woman, my curiosity growing with each interaction we have—and I didn't think I'd ever consider that after losing my wife.

I thought Sarah was the only great love that I'd get.

And I know I'm far from feeling love for Vienna, but I'm definitely feeling interest—and in a way, that almost feels more conflicting for me because that's the last thing I should want, given our complicated relationship.

But my mind keeps sprouting questions, like what was her childhood like? Why did she want to be a teacher? And has she done anything else liberating since the night at The Charming Bull? Or does she regret all of her choices that night, including leaving me without saying goodbye?

"You know, when I was a kid I collected pine cones," Vienna says, pulling me back to the present.

Ellis looks at her. "Really?"

"Yup. And I used to name them all."

Ellis glances down at her rocks. "I think I have too many rocks to name them all."

Chuckling, I cross my arms over my chest where I'm standing in the kitchen. "I think I have to agree with that, sweetie."

"What did you name them?" Ellis asks Vienna, ignoring me, which is fine. Honestly, watching the two of them chat is plenty entertaining. Besides, it gives me more time to admire Vienna's smile and laugh.

Fuck. I'm in over my head here, aren't I?

Yup. And if Laney were here, she'd point it out right in front of your neighbor you can't stop thinking about.

Needing a distraction, I turn back to the sink full of dishes and lather up the sponge with soap. Before I can pick up a dish, though, Vienna shrieks from the table. "Oh God!"

My instincts kick in and I drop the items from my hands, crossing the room in a flash only to find Vienna standing up, her entire stomach and lap covered in water and Ellis looking terrified.

"What happened?" I ask.

"I—I spilled," Ellis says through her tears as she throws down her paintbrush and takes off for her room, crying louder until I hear her door slam shut.

"Shit," Vienna says, standing there as colored water dribbles from her clothes onto the floor. "Give me a towel, Rhonan. Please?"

I dart into the laundry room, grab a clean towel from the basket on the washer, and then rush it back over to Vienna. She dabs at her clothes, not saying a word, then wraps the towel around her and takes off down the hall.

"What the... Where are you going?" I call after her, but she ignores me.

"Ellis?" I follow her as she knocks softly on my daughter's door, opening it and stepping into her room just a few seconds later. "Ellis?"

"I—I'm sorry. I didn't mean to make a mess," Ellis says through her tears.

Vienna drops to her knees on the side of Ellis's bed, reaching for her hands. "Honey, I know. I'm so sorry I yelled, but I was not yelling at you. Not one bit."

"Really?"

Vienna brushes Ellis's hair from her face. "Yes, sweetie. I was just surprised. The water was cold and it made me jump, but it was an accident. Accidents happen."

"I ruined your shirt and pants."

Vienna shrugs, but there's a smile on her lips. "They're just clothes, and I can wash them. If that doesn't work, I just buy new ones. No biggie." Ellis nods, but her eyes remain locked on her lap. "Now, can you come back out so we can finish painting rocks, please?"

Ellis lifts her eyes, meeting Vienna's before meeting my own. "Can—can Daddy paint with us?"

Vienna twists to face me, and when our gazes lock, this sudden urge to rush over to her, pull her from the floor, and smash my lips to hers overwhelms me.

This woman was more concerned over my daughter's feelings than her clothes. She wanted to make sure that Ellis knew that what happened was an accident, and *that* was her first reaction to what happened—not to scream and yell, not to rush home to change.

No. She was entirely focused on making sure my kid was all right.

Yeah. I am well and truly fucked.

Clearing my throat, I nod. "I can paint some rocks."

Ellis's smile reappears, and fuck if it doesn't make everything else going wrong in the world feel small. She leaps from her bed, and grabs

Vienna by the hand, pulling her past me as the two of them laugh and head right back to the kitchen. Once I return to the room, I find Vienna pulling her towel off and dropping it to the floor, sopping up the remaining water.

"Daddy, can you get us more water, please?" Ellis asks.

I reach for the plastic container. "Yeah, sweetie. But let's not fill it up as much this time, okay?"

After I fill the cup only a fourth of the way full, I bring it back to the table and take a seat in the chair opposite the girls. It dawns on me at this moment I'm grateful the chairs are all wood and don't have cushions on them that can get stained by these types of messes.

"You know what I was thinking would be fun? What if we painted a rock with a wedding dress and one with a tuxedo on it for your Auntie Laney and Uncle Fletcher for their wedding?" Vienna suggests.

"You mean the wedding you suddenly got invited to?" The words leave my lips before I can even think twice.

Vienna arches a brow at me. "You heard about that, huh?"

"Yeah. Just wondering when you were going to tell me. I mean, we are neighbors, after all."

Vienna dips her brush into the red paint, not meeting my eyes when she replies. "I didn't realize that being neighbors meant telling you about my plans. I mean, your sister is the one who invited me, which I did not ask for, by the way."

Ellis taps Vienna on the shoulder. "You get to see me in my princess dress at the wedding, Ms. Lewis."

Vienna rubs her nose against Ellis's. "I know. I'm sure you're going to be the best flower girl ever."

"I am," Ellis says confidently. "And my daddy gets to walk down the aisle too, in a tug."

"Tux," I correct her before looking back at Vienna to find her staring at my lips. When she sees that I've caught her, she darts her eyes back to her rock. "One of my least favorite garments to wear."

"That's a shame," Vienna says. "A man in a tux is one of my favorite things to see." She licks her lips, glances back up at me, and the hint of mischief in her eyes makes my dick twitch in my jeans.

Fuck. Is she...flirting with me?

"Are you gonna wear a princess dress?" Ellis asks the woman that is making my dick hard in front of my daughter. Thank God there's a table covering it, but still.

"I don't know. I'll probably have to go shopping for something. I didn't bring anything like that with me to Blossom Peak." Vienna peers over at Ellis's rock. "Are you still wanting to paint that rock as a watermelon?"

"Yeah."

"Then we need to make black dots for the seeds."

"I hate the seeds," my daughter says, scrunching up her nose.

Vienna chuckles. "Me too, but it's going to make the rock look so pretty." She helps my daughter carefully clean her brush, dip it in black paint, and then paint a border of green around the edge to mimic the rind of the fruit.

Meanwhile, I'm over here just painting my rock green, not sure what else to do because my mind is fixated on so many other things right now—Vienna's eyes, her smile, her tongue that keeps peeking out to lick her lips.

"Daddy?" Ellis's voice breaks through my thought spiral.

"Yes?"

"What are you making?"

"Uh..." My eyes dip down to the rock that I've kept smearing the green paint over.

"What about a leaf?" Vienna suggests.

"A leaf?"

"Yeah, you can just paint a few brown lines through it and then we can put it next to my rose." She holds up her rock painted in red, pink, and white, the blend of the colors so intricate to give the illusion of petals.

"Yes, Daddy! Make a leaf so your rock can go next to Ms. Lewis's!" Ellis practically jumps from her seat at the idea.

"Okay, Ellis. All right. Sit down before you fall, please."

The three of us continue painting and chatting about nothing really—things that happened at school or in Ellis's class, the weather, and the upcoming events at the winery.

"Since I'm supposed to tell you my plans now, I thought you should know that your sister also invited me to the yoga night at the winery in two weeks."

I try to hold back my laugh but fail. "She did, did she?"

"Yup. And I was told that I'm supposed to convince you to join since you never have."

"I've already shared my feelings about yoga with you."

"Yes, you did, but then I began to think that maybe part of the reason you don't want to join in on the fun is because you don't want to get shown up by a girl." She arches a single brow in my direction.

"I like yoga!" Ellis chimes in, but my gaze remains locked on Vienna.

"Nice try. Did my sister suggest you say that?"

Vienna laughs. "No."

"You're a terrible liar."

Vienna's smirk builds, and fuck—all it makes me want to do is kiss it right off her face—the desire so natural that I wonder what would happen if I did. How would she react? Would once be enough?

No, it wouldn't.

But if we were dating, I could do it any time I wanted.

Where the fuck did that thought come from?

"I'm not lying. She didn't tell me what to say, just that I should try to persuade you to participate."

"Daddy?" Ellis interrupts us once again.

"Yes, Ellis?"

With her hand held up in front of her, covered in every color of the rainbow, she says, "I think I need to wash my hands."

Vienna laughs. "Yeah, I think that's a good idea. The rocks are done anyway, so now we need to let them dry."

My gaze flickers all over the table to the array of colors. These rocks were just brown, gray, and black before tonight. Now they're full of life and color—sort of like the woman sitting across from me.

I stand from my chair and round the table, picking up my daughter and carrying her in outstretched arms to the kitchen sink where I help her scrub her hands clean of the paint. Whatever we don't get off here she can clean off in the bath.

Glancing over my shoulder, I see Vienna beginning to move the rocks onto a slat of cardboard I laid out for them to dry, clicking caps back on bottles of paint, and swirling the brushes in the water to clean them.

Once Ellis's hands are clean, she leaps down from her stool at the sink and runs to the bathroom. "I have to go potty!"

Vienna laughs.

"I bet you didn't need to know that," I say, watching her as she walks the cups of water over to the kitchen sink, pouring them inside. She's so close to me now that I can see the tiny flecks of paint that are covering her hands and face.

"Um, I teach a class full of five-year-olds, so I hear those words about eighteen times a day. I just didn't know that would become a part of my day-to-day life when I took this job, but I'm not complaining." She smiles up at me, resting a hand on her hip.

My eyes dance all over her face, fixating on her lips for the thousandth time, but I keep my restraint intact. Until I decide what I want to do about this growing desire for this woman, I need to keep my hands and lips to myself.

The corner of my mouth lifts in response to my internal thoughts, but Vienna catches it. "What?"

Raising my hand, I brush my finger against her cheek in an attempt to rub the paint away, but it's dry. "You have paint on your face."

Her breath hitches from my touch, and without a second of hesitation, she reaches up and wraps her hand around my wrist while my finger is still pressed against her skin. "Hazards of the fun, kind of like getting water spilled all over you."

I drop my voice lower when I speak next. "Thank you for the way you handled that, by the way."

"You don't have to thank me, Rhonan."

"Yes, I do," I say, rubbing my thumb over the spot of paint again, even though I know it won't do anything. But fuck, touching her, staring down into her eyes—it's making this pull to her nearly impossible to deny.

My thumb moves from her cheek to her bottom lip where I gently tug it down, making her breath hitch again.

Our eyes are locked on each other's mouths, and for a second, I can feel myself moving closer to her, like there's no control over my body. Just a few more inches and I could taste this woman finally—swirl my tongue with hers, nip at those pouty lips, hear her moans that I'm sure could lull me to sleep at night.

I watch Vienna's eyes flutter closed, but just before our lips touch, my daughter enters the room, throwing water on me this time—metaphorically, of course.

"Daddy?"

Vienna and I jump away from each other as if we've electrocuted one another. She clears her throat and turns away, heading back over to the table as I fight to conceal my hard-on in my pants.

"Yeah, sweetie?"

"Can I have dessert?"

I glance at the clock on the microwave hanging over the stove. "Uh, yeah. That's fine, but then it's time for a bath."

"Okay." Ellis heads to the pantry to pull out the container of cookies she and Joanne baked yesterday, but I glance back at Vienna, who's tossing her purse over her shoulder.

"I'm going to head home," she announces, focusing her attention on Ellis.

"No, you need to stay longer."

"I can't, sweetie. I need a shower too. The water is making my pants stick to me."

My thoughts veer to Vienna in her shower—you know, the one that I fixed for her—which doesn't help my cock calm down.

"Oh." Ellis nods. "Okay. Do you want to take a cookie?" Holding out the container to her, Vienna walks up and chooses one.

"Thank you so much."

"You're welcome. Thank you for painting rocks with me. It was fun."

Vienna leans down and bops my daughter on the nose. "It was. I can't wait to do it again."

"Me either," Ellis says as she giggles, bopping Vienna on the nose as well.

When she stands, Vienna nods toward me. "Have a good night, Rhonan."

"You too, Vienna."

"But just know, I'm going to get you to come to yoga somehow."

"Is that so?"

Nodding, she grins. "Yup. I'm determined."

My grin begins to match hers. "Good luck with that."

And then she's gone—far enough away that I can't kiss her, even though that's all I can fucking think about.

Chapter 13

Vienna

Novelty Cakes & Meeting with a Lawyer

The bell on the door rings above me as I walk into Bites & Bliss Bakery, eager to satisfy my craving for sugar. Today, a few of the front-office staff at the school were talking about how amazing the cheesecake is from here, and sadly, I haven't been able to think about much else.

That's a lie. You've definitely had something else on your mind, Vienna. Care to share with the class?

Shaking off my internal thoughts, I head toward the counter to wait in line, scouring the bakery case for their other options, but my mind drifts back to Rhonan for the thousandth time.

I wonder if Rhonan likes cheesecake.

It's only been two days since I spent the evening at his house painting rocks with him and Ellis. And if I didn't know any better, I'd say the sexual tension between us escalated that night, especially as we were standing in his kitchen with his hand on my face.

For a split second, I thought he was going to kiss me. And the worst part about it, I was desperate for him to—to show me what his kisses feel like because the longer time passes since the night we met, the needier I am for us to finish what we started.

A man breezes past me, bumping into my shoulder. "Oh my gosh, I'm so sorry," he says as he moves to steady me.

Our eyes meet and something about his gaze spikes my adrenaline, but I instantly convince myself to calm down. It's hard not to be paranoid when you've gone through some shit no one knows about. "No worries."

"Truly. I didn't mean to bump into you."

I smile at him. "It's okay. I'm fine. Have a nice evening."

"You too." He nods and then heads for the door.

"Vienna?"

Twisting back around, I'm surprised to see Dilynne Clark ahead of me in line. "Oh! Hi, Dilynne."

"Hey. You all right? I saw that guy bump into you."

"Oh, yeah. No biggie. How's it going?"

"I was just about to ask you the same thing." She taps her chin. "I think the last time I saw you was at the winery."

My mind searches through our encounters. "Yeah, I think you're right."

"Laney told me that you went to her salon last week, though." She waggles her eyebrows. "Isn't my best friend a wizard with hair?"

Chuckling, I nod. "She is."

"She also told me that she invited you to her wedding."

Sighing, I reply, "She did, even though it was completely unnecessary."

The line moves forward, so Dilynne takes a few steps, and I follow her lead before she turns back to me. "Um, I think it's completely necessary. It's bound to be a good time, you'll get to hear my maid of honor speech, and this means I get to invite you to the bachelorette party as well."

"Oh, gosh. You don't have to…"

Dilynne reaches out and places her hand over my mouth. The move catches me off guard, but I'm quickly realizing that this woman doesn't take no for an answer. "Nonsense. You're coming. End of discussion."

Once she removes her hand from my mouth, I shrug. "Okay, fine. Twist my arm, why don't you?"

She laughs and pulls her cell phone from her pocket. "Let me get your number so I can send you the details." We exchange numbers and then put our phones away. "There, now you have no excuse. And don't try to come up with one. I'm very good with a wrench and will use my talents if necessary."

"I sincerely hope that you're joking," I say, fairly certain she's just being sarcastic, but also getting a little scared the longer I stand here.

She winks at me. "Don't try to bail and you won't have to find out. Besides, you're going to want to see the cake."

"The cake?"

She tosses her head toward the bakery case. "That's why I'm here, to put in the order. Carolina is a wizard with novelty cakes, and after my last cake for the bachelor and bachelorette party for Elliot and his hideous ex-fiancée, I feel like I need to keep the tradition going."

"Elliot was engaged?"

Dilynne rolls her eyes. "Yes, and lucky for him, the bitch cheated on him with her boss and left him the day of the wedding."

Confusion rests between my brows. "I'm sorry, but how is that lucky?"

Dilynne plants her hands on her hips. "Look, I know you're new to town, but let me be clear—not all people in Blossom Peak are good humans, and Tori was one of the worst. Honestly, I still can't believe that Elliot wanted to marry her, but I think he just fell under her spell."

Is that what I'm doing with Rhonan? Am I so disillusioned by the idea of him that I'm missing the important things?

No, Vienna. Rhonan is a good man, a good father. He's not Cole.

God, I just hate that my past has made me question my instincts.

"So yes, I know it sounds harsh, but in a way he's lucky it ended that way. I would have hated to see what would have happened if they'd actually gone through with it. His heartbreak would have been exponentially worse than it already was."

Sighing, I nod in agreement. "Yeah, you're right. Especially because once you're in a commitment like that, it's not easy to leave."

"Agreed. So, how's it going still lusting after Rhonan Hart?" My eyes widen as Dilynne chuckles while I deal with the surprise in her change of topic. "Yup, I know about that too."

"I guess he wasn't kidding when he said his friend group loves to share everything about everyone's lives."

"Our group is a family, Vienna," Dilynne declares, her tone clear, but not harsh. "We've known each other since childhood, and we've been through a lot of shit. So, yeah, we share everything because we look out for one another."

My heart twists in my chest. The only person I ever felt that way with was Lydia.

"Then I guess I'm jealous of that. Good friends are hard to come by."

Dilynne studies me. "You're right about that, but that doesn't mean we all don't deserve them. And you know, we always have room for one more."

"Dilynne?" A woman's voice from the other side of the counter pulls both of our gazes to her. A petite Hispanic woman wearing a purple shirt and white apron with short, dark, curly hair has both of her hands planted on her hips and a smirk on her lips as she greets Dilynne.

Dilynne rubs her hands together. "Carolina, Carolina. Are you ready to make another cake for me?"

Carolina's grin spreads, the hint of mischief building in her eyes. "You know it. What are you thinking this time, hun?"

"The usual, but we're gonna add a few details that I think the bride and groom are gonna love." Dilynne turns back to me, wrapping her arm around my shoulder and pulling me forward. "Have you met Vienna yet?"

"I have not." Carolina wipes her hand on her apron before holding it out to shake mine. "Pleasure to meet you."

"Likewise."

"She's Mrs. Allen's substitute teacher for the rest of the year, and Rhonan's new neighbor," Dilynne explains, winking in Carolina's direction.

Great. Now another person is gonna be suspicious of our relationship.

Rhonan said people are already probably talking, Vienna, so does it really matter?

"Oh, lucky you," Carolina says. "How are you enjoying the view?"

I glance out the window, taking in the cherry blossom trees and the sun setting in the distance just between the crest of two mountains before directing my gaze back to her. "Oh, I love it here."

Carolina chuckles. "Yes, Blossom Peak is beautiful, but I was referring to the view of your neighbor. Rhonan Hart is Grade A eye candy around here. You'd be shocked at the number of conversations I overhear between women lusting after that man."

Dilynne snaps her fingers. "He may be Laney's older brother, but even I can admit that he's a catch."

"Exactly. I just wish he would open himself up again. It's a shame what happened to Sarah, but a man like that doesn't need to be alone forever," Carolina adds.

That dull ache returns to my chest when I think of how heartbreaking it is that Rhonan and Ellis both have lived a life without her, but it's quickly accompanied by jealousy at the thought of him with another woman that isn't me.

Calm down, Vienna. No need to get territorial over a man who just wants to be your friend.

"You know, Ellis is an incredible kid," I interject. "A true testament to how well he's done as a single parent."

Carolina nods. "Still, he needs someone to take care of him too." She shakes her head, blinking away her emotion, but her words spin on repeat in my mind.

I wonder when was the last time Rhonan did something for himself.

"Anyway, back to the cake."

Dilynne glances back at me. "Why don't you go ahead and order because I might be here for a while..."

"You sure?"

"Yup."

"Okay. I just need a slice of cheesecake, please."

Dilynne laughs while Carolina moves to the counter, picking up a box that is far too big for one slice of cheesecake. "Oh, Vienna. One does not order just a *slice* of Carolina's cheesecake."

"Uh, why?"

"Because one slice isn't enough," Carolina finishes for her. "Trust me, you're going to need the entire thing."

Before I know what's happening, I'm paying for an entire cheesecake that there's no way I'll be able to eat by myself and stepping back onto the sidewalk as cherry blossoms float through the sky in the breeze.

My feet begin to carry me toward my car, but my eyes catch the sign for Thorne Family Law Group across the street and my mind drifts to thinking about what Dilynne told me about Elliot and his failed relationship. I didn't anticipate feeling a connection to him in this way, but my heart hammered in my chest while hearing his story.

Before I can overthink my decision, I cross the street and enter the building of his family's law practice, finding it fairly empty. It is a Friday evening, so everyone's probably gone home already.

Sighing, I decide I'll try another night, but a familiar voice calls out to me. "Vienna?"

Spinning on my heels, I lock eyes with Elliot. "Hey, Elliot."

Elliot glances around the entryway. "Are you lost?"

"Uh, no."

"That didn't sound too convincing."

I shake my head. "Sorry. No, I'm not lost. I, uh... Well, I was wondering if you had a moment to speak with me, but then I realized it's Friday evening and you're probably itching to get home, so..."

Elliot holds up a hand. "Trust me, I'm not itching to go anywhere at the moment. What's up?" He looks me over. "Are you all right?"

I hoist my purse up higher on my shoulder and switch the bag with my gigantic cheesecake to my other hand. "Yeah, I'm fine. Sorry, I guess I'm just nervous."

"No need to be nervous," he says through a laugh. "I helped fix your showerhead for you, remember?"

Chuckling, I nod. "Yeah. But..."

He waves for me to follow him. "Let's go sit down in my office so you can relax and then tell me what's on your mind."

I follow Elliot down a long hallway into his office, a more than ample space filled with floor-to-ceiling bookshelves and the biggest mahogany desk I've ever seen. The walls are lined with his framed degrees and accolades he's earned throughout the years, and one of the walls is almost entirely taken up by a window that looks out toward the mountains that surround the town. "You want something to drink?"

"Water would be great."

He walks over to the mini fridge in the corner next to a couch, retrieves me a bottle of water, and places it on the desk in front of me as I take a seat in one of the cushioned chairs opposite his desk.

After he takes his seat on the other side, he says, "Now, how can I help you?"

"Well, you came up in a conversation with Dilynne earlier, and that reminded me that you're a lawyer. So I wanted to see if maybe you could help me."

Elliot's jaw ticks. "Dilynne tends to have trouble keeping her nose out of other people's business, but you'd think I'd be used to it by now. Although, not sure why she's always talking about me."

"I don't think she meant anything harmful by it. In fact, she seemed relieved that you avoided more hurt."

He rolls his eyes, forcing a smile after. "I know you didn't come in here to talk about one of the most annoying people on the planet, so let's focus on how I can help you."

Sensing his annoyance grow, I nod and then direct my focus back on my question. "Okay, but I need to know that what I discuss with you here stays between us."

"Of course. Anything you share with me is protected by attorney-client privilege, Vienna."

I let out a sigh of relief. "Good, because I don't want anyone to get involved that doesn't need to."

Elliot studies me with a pinch in his brow. "Do you mean Rhonan?"

I stare back at him, debating whether I should answer him honestly. But my conscience wins out. "Yes."

"Is there a reason?"

"Not one I should discuss with you."

He leans back in his chair, folding his hands together over his chest. "You know that if you hire me as your lawyer, you're going to have to share details with me, Vienna."

"I know, but I also know that what I'm about to share with you could put both of us in danger if it got out."

He sits upright in his seat again. "Are you in danger?"

"I—I honestly don't know, but I figure the best thing I can do is be proactive to keep everyone around me safe." *Most of all, Rhonan and Ellis.* "And I do know that you are familiar with being lied to and manipulated, so I thought you might understand."

He swallows roughly. "Talk to me, Vienna."

I take a deep breath and then admit why I'm here. "I need you to help me divorce my husband."

Elliot's mouth drops open, but he recovers quickly. And before I leave his office, I realize that getting out of my disastrous relationship would come at a greater price than I even imagined.

Chapter 14

Rhonan

My Worst Fear & One Hell of an Apology

Walking into my house after a long shift sends a wave of relief through me. It's been a long few days at the station, and I'm more than eager for some rest before I have to go back tomorrow.

Brody is on vacation this week, and Daniel's wife is going into labor, which means I'm working more than I'm used to. Truth be told, the distraction from real life has been nice, but that means I haven't had much time with Ellis, and I miss my daughter fiercely.

"Ellis? Joanne?" I call out as I step through the front door and shut it behind me, but all I'm met with is silence. Assessing the empty house, I hang my keys on the hook by the door and peer outside to the deck, where I find Joanne pacing around the backyard.

"Joanne?"

She spins to look up at me from the grass below as I make my way toward her. "Oh God, Rhonan." The desperation in her voice makes my heart rate climb instantly.

I rush down the stairs to her. "What's wrong?"

Tears cloud her eyes and her bottom lip is trembling. "I—I can't find Ellis."

"What do you mean you can't find Ellis?"

"She was out here playing, and I had to use the bathroom, so I went inside. When I came back out, she was gone. I'm so sorry."

I pull her into my chest, rubbing her back affectionately. "Hey, it's okay. I'm sure she's not far."

"I don't know, Rhonan. I called out for her as loud as I could, but I haven't heard her or seen her. The gate is still locked, and I…"

"Did you call law enforcement?"

"I was about to, but…"

"Okay, just wait while I check the front yard. You go inside the house and search all the rooms."

"What if she passed out? Or what if—"

I don't let her finish that thought because at this moment, I'm living through one of my worst nightmares as a parent. Gripping her shoulders, I say, "We'll find her, Joanne."

As soon as the words leave my lips, I race back up the stairs on the deck and run through the house, hearing Joanne yelling Ellis's name behind me. The screen door slams against the outside of the house as I barrel through the front door in search of my kid—*my everything*.

Fuck. This can't be happening.

Cupping my hands around my mouth, I project my voice as loud as I can. "Ellis! Ellis!" But I get nothing in response. Twisting my head back and forth, I look up and down our street. There's no sign of cars or her bike. The garage is closed, so the likelihood that she took off on her bike is low. Joanne would have heard her open the garage, and she knows damn well she's not allowed to ride without an adult watching her.

"Ellis!" I jog up the road to the bend, thinking maybe she took off after the ice cream truck.

"Rhonan!" Joanne calls out to me from my house as I run back toward her.

"Anything?"

"She's not in the house. I even checked her normal hiding places, but..."

"Shit."

Sobs wrack her body. "I'm so sorry, Rhonan."

"Stop it. We have to be missing something. There has to be..." The sound of music playing from Vienna's house stops me mid-sentence. "Vienna."

My feet carry me as fast as I can go to my neighbor's house, not even bothering to knock on her door as I burst inside.

"Jesus Christ!" Vienna shrieks as I barrel through her door, finding her standing in her kitchen, music blaring from a speaker—and my daughter standing right next to her.

"Daddy!" Ellis jumps down from a stool and races over to me.

"Ellis Seraphina Hart! What the hell are you doing over here?"

The music cuts out, making the sound of my voice echo throughout the house.

"Rhonan," Vienna starts, but I glare up at her and cut her off.

"No! You don't get to talk right now." Her head rears back, but I turn back to my daughter. "Ellis, you had me and Joanne scared to death! You can't just take off without telling us!"

"Rhonan..." Vienna attempts to interrupt me again, but I point a finger at her this time.

"No! Don't talk! You have no idea what was going through my mind just now!"

"Daddy, stop yelling," Ellis says, tears forming in her eyes.

"You just left our yard," I say, my voice cracking despite myself. "And didn't bother telling anyone. You know better than that, Ellis!"

"Rhonan." Joanne's voice comes from behind me, breathless with relief.

Ellis runs into Joanne's arms.

Joanne drops to her knees, catching Ellis like she might vanish again. "Oh, thank God. We were so scared." She presses her face into Ellis's hair.

"I'm sorry," Ellis whispers, crying now in earnest.

Joanne pulls back just long enough to cup her face, tears streaming. "You're safe. That's all that matters."

My chest feels too tight to breathe.

"Take her home," I bark.

Joanne looks up at me with a warning in her eyes, but she doesn't say anything as she rises, keeping Ellis tucked tight against her side.

I watch them leave and then turn back to Vienna. "You had no right!" My tone is harsh and laced with disdain because I need someone to blame for the fear that is racing through me right now.

"Right to what?"

"My daughter...she's..." Grinding my teeth together, I take a few steps toward her and move my face closer to hers. "Since you don't have children, you can't even imagine what I'm feeling right now and probably never will."

She winces, like my words physically hurt her. "Well, I—"

Shaking my head, I stare down at the ground while trying to get my heart rate under control. But when I look back up at the woman that I have been fantasizing about for over a month, I now know why I can't give in to what I feel. "You have no idea what it's like to have a child, to fear losing someone you love after actually experiencing it."

Vienna's eyes narrow at me as she swallows roughly, crossing her arms over her chest. But her reply surprises me, even though it shouldn't. "You know what? You can leave now, Rhonan."

We stay like that, staring at each other while my chest feels like it's splitting in two. Finally, when I can't take the disdain she's returning with her eyes, I break the eye contact and push back through her door, stomping over to my house.

"Fuck!"

I barrel through the front door of my house, finding Joanne holding Ellis on the couch, my daughter still crying.

And that's when the rage fueled by fear begins to dissipate. My shoulders fall, my feet carry me over to her, and the adrenaline evaporates, replaced by shame. "Ellis..."

Her bottom lip trembles and snot leaks from her nose as she stares up at me. "I'm—I'm sorry, Daddy."

Dropping to my knees in front of her and Joanne, I take my daughter into my arms, attempting not to crush her as I hold her to my chest. "God, Ellis. You—you scared the shit out of me, sweetie."

"I'm sorry..."

"You can't run away like that."

"I—"

"Rhonan," Joanne says, pulling my attention to her. Rocking back and forth, I press my lips to my daughter's forehead while waiting for Joanne to speak. "I guess Vienna and Ellis were talking over the fence and Ellis wanted to play with Roscoe. Vienna told her to ask if it was okay, but she didn't see me outside, so she lied and said it was fine." She tilts her head at me. "This wasn't Vienna's fault..."

"I just wanted to see Roscoe, Daddy," Ellis says on a shaky breath.

I push her hair from her face, cradling her cheek in my hand. Fuck, I don't think I've ever been this scared in my life. "You know better. You know that we don't lie."

"I know." She nods, looking away from me. "You scared me. You yelled..."

My shoulders drop again as I fall back to the ground on my ass. "I'm sorry I yelled. I was just so freaking scared, sweetie."

Her little arms wrap around my neck. "It's okay. Everybody makes mistakes."

As if her words were the realization I needed, my mind instantly veers toward Vienna and what a fucking asshole I just was to her.

Shit.

"Yeah, they do."

Ellis leans back and puts both of her hands on the side of my face. "I love you, Daddy."

"I love you too, Ellis." She kisses my cheek and then buries her head in my neck as I sit there, closing my eyes and breathing her in.

The fear begins to subside, and as soon as I feel ready, I release my daughter and Joanne takes her to the bathroom to clean up her face.

I hang my arms over my knees as my head falls forward, trying to take in a breath. But the pain is still there. It never truly leaves. It's a hurt that is a part of me that gets inflamed in instances like this, scars on the inside that no one else knows are there unless I tell them.

But now I've projected my fear onto yet another person.

The shitty part is—Vienna didn't even deserve it.

And now I don't know if an apology will be enough to undo the hurt I've caused her too.

***

I stifle yet another yawn as I walk through the front door of my house, my head down even though I'm fighting like hell to keep my eyes open.

I slept like shit last night, replaying my words as I yelled at Vienna, remembering how fucking terrified I was when I couldn't find my daughter and how out of line I was to blame her. Work was rough to get through today, but luckily, I now have a few days to recover.

Sighing, I hang my keys on the hook by the door, but the laughter coming from the kitchen stops me in my tracks.

What the...

"More sprinkles!" Ellis exclaims, clapping her hands together.

"I like your thinking, Ellis."

Awareness creeps up my spine because the last person I anticipated being in my house right now is the woman I screamed at only twenty-four hours ago.

When I round the corner and find Ellis, Joanne, and Vienna in the kitchen, the countertop covered in cupcakes, confusion rushes through me.

"Daddy!" Ellis jumps down from her stool and slams into my legs, wrapping her arms around me.

"Hey, sweetie. How was your day?"

"Good! Ms. Lewis asked if I'd like to help her make cupcakes for her friend's birthday, and I said yes!"

The desire to lift my eyes to the woman I can sense staring at me is frighteningly strong, but I refrain.

Way to be a fucking coward, Rhonan.

Joanne isn't going to let me off that easy, though. "She made sure to ask for permission this time before she took off."

I meet Joanne's gaze and nod. "Good, but why are you baking them here?"

"I figured you'd be more comfortable with that," Vienna interjects, pulling my eyes to her finally—and fuck, I wish she hadn't.

Her eyes are narrowed at me, like if she could, there would be lasers projected out of them right at me.

You messed this one up good, Rhonan. Nice job, dickwad.

"I—" But before I can respond, Ellis starts talking again.

"Ms. Lewis, are you gonna take the cupcakes to your friend now?"

Vienna directs her gaze back to my daughter, reaching for her hand. "I wish I could, sweetie, but unfortunately, I can't."

"Why not?"

Vienna inhales deeply before staring up at the ceiling and then back down at my daughter. "Today is my friend's birthday, but that friend is up in heaven."

Ellis's eyes widen. "My—my mommy is in heaven."

Vienna rubs her thumb across Ellis's hand. "I know."

"What was your friend's name?" Ellis asks as I swallow down the lump in my throat, guilt consuming me even more as I watch and listen to them.

"Lydia, and she was my best friend in the whole entire world."

"And now she's an angel," Ellis whispers.

"Yes, sweetie. Now she's an angel. But..." Vienna inhales again, as if trying to fight back her emotions. "Lydia loved cupcakes, especially cupcakes with sprinkles. So, since I was missing her today, I thought I could make some for her and share them with you since I know you love sprinkles too."

Joanne reaches up to brush a tear from her cheek, and that's when my stomach turns even harder.

Ellis reaches for the bottle of sprinkles. "These cupcakes need more rainbow sprinkles then."

Vienna and Joanne start laughing, but I can't watch anymore. Turning away, I head down the hallway to change out of my uniform while berating myself for the hundredth time about what an insensitive asshole I was.

Yesterday was not my finest moment, I'll be the first to admit that. But just like I tell Ellis, everyone makes mistakes. It's what we do next that matters the most.

By the time I shower and have a fresh pair of jeans and T-shirt on, I return to the kitchen to find Ellis coloring on a piece of paper and Joanne washing dishes in the sink.

And no sign of Vienna.

"Hey."

Ellis peers up at me from her coloring, but only briefly. "Hi, Daddy."

Scratching my neck, I say, "Uh, where's Vienna?"

Joanne glares at me over her shoulder. "She went home."

"Why?"

"Wanted to be alone. She left some cupcakes for us." Joanne wipes her hands on a dishtowel as she walks over to me and lowers her voice while placing her hands on her hips. "Feel like an ass yet?"

I grind my teeth together. "No need to rub salt in the wound."

Joanne huffs out a laugh. "You may have wounds, Rhonan, but what you fail to realize sometimes is that other people do too."

Ellis pulls on my shirt. "Daddy?"

I drop my gaze to her. "Yeah, sweetie?"

"I drew this picture for Ms. Lewis." She holds out the paper to me, showing me what looks like two female stick figures standing next to each other, both with wings.

"What did you draw?"

"That's Ms. Lewis's best friend and my mommy, up in heaven together."

My shoulders fall. "Oh. That's…"

"Can I give it to her?"

"Uh…"

"Please, Daddy?"

"It's almost bath time, Ellis."

Joanne clears her throat. "Why don't we have Daddy take it to her while you take your bath? And that way, we can have another cupcake once you're done."

Ellis nods enthusiastically. "Okay!" She pushes the paper against my stomach. "Make sure she knows it's from me though, Daddy."

"I—" My eyes trail Ellis as she runs down the hall, but Joanne steps right in front of me so I have no choice but to look at her.

"You owe that woman an apology, Rhonan." Her brow arches painfully high on her forehead. "I only heard a snippet of what you said to her, but I can imagine what else you spewed out of fear."

"Fuck, Joanne."

"You need to grovel," she continues. "Vienna is a special woman. Apologize and grovel like you've never groveled before." With one more lift of her brow, she heads down the hall to the bathroom where Ellis has already turned the water on.

A heavy sigh leaves me, but I know that Joanne is right. And the longer I put it off, the worse things are going to get between me and Vienna.

With Ellis's drawing in hand, I push open the front door and slowly cross my yard, reaching Vienna's too quickly to prepare what I'm going to say. Nonetheless, when she opens her front door, nothing could have prepared me for the sadness on her face and my lack of knowing what I could say to make things right.

Vienna swipes tears from under her eyes. "What do you want, Rhonan?"

Clearing my throat, I straighten my spine. "I came to apologize."

"For?" she asks, crossing her arms over her chest.

"For yelling at you yesterday."

One of her eyebrows lifts, and I'm suddenly aware of what a natural move that is for all of the women in my life. "Is that all?"

"Well, I—"

"You know what?" she says, cutting me off. "No. It's my turn to talk." She clears her throat and jabs her finger into the center of my chest. "You had no right to yell at me the way you did yesterday."

"You're right."

"I know!" Her voice rises in volume. "And guess what? You were wrong!"

"About what?"

She points toward the side of her where my house lies. "I do know what it's like to lose someone I love. Lydia was my family. She may not have been related by blood, but her death destroyed me."

"You're right. I—I didn't know."

Her hands fly into the air now, her anger radiating off of her and, despite knowing how pissed off she is at me, I can't help but find her anger fucking hot—the intensity of her gaze, the quickness of her breaths. That I fucked up and she has no problem letting me know that.

"I know you didn't! Because you just assumed! You just stomped over here like an ogre and—"

I don't think, I just move.

I close the distance between us and crush my lips to hers. When my tongue darts out to find hers, she shoves me away, but her eyes are wild and her cheeks are flushed. "What the hell, Rhonan?"

The only sound resting between us is our heavy breathing, our chests rising and falling with each labored inhale. Our eyes bounce between one another, the silence deafening even though that seems impossible.

But before I can say anything else, Vienna launches herself at me, jumping into my arms and wrapping her legs around my waist, smashing her lips back to mine.

My adrenaline kicks in, closing her front door behind me and then spinning around, pinning her up against it while our tongues clash and my cock presses against my zipper. I thrust my erection right between her legs, spurring a moan from deep in her throat, but Vienna doesn't miss a beat. She writhes against me, creating the friction I know she needs.

"God, you're infuriating," she mumbles against my lips.

"I'm aware. You're not a saint either, you know."

Vienna deepens our kiss, yanking on the strands of my hair between her fingers. "God, Rhonan. Yes."

Our mouths continue to move over one another, and even though I know I should stop this—whatever the hell *this* is—my body won't let me.

"I need you to know how sorry I am," I say, lifting my lips from hers and waiting for her to open her eyes. When she does, the green hue I've grown to find comfort and intrigue in is darker than I've ever seen.

She's needy, and fuck if I don't want to apologize to her in other ways.

"Fuck it," I grate out, fully committed to how I'm going to make my point.

Lifting her from the door, I carry her down the hallway to her bedroom, familiar with the layout of this house after fixing her showerhead all those weeks ago.

"Rhonan...what are you doing?"

When I reach her bed, I toss her onto it, pinning her hands above her head as I hover over her. "I'm going to apologize to you, Vienna... And when I'm done with you? You won't question the sincerity of it because you're going to be lying in a dent in your mattress too fucking spent from coming so hard."

Her eyes widen. "Rhonan..."

Dragging my nose up her neck to her ear, I whisper, "Tell me you want this. Tell me you want me to make you come."

"I do, I just..."

I lean over her again, still restraining her hands above her head. "Don't overthink this, Vienna. We've exercised restraint up until this point, but I'm really fucking tired of pretending I don't want you." Reaching for one of her hands, I move it right over my cock straining against my jeans. "Tell me you feel the same."

A moan leaves her lips as she nods. "I do. God, Rhonan. Fuck me...please."

I don't waste another second before my lips find hers again as Vienna continues to rub her hand up and down my cock.

"Jesus, baby. This isn't going to be gentle."

"I don't want gentle," she mumbles against my lips. "I want it hard."

"I hope you know what you're asking for." Vienna pushes up from the bed to reach my lips, and with my free hand, I make fast work on the button on her jeans. "Strip for me, Vienna. I need to see this fucking body again."

I release her other hand and she instantly pulls at her zipper, pushing her jeans down and kicking them off while our mouths remain connected.

Without hesitation, I find the string of her underwear at her hips and rip them apart before dropping my head between her legs and burying my face in her pussy.

She buries her hands in my hair. "Oh fuck, Rhonan. Yes…"

"You taste like heaven, Vienna." I drag my tongue up her slit, swirling it around her clit and then repeating the process. But then an idea comes to me.

Standing up straight and adjusting my cock, I pull Vienna up from the bed and trade places with her, lying down and resting my head on her pillow.

"Rhonan?"

"Come ride my face, sweetheart." She hesitates a second as she bites her bottom lip. "Give me that fucking pussy, Vienna. *Now.*"

My command sparks something inside of her because she immediately obeys, swinging her hips as she walks toward me, lifting her shirt over her head and undoing the clasp on her bra, tossing it to the side before she climbs on the bed and straddles my face. "Is this what you wanted?"

"Yes. Now, let me show you how fucking sorry I am." I yank her down to me, pulling her as close as I can before feasting on the silky flesh between her legs.

Vienna leans her head back, panting. "Yes…yes…" I suck her clit between my lips, flicking my tongue over the bud, loving the way she shivers in my grasp while my hands guide her hips over my mouth. I can feel her dripping over my lips and down my chin, and I'm loving it.

This woman. This sexy as hell woman is all I've been able to think about and tasting her is only going to fuel my obsession with her. Now that I know what she tastes like, I'm going to want to live between her legs. Now that I've heard her moans, I'm going to need to hear them every day.

And now that I know that she's just as desperate for me as I am for her, I'm going to have to face what I'm feeling.

Vienna tenses in my hands. "Yes, right there." I move one of my hands behind her, sliding it between her ass cheeks and down until I can tease her entrance, slowly pushing a finger inside as she continues to swivel her hips over my tongue.

She drops her head down so our eyes meet, her lips parted, her breaths turning quicker as she keeps riding my face. "You're gonna make me come, Rhonan."

"Do it. Soak my fucking face, Vienna."

My tongue gets back to work, and after a few more moments, Vienna lets out a scream that I'm afraid our other neighbors might hear.

But that sound? Fuck, I didn't know I needed that sound in my life.

When her body goes slack, I lick through her pussy once more and then help her slowly ease to the bed, licking my lips as I reach for my zipper and then freeze.

"Fuck, I don't have a condom."

"I do," she breathes before reaching for the drawer on her nightstand and tossing one in my direction. She lies on her back, her legs pressed together in an attempt to be modest, as if I didn't memorize every inch of her already, especially the soaked pink flesh I just got up close and intimate with. "Let's just say I wanted to be prepared, just in case you..."

"Gave in?"

She nods. "Something like that."

I reach behind me, pulling my shirt over my head and then shoving off my jeans and briefs as quickly as I can, covering my cock with the condom, stroking my length as Vienna watches me from the bed, her eyes locked on my erection. "You sure you want this?"

She stuns me as she reaches between her legs, runs her fingers through her pussy, and then holds them up for me to see. "What do you think?"

Leaning forward, I capture her fingers in my mouth, licking them clean. "I think you're about to get fucked, Vienna."

The truth is, *she* fucked me up a long time ago and I'm just now realizing that I don't fucking care. Something within me has shifted, and it's all because of the woman spread out on the bed beneath me, offering herself to me unconditionally.

But it's not just her body that I want—*it's her*. My head is catching up to my gut and the stubborn organ in my chest that's continued to protest all of the feelings this woman brings up within me.

"Please, Rhonan," she whimpers, bringing me back to the moment.

Crawling over her on the bed, I line my cock up to her entrance, teasing her by pushing forward just enough and then pulling back out, running my head up her slit to her clit and rubbing her there as well. "Your pussy is fucking perfect. I'm ashamed to admit how much I've thought about this."

She closes her eyes and whines. "God, stop teasing me. I thought you were supposed to be apologizing to me..."

I gently grasp her by the chin, waiting for her eyes to pop back open, and when they do, the vulnerability that passes through both of us nearly shocks me. "You have no idea how fucking sorry I am, Vienna. Truly."

She cups the side of my face, her eyes bouncing between mine. "I forgive you."

"Good." I thrust forward, burying myself inside of her in one fell swoop as she cries out. "Because I need to make you come again."

Her nails dig into my back and her head is tossed back as far as it can go. She shrieks each time I piston my hips forward, hitting her deep and hard like she needs. "God, just like that, Rhonan."

"This pussy was aching for my cock, wasn't it?" I keep up my pace, fixating on her face and mouth as I watch her take every inch of me and loving the sounds she makes as I fill her over and over again. "Hard and fast...that's what you wanted, right?"

Her hands find the sides of my face again, bringing my nose to hers. "Yes. God, it's so good, Rhonan."

"I love having you spread out beneath me like this, stretching you open, filling you up." My lips latch onto her nipple, sucking the bud between my teeth. "You ran away from me that night..."

"I know. I'm sorry too."

"Maybe it was for the best...because I wouldn't have been able to appreciate you like this before. But now?" Her moans grow louder. "Now I'm going to take my time showing you the attention you deserve."

I pull out of her and throw her legs back by her head. "What the..."

Dropping my mouth to her pussy, I flick my tongue over her clit again and lap at her until she's gasping. "So fucking wet..."

"Fuck, Rhonan. God, please..."

I hover over her again and slide inside easily, pinning her hands above her head once more as I kiss along her collarbone. "So fucking pretty when you beg."

"Fuck, I'm close." I release her hands as she reaches between us, rubbing her fingers over her clit.

"That's right. Rub that clit, baby. Fucking soak my cock with your cum." I speed up, watching her breasts bounce with each of my thrusts, pulling her nipple in my mouth as her hand moves faster between us. And then she's screaming, clenching around me, making me follow right behind her as I fill the condom with my release.

"Fuckkkk…" I drag out until every last drop has left my body, and then I collapse, rolling off of her.

We lie there, breathing heavily until we turn to face each other at the same time.

"You're forgiven," Vienna says on a shaky breath.

"Good." I stare back up at the ceiling, trying to get my heart rate back under control. And I'm waiting for the guilt to slam into me like it has the last two times, but it doesn't.

Fuck.

"Rhonan?" Vienna's voice cuts through my racing thoughts.

"Yeah?"

"What happens now?"

Her question shouldn't catch me off guard, but as soon as I twist back to face her, I can see the uncertainty in her eyes.

We do that again.

It's the only thought in my brain at this moment, because I know without a doubt that I'm not going to be able to resist this woman anymore now that I've had her beneath me.

But before I can say anything, I hear my phone chime from the pocket of my jeans. "Fuck, I—I need to get back home."

"Oh…okay, yeah."

Once we clean up and redress, an awkward silence rests between us. Vienna walks me to her door, where I find the picture from Ellis on the floor—a victim of the desperation we gave in to. "Shit." I lean down and pick it up, twisting to hand it to her. "By the way, Ellis made this for you."

Vienna studies the paper in her hands, tears forming in her eyes. "That girl has the biggest heart. I hope she never changes."

"Yeah, I know. I have no idea where she got it from, honestly."

Vienna tilts her head at me. "That's funny—because I do."

I reach for the door, not wanting to leave but knowing that I have to. "Good night, Vienna."

"Good night, Rhonan."

Once her door is shut and I hear her lock it, I make my way back home slowly, replaying everything that just happened and what the fuck I'm supposed to do about it now.

I don't regret sleeping with her. Not one fucking bit.

In fact, I feel like it was only inevitable at this point.

But now what?

As soon as I walk in the door, I find Joanne standing there, her arms crossed over her chest and a knowing look on her face.

"Yes, Joanne?"

"You've been gone for a while."

Shit. I didn't even think about how much time had passed while I was there. I push a hand through my hair, which draws Joanne's attention to the sight. Her brow lifts.

"We were...talking."

She narrows her eyes at me. "And did you grovel?"

I attempt to fight my smirk, but my effort is in vain. The corner of my mouth lifts because I can still taste Vienna on my lips. "I did."

Joanne purses her lips and then nods. "Good man. Perhaps not all hope is lost for you."

Hope.

That's not an emotion I'm too familiar with, but perhaps Joanne is right. It's something I need to be a little more open to.

And now that I know that Vienna wants me too, that's something I can move toward with more faith than I've had before.

Chapter 15

Vienna

Weird Feelings & A Dingleberry

"We need another idea for a booth at the Spring Festival." Jody Hansen, one of the fifth-grade teachers, is standing at the front of the cafeteria, leading the discussion during our staff meeting. It's a Monday afternoon and all of us are itching to go home, but Jody is determined to keep us until her list has been completed.

Honestly, this meeting could have been an email.

One of the second-grade teachers raises her hand. "What about a Flowers for Mom booth? The kids can make bouquets for their mothers for Mother's Day, since it's the Sunday after the festival, and we can ask Yancy's Florals to donate blooms to the booth."

A murmur of conversation filters through the room.

"I love that idea!" Jody says, but sadness builds in my chest. She scratches down something on her clipboard and then announces, "Perfect! All right, that's it for me. Be on the lookout for an email with more details as it gets closer."

Oh, now she decides to use email as a form of communication.

The staff scatters like cockroaches that have just seen light, but I stay back and wait until Jody is finished with a conversation to approach her. "Jody?"

"Hey, Vienna. Are you hanging in there? Are the kids driving you insane yet?"

I huff out a laugh. "They certainly have a lot of energy, but it's nothing I can't handle."

"Glad to hear it. How can I help you?"

"Well, I just... I have a concern about the Flowers for Mom booth."

A pinch develops in her brow. "Okay..."

"What about kids like Ellis Hart, who don't have a mom to celebrate with? Don't you think that would be a little insensitive?"

Jody sighs. "I understand what you're saying, but unfortunately, that's just part of life. We can't shield her from Mother's Day, Vienna."

"I know, I just think it would be more considerate if we left Mother's Day out of the festival."

"Look, I know you have a soft spot for Ellis, given you're her neighbor and all..."

Yeah, well, I also have a soft spot for her father.

"But I'm not going to sacrifice an opportunity for a bunch of kids just because of one."

Nodding, I say, "Okay. Just...thought I'd bring it to your attention."

Pulling my bag up on my shoulder, I turn to leave, trying to keep my emotions in check, but I struggle to do so. Jody is right in one respect, though. I know Ellis can't be shielded from the reality of her situation, but the more time I spend with her, the more it resonates with me.

My mother and I aren't super close, and since I'm an only child, I feel alone more often than not. Lydia was the closest thing I had to a sister, and when she died, the reality of my solitary situation was amplified.

I guess I just want to protect Ellis from feeling the same way.

Walking into the main office, intending on getting to my car as quickly as possible, I'm caught off guard when I see a man standing on the other side of the receptionist desk. The front receptionist isn't around, so when our eyes lock, he smiles in my direction.

"Sorry, the school is closed."

He nods. "I can see that. I was just trying to get some information about the school. My wife and I are thinking of moving to Blossom Peak, but I'd like to know a little bit more about the programs you have here."

"Oh, well..." I point to the wall by the door where several papers are printed out with most of the information he's interested in. "I'm just a substitute, but I know there's a bunch of information on those handouts over there."

His eyes drift to the wall and then back to me. "A substitute?"

"Yeah. One of the teachers is on maternity leave, so I'm filling in."

Leaning over the counter, he rests his forearms there, tilting his head at me. "Just a sub? Why not a full-time teacher?"

"Oh, well, I'm sort of new in town." Honestly, I still haven't classified this town as my home because my intention was for my stay to just be temporary, but now...

His eyes move up and down my body. "Well, you certainly look like a teacher the kids would like."

His comment makes me uneasy. "Uh, thank you?"

"I bet you're a good mom too," he adds.

Sadness overwhelms me, quickly followed by more uneasiness. "I—I really need to be getting home."

He pushes himself up off the counter, adjusting his pants on his waist. "Of course. Thank you for the info, Ms...."

"Lewis," I finish for him.

There's a twitch in his eye as he says, "Thank you, Ms. Lewis."

I watch him walk to his car and wait for him to leave the parking lot before I make my way out to my car, releasing the breath I was keeping trapped in my lungs.

I'm sure he was just like any other tourist passing through, but something about that man gave me the creeps.

Well, good thing your neighbor is a sheriff, right, Vienna? Perhaps you need to tell Rhonan about your visitor...

While driving back to my house, I consider whether it's even worth bringing up. I was probably just being paranoid. The man was just asking questions and trying to be friendly. Yeah, that's it. I'm just way too up in my head right now, especially since I haven't heard from Rhonan since we slept together, and it's been over twenty-four hours.

Today has been an emotional rollercoaster, so I'm more than excited about the idea of sitting on my back porch with a glass of wine and playing fetch with Roscoe to end it on a high note.

And if I happen to get a glimpse of Rhonan while I'm outside, then it will just be a happy coincidence.

Yeah, keep telling yourself that, Vienna.

But when I pull into my driveway, I notice Rhonan's truck isn't parked in his.

Disappointment floods my chest, but I brush it off and go inside, change my clothes, feed Roscoe, and pour that glass of wine.

As soon as I take my seat in the chair on my porch, Roscoe brings his ball over to me. "All right, boy. Let's play." Leaning my arm back, I catapult the ball as far as I can, smiling while watching Roscoe chase after it. He eagerly grabs it in his mouth, and rushes back to me, dropping it on the ground so I can throw it again. "Good, boy! You're learning!"

"Damn, I'm impressed." A voice from the other side of the fence makes me jump, and when I turn my attention over there, I'm shocked to see Rhonan watching me from the other side, his arms resting over the top of the wooden slats.

"Jesus, warn a person that you're watching them, will you?"

The corner of his mouth lifts. "I thought that's what I was just doing."

"Daddy!" Ellis shouts from his yard.

Rhonan glances over his shoulder. "What's up, sweetie?"

"Is Ms. Lewis home yet?"

"Who do you think I'm talking to, Ellis?"

"Roscoe," she replies without missing a beat, making me laugh.

I stand from my porch, wine in hand, and cross the yard, Rhonan's eyes trailing me the entire time. I can feel my lips quirk to the side as he tracks my movements, his gaze making heat pool low in my belly until I'm only a few inches from him on the other side of the fence.

"Hey, there," I say, our gazes still locked.

His eyes dip down to my lips before he speaks. "Hey."

"Ms. Lewis?" Ellis asks, her silhouette visible through the slats in the fence.

"Yes, sweetie?"

"Can I play with Roscoe?"

My dog claws at the fence when he hears her. I peer down at him. "What do you say, boy? You wanna go play with Ellis?" Roscoe barks in response. I turn to face Rhonan and shrug. "I think he's made his choice loud and clear."

Rhonan tosses his head to the side. "Meet me at the gate."

As I walk into Rhonan's backyard, my arm brushes his chest. Roscoe takes off toward Ellis and her laughter fills the air, but Rhonan grips my hand before I can walk away from him.

His nose drags along the column of my throat. "Fuck, you look gorgeous."

"Thank you," I say, feeling warmth bloom across my cheeks.

"How have you been?" His nose moves to my hair now.

"Good."

"That's good."

"Rhonan…" I warn softly, though I don't pull away.

"I need your number, Vienna." He leans back and our eyes meet.

"Okay…"

"I realized after I left your house the other night that I don't have it. I'd have asked for it sooner, but I was working all weekend."

Realization dawns on me that his silence over the past few days was probably due to both of those factors.

"Oh."

He toys with my bottom lip. "Yeah. Oh."

Nodding, I watch him take his phone from his pocket and then I rattle off my number to him, feeling my phone vibrate as he calls me. "There. Now we can text like other adults in this century do."

I chuckle as he releases me and then secures the gate behind us, leading me up the deck to the chairs. "You know, I didn't think you were home tonight either. I didn't see your truck in the driveway."

"Keeping tabs on me?"

"No," I lie. "I am just observant."

Rhonan shrugs, but there's a hint of a smile on his lips. "Joanne took my truck tonight. Her car was making a funny sound, so we're taking it to Dilynne's garage in the morning."

Taking my seat, I stare up at him. "I see."

"Would you like more wine?" He gestures to my glass that only has a little left.

I drain the glass and then hold it out to him. "Sure."

"Great. I'll be right back." I watch him walk into the house and then turn my attention to Ellis and Roscoe. But that's when I notice that Roscoe is running around in a circle, sniffing his butt.

"Ms. Lewis!" Ellis runs up to me. "Roscoe is running around in a circle."

Standing from my chair, I reply, "I can see that." I wait for him to stop, but when he does for just a few seconds, he goes right back to chasing his tail. Yet, he's not exactly after his tail. No, his nose is certainly positioned right at his back door.

I walk down the steps and onto the grass. "Roscoe, baby. Come here." But he doesn't close the distance between us. Instead, he starts dragging his butt across the grass. "Okay...well, that's new." As soon as I get closer to him, I finally see what's got him all riled up. "Oh my gosh."

Ellis is giggling. "Your puppy is so funny, Ms. Lewis."

"Uh, he is," I say, trying to stifle my laugh. "But it looks like Roscoe went to the bathroom and he didn't get all the way clean."

My eyes land on the piece of feces dangling from the hair around his butthole.

Rhonan's voice appears from the deck. "What's going on?"

"Roscoe has poop on his butt!" Ellis yells back.

Rhonan's nose scrunches up. "Gross."

I turn my head to face him. "What do I do?"

"Uh, clean it up?"

"With what? My hand?"

Rhonan sets the wine glasses on the small table between the chairs. "Hold on." He goes back into the house, and when he returns, he brings me wet paper towels. "Here."

"Thank you." I take the paper towels from him and walk toward Roscoe. "Come here, boy." But my dog is still running himself in a circle, trying to solve his own problem.

Ellis speaks. "You have to chase him, Ms. Lewis."

"If I chase him, he'll just run away."

"I can help." Ellis rushes toward Roscoe. "Come on, Roscoe! Let's clean up your butt!"

I can't control my laughter, but Roscoe is too fast for Ellis to catch. I lunge toward him, but he fakes me out and darts to the side.

"I just want you to know that this is what I looked like that morning before Career Day when I was trying to get him out of my yard."

I glare at Rhonan over my shoulder. "Not helping."

Sighing, he heads toward Roscoe where he's dragging his ass along the grass again. "Come here, boy. I just wanna help you get that dingleberry off your butt."

"Dingleberry?" I ask.

Rhonan nods, but his eyes are still focused on my dog. "That's what this thing is called."

"You learn something new every day."

"Can you eat a dingleberry?" Ellis asks.

I turn down to look at her. "No, honey."

"Then why is it called a berry?"

"Come on, Roscoe," Rhonan says in the highest octave I've heard his voice yet. "Come here." He gets within inches of my dog, but then Roscoe takes off again. "Come here, you little shit!"

"Daddy, you said a bad word!" Ellis shouts as Rhonan chases my dog around the yard.

"Motherfucker." Roscoe darts through the playground, making Rhonan lose his balance and almost fall over.

"Be careful!" I call after him.

"Your dog is a menace!" he calls back.

"He's scared. He doesn't understand what's happening. Come here, Roscoe!"

Roscoe comes up to me, nudging his head between my legs, so I squeeze my thighs together, trapping him. "Rhonan, quick!"

Rhonan rushes over, holds Roscoe by his hips, and wipes him clean. "Got it."

I release my dog and the first thing he does is inspect his backside. Once he's content with the lack of poop there now, he looks around for Ellis and then heads back in her direction.

"Yay! No more poop on your butt, Roscoe!" Ellis scales the stairs that lead to her playhouse. But the sound of gagging pulls my attention to the side.

"Rhonan?"

"Fuck," he says after gagging once more. "This shit stinks."

"Yeah, well... It's shit."

Rhonan continues to gag as he walks over to the trash can and tosses the paper towel inside. Another gag. "I need to wash my hands."

"Are you going to be okay?"

He nearly folds over in half as his dry heaves come quicker. "Fuck. I...I need a minute."

My laughter escapes me as I head back to the chairs on the deck to wait for him. After a few minutes, he returns and takes the seat beside me.

"How on earth did you handle changing Ellis's diapers?" It's the only question that's been on my mind since I watched this man dry heave from dog poop.

Rhonan pushes a hand through his hair, widening his legs. "Like that."

My chest bounces with silent laughter. "That must have been entertaining."

"Let's just say I was beyond grateful to have Joanne to help. Vomit will also do that to me."

"Now that, I can see." Shuddering, I continue, "If I even hear someone throw up, it triggers me."

Rhonan groans. "Can we please change the subject?" He hands me one of the glasses of wine he brought out earlier. "I really want to know what you think about this wine."

Hand outstretched, I intercept the wine from him. "Really?"

"Yeah. When you said you liked our cabernet, I knew this would be the next wine I'd have you taste." Lifting his glass to his nose, he inhales deeply, so I do the same. "Did you know that you're supposed to smell your wine before you drink it?"

"Yes. I've done lots of wine tastings."

"Good. Now swirl."

I can't deny that his commands about how to drink my wine are making me remember his commands in my bed the other day.

I follow his lead.

"Good girl. Now sip."

Tipping the glass, I let the burgundy liquid hit my tongue, moaning out loud when it does. After swishing it over my tongue, I swallow and smack my lips. "Wow."

Rhonan smiles proudly after he swallows his drink. "Right?"

I inspect the wine. "What is that?"

"It's called our GSM—Grenache, Syrah, and Mourvèdre. It's inspired by a French blend done in an Australian style."

I take another sip. "So unique."

"I know. The French Oak that it cures in gives it the spice, as well as notes of plum and dark cherry. But the berries and acid added at the end give it that earthiness, yet clean finish."

"I'm impressed."

"How so?"

"Your wine knowledge."

He arches a brow at me. "Well, my family does own a winery."

"Yeah, but I just got the impression that your dad runs the place."

"He does, but Laney and I grew up there, so we learned about every facet of winemaking too." He lets out a sigh, staring down at his glass. "I think I just realized that I—it's been a long time since I've shared my knowledge of wine with someone."

I reach over and squeeze his arm. "Thank you for sharing that with me then."

Rhonan stares out at Ellis playing with Roscoe, directing him to crawl down the slide. "What's your favorite color?"

His question surprises me. "Uh, yellow."

"When's your birthday?"

Confusion builds, but I humor him. "September sixth."

"What's your favorite food?"

"Lasagna."

He nods. "Fuck, I love a good lasagna too. First pet?"

"Roscoe," I reply, which makes him spin back to face me.

"Really?"

"Yeah."

"You—you haven't had a pet before him?"

"Nope."

"Not even as a kid?"

I tilt my head at him. "What's with all of the questions, Rhonan?"

He shakes his head and leans forward in his chair, resting his fore-arms on his knees while staring at me. "I feel like I need to get to know you better."

"And you think those are vital things to know?"

He leans forward in his chair. "Honestly? I feel like I already know most of the important things about you. Those things are just the details. You once said that the little things and moments are what matter to you, so..."

"You—you remember that?"

His eyes lock on mine. "I remember everything about that night, Vienna."

"And what do you feel are the important things about me?"

The intensity of his gaze practically strips me bare, but his words certainly do the job. "Well, since you've re-entered my life, I know that you have the patience of a saint to be a teacher to five-year-olds, including my daughter. I know that you are witty and care about other people's feelings far more than your own. I know that your energy is welcoming and bright, and you hold on to things that are important to you." He pauses, licking his lips. "And I know that when I'm near you, I feel like gray isn't the only color in the world. You brighten up any room you enter with your smile and heart."

I gasp softly. "Rhonan..."

"I've got pieces of you... Now, I want to see the whole picture."

Shit. How can I let him see more of me without letting him see everything?

You don't need to tell him everything right now, Vienna. You don't even really know what's happening between the two of you, and who knows what may happen down the line? You may need to leave this town too.

"I, uh..."

"Daddy, look at me!" Ellis screams from her playground as she pumps her little legs, raising herself higher in her swing.

"Be careful or you might shoot off into outer space!" he calls back to her.

"I wanna go to the moon! Can we go to the moon, Daddy?"

"No, it's very expensive."

His reply makes me laugh, but then he's turning back to me. "Sorry. Hazards of being a parent—there's no such thing as a conversation without interruptions."

"So I've gathered."

He shakes his head. "Here's another question. Why substitute teaching? I remember you telling me that your new job was teaching, but I figured it wouldn't be a part-time gig."

Swallowing down the lump in my throat caused by memories, I lean back in my chair and take a sip of the wine again. "I went to college and got my degree in early childhood education but never got a chance to do anything with it."

"Why not?"

"It's...a long story."

Rhonan leans back in his chair and fans his hand out toward the yard. "I've got some time."

"Seriously, I'm not sure it's something I'm ready to get into."

He nods, turning away to check on Ellis. Silence descends upon us, but then he twists back to face me again. "Then can you tell me about Lydia?"

I blow out a harsh breath. "Oh, Lydia. God, I miss her."

He lifts his glass to his lips. "Tell me about the cupcakes."

"Every year on her birthday, we used to always go out and get cupcakes from this local bakery. The more rainbow sprinkles, the better.

Lydia loved rainbows and told me to always look for them when life got me down."

Rhonan shakes his head. "Personally, I hate sprinkles. They get stuck in my teeth and then I feel like I'm gonna get cavities."

"Your obsession with cavities is probably why your daughter loves sugar so much."

He shrugs. "Hey, I'm a thirty-two-year-old man and I've never had a cavity. I'd say I'm doing something right."

My brows lift. "Wow. Okay, you definitely deserve bragging rights for that."

"I know." He smirks. "So, back to Lydia."

Sighing, I lift my glass to my mouth again and take a sip of liquid courage. "We met in high school freshman year. She was a few inches shorter than me, beautiful olive skin and long, dark hair, and she stood up for me when no one else would."

"What do you mean?"

"There was a boy in our grade who kept telling people that we'd sixty-nined. Honestly, I didn't even know what that meant at the time, but Lydia overheard him saying something at lunch one day and could sense how it was making me feel. So, she waltzed up to him and told the guy that even if we had, he probably didn't satisfy me."

But Rhonan certainly knows what he's doing in that regard, doesn't he, Vienna?

"But the best part was when she told him the only time he should worry about sixty-nine was when it comes up in his math homework since he was failing that class."

"I think I would have liked Lydia."

"The only sass I possess is because of her, and after that day, she and I were inseparable."

"You know, me and the boys met when we were freshmen too."

"Is that right?"

"Yeah, and we were so naïve at that age about how life can change that we made a stupid pact which involved never dating each other's sisters."

"But isn't Laney…"

"Marrying Fletcher?" He blows out a breath. "Yeah. Let's just say that I didn't take it well."

"Well, your sister may have mentioned that you're the king of holding on to the past."

Rhonan pushes a hand through his hair. "Not a title I'm proud of, but yeah."

"I get it."

His eyes meet mine again. "You do?"

"Yeah. History elicits emotions, and sometimes, it's those feelings that we're trying to hang onto, not necessarily a person or an event."

"It's both for me," he replies, his voice low.

"I can see that too, given what you've been through." Both of us grow quiet. "But, if it's any consolation, I'd say it's obvious that Fletcher loves your sister. I don't know them that well, but it only took me seeing them together for less than five minutes to come to that conclusion."

"I know he does. It's taken me months to really accept it, though. She's my baby sister. I've looked out for her since she was born and felt even more protective over her after our mom died. The last thing I want is for her to get hurt—again."

"She's lucky to have an older brother like you."

"Do you want kids someday?" he asks me, making my heart twist in my chest.

"I do, but I'm just not sure that's in the cards for me."

"How come?"

Opting to avoid a discussion I'm not ready for but still wanting to tell him a hint of the truth, I say, "I haven't found someone I want to have kids with yet, and I'm not sure how long that's going to take."

His eyes meet mine and his voice sounds like gravel when he speaks. "Well, I can say without a doubt, that any child would be lucky to call you their mom. I've seen the way you are with Ellis, and…" He clears his throat. "You're very good with kids. Not everyone can say that."

Tears threaten to spill over. "Thank you."

"Ms. Lewis?" Ellis says as she races up the steps of the deck, Roscoe on her heels.

"Yes?"

"Do you want to see me do a cartwheel?"

"I would love to."

Ellis runs back down to the grass and attempts a cartwheel, but it ends up looking more like she's rolling on the grass, tucked up into a ball.

With a smile on my lips, I set my wine glass down and move down to the grass to help her. "That was a great try. Can I show you something to make it even better?"

"Okay!"

Standing next to her, I straighten my spine. "You want to stand up straight when you start and keep your legs straight as you throw yourself forward." I demonstrate what I mean, landing a cartwheel pretty well considering I haven't done one since I was a kid myself.

Ellis claps behind me. "That was so good!"

I bow dramatically. "Thank you."

"How do you keep your legs straight?" Ellis stands up on her tiptoes but falls over.

I laugh, moving to help her up. "Lots of practice. But you know what really helps?"

"What?"

I peer up at Rhonan where he's standing on the deck, his arms crossed over his chest, watching us. "Yoga."

Rhonan rolls his eyes at me as he descends the stairs. "Nice try."

I shrug and then lean closer to him so only he can hear what I say. Ellis is still trying to do a cartwheel in the background, but I'm determined to make this man change his mind. "Wouldn't you agree that my strength and flexibility have certain perks?" I ask, arching a brow at him.

His eyes narrow as he licks his lips. "Are you baiting me right now?"

"No, just making a valid point."

He takes a step closer to me. "Taunting me with the many ways I could fold you while I fuck you is not going to work the way you think it will."

"Is that so?"

"No. I'm lying. It's going to work exactly the way you think it will."

Laughter escapes my lips. "Then maybe you need to come over later and demonstrate what you're referring to." I lean back and stare up into his eyes, the blue orbs darker as his penetrating gaze heats me up from the inside out. But I'm dying for a repeat of the other night. I have no clue what's happening between us, but I'm certain that I at least want that to happen again.

"I have to wait until Joanne gets home, which won't be until after nine."

"I go to bed at ten."

His jaw ticks. "Then look out for my text later."

I lick my lips. "Perfect."

"And Vienna?"

"Yeah?"

"You might want to stretch for what I have planned for you."

Hell yes.

Chapter 16

Rhonan

Testing Out the New Showerhead

I barely recognize myself as I stand in front of the mirror in my bathroom, freshly showered, teeth brushed, dressed in gray sweats and a white T-shirt. My heart is thrumming against my sternum as I run a hand through my hair and then reach for my deodorant.

I'm about to sneak out—of my own damn house—to go next door and fuck my neighbor. I didn't even do stuff like this when I was a teenager. Who the fuck even am I right now?

And more importantly, what the hell is this woman doing to me?

Vienna.

As soon as I kissed her the other night, I knew there was no turning back. My body took the reins, and now, I feel like an addict chasing his next hit.

I can barely go five minutes without her crossing my mind, and talking with her tonight only fed this new addiction of mine. I have to taste her again, but I also have so many other ideas of ways to show her how crazy she makes me that I'm afraid the list will have no end.

But am I ready for more than whatever we're doing right now?

I wish I could land on the answer to that question. Instead, I'm letting my body fuel my decisions.

Satisfied with how I look and how much time has passed since Ellis and Joanne both went to sleep, I carefully open my bedroom door and softly step down the hallway, leaving my house as quietly as I possibly can.

I dart my gaze from side to side as I cross my yard, as if someone might be watching me and alert the entire neighborhood.

When I reach Vienna's house and knock on the door, she answers it in nothing but a towel. "I was beginning to think you weren't coming," she says, holding the door open, then closing and locking it behind me.

"I was waiting to make sure that Ellis and Joanne were asleep." My eyes dip down her body and then back up. "Were you about to get in the shower?"

"I was."

Even though I just took one myself, an idea comes to mind. Reaching behind me, I rip off my shirt and toss it to the side. "Well, how about I join you?"

She licks her lips and drops her towel, baring herself to me—her gorgeous breasts, her hips I can't wait to grab onto again, and that pussy that is making my mouth water at the thought of tasting it again. "As long as you dirty me up before you wash me clean."

I crash my mouth over hers, pulling her into my body and walking her backwards down the hall as our lips and tongues tangle. Reaching between us, I find her slit and stroke my finger through it, finding her ready for me. "You're already soaked."

"I've been waiting for you."

"Fuck. Knowing you were thinking about me is making my cock even harder."

When we enter her room, I take her by the hand and lead her into the bathroom, turning the shower on to warm up the water, then lift her by her hips and set her on the counter. "Spread those legs for me, sweetheart."

Vienna tracks my movements as I kick off my shoes and shove my sweats and briefs down my legs, pushing them to the side before dropping to my knees right in front of her. I drag my finger through her slit again, rubbing my thumb over her clit and lean forward, sucking it between my lips.

Her moan makes my dick twitch. "Rhonan..."

"Say my name again, Vienna."

She buries her hand in my hair. "Don't stop, Rhonan."

Time feels like it stands still as nothing but the sound of Vienna's moans and the water running fills my ears.

God, I was a fucking fool to think I could stay away from this woman. One time with her would never have been enough for me.

And since I haven't felt that way with anyone else since Sarah, I think it's time I start listening to my gut.

I slide two fingers inside of her, stroking her softly as my tongue flicks her clit, building her up slowly, teasing her as the sting of her pulling on my hair grows.

She looks down at me between her legs, mouth parted and breath ragged, and when our eyes lock, I feel her clench around me.

"Rhonan...fuck, I'm coming!"

Her screams drown out everything else, echoing off the walls, but I know without a doubt, I need to hear her scream for me like that again.

Lifting her from the counter, I carry her over to the shower and place her gently on the ground as the water rains over us. I push her hair from her face and then her eyes open, peering up at me with such awe that it makes my fucking heart twist in my chest.

"God, you're really good at that."

I drag my nose up the column of her throat. "You are so fucking sexy when you come."

She reaches down between us and begins stroking my cock. "Now it's your turn."

Dropping to her knees, she pushes her hair back from her face and licks her lips, bringing the tip of my cock to her mouth before swirling her tongue around it. "I want to taste you."

"Jesus, Vienna." I lift her chin with two of my fingers. "You look so fucking good on your knees." She takes my length in her mouth as far as she can go, gagging as she releases me and repeats the move. "Fuck, just like that, baby." Over and over, she sucks me in hard, swirling her tongue around my tip and then pulling me back out. "You keep doing that, and I'm gonna come down your throat."

"Yes, Rhonan," she murmurs just loud enough for me to hear her over the water, taking me back in her mouth while pumping my length at the same time.

Jesus Christ. My mind is about to explode watching this woman worship my cock. It's making me realize why sex is so good with her—trust and yearning.

She trusts me and we both want each other so badly that being with her brings new meaning to the word desperation.

"Touch your clit while you suck me off," I say, wanting to watch her fall apart as she makes me lose my ever-loving mind. She reaches between her legs and her fingers begin to dance over her clit as I cup her jaw, stroking her with my thumb as she continues to bob up and down. "That's a good fucking girl. Now swallow my cock and take every last drop of my cum."

Vienna's mouth grows hotter and wetter around me, her suction growing tighter as her hand moves in between her thighs and I feel that familiar tingle at the base of my spine. After a few more moments, I feel that first spurt of cum leave my body and I groan, my sounds now echoing off the shower walls as Vienna hums around my cock and swallows every last drop.

When she releases me from her mouth, her chest is heaving. I stare down at her and notice that she's still rubbing her clit. "Fuck, did you come?"

"I was close, but I wanted you to finish."

I lift her from the floor and cup her jaw again. "Your pleasure always comes before mine. Do you understand me?" Her eyes widen as she nods. "Good. Now turn around, prop your foot on the ledge, and let me finish you off." Reaching behind me, I grab the removable showerhead from the wall and position it right between her legs. I slide my other hand down her backside until I find her entrance, and slowly push my fingers inside of her, moving the showerhead against her clit and pumping my fingers at the same time.

Her hands fly to the wall in front of her. "Oh God, Rhonan. More..."

I pump harder and flick the switch on the side of the showerhead, making the stream more intense. "Is that what you need?"

"Yes." She leans her head back against my shoulder and I fuck her with my fingers while letting the showerhead do its work. Her legs start to shake, and then her moan is long and drawn out as she comes all over my hand. "Fuck...yes..." I pump my fingers harder until her body goes slack, dropping the showerhead to catch her so she doesn't fall.

"Oh my God."

I kiss her right beneath her ear. "Fuck, Vienna..." Glancing to the side, I find her shampoo. "Time to clean you up."

"I can do it..."

I press a finger to her lips. "Let me."

And so she does. I clean us both up, holding my lips together so I can't let out all of the thoughts swirling around in my mind until I can make sense of them—because if there's one thing I'm acutely aware of now, it's that this woman makes me think and want things I haven't in years.

But until I can firmly decide what that means, these uncertainties need to be kept to myself.

***

By the time we get out of the shower, it's way past ten o'clock, so we say a quick goodbye and I retreat back to my house.

I just didn't expect to run into Joanne in the kitchen when I returned.

"Wh—what are you doing up?" I ask her breathlessly.

She lifts her glass of water to her lips, a smug smile resting there. "Funny. I could ask you the same thing."

"I—I just went for a walk."

Glancing to the clock on the microwave, she directs her gaze back to me and says, "At almost eleven o'clock at night?"

"I...couldn't sleep."

"You also can't lie for shit," she fires back, setting her glass on the counter and then crossing her arms over her chest. "Rhonan, I'm not a fool."

Sighing, I push a hand through my hair and move to the kitchen, taking a seat at one of the barstools on the other side of the counter. "Fuck, Joanne."

"You were at Vienna's, weren't you?"

"Would you judge me if I said yes?"

Her face instantly softens. "Rhonan, if you think I would judge you for living your life, then you must not know me as well as I hoped you did."

"You're right...I'm just..."

"Up in your head?" I nod. She rolls her eyes. "What else is new?"

"I don't know what I'm doing, but I can't stay away from her."

"That's not necessarily a problem." She clears her throat and arches a brow. "Is it just physical?"

I don't even have to think about the answer to that question. "No, especially since it didn't start out that way."

"And what does that mean?"

I briefly catch my nanny up on how Vienna and I initially met. She fights to hide her smile. "Well, I'm proud of you for putting yourself out there. Obviously, there's something between the two of you if you keep going back to her."

"Yeah, but am I fucking crazy, Joanne?" She shrugs, so I continue. "I have a kid, a job that takes up a huge chunk of my life, and she's my daughter's teacher."

"Not truly," she counters. "But you do know that there are adults every day who have relationships that also have demanding jobs and children, Rhonan. You're not unique in that case."

"Yeah, I know, but..."

"It sounds to me that you're just trying to come up with excuses so you don't get hurt."

The woman might as well have catapulted a brick at my chest with the way her words slam into me—because she's fucking right.

I don't want to get hurt again, but my desire for Vienna is too strong to ignore.

"What would your mom have told you to do?"

Her question slices through my chest like a knife. My mother—God rest her soul—knew me better than anyone. The first time I had a girlfriend and that relationship ended, she's the one that helped me through it.

Just thinking about it right now brings the scene back to me—sitting next to her on my bed, fighting off tears because I didn't want to cry in front of my mom, her gentle voice reassuring me that great love is worth the hurt and lessons your first relationships will teach you.

I just never imagined life would teach me the lesson of losing people I love too.

Clearing the emotion from my throat, I reply, "She would have told me never to give up on love."

Joanne's soft smile is accompanied by unshed tears in her eyes. "Your mother was a wise woman."

Staring down at my clasped hands, I nod. "She was."

"So, all I'm trying to get you to realize is that you have a chance here to have something real again, Rhonan. But don't lead that woman on if you're not ready for the possibility. Vienna deserves better than that."

I know she does—and that's what scares me the most—because I don't know if I'm ready to give her what she deserves.

***

"Hell yeah! Twenty-one, bitches!" Elliot tosses his hands in the air as if he's on a rollercoaster, celebrating his hand.

Henley chuckles as he lifts his beer to his lips. "Someone's in a good mood tonight."

Elliot smirks. "Well, someone needs to be because Rhonan is being grumpy enough for all four of us."

All eyes land on me as I scowl in Elliot's direction. "I'm fine."

"You sound like your sister," Fletcher chimes in. "And I've been with her long enough now that I know when she says she's fine, means anything *but* that." He lifts his water to his lips. "Wanna talk about it?"

"Not really."

Henley glances at Fletcher. "He probably should. It would help."

Elliot huffs out a laugh. "This coming from the guy who once was the most closed off of any of us."

Henley taps the table in front of him. "Key word being *was*. I've seen the light now, gentlemen."

"No, you've seen the power of the vagina," Elliot fires back. "And the only reason I can say that is because I was once hypnotized by one too. It clouds your judgment and makes you think life is all rainbows and sunshine."

"Really? And how's operation get-your-dick-to-work-again going for you?"

Elliot's smug smirk falls from his lips. "My dick works just fine. In fact, I made an appointment for next week to get my piercing."

Fletcher pauses while bringing his water to his lips. "I'm sorry. Did you just say piercing? As in, you're getting your dick pierced?"

Elliot glances over at me. "Yup, and Rhonan said he'd go with me."

I find my voice finally. "Uh, I never said that."

"Is getting your dick pierced the equivalent of having a mid-life crisis after a relationship ends?" Henley asks. "I just want to prepare myself if this is something I need to look out for, not that I would ever let Elodie go, but just to be safe."

Elliot glares at him. "Fuck you."

But Henley's not done. "More importantly, is your dick even big enough to get pierced? I mean, it has to have something to grab onto, right?"

"Funny. I heard your dick is the size of a Tic Tac," Elliot says to him.

Henley taps his chin in thought. "Huh. That must be why your mom's breath smells so good then."

Elliot lobs a stack of chips across the table at Henley as he stifles his laughter. "Don't fucking talk about my mom."

Fletcher stands and shoves his hand between the two of them. "All right, you two. Knock it off before someone gets their feelings hurt."

I run a hand through my hair. "Jesus Christ. I thought we were here to play blackjack."

"We're also here trying to have some fun, but apparently you didn't get that memo," Henley says to me.

"I'm fine," I grate out again while this ever-present frustration I've been battling the past few days is still simmering just beneath the surface.

It's been two days since I snuck over to Vienna's house and defiled her in her shower. But after my talk with Joanne, I knew I needed to create some distance between us while I figure my shit out.

Fletcher called yesterday saying that Laney and the girls were having a girls' night tonight, so the boys and I decided to get together and play some blackjack at the same time. Henley's parents are babysitting his daughter, and Ellis is at home with Joanne.

Now, I'm sort of wishing I would have just stayed at home to stew on my dilemma in silence once Ellis went to sleep.

"Cut the bullshit, Rhonan," Fletcher says. "It's us. You can talk to us. Remember, we fucking promised not to hold stuff in anymore."

"And if we're making bets, I bet I know what's got you all twisted up anyway," Henley adds.

Elliot casts a look in my direction but doesn't say anything.

Pushing a hand through my hair, I lean back in my chair and fold my arms across my chest. "Fine. I sort of...slept with Vienna."

The corner of Fletcher's mouth lifts, but he keeps his pleased smile in check. "Sort of?"

"Yeah. Do we need to review with you how sex works?" Henley adds.

I flip him off. "You know what? I think I liked you better before you fell in love with your nanny."

Henley laughs. "Aw, come on. I wasn't that bad."

Elliot scoffs. "Dude, you and I were in competition for the grumpiest of the group. Pretty sure even your sister referred to you as a gorilla."

Henley narrows his eyes at Elliot. "Did you just mention my sister without insulting her? Are you feeling okay?"

Fletcher clears his throat. "All right, let's cut the shit. Everyone, lock in. Rhonan needs us and it's time to be serious." Henley and Elliot sigh but toss their chips and cards on the table before regaining their composure. "Thank you. Now, Rhonan, what's going through your head, man? Let us help you."

I dart my eyes around to my three best friends, hating how it's now my turn to speak, to lean on them, especially for something like this.

When my mom died, they were there for me. When I lost Sarah, they were there too.

But this?

It's not like I've lost someone again. This is just me stewing on my fear. I'm not sure how they're supposed to help me through that.

"I slept with Vienna...twice."

Henley nods, but I can see the hint of a proud smile on his lips. "Okay..."

"And now I don't know what to do about it."

"How exactly did you two end up in bed together?" Fletcher asks.

I blow out a breath and recall the incident that led to me going over to her house to apologize, which led to me sneaking over another night because I couldn't fucking stay away from her any longer.

Henley smirks. "Well, that's one way to apologize. Works pretty well, if I do say so myself. But let's be honest. That's not the reason why you two ended up naked together."

Elliot raises his brows. "Yeah, sorry to break it to you, Rhonan, but I told you that day at her house that even I saw the chemistry between you two. There's no denying it."

"Yeah, well it's been two days and nothing else has happened."

"And why is that?" Henley asks.

"Because Joanne caught me sneaking back over to my house the other night and basically told me that I need to figure out what I want. Otherwise, I'm just leading her on."

Fletcher nods. "She's not wrong."

"I just don't know what to fucking do."

Henley shakes his head. "Yes, you do. You're just being a chicken shit about it."

I glare at him. "That's rich, coming from you."

He holds his hands up in the air. "How many times did you guys tell me to stop fighting what I was feeling for Elodie? And how many times do I have to tell you that you were right?"

Fletcher huffs out a laugh. "About a million."

Henley points a finger to his chest. "Exactly. And it took me way too fucking long to do something about it, but I'm so fucking grateful because now I have a woman in my life that I can't live without. I never knew life could be this good. My entire world flipped upside down in a matter of months with Remy and Elodie in it, but in the best fucking way. I'm telling you, I figured out that the key to being happy is to *choose* to be happy, and it was worth the bullshit I had to confront." He leans closer to me. "Don't waste fucking time like I did, Rhonan. Ask the woman on a date."

"Fuck." I bury my head in my hands. "Do you realize that the last date I went on was with Sarah?"

Fletcher clears his throat. "She would want you to move on, Rhonan. To find someone else to be happy with."

I lift my head and meet his eyes. "And I feel like I'm too fucking broken to ever feel that way again." The second those words leave my lips, I see the realization of what I just said in all three of my best friends' eyes.

"You think you're fucking broken?" Fletcher asks with a pinch in his brow.

Clenching my jaw tightly, I divert my gaze to the other side of the room, avoiding their eyes because the way that they're looking at me makes me feel like I'm under a goddamn microscope.

"Broken? You think that you're *broken*? Hell, I feel like "I'm Still Standing" by Elton John should be your fucking theme song," Henley says, pulling my attention back to him. "I sure as hell know that I wouldn't be standing without you."

"What the fuck do you mean?"

He looks at me as if I'm fucking stupid. "When Meghan dropped off Remy with me, who was the one who helped me land on my feet?" I don't reply. "You, dumbass."

"You're one of the strongest fucking people I know, Rhonan," Fletcher adds. "After what you've been through? I'm not sure I could survive that and have as much strength as you do."

Elliot nods. "And I know that I selfishly wanted you to stay single with me, but..." He blows out a breath. "If you have a chance to build a life with someone new, you need to fucking take it. Just...be careful. Speaking from personal experience, and all that. Make sure you two fucking talk about all of the important shit." There's a hint of seriousness to his tone that terrifies me a bit, but I also know that after what Elliot went through with Tori, his ex-fiancée, he has every right to warn me to be cautious.

"I'm not fucking strong. I'm terrified," I say, barely loud enough for them to hear. "I live in terror every day that life is gonna take someone else away from me." My eyes lift to find Fletcher's. "I don't want to risk having another person I'm petrified to lose."

"Then you're letting the fear win," Henley says. "Trust me, Rhonan. I know it's easier said than done, but the only way you move past it is to move through it. That's what I did when I found out I was a dad, and I'm pretty sure you're the one who told me that being a parent was going to teach me a lot about myself, but I think being in love taught me more."

Love.

Those four letters make my chest grow tight. I told myself that after I lost Sarah, I would never put myself in the position to love and lose someone again.

"Love is something I shut myself off from completely when Sarah died."

Fletcher nods in understanding. "I get it, but there's always a choice, and we wouldn't all be human if we didn't make shitty choices from time to time. And then some choices literally change the course of our lives. Look at me and your sister, man. Twelve years ago, I could have made one different decision and it would have changed so much. I regret it, man. I know we ended up where we're at now, and I'm so fucking grateful. But if I could go back? I'd do things differently. I don't want you to live with the same regrets."

Elliot scoffs. "I know I would choose fucking differently. I would have listened to my gut."

Henley furrows his brow. "What do you mean?"

Elliot scratches at the scruff on his chin, blowing out a harsh breath. "I had a feeling something was off with Tori, but I didn't want to believe it."

The three of us share a look. "What? Why have you never said anything?" Fletcher asks.

"Because I didn't want to fail," he admits, his brow deepened by his scowl. "I committed to a woman for the first time in my life, and I didn't want to fuck it up. I wanted to prove to everyone that I could handle a commitment like that. I wanted it to be worth the risk, so I just...let things ride, and look how that fucking turned out." He pushes a hand through his hair. "God, I'm a fucking piece of work. Thirty-two years old and still worried about letting my fucking parents down."

"Work in progress," Fletcher corrects him, darting his eyes among the group. "We all are. No one said we had to be perfect, and I think we can all agree that's never gonna happen."

Henley scoffs. "Ha, speak for yourself."

Fletcher shoves him from the side as he laughs. "Jesus, focus, man."

"Sorry."

Fletcher shakes his head before focusing back on me. "But our goal was to change for the better right? And as long as we continue to do that, none of us can fail," he says, locking eyes with Elliot as he finishes.

Inhaling deeply, he cracks his knuckles and sits up straighter in his chair. "All right, now that we know what you two both need to work on, let's focus on Rhonan since he has a woman at stake here and the last thing he needs to do is keep the ongoing silence between them."

Henley nods. "I agree, but I'm telling you...all he needs to do is ask Vienna on a date. It's the easiest first step in his situation since they're already banging each other's brains out." My mind instantly drifts to my sexual escapades with Vienna thus far, and yeah—there's definitely been some banging going on.

"And what if she says no?" I counter.

Henley looks at me as if I'm stupid. "Do you honestly think she will?"

Fletcher shakes his head before I can respond. "No way. Laney says the feelings between you two are definitely mutual."

"Ah, yes. My sister. The master of meddling in my life."

Fletcher points a finger across the table at me. "Careful what you say about my fiancée, buddy. You may be one of my best friends, and I know she's your sister, but I'm about to marry her, so I'm obligated to agree with and support everything she does."

I tilt my head and then glance over at Elliot. "And I'm the one who's been hypnotized by a woman?"

Elliot shakes his head, shrugging. "Dude, you're on your own with this one. Fletcher and your sister being together isn't something any of us could have predicted."

"She's the love of my life and your little sister, who just wants you to get out of your own way. You can't fault her for that."

"I can blame her for whatever I want. Perks of being related."

Fletcher huffs out a laugh as he leans back in his chair, crossing his arms and smirking at me. "Then I guess I shouldn't tell you where she is tonight."

My pulse picks up. "What do you mean? They're having girls' night, right?"

Henley chuckles. "Oh, they're having girls' night all right, but at someplace new."

Dread fills my stomach now. "And where exactly would that be?"

Fletcher's grin slowly creeps up at the corners as he says, "Vienna's house."

Motherfucker.

Chapter 17

Vienna

Girls' Night & Scheming

"Vienna!" Laney greets me a little too enthusiastically as I open the front door to my house. But the other two women standing behind her shock me even more.

"Oh, uh...hi there."

Laney glances behind her and then back to me. "I brought Dilynne and Elodie with me. I hope that's okay."

Shaking off my shock, I open the door wider and usher the three of them into my house. "Yeah, of course that's fine. I'm just surprised is all."

Dilynne lifts her chin in my direction as she walks past me. "Moving forward, you should just know that Laney and I are a package deal, and now that Elodie is shacking up with my brother, she's included in that package." Wrapping her arm around Elodie's shoulders, she pulls her toward the kitchen. "And we always bring food and wine, so there is a silver lining to getting more guests than you expected."

When Laney called me yesterday and asked if I'd be open to hanging out this evening, I thought she meant just her and me. Truth be told, I was nervous given the state of things with her brother right now, but I figured I could maybe get some help from her in that department and enjoy some female company.

Now, I guess my female company has multiplied. At least they brought food and alcohol.

Laughing, I follow them into my small kitchen, watching Laney begin to unpack styrofoam containers from Blossom Brews and bottles of wine from her family's winery. The smell of greasy food hits my nostrils as I inhale deeply. "Please tell me you at least brought onion rings."

Dilynne chimes in. "Ha. I would have divorced her if she hadn't." Popping the top on the correct container, she extracts one of the perfectly fried rings and pushes it into her mouth.

Nodding, I reach for one myself. "Yup. Laney, you're forgiven. These have become my new obsession since moving here." I'm not proud of how many nights I pick up food from Blossom Brews now.

Laney watches as Dilynne and I begin to inhale the onion rings, moaning out loud between bites.

Elodie clears her throat and leans closer to Laney. "Should we let them be alone?"

Laney laughs. "No, and if they don't save me at least three of them, I'm keeping all of the wine for myself."

I freeze but Dilynne just shrugs. "You can keep your booze. I'd rather slip into an onion ring coma tonight. My fucking period will be here in two days, so I need all the grease."

Elodie groans. "God, me too. We must have started to sync up our cycles."

"The ESP of our uteri is real," Dilynne mumbles around a mouthful of food.

Laney takes a step back from them. "Don't come near me then. I need my cycle to stay the way it is so I'm not on my period on my honeymoon."

"The wedding is only a month away. Are you getting more excited?" I ask, trying to interject myself into this girl talk, but honestly? I'm out of my element here. Lydia was the only friend I was ever comfortable talking about my period with—or lack thereof since my cycle was never quite regular. And my mother? She wouldn't be caught dead talking about any part of the female anatomy. It's a miracle I even knew anything about sex or my body before Lydia handed me my first Cosmopolitan magazine and taught me virtually everything that I know.

Laney's eyes practically turn into hearts. "I honestly can't wait until I get to call that man my husband. It's been a long time coming."

Dilynne nods. "Yes, it has. Personally, I'm more excited for the bachelorette party."

Laney narrows her eyes at her best friend. "I swear, Dilynne Marie, if you got a stripper, I will never forgive you."

Dilynne rolls her eyes. "Pull your panties from your ass, Laney. There isn't going to be a stripper, but I did find us some entertainment."

"What is it?"

"Nope." Dilynne points a finger in her direction, wiggling it around. "You have to wait and see just like everyone else."

Laney turns to me. "Just for future reference, don't commission Dilynne to plan a party for you...ever."

Dilynne puts her hand up, blocking Laney from my view. "Don't listen to her. She's just a control freak who hates surprises."

Elodie and I are laughing at their antics just as Elodie reaches for a bottle of wine. "I think we could all use a drink, yes?"

Once the corks have been popped and we all load our plates with food, we settle into my living room, fitting snugly on the couch and the one other chair I have. "Sorry there's not more furniture."

Elodie shakes her head. "Don't apologize. You probably don't usually have this many people over."

"I don't have people over at all."

All three pairs of their eyes land on me. "Seriously?" Laney asks. "You didn't hang out with your girlfriends back in D.C.?"

"I, uh...only had one really close friend there."

"And she hasn't come to visit you?" Laney continues.

I swallow down the lump in my throat and reply, "No. Actually...she died about six months ago," I admit to the first people besides Rhonan.

The three of them simultaneously gasp. "Oh my God, I'm so sorry," Elodie speaks first. "Was she your friend that you said was from Garnet Valley?"

"Yes," I reply.

"What was her name?"

"Lydia Rodriguez."

Elodie's brows pinch together. "I don't think I knew her."

"She lived there when she was younger and then moved to D.C. with her dad when she was twelve. We met in high school, and we were inseparable ever since. You know, until..."

Dilynne shoves Laney from the side of the couch, nearly knocking her over. "What the hell was that for?" Laney barks.

"You better not die before me, okay? I'll never forgive you."

Laney looks perplexed. "Why would it matter? I'd be dead."

Elodie glances over at me and shrugs. "She's not wrong."

"Besides, if you die before me, I know you'll come back and haunt me, and that's the last thing I'd want," Laney fires back.

Dilynne's smile is crooked. "Yeah, you're right about that. Every time you hear a noise, you'll always wonder if it's me."

"I'd just watch out for the smell of car grease and then I'd know it was you for sure."

"God, you remind me of Lydia," I say to Dilynne through laughter and unshed tears.

Her hand reaches out for mine, squeezing it. "Then I'm honored. Best girlfriends are the sisters we never got to have, or at least the ones we wouldn't dropkick if we had the chance."

All of us laugh. "Yeah, I'm an only child, so Lydia was definitely like my sister." *And the only friend who stood by my side when I made some questionable choices in my life.*

Dilynne glances at Laney and then turns back to me. "I know the feeling."

Elodie clears her throat. "I know no one can ever replace her, but you have us now, Vienna." Her smile is soft and comforting. "These two took me under their wings when I moved here back in August, so I know how it feels to be alone in a new place. Don't be afraid to call any of us if you ever need anything, okay?"

"I—I really appreciate it." Blowing out a breath, I blink away my tears that I kept from falling. "God, I didn't realize how much I needed some female interaction. Being around five-year-olds all day is draining and affecting my ability to have a conversation with adults."

Dilynne laughs. "I don't know how you do it. I would scream back in their faces if they started whining." She shakes her head. "Me and kids don't mix. That's why I never want any."

"It's definitely a struggle some days," I say. "But seriously? No kids?"

Dilynne shrugs. "I like my life the way that it is, and I don't need to have children to feel fulfilled. Now, if some man wanted to buy me Jay Leno's car collection in place of an engagement ring, I might consider marriage too."

I chuckle as Laney rolls her eyes and Dilynne focuses back on me. "I take it you want kids then?" Dilynne asks.

The cheer I was feeling earlier gets cut in half. "Yeah, but I don't think it's in the cards for me."

"I used to think that way too," Laney says. "But I'm a converted believer now that timing is everything. And I honestly can't wait to have babies with Fletcher."

"And when you do, I will maintain my status as the best aunt on the fucking planet," Dilynne adds. "I certainly love my little Ellis and Remy and will fuck anybody up that ever breaks their hearts."

Elodie rolls her eyes at Dilynne this time, but with a grin on her lips. "You might have to worry about Dilynne going down to the elementary school now to fight a kindergartener, Vienna."

I shrug. "Honestly, I could think of a few that could use some discipline, that's for sure."

Dilynne shudders. "Seriously, I don't know how you do it."

"And I bet having Ellis next door doesn't give you much of a break either," Laney adds.

The soft spot I have in my chest for Ellis swells from the mention of her name. "Oh, gosh. I could spend all day with that little girl and never get tired of her."

Laney smiles proudly. "She's such a character. I can't wait until she gets older and I can teach her all of the important things about being a girl. It's one of the duties as her aunt that I'm most concerned about since Sarah isn't around, you know?"

I cover the center of my chest with my hand. "I think about that all of the time. My heart just breaks for her. I mean, even though I'm not super close with my mom, the thought just makes me so sad."

"Well, she has us, and Rhonan is doing a phenomenal job," Elodie interjects.

"Speaking of Rhonan, have you seen my brother lately?" Laney adds, failing at her attempt at being sly. Dilynne arches a brow at me and Elodie weaves her hands together on her lap while she stares.

Suddenly, I feel like I'm under an interrogation, which only makes my cheeks heat up even faster. Needing to compose myself, I reach for my plate and head toward the kitchen. "Oh, uh...I'm not sure."

By the time I place my dish in the sink and turn back around, all three of the girls are right behind me with curious expressions on their faces.

Laney purses her lips. "You're not sure if you've *seen* him?"

"I mean, I haven't. No. I thought you asked if I knew how he was."

Dilynne snaps her fingers and points at me. "Oh my God. You've slept with him, haven't you?"

"What?" I ask with a nervous laugh.

Laney practically squeals. "I knew it!"

Elodie snaps her fingers. "Damn it, Vienna. I bet that you were able to keep it together, but you gave in." She shakes her head but then leans forward and winks at me. "But it was worth it, right?"

My mouth drops open as I stare at these three women, realizing that I was just coerced to tell the truth and I'm not even sure how it happened. "How—how can you tell?"

Laney waves her finger up and down my body. "Because I've had that look, the look of being freshly fucked." Her nose scrunches up. "And now I just realized I'm referring to my brother being good at sex."

Elodie nods. "Yup. I've seen that look in the mirror too. You've been dickmatized, Vienna."

Clearing my throat, I reply, "I'm not...dickmatized. It just sort of happened."

Dilynne rests her hand on my shoulder. "His dick can't just magically enter your vagina without consent and you spreading your legs, honey. But look...we listen and we don't judge here. Honestly, I'll always advocate for a woman having great sex. The world would be a better place if every lady was getting banged into her mattress on the regular. And I'm glad that grumpy Rhonan is getting some because he was starting to give Elliot a run for his money in that department."

"Elliot seems to be doing a little bit better lately, though," Elodie interjects.

Dilynne rolls her eyes. "He's still a giant pain in the ass and always will be as far as I'm concerned."

"I get the feeling that you and Elliot don't like each other," I cut in.

Dilynne gasps dramatically. "Why, whatever gave you that idea?"

Laney mutters, "Please don't get her started, Vienna. We could be here all night."

"Did you two date or something?" I ask.

Dilynne nearly bends in half as she laughs. "Oh, shit. That's hilarious. The answer to that question is no, dearest Vienna. Elliot wouldn't know what to do with all of this." She waves her hand up and down her body.

"Let's focus back on you and Rhonan banging each other," Elodie says with wide eyes, clearly invested. "This is how you two must have felt when Henley and I were tiptoeing around each other, huh?" She casts her gaze to Dilynne and Laney.

Sighing, I bury my head in my hands. "Dear God."

Laney wraps her arms around my shoulder. "Hey, in all seriousness, we're just trying to help. You can talk to us, Vienna."

When I lift my head and find all three of them staring at me, I sigh in defeat. It's not like I have Lydia to talk to, and these three know Rhonan better than I do. Perhaps they can give me some insight.

"Fine. I'm—I'm sort of confused because we haven't really even talked about what us sleeping together means, and both times we've had sex this past week, he's had to leave really quickly... But the sex?" I sigh wistfully. "I didn't know sex could be like that."

The sex with Rhonan has been incredible—so much so that I barely recognize myself when he touches me. The moment he opens his mouth and tells me what to do, I instantly obey. He makes me comfortable asking for what I want, safe enough to let go and try something new—and I swear, I've never had more than one orgasm during sex before—if I even had one at all.

Dilynne snorts while crossing her arms over her chest. "Surely you've observed how closed off Rhonan Hart is."

"Um, yeah..."

"So do I need to spell it out for you?"

"I think so..."

"He's not going to just sleep with someone if it doesn't mean something."

Laney nods. "She's right. My brother has always been a bit of a monogamist, and losing Sarah was very tough for him. According to Fletcher, he has only slept with two other women since she passed. He's just not cut out for casual sex."

"Should I be concerned that you know this much about your brother's sexual history?"

Laney laughs, but Elodie and Dilynne shake their heads. "No. Trust me, Dilynne and I have been looking after him for years. And even

Elodie knows in the short time she's been around how my brother thinks. Every decision he makes is calculated. He's never been the spontaneous type."

And that's the part that scares me—because there is very little about my life right now that is grounded. Hell, the only reason I ended up in Blossom Peak is because of a spontaneous decision I made to apply for this job. And given that there are other details of my life that are still in pieces, I'm not even sure what a future could look like here without being completely honest with him, especially about Cole.

My eyes find Laney's. "I feel strongly for him, but I'm scared."

"Why?"

Dilynne reaches for the open bottle of wine, filling all of our glasses again as we make our way back to the living room, returning to our seats. "Lay it out, Vienna. Again, no judgment."

Staring down into my wine glass as if it holds all of the answers, I take a minute to debate just how many details I should share.

"I—I just left a relationship shortly after Lydia died, and it wasn't a great one," I start.

Laney nods. "Okay..."

"My ex was...controlling, but charming. I fell for him hard and fast, and then it was too late when I realized who he really was. He was jealous, and it took me years to realize that wasn't a good thing. When I finally did, it's like I was stuck. He alienated me from my family and the few other friends that I had besides Lydia, but when things started to take a turn for the worse, I finally got the courage to leave."

"He didn't hit you, did he?" Dilynne asks. "Because if he did, you give me his address right now. I'll grab my tools, and he won't know what's coming."

I shake my head rapidly. "No, he never hit me...grabbed me really hard a few times, but that was it." Reaching up, I rub the skin on my upper arm from where I felt his touch the last time.

Elodie reaches for my hand this time from her spot on the couch. "Then I'm proud of you for doing that—leaving him. It takes a lot of guts."

Her words instantly make tears fill my eyes—because those are the words I never got to hear from Lydia and feel like I need now more than ever.

Lydia died before I left Cole.

It was a week after she was gone that I finally found the courage to leave, and then it took me months to get my ducks in a row.

But she never got to cheer me on when I did.

And I have no one to blame for that but myself.

Laney says, "I'm so sorry you went through something like that, Vienna. We all have past relationships that have affected us and shaped us in some way. But I say this with the most sincerity I can muster..." She takes a deep breath. "My brother would never treat you like that, and when he lost his wife, I saw a part of him shut off completely. Since you've been around, I've started to see glimpses of it again."

"And what part is that?" I ask on a shaky breath.

Laney smiles. "His ability to find joy. When he talks about you? There's a twinkle in his eyes and I can see him fighting the curl of his smile. He's so determined to hang on to his struggle that he probably doesn't even realize he's doing it. But I've noticed and so has Fletcher." She reaches for her phone and opens the screen to check her messages. "Speaking of my fiancé, he says that he just told Rhonan that we're over here having girls' night with you and he looks like there could be steam coming out of his ears."

Dilynne stares up at the ceiling. "Yup, I could definitely see that."

"Well since we haven't talked, it's not like I could have told him that I planned on hanging out with Laney tonight," I say.

"Exactly. Don't worry, though, I know how to handle my brother." Laney flips her hair over her shoulder. "He's going to accuse me of meddling in his life, but honestly? He'd be lost without me."

"And Joanne," Elodie interjects.

Laney points at Elodie. "True. But here's what we're going to do, Vienna," Laney continues. "You're going to keep doing what you're doing, and let me, Dilynne, and Elodie handle him."

"Uh...what do you mean?"

The three of them share a look before Dilynne turns to me and smirks. "We're going to light a fire under his ass so he'll finally admit that he wants to be with you."

"And how are you planning to do that exactly?"

Laney rubs her hands together. "The best way for a man to get over his own fear is to make him scared of something else."

"I—I'm not sure that I like the sound of this."

Dilynne chuckles. "Honey, just let us handle everything. We're gonna make Rhonan Hart drop to his knees for you. And when he does, you can thank us later with a cheesecake from Bites & Bliss on our next girls' night."

Saliva instantly pools in my mouth. "Oh my God, that was the best cheesecake I've ever had in my life."

"I know. But that's just because you haven't experienced a man begging for you yet," Elodie says, waggling her eyebrows. "And Rhonan Hart doesn't even know what's about to hit him."

Chapter 18

Rhonan

Yoga Manipulation

"The new cart is a machine." My dad stands proudly next to the popcorn cart that Fletcher got him last fall to replace the old one my mother bought when we first started Hart Winery events. "I didn't realize the new state-of-the-art technology that was available in things like these."

"Glad it's working well, Dad."

I can feel his eyes on me as I survey the grounds of the winery, thinking about what else can be done before the event starts tonight. Normally, my father only brings out the popcorn cart for movie nights, but Ellis begged him to have it available every time there's an event, and Elodie agreed the idea was spectacular because both of them are obsessed with popcorn.

"Daddy! Watch me go down the slide!"

I turn my attention back to Ellis as I watch her slide down the twisted slide on the playground at Hart Winery for what feels like the hundredth time.

Spoiler alert—it looks the same each time.

"You're a professional," I call back to her before directing my gaze back to Henley, who's holding his daughter in his arms.

"Is this what I have to look forward to?" he asks.

"Yup." I reach out and play with one of Remy's short pigtails. "Sometimes I miss this age because Ellis spoke far less."

Henley chuckles. "Yeah, she doesn't ever seem to stop talking now, does she?"

"Ms. Lewis!" Ellis shouts, jumping from the swing and running over to where Vienna is standing.

And fuck me sideways.

She's wearing a hunter green spandex outfit that should be illegal.

Well, she's here for yoga, so what did you expect her to be wearing, Rhonan? A muumuu?

Ellis wraps her arms around Vienna's legs the second she reaches her. "Hey, sweet girl." Vienna squeezes her back. "Long time, no see."

Ellis peers up at her. "I just saw you at school."

Vienna bops her on the nose. "I know, it's a joke."

"Oh." Ellis shrugs and then races back to the playground. "Ms. Lewis, watch me go down the slide!"

Vienna starts heading in my direction, but her eyes remain locked on my daughter. "I'm watching." She waits for Ellis to traverse the entire slide before clapping. "Amazing! You're the best slider ever!"

Ellis takes a bow. "I know!"

Laughing, Vienna approaches me, meeting my eyes finally. "Hey there, neighbor."

I have no control over how my eyes dip up and down her body before I finally find some words. "Hello."

She moves her gaze up and down my body now. "Is that what you wore to do yoga?"

"I already told you, Vienna. I don't do yoga."

She tsks. "Such a shame. You're missing out."

Henley nods. "She's right, man. Once Carol gets here, I can hand off Remy and I'm ready to get my sweat on."

Joanne walks up to us, reaching out for Remy. "If you need me to, I can watch her too."

Remy reaches out for Joanne, landing safely in her arms. "I appreciate that, thank you," Henley says.

Vienna gasps, glancing between me and Henley. "Wait a minute. Your friends do yoga, but *you* won't?"

"Nope." Widening my stance, I cross my arms over my chest. "And trust me, they've all tried to get me to join, but it's not gonna happen."

"What's not gonna happen?" Elliot asks as he and Fletcher walk up to us, holding their yoga mats.

I fight my desire to give them both shit in front of Vienna. "Me doing yoga. I was telling Vienna that even you guys haven't been able to convince me."

Fletcher rolls his eyes at me. "You're such a stubborn ass, I swear."

"Hey, Vienna!" My sister comes walking over, her strides intense and purposeful. "There you are!"

"What's up?"

"That guy I wanted to introduce you to is here," Laney says, her smile blinding.

"Oh, yeah." Vienna turns back to all of us, but locks eyes with me. "See you guys over there." She follows my sister as they traipse off together, whispering to one another.

My blood pressure just skyrocketed.

"What guy?" I blurt out, my eyes still locked on Vienna as Laney leads her into the main building of the winery.

Fletcher shrugs. "Beats me. Must be something they talked about the other night when they were all hanging out."

"She can't talk to some other guy."

Henley wears a smug smile as he says, "And why not? I mean, technically she's single."

"And sleeping with me," I add.

Elliot hits me on the upper arm with his yoga mat. "Did you two talk about exclusivity? Because if not, then she has every right to…"

"Motherfucker," I mutter under my breath, glancing back at the playground to check on Ellis. "I swear to God, if—" But I don't get to finish my thought because Vienna comes out of the main building into the courtyard of the winery talking to some guy I don't even recognize. "Who the fuck is this guy?"

My three best friends turn to assess the situation before Henley speaks up. "I have no idea, man. Maybe he's new in town."

My sister crosses the courtyard, headed to her spot on the small hill where she'll lead the yoga class in about thirty minutes.

"Well, I'm going to find out."

When I showed up tonight at the winery to help out my dad and, of course, support my sister because Ellis likes to pretend that she knows how to do yoga with her aunt, I never imagined that rage would be a part of the evening's activities.

After blackjack the other night, I sent a text to Vienna that I was thinking about her. We chatted a bit about our days apart, but I couldn't visit her again because I had to work two back-to-back shifts. Now, it's Thursday night and the impending yoga event at the winery is underway.

I just didn't count on needing to confront my fears so quickly.

I planned on speaking to her once we were back home, alone and away from the crowds. I wanted to show her with my body how much I'd been thinking about her since we saw each other last.

And even though I still don't know how to communicate what I'm feeling to her, I was thinking that maybe it was time to talk about the two of us putting a label on what we are. I'm not even sure if that lingo is still relevant because it's been over five years since I've been in a relationship—just another reason why I feel so out of my fucking league here.

But here I am, stomping across my family's winery, intent on giving my sister a piece of my mind because I need someone to blame for what I'm feeling, and she's the one who took Vienna to meet this guy.

Dilynne and Elodie join my sister in her usual spot, whispering about something before I reach them.

"Oh. Hi, Rhonan," Elodie says, alerting my sister to my presence.

Laney pops up from the ground. "Hey, big brother. What's up?"

"You know what's up," I grate out through clenched teeth.

My sister's brows draw together as she glances at Dilynne and Elodie. "Uh, okay…"

I wave my finger in the direction of Vienna, but when my eyes land on her, there's now two more men talking to her. *What the actual fuck?*

I growl in frustration as Dilynne places her hand on my shoulder. "Use your words, Rhonan. We don't speak caveman."

Pushing her hand away, I take another step closer to my sister, lowering my voice. "Why did you introduce Vienna to a guy?"

Her eyes widen, but she still looks confused. "I—was I not allowed to, or something?"

"Laney…"

"What? You two aren't together, and Ryan said that he was looking to be set up. The only single person I could think of was Vienna, so…"

"What about Dilynne?" I say, pointing to her best friend.

Dilynne huffs out a laugh. "That boy is way too soft-spoken for me."

"I thought that's how you liked your men," Elliot interjects as he, Fletcher, and Henley all arrive where we're standing. "That way you can boss them around, right?"

Great, now the gang's all here.

Dilynne directs her icy glare right at Elliot. "You mean how you were with Tori?"

Elliot's smug smile falls from his lips, but Fletcher steps in. "Let's not start, you two. Rhonan seems to be on the verge of a mental breakdown right now, so we don't need another situation to manage."

Dilynne flips Elliot off, to which he returns the gesture, and then Laney rolls her eyes. "I don't understand why you're so angry about me introducing them," my sister continues speaking on our original topic.

"That's a lie, and you know it."

She smirks. "Oh really? And why is that?"

Suddenly, I feel everyone's eyes on me.

It's now or never, Rhonan. Time to shit or get off the pot.

"Because I want her," I declare out loud for everyone to hear—and something about letting those words out into the universe makes the knot in my chest loosen.

Dilynne yells. "Hallelujah, folks! Our man just had a come-to-Jesus moment! Everyone, give him a round of applause."

My sister nods proudly while clapping her hands. "Glad you can finally admit that." She tosses her head in Vienna's direction. "And now that you did, why don't you go get her?"

When my eyes lock on Vienna, there are now four men standing around her, intensely focused on her face and body, one of them clearly attempting to make her laugh.

Fuck this.

That woman is mine.

My feet carry me across the space, bypassing people attempting to say hello to me and hordes of people entering the property for yoga. But all I can focus on is the woman that I need to remind of our connection, the woman that I want to claim in front of all of these idiots so they know to back the fuck off.

When I make it to their group, Vienna's laughter cuts through my intense rage, calming me instantly.

"And that's when I said, maybe we should get a glass of wine then," one of the morons says like he's telling the punchline of a joke.

But when Vienna laughs this time, I can tell it's fake. That's not the same laugh that she has when she's with me and Ellis. It's not easy and natural, reminding me of the way birds sound when they whistle while flying—effortless and light.

No, it sounds like a cry for help, if you ask me. And I do have a habit of rescuing this woman when the time is right.

"Vienna," I say, cutting in on their conversation and pulling all of their eyes to me. My eyes remain on her, though.

"Oh. Hey, Rhonan."

"I need to speak with you."

She glances around at the men and then back to me. "Uh, I'm kind of busy right now."

"It can't wait."

She takes a step closer to me. "Is—is something wrong? Where's Ellis?"

Fuck. This woman's mind instantly went to my daughter and her well-being.

Yeah, I didn't stand a fucking chance at resisting her.

"Ellis is fine. I'm the one with the problem."

One of her many suitors glares at me, but I shoot him an equally harsh look and then plead with Vienna using my eyes.

Vienna addresses the men. "I—I'm sorry y'all. I need to step away for a moment."

As soon as she says the words, I grab her hand and pull her toward the main building.

"Rhonan!" Fletcher calls out to me as we cross through the courtyard, but I wave him off.

"Rhonan." Vienna's voice infiltrates my ears this time, but I'm too focused on getting this woman away from everyone so we can speak in private.

"Hey, son," my father says as I pass him in the tasting room, headed for the hallway that leads to the cellar beneath the building. "Everything all right?"

Pausing in front of him for just one second, I ask, "Is the cellar empty?"

His brows draw together. "Yes..."

"Okay, thanks." I pull Vienna behind me again and lead her to the heavy wooden door, entering the keypad on the lock and opening it up for Vienna to step through. "Watch your step."

"What's going on, Rhonan?" Her hand glides on the railing of the stairs as I step behind her, keeping my hand on her shoulder. When she finally reaches the cellar floor, she spins around, ready to give me a piece of her mind, but I crash my mouth into hers and back her up against the racks of barrels behind her, pinning her hands above her head.

White-hot pleasure races through me, traveling straight to my cock as I thrust my hips into her stomach, letting her feel how hard I am.

I don't think anymore. All the words, all the doubts that have been on a loop in my head for nearly two months vanish the second our lips touch—because this can't be wrong.

Not when it feels this right.

Vienna breaks our kiss, her chest heaving between us. "What the hell has gotten into you?"

"You have, Vienna. I'm waving my white flag."

"And what exactly are you surrendering to?"

I lock my eyes onto hers, those green irises glittering from the soft lighting above us. "I can't deny my fucking feelings for you anymore, woman. It fucking killed me watching those men gawking over you..."

Her eyes widen, but she still looks confused. "Right now? You—you came to this realization right *now*?"

I drag my nose up the column of her throat, nibbling on her earlobe when I get there. "You're lucky I dragged you away from those men before kissing you the way I just did. Trust me, I wanted to mark you right in front of all of them."

I don't miss how her body shivers in response to my words. "I—I'm sorry. We haven't seen each other in almost a week and now..."

I lean back and stare into her eyes again. "Have dinner with me," I blurt out, throwing caution to the wind, but it's now or never. I'm asking this woman on a date, just like my friends told me I should.

I just wish she didn't pause as she considers her answer.

Chapter 19

Vienna

If He Wanted To, He Would...Do Yoga

"Have dinner with me."

His words make me freeze because that's the last thing I was expecting to come out of his mouth in this moment. "What?"

Smirking, he toys with my bottom lip with his hand that is not holding both of mine above my head. "You know, that meal at the end of the day after lunch but before dessert? Dinner."

"That's..."

His grin falls as he murmurs. "I'm trying here, Vienna." There's a vulnerability to his voice that makes me stiffen once more. And then our eyes meet. "I'm trying to tell you that you mean something to me. I'm trying to trust that this is real. I'm just—"

He's trying.

For the first time since our apology sex, Rhonan is finally baring himself to me in a way that lets me know it's safe to fall with him.

He's not Cole, Vienna. This man is the antithesis of Cole.

My body knows that, but my head and heart are having a difficult time catching up.

And up until now, Rhonan hasn't really given me much of an indication that he wants more than that—a physically beneficial relationship.

So, asking me to have dinner with him is clearly his attempt at conveying that.

But is that what I want?

A sigh leaves my lips as he nibbles on the delicate skin of my neck. "But what about my job? I'm still Ellis's teacher. I—I thought we didn't want people talking."

"I don't care anymore, Vienna. I want people to know that we're together." His eyes meet mine as he releases my wrists and drapes my hands over his shoulders. "I want to be able to touch you in public, and I want every other man to know you're unavailable because you're *mine*—because if I have to watch other men hit on you again, I'm going to pry their eyes out of their heads and crush them beneath my boots."

I gasp out of shock. "My God, Rhonan."

He presses his lips against mine in a soft, reverent kiss. "I'm not going to apologize for being honest. That's how you make me feel. I can't hide it anymore, and I'm sure as hell done fighting it."

As our eyes remain locked, I think of all of the reasons why I should say no—Ellis, my past, and this double life that I'm living. But the only thing that is screaming at me right now is to let this man have me in a way that no other man ever has.

"So, what do you say?" The shakiness of his voice is subtle, but it's there. "Will you have dinner with me?"

"I—" Dropping my hands from his shoulders, I shake my head slowly. "No."

The confusion on his face is instant. "No?"

I plant my hands on my hips, huffing out my frustration. "Here's the thing, Rhonan. I need a man who's not afraid to put himself out there, to show me how much he wants me."

Reaching up, he scratches his nails through the scruff on his jaw. "Uh...I thought that's what I was doing right now?"

"I think there's one more thing you could do to show me that you're serious," I continue, loving how this all worked out so perfectly in my favor.

"Okay...and what would that be?"

"Yoga," I answer simply, watching his face transform from curious to downright pissed.

His eyes narrow. "Vienna..."

Shrugging, I begin to walk past him. "I really think it's a simple request, and if you're serious about this..."

Before I get too far, he reaches out for my hand and yanks me back into his chest, my ass pressed up against his cock, that's still hard and turning me on even more than his original words and kiss. "You're testing me, aren't you?" he growls in my ear.

"Every man has a weakness. I think I just found yours, Rhonan Hart."

"You might think doing yoga is the ultimate test for me, but *you* are my test, beautiful." He presses a kiss right beneath my ear and then one to my exposed collarbone, sending a shiver racing through me and not just from his touch—it's his confession.

I'm his test? Does that mean he wants to put his past behind him? Does he see a future for us?

But I'm still married to Cole.

Rhonan doesn't know the entire truth, and will he still want me when he does?

"I. Want. You." Rhonan's deep voice vibrates near my ear, pulling me back to the present.

One step at a time, Vienna. Futures take time to build.

Yeah, but they can be destroyed so easily.

When his lips meet my neck again, he says, "You've been testing my resolve since the moment I met you, but now I know without a doubt, you are worth all of the fight I've gone through to get to this point." Standing up straight, he releases me from his grasp and spins me around to face him, cupping my jaw. "If doing yoga is what I have to do to prove that I want this, then that's what I'll do."

I can't fight the pleased smile from curling on my lips. "Damn." I move my arms back around his neck. "You're making it really hard for a girl to resist you."

His mouth comes within an inch of mine. "You made it hard to resist you since the moment I picked you up off that floor."

"Yeah, you sure did pick me up, Rhonan Hart. In more ways than one."

***

With our hands intertwined, Rhonan leads me back to the main tasting room, where his father is behind the bar still. They share a look, but he avoids a conversation since he knows yoga has to be starting soon. They share a simple nod instead, and then we leave the building, making our way back out to the courtyard just in time to find Laney taking her spot on the hill to start the session.

Glancing down at his attire, Rhonan gives me an irritated look. "You know, I'm not exactly dressed for yoga."

"Well, if you hadn't been fighting this so hard and actually agreed to try it on your own without being bribed, you would have been better prepared." His grin of amusement makes my heart flutter, but then my eyes drift down to our clasped hands. "You're sure about this, Rhonan?"

I swear, I can see a wave of calm wash over him. "I really fucking am, Vienna." Lifting my hand to his mouth, he presses his lips to the back of it and then locks eyes with Fletcher across the grass. The smile he boasts is like that of a proud father, which instantly makes my cheeks heat because I wonder what he and the rest of the group think happened when Rhonan pulled me away. I don't get a chance to ask him as he leads me over to a mat near the front where his other friends are, along with Ellis.

Her tutu is bouncing around her waist when she sees me and her father walking toward her. "Ms. Lewis! I'm ready for yoga."

"I can see that," I say, releasing my hand from Rhonan's before unrolling my mat next to her and then motioning for Rhonan to do the same on the other side of her. "I definitely think your tutu is gonna help. I should have worn mine."

"You have a tutu?" Ellis asks.

I glance back up at Rhonan to find him staring. "Yup, and I think I would have given it to your dad to wear since he's going to need all the help he can get in just a few minutes."

Elliot, Henley, and Fletcher gather around Rhonan. "Uh, Rho?" Henley starts. "What are you doing?"

"What does it look like?" He smooths the rubber mat out with his boot before untying the laces and removing them.

Laney runs over to us now with Dilynne and Elodie on her heels. "Am I seeing things? Please don't tell me that I'm hallucinating because it looks like my brother is about to do yoga." She turns to me with wide eyes. "Is that what I'm about to see?"

"You don't need to make a big deal about it," Rhonan grates out.

Laney laughs. "Um, yes I do." She turns back to Dilynne and Elodie. "My brother is about to do yoga."

Dilynne pops her shoulder. "Then the plan must have worked."

Rhonan straightens his spine, focusing on Dilynne. "What plan?"

Fletcher covers his mouth to stifle his laughter. "Oh, shit."

Spinning to his friend now, Rhonan repeats, "What plan?"

Dilynne snaps her fingers twice, regaining Rhonan's attention as Ellis hugs my legs right beneath me. I smooth her hair away from her face while trying to pay attention because even though I knew the girls had something planned for the evening, I didn't know the details. But apparently, they were right about knowing Rhonan and the push he needed.

"Rhonan, you fail to realize that the male mind is actually very easy to hack into," Dilynne starts. "And you, sir, were acting like your own worst enemy, so the girls and I decided to help you get out of your own way."

"And how exactly did you do that?"

"By showing you what you could lose if you didn't get over your fear," Dilynne explains, directing her eyes over to me. "Your neighbor is a catch, and other men were starting to notice, weren't they?" Her brow arches painfully high on her forehead.

"You mean..."

"Two of the men talking to her earlier were asked to, but the other two? They came over of their own accord." She pats his chest. "You can thank me later. I prefer tools as gifts, but I'm sure you already knew that."

Rhonan narrows his gaze on me, but then his eyes drop down to Ellis holding onto my legs and his face instantly softens. Without hesitation, he marches over to us, tips my chin up with his fingers, and presses his lips to mine. All of his friends—which I guess are mine now too—start cheering, drawing the attention of people around us.

When we part, Ellis gasps. "Daddy! You just kissed Ms. Lewis! That's gross!"

Our group laughs around us now.

Rhonan peers down at his daughter. "Well, Ellis...when a boy likes a girl, sometimes they kiss."

Her nose scrunches up. "That's still gross, Daddy. Johnny says he likes me and I would never let him kiss me. He's a dingleberry."

I burst into laughter as Rhonan pinches the bridge of his nose.

Fletcher steps closer to us now. "I'm sorry, did your daughter just say the word *dingleberry*?"

"Yes."

"Huh?" Fletcher scratches his chin. "Does that mean I'm forgiven for the stripper incident?"

Rhonan glares at Fletcher. "No, and you never will be."

"Stripper incident?" I ask.

Elodie places her palm on my shoulder and whispers in my ear. "You should probably have that conversation with Rhonan away from Ellis. She just stopped telling people she wants to be a stripper like three months ago."

Fletcher backs away from us with his hands up. "Just wanted to check."

Rhonan crouches down so he's at eye-level with his daughter. "Ellis, you can't call people a dingleberry." I fold my lips in to hide my smile as Rhonan continues. "But you also shouldn't let Johnny kiss you...ever. In fact, I don't think you should kiss a boy at all in your entire life."

I swat at him playfully. "Don't tell her that."

"Ms. Lewis?" Ellis says, pulling on the waistband of my leggings, ignoring her dad.

"Yes, Ellis?"

"If you and Daddy are kissing now, does that mean you're going to be my new mommy?"

"Oh, my heart," Laney whispers behind us, but I'm too busy trying not to let my own heart jump from my chest.

"Um..."

"How about you start calling her Vienna for now," Rhonan interjects as he stands, saving me from answering that question the wrong way.

Because how am I supposed to answer that at all? This man just admitted that he wants me for more than a physical relationship. That type of declaration is far from a marriage proposal.

And yet? The idea of not having this little girl in my life long-term is making me want to cry right here in the middle of the courtyard of Hart Winery.

Ellis's eyes light up from her father's suggestion. "Okay! I'm gonna call you Vienna now."

"But at school, she's still Ms. Lewis," Rhonan adds.

Ellis turns back to her dad. "Why?"

"Because that's how you refer to a teacher, by their last name."

Her brows draw together and then she shrugs. "Okay, but I'm still gonna call Johnny a dingleberry because he acts like a piece of poop stuck to a dog's butt," she says, skipping back over to her mat.

Rhonan shakes his head, but there's a smile on his lips as he cups the side of my face. "You sure you want to be a part of this?"

I press up on my toes and kiss him. "Abso-fucking-lutely."

***

"How are you doing over there?" I say in Rhonan's direction, watching him shake as he holds warrior pose and a bead of sweat travels down the side of his face.

"Good. Great," he grates out between clenched teeth.

Henley is shaking from his laughter on his mat behind Rhonan, and Elliot collapses as Rhonan nearly falls over.

"Not as easy as you thought, huh, big guy?" Henley taunts.

Rhonan flips him off over his shoulder as he struggles to regain his balance.

Meanwhile, Laney is guiding everyone to switch to downward dog, also fighting to keep her composure together.

"Is there sweat going down your ass crack yet?" Fletcher asks Rhonan from his left. "That's how you know it's working."

"I second that," Elliot says. "Just be glad you're not wearing a one-thousand-dollar suit while you're doing this for the first time because you came straight from work."

"Not sure jeans are any better," Henley mutters through a laugh. "What kind of idiot does yoga in jeans?"

"The kind that is pussy-whipped," Elliot mutters out of the corner of his mouth.

"Will you three shut the fuck up so I can focus?" Rhonan growls.

"Daddy, you said a bad word!" Ellis shouts loud enough that it gets picked up on Laney's microphone, making the entire courtyard laugh. "And what's a pussy?"

Rhonan tosses his hands in the air. "That's it, I'm done!" He turns back to the guys, who have all fallen onto their mats, clutching their stomachs with laughter.

Dilynne is also having a fit. "Holy shit, this is better than I ever could have imagined!"

Laney speaks into her microphone. "I am so sorry, everyone. It seems that my brother has forgotten his manners this evening. So, if you'd all transition into child's pose, we'll cool down and end a little early tonight." She shoots a glare in Rhonan's direction, and he rolls his eyes as he mimics the pose, making sure to glance in my direction for a beat, shaking his head in frustration.

But me? I'm having the time of my life. Not only have I never laughed this hard, but these people? They're everything good there is in the world. Lydia would have fit in with them so well.

But that thought right there tells me that maybe that's the reason why I feel so at home here—because they and this town remind me of her.

Maybe she led me here after all.

I just hope my past doesn't come back to test this newfound happiness of mine.

Chapter 20

Rhonan

First Date Confessions

I take a deep breath and straighten my tie, fighting off the ball of nerves that's taken up residence in the pit of my stomach. Tonight, I'm taking Vienna on our first date, and it still hasn't left my mind that this will be my first date since Sarah died.

Yes, I've slept with other women since then, but they didn't steal my attention the way Vienna has—or give me a reason to want to try again.

Ellis runs into my bathroom. "Daddy?"

"Yes, sweetie?"

"I can't find my Elsa pajamas."

"Did you check your drawer?"

"Yes, Daddy. They're not there."

I'd bet five hundred dollars that they are.

"Are they in your dirty clothes hamper?"

"No."

Turning to face her, I plant my hands on my hips. "Then just pick a different pair of pajamas to wear tonight."

Ellis flings her hands down at her sides. "I can't! Uncle Fletcher told me that I have to bring my Elsa pajamas because we're watching *Frozen*. Plus, they will match my new shoes and bracelet."

A few weeks ago, I bought Ellis a pair of *Frozen*-themed Crocs and a matching bracelet. She was ecstatic, but I had an ulterior motive with the purchase that no one else knows about.

"You can watch the movie in different pajamas, Ellis."

"No, I can't!" Tears start to form in her eyes. "I need my Elsa ones!"

Dear God, help me.

Sighing, I step out of the bathroom and make my way into her room, only to find her entire dresser emptied on the floor. "Ellis Seraphina…"

"I told you that I looked everywhere!"

I pull my phone from my pocket and text Joanne, asking if she knows where the coveted pajamas are, and then text Vienna that I might be running a few minutes behind.

She texts back immediately.

Vienna: *No worries. I'm still figuring out what to wear.*

Me: *How about nothing?*

Vienna: *Not sure that the restaurant will approve of that. Besides, I thought you didn't want other men looking at me?*

Me: *Fuck. You're right. But don't stress about it. I'm sure you'll look incredible in whatever you decide on.*

Vienna: *Who knew you could be so sweet?*

Me: *Trust me, a lot of people wouldn't believe you if you told them that.*

Joanne texts back at that moment, telling me that the pajamas are already in Ellis's overnight bag.

"Did you check your bag, Ellis?" I say, preparing to text Vienna back.

"No." She races over to her bag and starts ripping things out of it, squealing when she finds the pajamas. "There they are!"

"Great, now they've been found, so you get to clean up this mess that you made."

Her shoulders fall. "Why?"

"Because this is not where your clothes go. Now clean up so we can get going."

"Ughhh..." Her whine practically echoes off of the walls, but I wait to leave until I see her actually picking her clothes up, hurrying back to my room to finish getting ready.

Me: *Pajamas have been found, which means we're back on schedule.*

Vienna: *Shit, okay. I'm making a decision.*

Laughing, I put my phone back in my pocket and grab the gel from the counter to style my hair.

Before we left the winery the other night, I asked my sister if she and Fletcher would be willing to watch Ellis this weekend sometime so I could take Vienna out. Joanne had already made plans with her family to celebrate her niece's birthday, so I knew she wouldn't be here to help. Lucky for me, Laney was more than eager to help me out. So, once I walk next door and "pick up" my date, we're headed to my sister's house to drop off Ellis, and then we have reservations at a steakhouse in Asheville that I have a feeling Vienna will love.

"I'm done, Daddy," Ellis announces when she reappears in my bathroom.

I finish combing the last few pieces of my hair into place, wash my hands, and verify that her mess has been cleaned up for myself.

"You did a good job, sweetie," I say as I grab her bag from her bed and make my way out to the main part of the house. "Did you put everything back where it goes?"

"No, I just shoved everything inside drawers until it fit."

I sigh. "Well, at least you're honest. We can fix it later."

Ellis jumps up and down beside me. "Is it time to pick up Ms. Vienna?" she asks, mixing up the two names she is now allowed to call the woman we're both enamored with.

"Yes."

She runs over to the basket of rocks and picks up the one that she painted like a rainbow for her last night. "Okay, I've got my rock."

I grab the bouquet of red roses from the counter as well. "And I've got the flowers."

Ellis races to the door now. "Let's go, Daddy! You don't want to be late."

Laughing, I lock the door behind us, drop off Ellis's things in my truck, and lead my daughter across the yard into Vienna's, trying to keep up with her. Ellis knocks on the door while I'm still in the driveway. But luckily, Vienna doesn't answer until I catch up to my daughter.

And when she opens the door, my tongue nearly falls to the floor.

Fuck, this woman takes my breath away.

Standing in front of me, her blonde hair down in soft waves and her face fresh with the most natural amount of makeup, I can't stop staring at her. But then my eyes trail down her body, taking in her outfit.

She's wearing an off-the-shoulder black top that shows off just a sliver of her cleavage, and a long floral skirt with black high-heeled boots. The outfit is stunning on her figure, and perfect for where we're going—classy, yet still sexy, and hinting at everything I know is underneath those clothes.

Keeping my promise to myself is going to be far more difficult tonight than I thought.

"I don't know what other outfits you were contemplating, but I one hundred percent approve of this one."

Her cheeks turn pink as she tucks a strand of her hair behind her ears. "Thank you."

"I brought you a rock, Ms. Vienna." Ellis holds out the rock to her. "It's a rainbow."

"I see that." Vienna smooths her thumb over the stone. "You did a beautiful job. I love it."

Ellis clasps her hands in front of her, twisting from side to side. "And Daddy brought you flowers."

I hold the bouquet out to her, and she leans forward to smell them before taking them from my hands. "Thank you. These are gorgeous."

"Not as gorgeous as you, Vienna." I step toward her and press a kiss to her cheek. "You took my breath away just now."

Her eyes meet mine. "Funny. I didn't think anything but yoga could do that."

Fuck, this woman is something else.

Chuckling silently, I smooth my hand around to her lower back and pull her close, lowering my voice even more. "I guess later I'll have to remind you that I can steal your breath in other ways."

"Daddy, I don't want to miss the movie!" Ellis shouts, interrupting our moment. And it's probably a good thing that she does because the longer I stand here and admire this woman, the more I want to skip dinner and just eat her instead.

"What movie are you going to watch?" Vienna asks Ellis once we're all in my truck and on the way to my sister's house.

Ellis kicks her feet in her booster in the back seat. "*Frozen*. It's Uncle Fletcher's favorite."

By the time we've arrived at my sister's house, Ellis has given Vienna a well-thought-out summary of the movie. "And we're gonna make popcorn with marshmallows and rainbow sprinkles," Ellis says as Vienna leads her up to the front of the house by the hand.

Vienna's face lights up. "Oh, that sounds amazing. We should try that one night."

"Yeah, if you never want her to go to sleep," I mutter out of the corner of my mouth as Laney answers her front door.

"Running late?" she says, assessing the three of us.

"I couldn't find my Elsa pajamas because they were already in my bag," Ellis announces before dipping inside right past my sister and Fletcher.

"She insisted she looked everywhere for them, which included her tearing every last article of clothing from her dresser." I meet Fletcher's eyes. "Word of advice, next time tell her that any pajamas will suffice."

Fletcher shakes his head. "No can do. Wearing Moana pajamas to watch *Frozen* is clashing vibes, Rhonan. And as a girl dad, I'm surprised you don't understand that."

Vienna laughs beside me.

"One day when you two have a kid, I'll make sure to get my payback." Tapping my temple, I say, "I'm filing this all away for later."

Laney crosses her arms over her chest, smirking. "Oh, calm down. You know, you should be thanking me, not threatening me right now." She moves her finger back and forth between us. "If it weren't for me, you two wouldn't be going on this date right now, for many reasons other than you were lacking a babysitter."

I step forward and kiss my sister on the cheek. "Fine, I'll let it slide."

She places her hands over the center of her chest, peering up at me with so much emotion in her eyes, I'm afraid she might cry. "Have a wonderful time tonight, and no rush in picking Ellis up in the morning, okay? We have plans to make breakfast and take her to the park if the weather permits."

"I appreciate you," I say, moving my eyes to Fletcher as well. "Both of you."

"The pleasure is ours," Fletcher says with a nod. "Ellis, come say goodbye to your dad and Vienna."

The pitter-patter of tiny feet on the floor alerts us to her arrival. When she pushes through the door, she moves to Vienna first, something I wasn't anticipating, but makes my chest tight in a good way. "Bye, Ms. Vienna. Have fun!"

"I will, Ellis." She leans down and presses a kiss to the top of her head. "You have fun too!"

Ellis peers up at her and widens her eyes. "I'm gonna eat all the cavities tonight!"

Laughing, I pull my daughter over to me, wrapping her in my arms and inhaling her for just a few seconds longer than normal. "Behave yourself. Use your manners and make sure to brush your teeth." I bop her on the nose. "I love you, Ellis."

"I love you too, Daddy." With a quick kiss to the tip of my nose, she runs off again.

"Be safe. Call us if you need anything, all right?" Fletcher adds.

I glance over at Vienna and take her hand in mine, realizing how long it's been since I've been able to glance beside me and find someone there that I wanted more than the fear. "Trust me. I think we'll be fine."

***

The drive to Asheville goes by in a blur as Vienna fills me in on all of the latest kindergarten drama.

"Who knew that five-year-olds could have such complex relationships?" I say as I open the passenger side door to my truck, helping her down once we've arrived and parked at the restaurant.

"Pretty sure adults still have them too."

With her hand in mine, I lead her to the front door of Pete's, a steakhouse that I haven't been to in years, but my mouth is already watering at the thought of tasting the mesquite and hickory butter they melt on their steaks. I give my name to the hostess for the reservation and within seconds, we're being led back to a booth.

The dim light above us makes the space feel intimate, and as soon as we get our glasses of wine and place our orders, I encourage Vienna to scoot closer to me.

"So, what do you think so far?" I ask her as she takes a sip of her wine.

"You sure know how to be romantic when the time calls for it."

I lean forward and whisper, "Don't worry. I can still be dirty later."

Her eyes close as she hums, my lips pressing softly to her skin. "Good. Just wanted to make sure that you're still in there."

Chuckling, I lean back but keep my arm along the back of the booth. "Honestly, I can't remember the last time I felt this nervous, Vienna."

"Could have fooled me."

"The last first date I went on was with my wife."

She sets her glass down on the table and gives me her full attention. "Will you tell me about her?"

My chest grows tight. "Are you sure?"

She places her hand over the top of mine on my leg. "Of course. She's Ellis's mom, which means she will always be a part of your lives."

Sighing, I nod. "I know. Honestly, it's been five years and sometimes it feels like it was just yesterday she was telling me we were gonna have a baby." I can see a hint of something in Vienna's eyes, but I keep talking. "Things happened fast between us. I joined the Marines after my mom died. Even that seemed easier than facing a life without her."

"I want to hear about your mom too," Vienna interrupts me.

I can't help but smile thinking about my mother. "My mom was so full of life. The winery was her third child, as we liked to joke with her about. But honestly? I think she took her love of wine and people and brought those two things together. If she were still alive, I wonder how much bigger the winery would have gotten."

She rubs the top of my hand. "I've been in awe every time I go there at what your family has built and how enamored Blossom Peak is with it too. There's community and genuine relationships everywhere on those grounds. I think your dad, and you and Laney, have done a wonderful job keeping it prospering."

My eyes drop to my lap. "I ran away when he needed me the most, Vienna. I didn't want to be here without my mom, so I joined the Marines and barely looked back. If there's one regret I have in my life, it's that. I left my sister and dad when they really needed me, but I..." My words trail off, my admission hanging in the air.

"What?" she cups my face with her hand, pulling my gaze back to hers.

"I couldn't save her." I know those words sound so childish because the circumstances were unavoidable. But I still felt powerless when she died.

"How did she die?"

"A brain aneurysm

Her shoulders fall. "You realize that there's nothing you could have done about that, Rhonan...right?"

"The rational part of my brain does, but the pain that rests in here?" I tap the center of my chest. "Some part of me just felt so helpless because of it that I searched for that control in other ways."

"Like the service," she says.

"Yeah. So being away from home gave me just enough of a distraction from real life, until I realized that now I was actually responsible for other people's lives and deaths."

Vienna brings her wine glass to her lips, taking a drink. "Didn't think that one through, did you?"

"I never said I was the sharpest tool in the shed, Vienna."

She chuckles. "Continue, please."

"During my four years in the Marines, I lost friends who were practically brothers. Even though I tried to escape loss, it followed me. When it was time to decide if I wanted to reenlist or leave, I met Sarah on a trip home from overseas to Camp Lejeune, where I was stationed. She grew up in Carrington Cove, this small town on the coast. Have you heard of it?"

"I have, actually. That was the other place I was contemplating running off to besides Blossom Peak." Her eyes widen after she finishes speaking.

"Everything okay?"

She clears her throat. "Uh, yeah. I'm fine."

"You sure?"

Nodding, she licks her lips. "Yeah. Continue your story, please."

I push my curiosity aside for now. "Well, Carrington Cove is where my mom died. She and my father took a long weekend just the two of them, which they never did, and that's where her aneurysm burst."

Vienna sucks in a breath. "Oh my God."

"Yeah. So when Sarah told me that, I took it as a sign, like my mom had sent me this woman to bring me back home." I take another drink.

"We fell hard and fast for one another, and she was the reason I chose not to reenlist. I wanted a life with her. For the first time in four years, I had felt something other than grief and anger. She lit up any room she walked into and had a smile that rivaled Julia Roberts'," I say, remembering what her smile looked like, how she sounded when she laughed, and what it felt like to hold her in my arms. Vienna's thumb moves over my hand again. "She reminded me so much of my mom, and I know she would have loved her. It was fast, but I proposed to her within a year, and soon after we were married, we found out we were expecting Ellis."

A tear slips down Vienna's cheek, and I brush it away. "She gave you one of the best gifts anyone can give you, Rhonan—the unconditional love of a child. Trust me, there are people out there that will never get to experience that but wish they could."

"I know she did, but never in my wildest dreams did I think I would be raising my daughter without her. That day..." I shake my head while gathering my thoughts. "It was the best and worst day of my life so far."

"I can't imagine how you can even begin to navigate something like that."

"Honestly, Vienna...I'm not sure that I have." Reaching out, I stroke the side of her face. "And no one has made me want to until you."

"Wow."

"Which is why I need to say thank you."

"What? Why are you thanking *me*?"

"Because you're helping me conquer my fears."

"I think you're giving me too much credit."

I shake my head. "No, I'm not. Don't you have things you're terrified of that have impacted your life?"

Her eyes move to her wine glass, but she doesn't pick it up. Instead, she stares at it in contemplation.

"I have two big fears," she starts. "One is regretting not taking risks." When she focuses back on me, she continues, "And the other is never having kids." There are tears in her eyes, but she blinks them away. "Let's just say I'm working on the first one more than the second, and that's definitely because of you, so I guess I should say thank you as well."

With my eyes locked on hers, something inside pushes me to reciprocate. "My worst fear is losing my daughter." I shake my head. "You got a glimpse of that fear firsthand the day she disappeared from the yard."

She places her hand on top of mine. "I can't imagine what that must have felt like."

"And I took it out on you."

The corner of her mouth lifts. "You already apologized for that, so no need to bring up old wounds."

I lean forward and press my lips to her chastely. Scooting closer to her in the booth, I wrap my arm around her waist and pull her into my chest now, getting lost in her magnificent green eyes. "You know, my other worst fear was that by dating someone new, Ellis would get attached to the woman and then things wouldn't work out. But Ellis was attached to you before I ever gave myself permission to pursue you."

"You're pursuing me, huh?" she teases.

"If you didn't know that, then I haven't been very clear." I reach up and cup the side of her face. "I want you, Vienna. And...I'm willing to see where this goes. I can't make any promises, and I'm sure I'm going to make mistakes. But for the first time in five years, I'm choosing not to let my fear make the decision for me."

Chapter 21

Vienna

Everything I've Been Missing

Oh God. He wants to see where this goes.

You need to be honest with him, Vienna—about everything.

"But the other reason I haven't dated is because I hated the idea that Ellis would think I was trying to replace her mom," Rhonan continues as my thoughts start to spiral.

"You—you were worried that Ellis would think that? Or was that another worst-case thought?"

He drags his free hand over his mouth. "Both, I guess. Moving on is something I'm not familiar with at all, baby."

He just called me "baby."

Oh God, I'm so doomed.

"Moving on doesn't mean we're forgetting about people, Rhonan. At least I know for me, it helps me remember Lydia even more, like she's still with me for every decision that I make. Hell, I wouldn't be here with you if it weren't for her."

He nods. "And I'm grateful for that. I just have a hard time believing that everything happens for a reason. I used to, but then…"

"Something bad happened," I finish for him.

Nodding, he exhales heavily. "But seeing you with my daughter?" He toys with my bottom lip. "It's making me think maybe the entire reason I haven't moved on since Sarah is because I was waiting for you."

"You're laying it on thick tonight, Rhonan Hart."

He chuckles as he brushes my hair from my face. "I think you're the only person who could show me that it's okay to be happy again. I don't think I would have believed it if it were anyone else."

Before I start sobbing in the middle of this restaurant, I crash my mouth into his, kissing him and savoring every second of his touch because I never knew that I could feel this way about another human.

The lack of experience I have in love threatens to disturb my happiness, but every second I spend with Rhonan is rewiring my brain.

I'm such a fool.

I've wasted so much time.

No, time is never wasted, Vienna. It's spent learning lessons and using your newfound knowledge to live with purpose moving forward.

I swirl my tongue against his as we swallow each other's moans.

"You'd better stop that before I hoist you up on this table and eat *you* for dinner," Rhonan growls against my lips.

A throat clears behind us.

When we part, we find our waiter and two other servers standing there.

"Your—your meal is ready," the waiter says, clearly uncomfortable.

Rhonan adjusts himself under the table and I fix my hair as they set our plates in front of us.

Right after they leave, Rhonan mutters, "I think we were just judged really hard by those people."

My chest shakes with laughter. "I don't even care."

He leans over to me and presses one more chaste kiss to my mouth. "Good, me neither."

After we sample each element of our dishes, Rhonan wipes his mouth. "Okay, so I've told you about my past. What about yours?"

"Oh. I, uh..."

"Vienna," he cuts in. "I want to know. You know about all of my scars—it's time you show me a few of your own. What made you run off to Blossom Peak?"

He's right. The man just bared the worst moments of his life to me, and I know that if I want any chance of a future with him, I need to do the same.

Taking a sip of wine for strength, I prepare to tell him the important things. "You caught that phrase, did you?"

"I'm a sheriff. It's in my nature to pay attention to details."

"Yeah, well... I wouldn't say that I ran. I actually hate running, much like you hate yoga."

Rhonan growls. "It's actually stupid how difficult it was."

His comment makes me laugh. "I tried to warn you. But does this mean you're not going to do it again?"

He shakes his head. "No, actually, I'm going to prove that I can do it now. I hate not being good at something." He lifts another bite of his steak to his mouth. "Back to you though. Home was D.C., right?"

"Yes, and there was someone in my life that I left back there."

"A man?"

"Uh huh." I toy with my hands in my lap, debating how to explain this to him even though I've gone over this conversation in my head numerous times at this point. But right now? Nothing I've prepared to say is coming to the surface. "We met when we were young and in college. He was...charming, came from a good family, and my parents adored him. As an only child, you can imagine the pressure I might have felt to make my parents happy, especially since I felt like an afterthought to them."

"What do you mean?"

"Like, they chose to have a child but then acted like I was a hindrance to their life, not a blessing."

His jaw ticks. "I see."

"Anyway, Cole gave me the attention I guess I was so desperately seeking, so as soon as we graduated from college, I moved in with him and we got married."

Rhonan's eyes widen. "You were...you were married?"

"Yes," I say, not sure if now's the time to explain all the details about that. "Lydia never liked Cole," I continue. "And as my best friend, I should have listened to her more, but I was blinded by him, Rhonan. Until..."

His spine stiffens. "Until what?"

"Until things weren't good anymore," I say, not ready to get into everything else that made my marriage fall apart.

"Did he get physical with you?"

"No, but he was emotionally and verbally abusive. I lost so much of myself that it was too late when I finally realized that I didn't even recognize myself anymore." Telling him this makes me want to hide under the table, like he's going to look at me differently now, like he might feel that the Vienna Lewis he's gotten to know can't possibly be the woman I'm describing right now.

Rhonan pulls me into his chest, burying his hand in my hair and breathing me in deeply. "I am so sorry, Vienna. But I respect you for leaving a relationship that wasn't healthy. That takes a lot of courage and strength."

His words quiet those doubts I was just thinking of almost instantly.

"You deserve so much better than that," he continues.

"I know that now," I whisper back.

He releases me and smooths my hair from my face again. "What made you finally decide to leave?"

"It was Lydia, actually. A few days before she died, she said, 'I'm not going to be here to look out for you anymore, Vienna. So I need you to start looking out for yourself.'" The memory makes me grow emotional. "She died before I left, but I finally did because when you lose someone, it can make you reassess the way you're living, you know?"

He nods. "And do you feel like you're doing that? Living differently?"

I take a second to consider my answer. "I do in some ways. I mean, I never would have ridden a mechanical bull before losing her." We both smile at the memory. "But let's just say that you're not the only one with something to fear, Rhonan. I'm afraid that I'm going to let myself get blinded again from the truth, and it terrifies me."

He frames my face with his hands. "I can fucking promise you that I will never make you question how I feel about you, or how real this is."

This man. God, I think—I think I might love him.

"Pinky promise?" I hold out my pinky to him, watching the corner of his mouth lift before he intertwines his pinky with mine.

"I promise, Vienna. You're mine now."

Rubbing my nose against his, I say, "I never really liked that possessive title before you, Rhonan."

"Anything before me was just practice for the real thing then. Let's think of it that way."

"I like that."

His lips find mine, kissing me softly as I taste the food and wine on his tongue.

"You know, we're going to have to watch the kissing in front of Ellis moving forward," Rhonan says when we part and I pick up my fork again.

"Because she thinks it's gross?"

"Yeah."

"That might be hard," I say, placing a piece of my steak in my mouth and smiling as I chew. "I sort of like kissing you. But I adore your kid too."

He licks his lips, smiling back at me. "You know, I love that you light up when you talk about my daughter. Honestly, it's one of my favorite things about you and a big part of the reason I feel comfortable pursuing this. But I want to know what lights *you* up, Vienna. What makes you light up on the inside?"

I finish chewing. "What do you mean?"

"Like, for me? There is nothing that makes me happier than hearing Ellis's laugh."

"Oh, I agree."

"But also, the meatball sub from The Happy Belly Deli."

"Is it that incredible?"

He moans as he closes his eyes. "You have no idea, baby."

"I think you and Joey from *Friends* could be best friends."

"We could, I assure you."

"What else?"

He looks toward the ceiling as he thinks. "I mean, I love when my father gets excited about a new blend of wine that he's working on and shows me what he's thinking before everyone else. And, I love when I get to turn the sirens on in my cruiser because, contrary to what you might think, I don't get to do that very often."

"Not too many crimes and emergencies in Blossom Peak, are there?"

"Nope. But now it's your turn. Tell me what makes you tick, Vienna."

The casually laid-back man sitting in the booth with me is someone I barely recognize, but damn, do I like the vibe of him too. I mean, the grumpy, closed-off single dad was a turn-on to begin with. But this man? The one who's relaxed and genuine? The one who is honestly interested in *me*?

Yeah, this is the man I'm head over heels for.

"Well, I love the smell after it rains," I start, thinking about what would be things that make me appreciate being alive. "I love coming home to Roscoe."

"I still can't believe you never had a pet before him."

"Cole hated animals," I say without thinking.

Rhonan's smile falls. "I hate him even more now. What kind of person hates animals?" Clearing his throat, he says, "But continue, please."

Tapping my chin in thought, I think for a moment. "I think the first sip of coffee in the morning is one of life's greatest treasures." He laughs at that one. "And rainbows," I say, thinking about how Lydia always told me to look for them. "There's just something about them that fills me with hope."

"Rainbows or rainbow sprinkles?"

I laugh. "Both."

Nodding, he finishes his glass of wine. "Anything else?"

My eyes light up when I remember one of my favorite things ever. "Oh, yes. Now, this is important." He nods, waiting for me to continue. "I am a huge sucker for the moment in a movie or a book when the guy gets the girl, or vice versa. That blip when the conflict is done, and they can finally be together?" I clasp my hands over the center of my chest as I sigh. "It gets me every time."

The corner of his mouth lifts in a slow, satisfied smile. "Movies, huh?"

"Yes. It just never gets old."

"I'm glad you think so, because I have a movie in mind that we're gonna watch together tonight."

***

Rhonan cues up the television and finally steps out of the way so I can see what he chose.

I gasp. "Top Gun Maverick?"

"You said it was better than the first one, so I have high expectations." He moves toward the couch to sit next to me, resting his arm along the back of it.

"I—I can't believe you remembered that I said that."

He lifts his hand to cup my jaw. "I told you, I remember everything about that night, Vienna."

"Me too."

Sexual energy races between us as I move to straddle him, but he stops me before I can get into position. "Vienna, don't."

Disappointment races through me as I take my seat again. "Oh, okay. I just..."

He presses a finger to my lips, silencing me. "Don't think for a second that I don't want you." He takes my hand and places it on his cock, hard and ready in his slacks. I have to clench my thighs together to ward off the need building low in my belly. "But I want to make sure you understand that sex is not the only thing on my mind. Do I plan on fucking you later? You bet your ass. But right now?" He tilts his head to the side as his eyes move all over my face. "I just want to experience something normal with you."

"Normal?"

"Yeah, you know... Watching a movie, cooking dinner together, cuddling on the couch." He bites his bottom lip. "I haven't had that in a long time."

Is now when I tell him that I never had that because my husband was an asshole that flipped a switch on me the second we were married?

"That sounds perfect, Rhonan," I reply instead, falling even deeper for this man as he wraps his arm around me, settles into the couch, and holds me while we watch a movie together that I think will be my favorite movie of all time now, for obvious reasons.

***

"Holy shit," Rhonan breathes out as if he were just holding his breath. The movie just ended and when the final task for the pilots started, Rhonan was sitting on the edge of the couch, all cuddling forgotten.

One thing I've learned about Rhonan Hart tonight is that he's a talker during movies, which is both endearing and also kind of annoying. At least I've already seen this movie, so it didn't bother me as much as it could have. But moving forward? That's something I'm going to have to talk to him about.

"That was intense."

"Right? So good though," I say as Rhonan finds the remote and stops the movie from playing during the credits. When he turns to me, he looks as if he's still struggling to breathe. "Are you okay?"

"Yeah. My adrenaline is just flowing right now."

I place my hand over his chest, finding his heart beating wildly. "You were invested."

"I was." He reaches out and frames my face with his hands. "But now I think I need to burn some of this adrenaline off."

I glance up at the ceiling playfully. "Huh. I wonder how you could do that..."

His eyes dip to the cleavage peeking out of the top of my shirt, and he traces the delicate skin with his finger. "I have a few ideas."

"I'd love to hear them."

A low growl travels up his throat before he yanks my bottom lip down with his thumb. "How about I just show you?"

We lean forward at the same time and capture each other's mouths in a desperate kiss that has been building all night. It's been nearly a week since the last time we were naked together, and my body is eager to be reminded of how his touch controls me.

He buries his hand in my hair, manipulating my head as he owns me with his mouth—deep strokes of his tongue, soft nips, the drag of his teeth across my bottom lip. Each move makes me struggle to take in air.

When we part, he stands from the couch and starts undoing the buttons on his shirt. "Get naked, baby."

I reach to my ribs and slide the side zipper down before lifting the shirt up and over my head, revealing my strapless bra to him—a black satin number with lace.

When he's undone the last button on his shirt, he strips it from his arms and drops it to the floor before tipping my chin up, locking his eyes on mine. "You are so fucking sexy, Vienna."

"Right back at you, Rhonan." I drag my hands down his chest and abs, stopping at the clasp on his slacks to release it. I can feel his hard length under my hands, so I make quick work of his zipper and then reach behind him to push his slacks and briefs down, revealing his hard length right in front of my face.

I keep my eyes on him as I bring his tip to my mouth, licking around it softly, dragging my tongue from the base of him all the way to the tip, swirling my tongue as I take him all the way to the back of my throat.

The deep moan of satisfaction that leaves him urges me to continue. "This fucking mouth." He strokes the side of my face with his thumb. "So fucking perfect." I worship his cock for a few more minutes before he pulls away from me. "If you keep doing that, I'm gonna come down your throat, and I'd rather be buried inside you when that happens."

Licking my lips, I nod. "I want that too."

"Stand up."

Keeping only a few inches of space between us, I follow his order while keeping my eyes on his. His hands move down my arms, softly tracing my skin, like he's memorizing the feel of me. When he reaches behind me and pops the clasp on my bra, the fabric falls to the floor between us.

He cups my breasts, toying with my nipples as he leans down and kisses my shoulders, my collarbone, and up my neck right to my ear. "So fucking beautiful."

"Rhonan..."

"Patience, baby. For once, we don't need to rush. I'm gonna take my time, worship you the way you deserve, play with you until you're so desperate for my cock that you're begging for it." He nibbles on my earlobe.

"Not fair."

"I know it's not, because that's how you make me feel every day, Vienna—desperate. For more of you, for more of this, for just...more."

Our eyes meet and then he's kissing me again, our hands roaming over each other's torsos. Rhonan kicks his slacks and briefs from his feet, and then he's dragging the zipper down the back of my skirt, letting it fall to the floor before cupping my ass in his hands. "Fuck, your ass is exquisite."

"You can thank yoga for that."

He laughs before grabbing the strings of my thong on my hips and tearing them apart, tossing the flimsy excuse for fabric to the side.

"Hey! I liked those."

"I'll buy you more." Cupping my face, he brings my mouth to his once more, holding me to his chest so tight that I can feel his hard, hot length resting between us, almost perfectly in line with my slit. When he realizes this too, he moves his hips back and forth, sliding between my lips just enough that I know he can feel how wet I am. "Fuck, your pussy is dripping already."

"I need you," I say, reaching between us to help him part my lips even more so his length can rub against my clit. If there were a more significant height difference between us, this position and movement probably wouldn't work. But his slow drags across my sensitive flesh are making my legs shake and building up the pressure inside of me.

"And you'll have me. But first, I need to satisfy my craving for a taste of this pussy."

Taking me by the hand, he leads me to his room and guides me to sit on the edge of his bed. I'm too mesmerized by the look in his eyes to realize that this is my first time in here.

"Prop your feet up on the bed and let me see you, baby."

I do as he says, feeling more exposed than I ever have, but not because of my nakedness.

No. This exposure feels like accepting the shift happening between us—the open desire, the need, and the trust.

I trust this man, and he's telling me that he trusts me too.

But there's still so much more I need to be honest with him about.

Focus, Vienna. There will be a time to bring that up, but now is not it.

Rhonan pushes my thighs open wider and with his eyes locked on mine, he drops to his knees and drags his tongue all the way through me. "Fuckkkkk…" he draws out before repeating the movement over and over again.

"More, please…"

Another long drag of his tongue. "I told you, you're gonna have to be patient, Vienna. Be a good girl and listen to me, and I promise, I'll let you come." He licks two of his fingers and then slowly pushes them inside of me, pumping them in a rhythm that makes my entire body quake.

"Yes, Rhonan."

His tongue returns to my clit. "Fuck, I love hearing you say my name while I'm eating your pussy," he mumbles as his tongue works me over.

"Rhonan…" I moan again. He growls in response.

"You'd better say my name when you come, Vienna." As he picks up his pace, I watch him focus on what he's doing—using his fingers expertly, moving his tongue against my clit with the perfect amount of pressure, and then he just…stops.

"Rhonan!"

He stands, pumping his cock and giving me the perfect view of his physique—his broad shoulders, his massive chest, those muscular arms, and that V of his hips that makes women drool, much like I feel myself doing at this very moment. "Are you on the pill, Vienna?"

"I—yes," I reply, with a hint of desperation in my voice.

"I just..." His voice strains when he says, "I want you bare. I don't want anything between us."

Pulling him toward me, I mumble against his lips. "God, I want that too."

"Lie back then, baby." I scoot toward the head of the bed as he crawls over me. Once my head is resting comfortably on the pillow, Rhonan rests his body between my legs and lines his cock up to my pussy, dragging the head of it over my clit. "You have no idea how crazy you make me feel, Vienna."

"I think I understand a little."

He shakes his head. "No. How intensely I crave you? It's like nothing I've ever felt before. But I'm not sure how I'm supposed to stop that."

"Don't stop," I breathe out, shaking my head.

His lips part as he lines his cock up to my entrance and pulses inside, giving me another inch of him with each thrust until he's filling me completely. "Fuck, baby. You're so hot, so wet, so fucking perfect." His thrusts get harder and deeper, sliding inside of me with very little resistance as he rests his forehead on mine and our bodies move in sync.

I never knew that sex could be this passionate, this carnal. This man moves in a way that makes me think his body was made for mine. He knows what I need, when to speed up and slow down, when to push harder and how to touch me in the perfect way that the ecstasy is almost too good to bear.

"Fuck me, Rhonan." I claw at his back as he finds his pace, sliding in and out of me, letting me feel every inch of him as he hits that sweet spot deep inside of me that I know will make me see stars. I was so close to coming earlier that it doesn't take me long to find the brink of that release again. "Oh God...I'm gonna come," I warn, bracing myself for the impact.

"Soak my cock, baby. Clench that pussy around me."

The orgasm slams into me fast and hard. Rhonan reaches between us to rub my clit and make it more intense. It lasts for so long that I almost feel like it's never going to end, and honestly, I don't want it to.

This life, this man—it's something I never could have dreamed of as a possibility.

But Rhonan Hart has shown me what real love can look and feel like.

I'm in love with him.

I think I have been for a while.

I just need to move on completely from my past now. It's not something I can put off any longer.

When my orgasm subsides, I open my eyes to find Rhonan smirking down at me. "Fuck, I love watching you come."

My entire pussy is so sensitive right now that I almost feel like I could come again. I wrap my arms around his neck and pull his lips to mine. "Your turn."

His forehead drops to mine again. "I'm not ready for this to end. You feel so fucking good." His hips continue to move in a tortuous pace.

I bring my knees up and wrap my legs around his back. "Please, Rhonan. I want you to fill me up."

"Fuck," he growls as he increases his speed again, pounding into me in the most perfect way—hard, but deep, flicking his hips so that he hits that spot deep inside of me again, building me up to come quicker than I thought possible. "I want you to come again."

"Keep going. I'm close." Reaching between us this time, I find my clit and circle the nub in the way I know will bring me over the edge. "Yes, right there..."

"Fuck, Vienna. Goddamn it."

"More..."

"Shit."

"Yes...fuck, yes. I'm coming!" I scream as Rhonan lets out a groan full of pleasure, fucking me through our orgasms, not stopping until we're both completely spent.

His body goes slack as we both struggle to catch our breath. When he rolls to the side, I turn my head to face him, finding him staring back at me.

"Still craving me?" I tease him, loving the way his smile appears so much easier now.

He pulls me to his chest. "I told you, that won't ever stop."

"Then let me know when you're ready for round two."

He points to his dick that's still hard. "Give me a few minutes to recover, will you?"

Laughing, we fight to regulate our breathing before my eyes land on the scar on his arm as I trace it with my fingers. "How did you get this?"

His smile falls as he directs his gaze to the mangled tissue. "A bullet. It grazed me, but the guy behind me didn't get so lucky."

I push his disheveled hair from his face. "I'm sorry, Rhonan."

Pulling me closer, he says, "Don't be sorry. We all have scars. Some are hidden on the inside, and some are visible on our skin. But something I'm beginning to understand is that they all have a purpose. And once you start to accept them, they don't seem so ugly anymore."

Chapter 22

Vienna

Is That a Magician?

I come out of the bathroom, tears already streaming down my face. "It's negative."

His jaw grows tight. "Seriously?"

I nod, darting my eyes to another place in the room other than his face and the anger resting there. "Yes."

"What the fuck, Vienna?" He picks up the picture frame on our dresser and slams it to the ground. "Are you fucking lying to me?"

Fury races through me. "Why on earth would I lie about something like that?" I toss the pregnancy test at his feet. "Look for yourself."

He picks up the stick, furrowing his brow. "I don't know what the fuck this means."

"One line is negative, two means positive. How many lines do you see?"

He glances at it again and then tosses it to the side. "Take another one."

"I've already taken five. They've all said the same thing."

"This is bullshit," he says, pacing the room while pushing a hand through his blond hair, the same hair that his father and sister have—the blond that all of the Cassidy family has.

"Maybe it's time we see some doctors, Cole," I suggest cautiously. "We've been trying for almost two years now and…"

"Fuck that. There's nothing wrong with me. It sounds like you're the problem."

"You don't know that…"

"Yes, I do!" His voice carries through the room as he gets inches from my face. Pinching the bridge of his nose, he grates out, "Think about how this looks. We've been married for so long and still no children. I have an image to uphold, Vienna. My job and the connections I make rely on it." When his eyes meet mine again, he looks at me with disgust. "Figure it out, or I'm going to."

All I see is his back as he leaves our room, slamming the door behind him. As soon as I'm alone again, I crumble to the floor, holding my knees to my chest.

All I've ever wanted is children, to raise them to know love like I never did.

But I don't know if that will happen now. And without a husband who is willing to approach this intentionally, I don't know if it ever will.

***

"You booked a magician for my bachelorette party?" Laney is frozen in place, watching our entertainment for the evening setting up his props in Dilynne's living room.

"Well, you said no strippers, so I figured this was the next best thing."

"How did you even arrive at that conclusion?"

Dilynne plants her hands on her hips, smacking her gum. "I had a customer come into the shop a few weeks ago, this little old man who wanted a tune-up on his car." She peers over at me, eyes widening. "It was a 1979 Camaro z28. I've never seen one in person, and when I did, I nearly came when I touched it."

"Yeah, that means nothing to me," I reply.

Elodie scrunches up her nose. "And that was an unnecessary detail to share with us."

Dilynne shakes her head. "I need better friends."

"Please get to the point," Laney says, directing Dilynne back to her story.

"Anyway, he wanted the car in tip-top shape because he and his wife were going on a date to see a magic show in Charlotte. How adorable is that?"

"Okay, that's actually kind of sweet," I say as I lift my glass of champagne to my lips.

"Exactly, and since my best friend is acting like a prude of a bride, I figured we should see what all of the hype about magic shows is, so I got the information from the little old man and here we are." She fans her hands over to the guy dressed in a black tux and top hat.

"I am not a prude for not wanting to see some man get naked when my fiancé fulfills every fantasy I have," Laney counters. "Plus, I let you order that monstrosity of a cake." When she points to the corner, the four of us look in that direction. "Dilynne likes to order novelty cakes for bachelor and bachelorette parties. For Elliot's, she put his and his would-be bride's face on the testicles of a penis."

"You didn't *let* me do anything. You and I both know that you weren't going to do a damn thing about the cake that I ordered. Honestly, I think I went a little tame with this one."

The rectangular-shaped cake was decorated to look like a postcard, but Fletcher's face is on the penis-shaped stamp in the corner. In the middle is a picture of Laney and Fletcher as kids, but when you lift that picture up, there's an image of Fletcher's calendar photo underneath. Laney appreciated that more than anyone.

"I get it, but there are plenty of single women here who would have appreciated a stripper and a penis-shaped cake," Dilynne fires back. "I exercised so much control by honoring your requests that I should get some credit for that. But sometimes you need to think about other people too, Laney."

Laney gasps, but there's a smile on her lips. "I can't believe you just said that to me!"

"Honey, if I can't be honest with you, then who can?"

Elodie and I laugh, watching their exchange as a bunch of the other girls murmur in conversation while sitting in chairs around the room.

Dilynne really did plan the perfect party for Laney. Her entire house is decorated in shades of gold and rose pink—Laney's wedding colors—and there are tables full of food, but most importantly, towers of onion rings on tables around the room. Endless bottles of champagne are chilling on ice, and there are cardboard cutouts hiding under sheets in the corner, which I can only assume are for a game later.

Normally a social situation like this would make me feel uneasy, but these girls are quickly becoming a source of comfort in my new life, yet another aspect I want to fight for.

"Fine. Then tell me why the cutouts are back," Laney says to Dilynne, planting her hands on her hips now.

"You'll find out later along with everyone else."

Laney drops her hands, reaches for her glass of champagne, and drains it. "You're lucky I love you."

Dilynne bops her on the nose. "Right back at you, future Mrs. Laney Adams."

Laney sighs wistfully. "God, I can't wait to marry that man."

Dilynne grabs Laney's hand and squeezes it. "Your dream is finally coming true, Laney. And no one deserves it more than you and him. This is one wedding I'm actually excited for." She directs her eyes over at me and Elodie. "And the next weddings I'll be happy for will be yours."

"Me?" I nearly drop my glass of champagne. "I don't think..."

Laney reaches for my hand. "Does that mean your date didn't go well? You gave me nothing when I texted you."

Dilynne pokes my cheeks that I know are turning pink in a flash. "I think her flushed cheeks speak for themselves."

"It was..." I think back to that night and how everything felt like it clicked into place for me, but I know Rhonan and I are very far away from getting our own happily ever after. "I mean, it was amazing, but it's still so new, and..."

Dilynne snaps her fingers. "Now I'm bummed that I changed the game up."

"What do you mean?" Elodie asks.

Dilynne points to the corner where the cardboard cutouts are standing. "Rhonan's handcuffs would have been perfect for Vienna tonight. I bet she knows how well he can use them now."

Laney wrinkles her nose. "Ew, that's my brother you're talking about."

Dilynne shrugs. "Don't act like you haven't been invested in him getting with Vienna since we found out about the two of them."

I can't hide my smirk, even though I'm grateful for the change in topic. "You know, being handcuffed isn't something that would have interested me before. But with Rhonan?" I fan my face. "I think I'd definitely be interested."

"Gross!" Laney shouts.

I lean forward and drop my voice. "Sorry to tell you, Laney, but your brother is a dirty boy in bed, even without handcuffs."

Dilynne slow-claps as Elodie and I laugh. "I knew Rhonan was a closet freak."

Laney covers her ears. "You're ruining my bachelorette party."

Dilynne laughs. "Hey, you wanted him and Vienna to get together, and it's happening. Be grateful. They're halfway on their way to wedded bliss." She lets out a frustrated groan. "My fuck buddy and I parted ways a few months ago, and I've been so busy working on the Porsche for Motorlux that I haven't been dicked down in a long time. I'm afraid I've forgotten what a good redwood tree might feel like between my legs."

Elodie spits out her champagne as she chokes. "Dear God, Dilynne! A redwood?"

"What?" She tosses her hands in the air. "Would you prefer magic wand?"

A throat clears behind us. When the four of us turn around, we find the magician standing there, looking slightly uncomfortable. "Uh, I'm ready when you are, ladies."

Dilynne claps her hands together, completely unaffected by this man overhearing our conversation. "Perfect! Let's get the show on the road! Ladies, gather 'round and prepare to have your minds blown."

Everyone refills their drinks and settles in for an adult-themed magic show.

Even though Dilynne wasn't able to satisfy our eyes with a male stripper, the magician made sure to include plenty of dildos, whips, and chains in his performance to leave us all hot and bothered. And then, he finished his act with the ultimate trick—making his clothes disappear.

"Oh my God!" Laney shouts as the man stands there, sculpted muscle and tan skin, in nothing but a thong.

Dilynne hoots and hollers. "Fuck yeah! Best magic trick ever!"

The magician spins around and shakes his ass before smirking over his shoulder. "The maid of honor paid me extra for that trick, and money talks."

Dilynne nearly falls out of her chair from laughter, while the rest of us cheer and give the man a standing ovation.

Once the entertainment has packed up and left, Dilynne brings out the cardboard cutouts of the guys, revealing the adjustment that she made to the original game.

"I can't with this girl sometimes," Laney says to me from my right. "She created this game when Elliot and Tori were getting married and had cutouts of objects for people to pin to their junk. Now, I guess we're pinning different hairstyles on them?"

"You know, since you're a hairstylist," Dilynne explains like it makes perfect sense as she continues to set up the cutouts.

Laney turns to me and takes my hand in hers. "Are you having a good time?"

"I really am," I say. "And I know you and I haven't known each other for very long, so it really means a lot that you've included me in this special moment in your life, Laney." I fight off the emotion clogging my throat.

She squeezes my hand. "Well, it means a lot to me that you've made my brother smile again, so let's say that we're even."

We share a laugh, and then I glance across the room where Elodie is trying to help Dilynne set up the cardboard cutouts of the boys, but the one of Elliot keeps falling down.

"He would be a pain in my ass, even in cardboard form," Dilynne mutters as she kicks Elliot sprawled across the floor. "Can't keep it up. I bet that's how it is in real life too."

Laney shakes her head and turns back to me. "Anyway, in all seriousness, how are things going with you and my brother? And please, spare me any more details of your love life."

I tuck my hair behind my ear. "Honestly, things are going so well that I'm terrified."

"Girl, I know that feeling."

"He took me on a date and told me that he thinks I'm the person he was waiting for to show him that he could be happy again, Laney." I take in a shaky breath. "I'm falling for him."

Laney squeals. "You two belong together. I can feel it."

"You think so?"

"I know my brother, and I knew it would take a special woman to pull him out of the storm he's been living in." She rubs my hand. "That's you, Vienna."

"I—I'm speechless."

"Don't be. Just keep being patient with him and don't let anything stand in your way. Otherwise, you'll live with regrets and that's something no one can ever take back."

Trust me, Laney. I know.

Chapter 23

Rhonan

Dick Piercings & Realizations

"Jesus, do you think the music could be any louder in here?"

Henley leans his mouth next to my ear. "Your old age is showing."

I push his shoulder and follow him deeper into the club. We just finished one of the best sushi dinners I've ever had, and now our group is walking through the main floor of Tonic, a nightclub in downtown Charlotte, to keep the bachelor party going. The reviews for this place were insane, and Fletcher agreed it would be a great place to kick back with everyone, so I made the reservations months ago. They're also going to set up poker and blackjack tables for us to play in lieu of dancing.

Guys from Fletcher's NFL team are flanking us as we walk through the crowd to the VIP area roped off for our party, and I've never felt so small.

I'm not a tiny man by any means, standing just over six foot and proud of the physique I've carved over the years. But being near a group of professional football players is making me feel like I would be the last guy in this crowd to be picked to play on the team.

Elliot comes up behind us, walking bow-legged still. I noticed something was off with him earlier, but I didn't think too much of it. However, now that I have time to study him, I can definitely tell that his gait is not normal.

"Why are you walking like you have a fucking stick up your ass?" I ask as we pass through the ropes and everyone starts picking which booths they want to sit in.

Henley turns back to the two of us. "Well, according to my sister, Elliot does have a stick shoved up there, so..."

Elliot flips him off. "Fuck you and your sister."

"I'm gonna tell her that you said that."

"I don't fucking care. Tell her I got the stick from her broom closet." Elliot carefully slides into the booth in the corner before turning back to me. "For your information, it's not my ass that's making me uncomfortable right now, it's my dick."

Henley's lips curl up in disgust. "Fucking gross. You have an STD or something?"

"No. I got my dick pierced."

I freeze before taking my seat next to him. "Are you fucking serious?"

"I told you I was going to do it, and since none of you would go with me, I went by myself. One of the tattoo artists held my fucking hand."

I wince. "You really let some dude stick a needle through your dick?"

"It was a chick who did the piercing, but yeah."

Henley shakes his head, his mouth still turned up like he's in pain for our friend as he slides in the booth next to me, our knees knocking since Elliot is spread out as much as he can. "I hope to God Elodie never leaves me if dick piercings are the new thing to do after a relationship ends."

Elliot flips off Henley again just as Fletcher comes over and takes a seat next to Henley. "What's going on? Why does Elliot look like he needs to take a shit?"

"I got my fucking dick pierced!" Elliot shouts loud enough for the entire room to hear. Some of the guys clap for him, others wince and ask him what the fuck he did that for.

Fletcher peers back at Elliot from across the table. "The consensus is that you're nuts."

"Did you get your nuts pierced too?" Henley asks through a laugh.

"No, just an apadravya piercing."

"What the fuck is that?" Fletcher asks.

Elliot reaches for one of the glasses of water that had been placed on the table before we arrived. "Look it up."

"Fuck no. I don't need to see other guy's dicks."

"Did it hurt?" Henley adds.

Elliot shrugs. "Honestly, the healing is worse than the piercing. But I'll be back up and running in a few weeks."

"I thought your dick was broken," I chime in.

Elliot glares at me. "My dick is *not* broken. And the next woman I take to bed is going to appreciate what I went through for her pleasure and mine."

"I heard ribbed condoms are supposed to help with that," Henley says, laughing still.

Fletcher high fives him but Elliot grows serious. "You just keep cracking your jokes, but once the girls find out what I did, don't come crying to me when they start asking you to do the same."

Fletcher and Henley's smiles fall instantly. "Why would the girls find out?"

"Because you fuckers are gonna go home and tell them like you do everything else." Elliot tosses his thumb in my direction. "You did it with Rhonan and Vienna's situation."

"Yeah, well I'm sure as fuck *not* going to tell Vienna about this because there will be no needles coming in contact with my penis. Ever," I say.

Fletcher nods in agreement. "Same here."

Henley contemplates his answer. "No, I'm good."

"Speaking of Vienna, you never told us about your date," Fletcher cuts in as Elliot and Henley turn their attention to me.

I bring my glass of water to my lips as I see the waitress headed in our direction for our drink order. "Was I supposed to?"

Henley slaps the table in front of him. "Hell yeah, you were. Come on, you finally made a move and we wanna know how it went. Your little display at yoga night was top notch, my friend, so I'm sure the date went well."

Narrowing my eyes at him, I debate how much I want to share with these guys. But at the same time, for once, I'm really fucking happy and, even though I don't want to admit it, it's in large part due to their encouragement.

"It was perfect," I start just as the waitress arrives at our table. We place our drink orders, then Fletcher nods for me to continue. "I took her to Pete's. The food was incredible and..." I push a hand through my hair. "I told her everything about my past—my mom, Sarah, the Marines..."

Henley grows serious. "Shit, Rhonan."

"I know." Blowing out a breath, I continue. "Then we went back to my place and watched a movie."

Elliot's brows draw together. "A movie? Is *your* dick broken?"

It's my turn to flip him off. "Not even a little. But it was important to her, and fuck. I forgot how much I've missed having someone to do something so trivial with, you know?"

Fletcher nods. "I get it. The nights when Laney and I hang out at home and watch tv, or cook dinner together are the best moments, in my opinion."

"After dinner when Elodie and I play with Remy in her room is my favorite part of the fucking day," Henley interjects, followed by a groan. "Fuck, I miss my girls."

I lock eyes with Fletcher. "I know this is your bachelor party and all, but I really wish I was back at home with Ellis and Vienna right now, man. I really fucking do."

Our drinks arrive and Elliot takes his from the waitress before she can even place it on the table. "Apparently, I didn't start drinking early enough in the evening for all of the lovesick puppy talk. I thought this was supposed to be a bachelor party?"

Fletcher kicks Elliot under the table. "Look, I'm sorry. I know you wish things had worked out differently for you, but that doesn't mean that you won't get a second chance at happiness." He flicks his chin in my direction. "I mean, hell. Look at Rhonan. He never thought he'd want to build a life with someone else after Sarah, and then he met Vienna."

I smile at the mention of her name again, but the ache in my chest intensifies because I meant what I said. I wish I were back at home with her and my daughter.

My girls.

Elliot snorts. "So you're telling me I have another five years of listening to you three drone on about how happy you are?" He shakes his head and drains half of his whiskey. "No thank you."

I slap him on the shoulder. "Don't shut yourself off to it, man. Trust me. It took me far too long to see what was in front of me the second I met her."

He eyes me curiously from the side. "So you told her about your past, but did she tell you about hers?"

"Yeah."

"Everything?" he presses.

"What do you mean, *everything*?"

Elliot shakes his head and brings his glass back to his lips. "Never mind."

I pull his glass down before he can drink. "Look, I know you were fucked over, but that doesn't mean everyone will be. Vienna is incredible. She's fucking made my whole life feel lighter, man."

Elliot sighs. "Trust me. I know you're happy. I'm just trying to look out for you. Pretty sure you're the one who wanted to do a background check on Tori, and I told you not to. If I would have listened to you, I probably could have spared myself some bullshit and embarrassment."

"Vienna hasn't given me a reason not to trust her, though."

"Wait. Are you telling me that you haven't done a background check on her?" Henley asks.

And that's when it hits me.

I haven't.

It honestly didn't even cross my mind because our connection from the beginning hasn't made me think straight exactly. I'm usually the first to suggest such a thing, given that I work in law enforcement.

"No," I answer honestly, but now that Henley is bringing this up, perhaps I've been letting my dick lead the show with rose-colored glasses. I turn my attention back to Elliot. "But now you're making me wonder if I should."

He puts his hands up. "I shouldn't have even fucking said anything. I just want to make sure that you're getting the whole story from her. That's all."

My pulse is pounding in my ears, fueling this desire to go home even more now to see her.

Fuck. *Have I* been blinded by this woman?

Am I missing something?

My gut is telling me no, but my head?

That fucker likes to stir shit up, and apparently, so do my friends.

***

"What's with the look?" Daniel asks Chief Banks as we sit in the debriefing room before shift changes. And even though our boss always has a crinkle in his brow, this one's a little deeper than normal.

The chief hoists his pants up on his waist, surveying the room. I'm at my usual seat in the back, waiting to hear what he has to say.

"I've been getting a few calls from people around town—Mrs. Higgins, Ned down at the hardware store, and even Carolina at the bakery has mentioned this."

Jake sits up taller in his chair. "What's going on?"

"Apparently, there's a man that's been hanging around town for the past few weeks asking questions. None of the business owners have been able to get a good picture of him without him noticing, but he's being described as around six feet tall, jet black hair with gray at the temples, and wearing the same tan Carhartt jacket."

"What kind of questions?" I interject.

"Stuff about the town, job openings, and cost of living, etcetera."

"That doesn't sound too alarming," Brody says.

The chief shakes his head. "I didn't think so either until someone said they saw him hanging out by the school."

"Okay..." I drag out.

Chief Banks throws his hands in the air. "I'm just letting you know about the calls I've been receiving."

"Sounds like you're reaching," Jordan says. "I know things are quiet..."

"Goddamn it, Jordan!" The chief yells. "Haven't I made myself clear about using the fucking q-word?"

The sound of metal screeching echoes in the room as I stand from my chair, pushing it backwards. "All right," I say. "Let's approach this rationally." Chief Banks glares at me, but puts his hands up in surrender. "It's better to err on the side of caution. Just keep your eyes open for this guy and approach him carefully if you see him. He's probably just a tourist interested in life here, contemplating a move or something," I add, partially trying to convince myself. "You know how people are that visit Blossom Peak. They fall in love with this place and suddenly are considering small-town life, only to go right back where they came from."

Daniel nods in agreement. "You're right, Rhonan. Better safe than sorry."

"Thank you, Rhonan, for helping me try to get these knuckleheads to see reason," the chief says to me before turning on his heel and heading for the door. "Glad to see someone else doesn't want a situation to occur that could have been prevented."

Once he's completely out of the room, Jordan turns to all of us. "Is he all right?"

"Who knows," Brody replies. "Could be that the state is breathing down his neck to retire."

"Where did you hear that?" I ask.

"I'm surprised you haven't heard about that yet," Brody says as a smirk forms on his face. "Although you seem to have been distracted by a certain blonde lately, so I guess you have a legitimate excuse."

"I'm not distracted," I say a tad too defensively.

Daniel comes up behind me and slaps me on the shoulder. "I'm pretty sure it's a good thing, man. You certainly have a pep in your step that hasn't been there in a while."

"Yeah, that's what getting laid will do for you," Brody adds through a laugh.

I step up to him, getting right in his face. "Don't speak about Vienna like that."

Brody's smile falters. "You're into her, huh?"

"What do you mean?"

"Like...this isn't just a fling for you. Fuck, man." He pats me on the shoulder. "That's great."

I push his hand away. "I don't need your fucking encouragement."

"No, I'm being serious," Brody says. "Jaylyn and I always wondered if you'd find someone that would help you move on after Sarah," he says, referencing his wife.

"Yeah, well..."

She has, I think to myself.

For the first time in five years, I'm thinking about the future—and not just the one where I watch Ellis grow up alone—but one where I have someone by my side through it all.

Brody slaps me on the shoulder before heading for the door. "I hope it all works out for you, man. Truly."

Yeah, you and me both.

After everyone clears out from the debriefing room, I head back to my desk to catch up on some paperwork, fighting to ignore the bomb my friends planted over the weekend.

All I would have to do is press a few keys, and the database would tell me everything I could ever want to know about the woman that I'm falling for more with each passing day.

But is it necessary?

Like I told my friends, I don't feel like she is hiding anything from me, but then I think about Elliot and how blindsided he was by Tori. I don't want to fucking end up like that too. If I got fucked over by this woman, I know for certain that I would never entertain a relationship again. My heart and head couldn't go through something like that again.

Staring at the blinking cursor on the screen, it taunts me with the truth—the whole truth, not just what Vienna has told me.

But do I honestly think that something is missing?

No.

The answer comes to me so quickly that I exit out of the database system and exhale the breath I was holding.

For once I'm going to trust my gut because the thing I know for certain is that the only thing that has been missing from my life—is her.

***

"Daddy, why do you look so grumpy?" Ellis asks as she and Vienna paint rocks at my dining room table.

I'm standing in my kitchen, cleaning up the dishes from the meal I just made for the three of us, but I haven't said much since Vienna arrived.

I'm afraid that if I do, I might blurt something out that she might not be ready to hear, but my mind can't stop fixating on.

I'm fucking in love with this woman.

Every time she's in my house and with me and my daughter, all I can think about is how I want this for the rest of my life.

And as soon as I came to this realization about an hour ago, I couldn't focus on anything else.

"Just have a lot on my mind, Ellis," I say as Vienna glances up at me too. And fuck, the sight of the two of them together is everything I feel like I've been missing—someone who cares for my daughter as much as they do for me.

"You should come paint rocks with us," Ellis continues as she smears red paint all over her rock. "I'm making a ladybug."

"And you're getting more paint on your hands than the rock," Vienna tells her. "Maybe you should wash your hands before you continue."

"Okay." Ellis hops down from her chair and runs down the hall to her bathroom.

I'm in the middle of wiping down the kitchen counter in front of me when I feel Vienna come closer. "Are you okay, Rhonan?" There's a cautiousness to her voice.

I reach for her by the waist and pull her into my chest, stroking my finger down the side of her face. "I'm fine."

"You don't seem fine," she says, reaching up to my chin, forcing me to look at her. "If you're not careful, you're going to give yourself even more wrinkles and then your sister is definitely going to push that face cream on you." She toys with my bottom lip and I can't fight the way my body reacts to her.

Chuckling, I lean down and press my lips to hers. "I draw the line at yoga, all right? Yoga won't prevent wrinkles, but it will prevent a shit ton of other issues."

Her eyes widen. "Has someone been researching yoga?"

"Not intentionally. It's just popping up on my internet feed now. Henley said the same thing happened to him after the first time he tried it."

Vienna laughs. "Well, I'm glad to see that you're embracing it instead of fighting it finally."

I'm embracing a hell of a lot more than yoga.

"Okay, I'm ready!" Ellis announces as she re-enters the room, interrupting our conversation.

"We'll talk later."

Vienna nods before pressing a kiss to my lips and returning to the table with my daughter.

Fuck, I can't wait until Ellis goes to sleep so I can show this woman exactly how she makes me feel—all fucking night long.

"Daddy, are you gonna paint with us now?"

Sighing, I toss the kitchen towel to the counter and take a seat at the table. "Sure, sweetie."

"Yay!"

After countless rocks are turned into ladybugs, turtles, and more rainbows, Vienna goes back to her house to check on Roscoe while I get Ellis through bath time and our bedtime routine.

Tucked in her bed, on the verge of falling asleep, my daughter looks up at me. "Daddy?"

"Yes, sweetie?"

"I missed you when you were at work and Uncle Fletcher's party."

"I missed you too, baby girl." Pushing her hair from her face, I can see her eyes start to flutter closed.

"I missed Vienna too."

"Yeah, me too," I croak out as I hear the front door open and close, which means Vienna must have come back.

"Are you gonna marry her?"

"I—I don't know, Ellis," I answer honestly. Plus, she's already been married and so have I, so I'm not sure where her head is at on the topic. But could I see her walking toward me in a white dress? Could I see me waking up next to her with my ring on her finger?

Yeah, I can definitely see it now.

"I think you should."

I fight to control my smile. "Is that so?"

"Yes. You love her, just like Uncle Fletcher loves Auntie Laney."

God, to be a kid when love and life seem so fucking simple. "What makes you think that?"

"Because you look at her like she's the most beautiful rainbow you've ever seen."

My heart threatens to jump out of my chest. "I love you, Ellis."

"You should give her your lucky rock," she mumbles, her eyes nearly closed now.

My hand covers my pocket where my rock resides. "But you gave me that rock."

"Yeah, because I love you. But you love Vienna, so you should give it to her."

Ellis's eyes completely close, so instead of responding, I place a gentle kiss to her forehead and then shut her door softly, returning to the living room to find Vienna sitting on the couch, focused on her phone.

When she senses me in the room, she jumps, covering her chest with her hand. "Jesus, Rhonan." Tucking her phone back into her purse, she peers up at me. "You scared me."

"Who else would be coming down the hall?"

She shakes her head. "No one, I guess..." Pushing her hair from her face, she smiles up at me. "I was just so engrossed in my phone that I didn't hear you."

I take a seat on the couch next to her, pulling her into my chest and inhaling her, my nose buried deep in her hair. "Well, you can be engrossed in me now." Leading her to straddle me, I wait until she's in position before I study her face. "God, I could get used to this."

Her eyes sparkle in the dim light from the lamp beside us. "Me too."

"I like coming home and knowing I get to see you." I drag my nose up the column of her throat. "It makes all of the stress go away."

"What stress?"

"Just life. Worries about being a good dad. Work."

"I thought your job was pretty lowkey?"

Leaning back, I meet her gaze. "Normally it is, but when Chief gets an inkling about something, he makes it the entire station's problem."

Her hand plays in my hair at the back of my neck. "What's going on?"

I shake my head. "Nothing. I don't want to add any worry to your plate."

"You know you can talk to me, Rhonan."

"I know, baby. That's one of the things that I enjoy most about having you here." Inhaling deeply, I say, "And the fact that you and Ellis have a connection too makes this seem almost too good to be true."

She huffs out a laugh. "I seriously love that little girl. She's like joy, sunshine, and rainbows all bottled up into a tiny person."

"Speaking of Ellis, do you mind watching her Monday night next week, please? Joanne needs the night off after this weekend with the wedding and all that."

"Of course. I—I would love to." She bites her bottom lip. "My, how things have changed in a matter of a few months."

"What do you mean?"

She arches an eyebrow. "Well, if memory serves me correctly, you were yelling at me weeks ago about not understanding the responsibility of having a child, and now you want me to babysit her." Tapping her chin playfully, she continues, "I honestly don't know what to think of this turn of events."

I tickle her ribs, making her squeal. "Hey, watch it. If memory serves me correctly, I apologized profusely that night with my tongue all over your pussy."

Her eyes grow darker and the heat between her legs grows hotter as she rubs herself over my cock. But I'm not done holding her, not done soaking up her warmth that is soothing my soul in ways I never thought possible.

"I'm not just obsessed with your body, though, Vienna." I push her hair from her face so her eyes are exposed to me completely. "It's been a long time since I've had someone to talk to, someone that I feel I can trust, and you've given me that again."

"Same, Rhonan." She places a chaste kiss on my lips and then rests her forehead on mine. "Lydia was my person, and when she died…"

"How did she die?" I cut in. "You never told me that."

Her eyes grow glassy. "Ovarian cancer. It was aggressive and she fought it hard, but by the time they started treatment, it was too late."

"Fuck, I'm sorry." Pulling her into me, I hold her tightly. "I would have loved to have met her."

"She was the best. She would have loved you."

"I owe her a lot."

She leans back and looks into my eyes. "Why's that?"

"Because she brought me you." The words drift from my lips so effortlessly that I almost say the other three words that have been on my mind these past few days.

"If I never would have fallen down at The Charming Bull, do you think we would have met?" she asks with a quirk in her lips.

"I'd like to think so."

"Does that mean you're beginning to think some things might actually happen for a reason?"

I frame her face with my hands and pull her within an inch of my lips, feeling her breath skate across my mouth. "Yeah, baby. I think I just might."

Chapter 24

Vienna

A Meatball Sub & A Choice

As soon as I take my seat at my desk, ready to open up my mediocre turkey sandwich for lunch, the classroom phone rings. It's Friday afternoon, tomorrow is Laney and Fletcher's wedding, and my energy level is so low, I'm trying not to fall asleep at my desk.

"Hello?"

"Vienna? You have a visitor."

"I do?"

Jessica, the front receptionist at the school, laughs. "Oh, yes. And he has a gun and handcuffs, so if I were you, I'd get here quickly."

My heart is racing, but I don't say another word before hanging up the phone, grabbing my keys, and rushing down the hallway to the front office, only to find Rhonan standing there in his uniform, holding a brown paper bag and looking far more delicious than anything he could have brought me to eat.

But then I see the logo on the bag, and my stomach does a little flip. "You brought me lunch?"

He holds the bag up higher. "Not just any lunch, but the meatball sub from The Happy Belly Deli."

I cross the space to him. "You brought me your favorite sandwich?"

Nodding, he says, "And soon, it's about to be your favorite too."

For some reason, this gesture makes me want to cry. Cole never did things like this for me—the small things, the everyday things, the things that make me question if he ever truly loved me.

I think you already know the answer to that question though, Vienna.

Rhonan cups my face just as Jessica clears her throat behind us. "Why don't you two go enjoy your lunch together while you still have time?"

Rhonan shakes his head, but keeps his eyes locked on mine. "I wish I could, but I'm on duty. I just wanted to drop this off and then I need to get back on the road. I'm on patrol today. Chief's orders."

"Well, this was very sweet of you."

"I guess I just needed an excuse to see you," he says before pressing his lips gently to mine.

My eyes close and I savor this feeling—the feeling of being cherished, appreciated—loved.

God, does Rhonan love me?

It's too fast, right?

I know how I feel, but this man has been through so much. I know he said he wanted to see where things could go with us, but I know what I want.

I want him.

I want Ellis.

I want a life in Blossom Peak.

When he leans back and looks at me, his eyes say so much more than his mouth ever could in this moment, so I hang onto that. "I wish I could see you tonight."

"I know, but..."

"Wedding traditions," he cuts in before taking me out of the office to the front of the school so they're aren't people listening for what he says next. "Fletcher wanted all of us boys to stay together tonight. But once this wedding is over, you're all mine." He drops his voice down to a whisper. "Tomorrow night I'm going to strip you out of your dress and fuck you all over your house. And then Sunday, we can go back to my place, cook breakfast with Ellis..."

"Pancakes with sprinkles?"

"Of course."

"We'll take her to Skye's the Limit. She loves the obstacle course, and then I'll cook dinner while the two of you paint rocks. We can watch a movie when Ellis goes to sleep..."

"Sounds perfect." And it does. It sounds like the life and relationship that I've always wanted but never had with Cole. I press one more kiss to Rhonan's lips and then take the bag from his hand. "Thank you again for this."

"Thank you for being someone I want to get addicted to my favorite sandwich." His wink makes the crinkles at his eye more pronounced before turning around, placing his aviator glasses back on his face, and exiting the front office.

"I don't need to tell you how lucky you are to have landed that man, now do I?" Jessica says, reminding me that she's been watching our entire exchange.

A wistful sigh leaves my lips. "No, I'm very much aware."

"Rhonan Hart has been single ever since Ellis was born," she continues. "If he's got his eyes set on you, I'd say that's a big deal."

"Trust me, I know."

"I'm happy for you then, Vienna. Everyone deserves a man that looks at them like that."

I glance back at the door that he just walked out of, a nagging thought in the back of my mind. "Not sure I'm the one who deserves it, though."

"Why not?"

Turning back to her, I plaster on a fake smile. "Just stuff from my past creating doubt." I shrug. "You know how that is, right?"

"Sure. Just don't dwell on the past too much. Otherwise, you're going to miss out on the present happening right in front of you."

With my lunch in hand, I hurry back to my classroom, unwrap the sandwich, and take the first bite as my mouth waters from the smell.

"Dear God…" I moan as the combination of flavors hits my tongue. I pick up my phone and instantly text Rhonan.

Me: *I get the obsession. Holy shit. SO good.*

Rhonan: *Glad to know you agree.*

Me: *I think this is the second-best thing I've ever put in my mouth.*

Rhonan: *The first better be my cock.*

Me: *Actually, I was referring to Carolina's cheesecake, but good to know your ego is intact.*

Rhonan: *Then maybe I need to feed you my cock again to remind you of how good I taste coming down your throat.*

I clench my thighs together under the desk.

Me: *You're right. I think I do need the reminder.*

Rhonan: *I definitely know that your pussy is my favorite meal now.*

Me: *Rhonan, I'm at work. You can't do this to me, get me all riled up when I'm not going to see you tonight.*

Rhonan: *I'm fucking hard right now too, baby. But just think of how good it's going to be when I get you alone Saturday night. Fuck, I miss you already.*

Me: *I miss you too.*

Rhonan: *Have fun tonight and be safe. I can't have anything happening to you. Not under my watch.*

Those aren't the exact words that have been on a loop in my mind, but for Rhonan? I'm not sure how much closer he could get to telling me how he feels.

Me: *I will. I promise. You be safe too.*

Rhonan: *Always. Have a good rest of your day, baby.*

Me: *You too.*

I place my phone on my desk and inhale the rest of the sandwich until that pest of a thought about my ex from earlier comes back to me. Picking up my phone again, I find the number I'm looking for and press call.

"Vienna?" Elliot answers after the third ring. "Everything okay?"

"I want you to send the papers, Elliot," I say while wiping my face free of sauce from the sandwich.

He blows out a breath. "Okay. Are you sure?"

My eyes land back on the clock on the computer, realizing I only have five minutes left before the end of lunch when I have to go pick up my students again from the playground.

"Yes, Elliot. Send them."

"But what about..."

"I don't care anymore. I can't hide forever, and I need to put that part of my life behind me."

I can hear the rustling of papers in the background through the phone. "Have you told Rhonan yet?"

"No, but I'm planning on it. Soon. Maybe after the wedding... I don't know." I bite my thumb. "Do you think he's going to be mad?"

"I mean, you told him that you were married, but still *being* married is a pretty important detail."

Sighing, I fight back my tears. "I know, Elliot. And I'm so sorry for putting you in the middle of this. I just needed someone who might understand and someone that could help me get out of this nightmare I was living in for far too long."

"I told you that day in my office that I do understand, Vienna, especially given who your husband is. The Cassidy family is powerful and if Cole behaved the way you said he did when you told him you were leaving, I don't blame you for being cautious. But I think if Rhonan knows, you'll feel better too. Plus, I hate keeping something like this from him."

I nod, even though he can't see me. "You're right. I promise, I'm going to tell him."

"If you need some support when you tell him, let me know. I have no problem being there for you."

"You're a good man, Elliot Thorne."

"Not so sure about that, but Rhonan is one of the best people on the planet and having you in his life has made part of him come alive again. Even though love didn't work out for me, I still want to see my friend get what he deserves."

"Thank you."

"I'll let you know when the papers have been delivered."

"Okay."

I end the call just as the bell rings, signaling the end of lunch for my students. Shoving my phone in my pocket, I grab my classroom keys and make my way outside.

"Ms. Vienna!" Ellis comes running up to me as I make my way to the spot on the blacktop where my students line up.

"It's Ms. Lewis when we're at school, remember?" I whisper to her.

"Ugh, I keep forgetting."

"It's okay."

"Are you gonna come over and paint rocks with me and Daddy tonight?"

"I can't, sweetie. I'm going to your Aunt Laney's house tonight for a girls' night."

She huffs, crossing her arms over her chest. "I don't know why I can't go if it's only for girls."

"Grown up girls," I reply right as I arrive in front of my class. "Okay, kiddos. Are you ready to go back inside?"

"Can we play a little while longer?" Johnny whines from the back of the line.

"Yeah!" One of the other boys echoes. "We were playing a game and it was really fun. I don't want to do math!"

The weather has been so rainy the past few days, even though we're at the end of May, but that means that the kids haven't been able to play outside for recess. Today the sun is shining, so maybe more time for them to run around and burn off their energy isn't a bad idea.

I turn to the other two kindergarten teachers. They shrug.

"You know what? Yeah, let's play outside for a little while longer!"

The kids scream in celebration and race back to the playground. Stacey comes up beside me. "Honestly, I was dreading going back inside with them right now, so thank you for making that decision."

"I do think they need some more time to run around. The past few days have been brutal."

"You're telling me." I stifle my yawn, and Stacey bumps her shoulder against mine. "You seem to be tired too. It wouldn't have anything to do with that handsome neighbor of yours, would it?"

My cheeks turn hot instantly. "Oh, well...uh..."

Stacey laughs. "That's what I thought. So things are going well with you two?"

I think back to the conversation I just had on the phone with Elliot, but then instantly veer to last night when Rhonan fucked me over the arm of my couch after he got home from his shift and earlier when he delivered lunch to me. My body heats up now from the memory. "They are."

"Does this mean you're sticking around? Word on the street is that we have two teachers retiring, which means there will be openings here. Not that I need to explain that to you, but it doesn't happen often in small towns like this."

"Oh." Excitement mixed with uncertainty builds in my gut. "Well, I would definitely be interested."

"Ms. Lewis!" A student named Sadie comes running up to me, yanking on my shirt.

"What's going on, Sadie?"

"There's a guy on the other side of the fence with a camera." Stacey and I both look in that direction, my eyes landing on the man she's referring to.

Wait. Is that...

"Ugh," Stacey says before I can finish my thought. But even though I'm pretty far away, I recognize the man's build and black hair with gray at the temples from the day he walked into the office at the school after our staff meeting. "This creep is back?"

"What do you mean, *back*?"

She crosses her arms over her chest, shaking her head. "He was here last week taking pictures too. I'm going to call the sheriff's office and see if they can send someone down to get rid of him."

A spike of awareness races up my spine, so I turn my back to him and fight to get my breathing under control.

This can't be a coincidence. That's the man I spoke to. He made me feel uneasy and now it's happening again.

Cole must know that I'm here.

I reach for my whistle hanging around my neck and blow on it. "Kids, it's time to go inside."

"What? Why?" Johnny yells from the top of the slide.

"Because..."

Stacey can sense the panic in my voice, so she interjects, "We're gonna watch a movie and eat popcorn!"

The screams of excitement are extreme, but her bribe does the trick. Little legs race to the buildings where the classrooms are, but Stacey stays behind with me, wrapping her arm around my shoulder while the other teacher lets the kids back inside. "Are you all right?"

"Yeah, I think so." Placing my hand over my stomach, I say, "I—I just got really nauseous."

"Did you eat something different than normal?"

"Uh, yeah actually. Maybe it just didn't agree with me?"

Stacey nods. "I get it. Happens to me all the time. I have a delicate stomach too. Why don't you go to the bathroom, take your time, and I'll keep all of the kids in my room. I have some antacids if you need them."

"I have something, but thank you. I appreciate it."

"Of course." She enters the building right before I do, glancing over my shoulder once more to see if the man is still standing outside of the fence.

But he's nowhere to be seen.

Did I imagine it?

No, Vienna. Sadie came up to you and told you about him. If a child saw him, he was there.

Just relax. There's nothing to stress about.

Cole is going to know where you're at sooner than later, and he's not the type to make a scene. It would ruin his precious reputation.

A United States senator can't have anything make him look unfit in the eyes of the public—including a wife who wants to leave him.

And yet that's the thing that I'm the most afraid of.

I might have left but I'm definitely not free. Not yet anyway.

But now I want that more than anything.

I just hope the price isn't too high to pay.

***

"This isn't working for me anymore, Cole." I'm proud of how strong I sound right now, even though I know his temper is simmering beneath the surface and one more word could make him begin to unravel.

He lifts his scotch to his lips. "Not the first time I've heard that one," he mutters.

"Well, this time I'm serious."

The asshole laughs at me. "You? Serious?" Standing from his chair, he crosses the room and gets within an inch of my face. "You think you won't change your mind tomorrow and then everything will be fine again until the next time you try to tell me what a shitty husband I've been?" He shakes his head. "How about owning the fact that you're a shitty wife who can't get pregnant with my child?"

The only thing I want to tell him right now is how grateful I am that I'm not having his baby, but I know that's the last thing I should say. And honestly? The fear of not being able to get pregnant at all haunts me every day. If I can't have children, I don't know how I'm going to handle that.

"So if you feel that way too, don't you agree this isn't working anymore?" I say instead, trying to get him to see reason.

But this man doesn't know the definition of the word. "Well, we made vows, Vienna. And I made a promise to serve my country, which means you are obligated to that promise as well."

"You don't need me to be a senator, Cole. All I am is a trophy and pawn to you anyway."

He chuckles. "Well, trophies and pawns help me win elections. Eye-candy and appearances show people that I value family and marriage." He swallows the rest of his scotch. "Which is why we need a family of our own, but you can't even seem to get that right."

"I'm done, Cole." Hoping that if I utter the words enough he'll start to hear them.

He reaches forward and grips my chin, squeezing my jaw tightly. Pain radiates up to my temple, but I fight off showing him that he's hurting me. "You're mine, Vienna. The second you signed that marriage license, I owned you. You can never leave me. You promised me forever, Vienna...and that's not something I'm ever going to let you forget. You may think you can be done with me, but that will never happen, and that's a fucking promise."

Chapter 25

Rhonan

Wedding Confessions

"Your little sister is getting married today." My father is straightening the chairs in rows on one side of the aisle in the courtyard of Hart Winery, while I'm working on the other side. All of the chairs are facing a white trellis that is covered in white and mauve roses where Fletcher and my sister will tie the knot later this afternoon.

"Yes, I know, Dad."

"All I've ever wanted is for the two of you to find a love like your mother and I had."

When I glance over at him, I can see unshed tears building in his eyes. "She's here today, you know that, right?"

He taps the center of his chest. "Trust me, I know, Rhonan. I feel her every day."

"She would be so freaking happy."

My father laughs. "Yeah, she would. She'd also be coming up behind me right now and correcting every chair that I just moved."

"You're not wrong about that."

"Just wait. Before you know it, you'll be giving Ellis away and then you'll understand why I'm so emotional today."

His words hit me square in the chest. "I'd prefer not to think about that right now, Dad."

"Avoiding it doesn't mean that it won't happen." He stands up tall again and surveys the rows. "All right, these look good."

"You know that you pay people who could have done that for us, right?"

He turns to face me. "I know, but it's what your mom would have done. Plus, it's keeping me busy. Everything is running smoothly so far, but I don't want your sister to worry."

I push a hand through my hair as I glance back at the main building of the winery where my sister, Ellis, and the rest of the girls are all getting ready in private. "I don't think she'd even care if something did go wrong, Dad."

He pats me on the shoulder. "Yeah, you're right. She and Fletcher have figured out what truly matters, and it sure as hell isn't a fancy party."

I huff out a laugh. "Yeah, a wedding does not make a marriage, right?" As I say the words, something occurs to me.

Fuck. That's how Vienna must have felt with her husband.

It makes my fucking chest ache for her—because even though I only had Sarah in my life for a few short years, our marriage was the complete opposite of what Vienna has experienced. Sarah was my best friend, she was the person I wanted to tell everything to, the person I never imagined my life without.

That's why it hurt so fucking much when I lost her—because never in a million years did I think that could be a possibility.

And now I'm realizing that Vienna is that person for me, and I'm fucking reeling from how good it feels.

"Dad?"

"Yeah, son?"

"Do you mind if I run something by you real quick?"

He studies me curiously. "Of course. Is this a conversation we can have here, or would you rather go to my office?"

"Office would probably be best."

I follow him inside, and once we're in his office, he pours us each a glass of Pappy Van Winkle. Fletcher made sure there was a bottle here for us today, even though he won't sample any of my favorite bourbon himself. The man doesn't drink after what he experienced with his father, and I can't say that I blame him for that choice.

"What's on your mind, son?" My father asks as he lifts his glass to his lips and takes a sip of the caramel liquid.

I stare into my bourbon like it might hold some wisdom I need to hear. "You remember when you told me a few months ago that I would know when it was time to move on?"

"Yes."

"Well, I think I'm ready."

His brow lifts. "You think, or you know?"

I blow out a breath. "Vienna is..."

My father chuckles. "Son, I'm not blind. I've seen the way you look at that woman."

"I'm fucking crazy about her," I admit. "But..."

"What's holding you back?"

"Elliot made a comment about how he felt like he knew Tori and then he ended up completely blindsided by her. I guess I just don't want that to happen to me too. And then naturally, I'm afraid I'll let myself dive in headfirst with her and end up devastated again."

My father stares off to the side of the room in contemplation. "It's a gift to exist, Rhonan, but there is no way to exist without experiencing some kind of suffering. Did you ever stop and think that the suffering was so you could appreciate the good?"

"No."

"Losing your mom is one of the worst pains I've ever felt. I didn't know if I could move forward, but each day got easier, and then you know what helped me really commit to moving on?"

"What?"

"It was the night you told me you were marrying Sarah. Something about that news made my entire life flash before my eyes, and I knew I didn't want to miss a second of watching you and your sister live your lives. It's not that I didn't already feel that way, but the grief was so heavy for so long, it was difficult to see through it. I was so focused on my pain that I was ignoring the joy that was still present in my life."

"That's how I've felt."

"Well, then now it's time for you to move on. Ellis deserves that. You deserve that. And so does Vienna." He leans forward in his chair. "You don't have to know everything about someone to know they're your person. That's kind of the point of being with someone—you have the pleasure of getting to know each other for the rest of your lives, potentially. There were still things I was learning about your mother up until her very last day."

"Even though you lost Mom in the end..."

"I don't regret our time together for a second," he says, answering the question I was alluding to. "I would do it all over again, even if I knew the outcome. That woman gave me love that most people never get to experience, and she gave me you and your sister." He takes a sip of his bourbon. "Suffering is part of life, Rhonan. Now the question is, are you going to keep moving forward with Vienna by your side and tackle the suffering together? Or are you going to continue to live under the dark cloud that's been hovering over you for the past five years and be alone still?"

I already know the answer to that question, but hearing this from my father today makes me feel so much more secure in my decision and feelings.

Opening myself up to someone again is the risk I have to take if I want to experience a second chance at love. I could lose Vienna too, but I don't regret my time with Sarah even though I lost her. And she gave me Ellis.

My life changed forever when that little girl came into it.

And Vienna has changed my life too.

A heavy sigh leaves my lips. "Thanks, Dad."

"I'm always here for you, son. And remember, therapy can help you process a lot of this too. I haven't pressured you about it after Sarah because I know you were busy with Ellis and finding your footing, but I think now it might be something you should consider. Out with the old thoughts and in with the new ones, you know?"

"Yeah, I think you're right."

My dad laughs as he lifts his glass to his lips. "Can't hear that enough as a parent."

"Trust me. I'm beginning to understand that feeling all too well. Ellis already thinks she knows everything."

"I'd love to tell you that it gets better, but that would be a lie."

"Yeah, I think I'd like to stay in the dark about that for just a little while longer."

Little did I know just how dark things could get.

***

"Fletcher," my sister starts to say her vows as she dabs under her eyes with a tissue. "I have loved you since I was fifteen, and I can't believe that I get to love you for the rest of our lives."

You can hear sniffles from the guests, and I can't deny that I'm getting a little choked up standing across the aisle behind Fletcher, watching my little sister battle through her vows with some emotional composure.

"You say that I'm your angel, but you are mine. You've watched over me and loved me for so long that there's no possible way we don't belong together in this life and the next. I can't wait to grow old with you, have babies with you, and show you what true love really is—because that's what you've shown me. I love you, Fletcher Jared Adams, and I can't believe that I finally get to be your wife."

My eyes find Vienna in the audience, who is wiping away tears under her eyes as well.

Fuck, *I* want those things with *her* too.

Goddamn it, I'm so in love with her.

"Laney," Fletcher starts, clearing his throat and pulling me back to the moment as my entire body ignites with awareness. I have to fight the urge to rush over to Vienna and tell her everything that's on my mind, because if I did that during my sister's wedding, she'd never forgive me—personal epiphany or not.

"Shit, I'm sorry. You're making me cry, angel, and I told you not to," Fletcher explains. Everyone lets out a laugh, but Laney sticks her tongue out at her future husband. Once the laughter has died down, he finds his footing again. "You know better than anyone how you saved me when I didn't think life would ever be kind. Your strength, your kindness, your love—it's everything I need. As long as I have you by my side, I know that we're golden. You have me—mind, body, and soul. I am yours, always have been, and always will be. I can't wait to watch you sign your name as Laney Adams. It's been a long time coming, and today is the start of our forever."

There is not a dry eye in the vicinity, including my own.

Something about watching my baby sister and one of my best friends promise to love each other is making every piece of the puzzle that's been taunting me for months slide right into place.

They're standing here today, making vows to each other with no clue how the rest of their lives will go. Something could happen to either one of them at the drop of a hat, and yet, they're declaring their faith in each other in front of their family and closest friends, telling us out loud that they're willing to take the risk.

So why can't I do that too?

I can't believe I ever doubted what I feel for Vienna, or how hard I've fought it. Funny how when you see someone else find their happiness, it can inspire you to find your own.

I know that tomorrow is never guaranteed. Life has taught me that plenty of times already. But I'm tired of living in fear or letting days and years slip away when the woman I met a little over two months ago is opening my eyes to so many possibilities for the future.

I loved Sarah, and I always will. But she's not here anymore.

Vienna is here though, and her soul is the one I want a chance at a future with now.

As soon as the officiant pronounces Laney and Fletcher husband and wife, cheering erupts, echoing throughout the courtyard of the winery. Guests settle in for a cocktail hour while the wedding party and family take photos, and then the outdoor reception starts. My sister wanted the reception to be outside, which was a risky decision, given you can never be too sure what kind of weather Blossom Peak can have during the first week of June.

But my mom must have pulled some strings upstairs because the skies are clear, stars twinkle in the distance, and there's not even a breeze to disturb the beautiful night.

When it's time for speeches, Dilynne proves she is and always will be, a tough act to follow. I'm sitting next to Fletcher at the head table, waiting for my turn. But my eyes keep moving over to check on Vienna and Ellis. My daughter is sitting on Vienna's lap eating her fourth cupcake with rainbow sprinkles, but tonight? I'm just going to let it happen. Cavities be damned.

Fuck. Being in love is making me soft about my morals.

"Fletcher Adams, I am happy to tell you that your nickname of Lucifer has officially been retired. Now, I'm going to call you Mr. Laney Hart." People raise their glasses in the air while laughing. "I always had faith that you and my best friend would find your way back to each other, but I didn't realize that when you did, it would mean having to trust you to take care of her." Dilynne clears her throat as she gets choked up. "Just know, that you may be her husband now, but this girl is my person and always will be. I'm willing to share her, though, and the only reason why I'm okay with this marriage is because I know you'll protect her as fiercely as I would. You two make people like me believe in love—because if she can go from calling you Lucifer to her husband, then there's hope for the rest of us."

"I knew I shouldn't have let her make a speech," my sister mutters on the other side of Fletcher, laughing through her tears.

Dilynne lets a tear slip free, which shocks those of us close to her. The woman is a professional at keeping her emotions in check, but I know that her love for my sister is what's making this night even more special.

"I love you both so much. Congratulations!"

The guests break out into applause and then Dilynne passes me the mic. "Your turn, Rhonan. Good luck."

I take my spot up at the front of the table and dart my eyes around, only to land on the two most important people in my life.

"Go, Daddy!" Ellis shouts, making everyone laugh once more.

Clearing my throat, I think back to what I wanted to say. "When I first found out about Fletcher and my sister, you could say I wasn't exactly thrilled." Everyone chuckles. "But when Laney explained their connection, I understood. It's rare in life to find someone you can lean on when times get tough. Life is going to test you, but with the right person by your side, you know you'll make it through." I swallow roughly. "I wish that Mom were here to see your love for one another. She would be happier than anyone else for the two of you."

"I love you," Laney murmurs just loud enough for me to hear.

"But what I want you to know is that the two of you have given me hope that everyone can get a second chance at happiness, and that's what I hope you build together—a life that may not be perfect but is full of love and contentment." I raise my glass in the air. "To Laney and Fletcher!"

"To Laney and Fletcher!" All of the guests repeat my toast and then my sister and her new husband share their first dance. When my dad and Laney share their dance, all I can think about is that one day, that will be me and Ellis.

My chest grows tight as I grab her and twirl her in my arms on the side of the dance floor. Once the DJ starts playing dance music for the rest of the night, I finally get a chance to find Vienna in the crowd alone as she brings a flute of champagne to her lips. "Hey, beautiful." I kiss her collarbone exposed by the off-the-shoulder cut of her sky-blue dress that highlights every one of her curves and breathe her in, letting peace wash over me.

"Right back at you, handsome." She spins to face me and wastes no time pressing her mouth to mine. "Mmm, that was nice."

"Enjoy nice me right now because later? I plan for us both to be really fucking naughty."

She shivers in my arms and then holds out her hand to me, lifting her pinky. "Pinky promise?"

I hook my pinky with hers and we seal the deal. She drains her glass of champagne and says, "Dance with me." It's more of a command than a question, but Vienna doesn't falter as she sets her empty glass down on a nearby table. She lets me take her hand in mine, and then I guide her to the dance floor, enveloping her in my arms as we sway to the slow song.

"This wedding is gorgeous," she says. "It reminds me of what mine looked like, only I know that this marriage will have a happy ending."

"I know my mom is happy that Laney chose to get married here. She'd have been thrilled. This was one of her main goals for the winery."

"Your speech made me cry, especially when you mentioned her." Vienna runs her nails through my hair on the side of my head. "I can only hope that she's smiling down at you and your family today."

"Would you ever consider getting married again?" I ask, nervous to know the answer but confident that I might.

Her eyes meet mine with no hesitation. "With the right person, yes. Would you?"

"With the right person," I echo her sentiment before clearing my throat. "Look, there's, uh...something I need to say to you."

She inhales deeply and then blows it out. "There's something I need to tell you too." A pinch in her brow develops, but I don't want to waste another second without letting this woman know how I feel about her.

"Can I go first?"

"Sure."

Taking a deep breath, I brace myself for everything I need to say. Stroking the side of her face, I bounce my eyes back and forth between hers. "I've fallen for you, Vienna." I can hear the sharp intake of her breath, but I keep going. "The moment I picked you up from the ground in that bar, you've had my attention. But the truth is, *you're* the one who's picked *me* up. You've helped me see through the clouds and find the rainbows. It's time that I surrender to this thing between us and give us a shot at a future, and the only person I want to try again with is *you*."

"Rhonan..." Her eyes are filled with unshed tears.

"I can see a life with you. And I know we have things to conquer first and so much to still learn about each other, but I'm in this, Vienna." I lift her hand to my lips, kissing the top of it and then the inside of her wrist. "It's you and me, baby. And Ellis, if you'll have us. Just tell me that you want this too..."

She swallows roughly as a slow smile spreads across her lips. "God, I do. I want that too."

"Thank fuck," I breathe out as I rest my forehead against hers. "That's all I needed to hear."

"But Rhonan..."

I lift my head. "Yeah." Then it clicks. "Oh yeah, you had something you wanted to tell me?"

She nods, biting her bottom lip nervously. "Yes. I just... Shit, this isn't where I wanted to tell you this."

"Tell me what, Vienna?"

And then she says three words to me, but they're not the ones I was thinking of.

"I'm still married."

Chapter 26

Vienna

Putting the Pieces Together, But There Are Two Pieces Missing

"You're still married?" Rhonan is pacing back and forth across the floor of the same wine cellar he dragged me to a few weeks ago, but the energy in the room is much different than it was that day.

After I blurted out my confession to him on the dance floor, he made sure Ellis was occupied and being looked after, then he brought me down here so we could talk privately.

"Legally? Yes. But Rhonan, my marriage has been over for a very long time."

"So, the man you told me about last week on our date is *still* your husband?"

"Yes," I say, my reply direct and my eyes locked on his. I'm not trying to make excuses. This is my fault for letting our relationship get this far without telling him the truth. But after hearing his words on the dance floor, the life he envisions for us and his daughter? I couldn't hold my truth back any longer.

He shakes his head, trying to put the pieces together.

"Vienna..."

"I hired Elliot to draw up a petition of divorce for me, Rhonan—because when I left Cole, I did it without telling him. Well, I kind of told him, but he wouldn't listen."

"What do you mean?"

I take a steadying breath. "I told you that I got married fast, but as soon as we became husband and wife, something shifted in Cole. I told myself it was normal, that wedded bliss was a fairy tale, but Lydia picked up on it and slowly started trying to get me to see what was right in front of my face."

"Which was?"

"That my husband was a selfish asshole who didn't deserve me." Rhonan's jaw ticks, but I continue. "I made excuses for his behavior all the time, and then when he approached me about having a baby, I thought maybe he was starting to change. Starting a family was something I've always wanted, but after months of trying to get pregnant with no success, he started to get mean."

"What the fuck?"

I nod. "Yeah. I can't begin to express how frustrating it is to want something so badly and fear that it will never happen. Even though looking back now, I'm grateful that I never got pregnant with Cole's child, I'm not sure if I ever will. The second I suggested going to see a doctor, he flipped out and grabbed me—hard. Lydia saw the bruises that he left and she flipped out on me. That's when I think I finally started to realize he was not a good person and things between us were never going to change."

His eyes find the ground as he thinks. "Wow, this is a lot to take in."

"There's more." When he looks back up at me, I continue. "Right after Cole grabbed me the first time, Lydia told me about her diagnosis. She begged me to leave him, but I couldn't fathom dealing with him and losing my best friend at the same time, so I dealt with his mentally, emotionally, and verbally abusive behavior for a few more months."

He finally closes the distance between us, cupping the side of my face. "You are so fucking strong, do you know that?"

I shake my head. "No, I'm not, Rhonan. I'm a coward, and I'm so mad at myself for not being strong enough to leave him earlier when I knew things were wrong, but I didn't want to believe it. I didn't want my marriage to be a failure. Plus, when you're married to a U.S. senator, divorce isn't an easy choice."

His eyes widen. "Wait, what did you just say?"

Sighing, I close my eyes and mentally kick myself. "Shit. I—I was getting to that part."

"Cole... Cole..." I can almost see the moment that everything clicks in his mind. "Fuck. So your husband is..."

"Cole Cassidy," I finish for him. "A senator for West Virginia and a horrible human being."

His eyebrows draw together again. "But your last name..."

"Lydia created a new identity for me before she died. It was delivered to me a few weeks after her funeral. She wanted to protect me and give me a shot at a new life, so she thought of everything—my license, passport, teaching certificate, birth certificate..." Shaking my head, I say, "She wasn't just looking out for me when she was alive, but she gave me the means to leave even after she was gone. And I figured the farther I got from West Virginia, the less risk of being recognized." I hold onto the lapels of his suit jacket a little tighter. "I'm so sorry that I hid all of this from you, but as soon as I met you, I just wanted to be *me*—the real me. Not Vienna Cassidy, not Cole Cassidy's wife, and not the shell of a woman I was when I was with him. You allowed me to be the person I forgot was hiding underneath all of the baggage I collected during my marriage."

"What about your parents? Couldn't your family have helped you?"

"My father is a judge in the court system, and my mother spends her days drinking at the country club to avoid the fact that my dad has two mistresses. Trust me, I would not have gotten any sympathy from them."

Rhonan blows out a breath before cupping the back of my head and holding me to his chest. "I'm so fucking sorry, Vienna."

"What are you sorry for?"

His head moves back and forth against mine. "For everything that you've gone through."

"Me? You've gone through so much more than I have, and yet..." I cut myself off. "Thank you, but I should have been honest from the beginning."

He cups my jaw and forces me to look at him. "I understand why you weren't."

"You deserve honesty, and I promise going forward that you'll have it from me. My past is messy, but I'm trying to move on. It's the only thing left to do."

"I understand that more than you know, but also? I really want to beat the shit out of your soon-to-be ex-husband."

Laughter bubbles out of me as the adrenaline running through my veins finally starts to subside. "Trust me, I would love to see that."

Framing my face in his hands, he says, "You're safe with me. You know that, right?"

"I do."

"You've changed my life, Vienna. And even though we've both suffered, it's time for us to have someone to handle the shitty parts of life with."

"Rhonan Hart... I don't know if I'll ever be able to explain just how much you mean to me."

Our lips meet and a wave of relief rushes through me. "Fuck, I need you." Rhonan mumbles against my lips. "I want..."

"Yes..."

Rhonan backs us up against the stacks of wine barrels and spins me so my back is to his chest. "Lift your dress." I do as I'm told as I hear the sound of him unbuttoning his slacks and pulling down his zipper. "Jesus, your ass is so fucking perfect." His hand connects with my skin, leaving a sting behind before he pulls at the strings of my thong on each hip, snapping it from my body.

I glance over my shoulder to find him tucking my useless underwear into the pocket of his pants as he pumps his cock. "Will you stop ruining my underwear?"

"Just stop wearing them." Dragging the head of his cock through my pussy to test my readiness, he finds me soaking already. "Fuck, your pussy is already wet for me." He lines himself up and pushes in, the sensation so tight from the angle we're at, but the heels I'm wearing are making our height difference work. I use the barrels in front of me for leverage as he pumps in and out of me. "God, I don't think I will ever get enough of the way your pussy squeezes my cock."

"Don't stop, Rhonan."

His hand travels over my shoulder and up the back of my neck, burying in my hair and tightening around the strands just hard enough that he can pull me back to him. Our mouths meet as he continues to slide in and out of me, over and over, letting me feel every silky inch of him.

I can feel my wetness drip down the inside of my thighs. My chest is heaving as I struggle to take in air. And Rhonan's eyes are locked on mine as he holds me to his chest.

His other hand grips my hip possessively as he thrusts, over and over, taking us both higher. I reach behind his neck and pull his mouth to mine over my shoulder again, mumbling, "I'm close."

"Rub that perfect little clit and get there so I can fill you with my cum."

His words ignite a spark in me as I bring my hand back and reach beneath my dress, finding my clit and rubbing in circles, building the friction I need to come.

"Fuck, Vienna. You're dripping."

"I'm almost there."

"Shit. Fuuuuck…"

"Rhonan!"

We shatter at the same time, gasping for air as pleasure rushes through both of us. He holds me to his chest, still buried inside of me as we let every tremor run its course. "You're mine now, Vienna. And I promise, I won't let anything happen to you."

It's as if he was testing the universe—because I had no idea just how wrong he could be, and neither did he.

***

"I want to paint a really big rock!" Ellis nearly tips the water cup over on the table as she leaps from her chair at Rhonan's dining room table.

"Well, let's find one in the basket."

She shakes her head as she moves from the dining room to the kitchen where I'm standing at the sink. We just finished eating spaghetti that I made, and Ellis naturally wanted to paint rocks with me after dinner.

It's Monday night, and as Rhonan asked me, I'm looking after Ellis for him while he's on shift. After Laney and Fletcher's wedding Saturday night, where I finally confessed everything to him, I wish I could say that I felt better about our future. On some levels, I do—the man accepted everything I had to tell him with such understanding that I became emotional when we lay in bed together that night. He held me as I let months of pain, grief, and anger pass through me. He assured me that he wanted to be responsible for keeping me safe now.

But today the divorce papers were delivered to Cole, which means my anxiety has been through the roof. I've even felt nauseous while wondering what his reaction would be. Honestly, I expected a phone call from him, but my phone has been quiet all day except for a few texts from Rhonan here and there.

"Ms. Vienna?" Ellis says, pulling on the bottom of my shirt and reminding me that she's on a mission.

"Yes, sweetie?"

"Can we please go outside and find a big rock? I want to paint it to look like me, and then we can put it in your backyard so Roscoe has a friend at your house."

"Aw, I love that idea." Reminders from Rhonan about staying home enter my mind, but I don't see any harm in walking around the neighborhood. "Okay, get your shoes and socks on."

"Yay!" Ellis runs to the front door and slips on her new *Frozen* Crocs that Rhonan got for her. She wears them any chance she can get. In a matter of seconds, she's right back beside me. "I'm ready."

"I can see that."

"Ms. Vienna?" Ellis grabs my hand as I reach for my cell phone on the counter, slip it into my pocket, and follow her lead to the front door.

"Yes, Ellis?"

"I'm really glad you're my teacher."

"Aw, me too, sweet girl." We stand at the edge of the sidewalks that line the streets in Rhonan's neighborhood and look both ways before we cross the street. Our hands remain locked as we walk down the road to an empty field nearby to hunt for a rock that Ellis deems big enough.

"And I'm glad that my daddy kissed you, even though it's gross."

I chuckle. "One day, you won't think that way."

Ellis grows quiet for a minute. "Can we make cupcakes for my mommy's birthday?"

Her question throws me for a loop. "When is your mommy's birthday?"

"June thirteenth."

"Then we should definitely make cupcakes for her birthday. Did she like cupcakes?"

"I don't know." My heart aches for her. "But I do, and your friend Lydia likes them, and since they're angels together, we should make some for them."

Swallowing down the lump in my throat, I nod. "I think so too."

"Are you gonna be my mommy?" The curiosity in her voice nearly tears my heart in two.

"No one can replace your mom, Ellis."

"But my mommy is in heaven, and I need a mommy here." She leans her head on my hip as we continue to walk, stepping along the path as the field grows closer.

My gut tells me not to respond because I'm not the one that gets to make that decision—Rhonan does. I know he said he wants a life with me, but there's still so much to figure out between the two of us, and the last thing I want to do is tell this beautiful little girl that I would love nothing more than to be her mom here on earth, and then not have that happen.

If there's anything I've learned in my twenty-eight years of life, it's that nothing is guaranteed.

Unfortunately, I don't get a chance to respond either way because a black SUV creeps up beside us, sending my pulse climbing.

I keep my head pointed straight so as not to alarm Ellis, but when I hear the window move down and the voice of the driver, every hair on my body stands up.

"Good evening, *Ms. Lewis.*"

I freeze, and Ellis nearly trips on the sidewalk beside me.

Slowly, I turn to face the man that I've seen on more than one occasion in town, and suddenly, that intuition that I was ignoring before rears its ugly head. But I don't respond.

"Lovely night for a stroll in Blossom Peak, isn't it?"

"Can I help you with something?" I manage to squeak out despite the dread filling my gut.

"You can get in the car without me having to force you," he says, his voice growing more irritated as I hear him put the car in park.

"And why would I do that?"

He lifts a gun just above the window so I can see it, but I stand in front of Ellis to hopefully prevent her from seeing it. "So I don't have to use this."

"She's five," I whisper. "I can't leave her."

He nods. "She comes too then."

"Ms. Vienna?" Ellis peers around me. "Who is that man?"

"Uh, he's a...friend. We're gonna get in the car with him for a little bit, okay?"

Nodding, he exits the SUV and unlocks the back door, opening it for me and Ellis to enter as my thoughts start to spiral and my eyes land on the gray at his temples standing out against his jet-black hair.

Oh my God, how am I going to get us out of this? Where is he going to take us?

And why is my location on my phone off in an instance when I wish it weren't?

Ellis peers back at me as I help her up. "But what about the rock?"

"We can find a rock later, okay?" Ellis jumps into the SUV and then I follow behind her, nearly falling because every part of my body is shaking right now.

"But I don't have my booster chair," Ellis says as she slides further into the vehicle.

"It's okay, Ellis. Just—just sit down for me, okay?"

"Ms. Vienna... I'm scared." The terror in her voice makes me grow emotional until I take my seat next to her and hear the car door shut.

But when I look up to the front of the vehicle, I see the man I was hoping I'd never have to come face to face with again sitting in the passenger seat—and then true nausea builds in my stomach because there's no telling what might happen to us now.

Chapter 27

Rhonan

My Worst Nightmare Times Two

"I don't think I could ever get sick of Carolina's baked goods." Brody shoves the last bite of his pizza roll into his mouth. He's not even done chewing his first one before he reaches for another.

Jordan nods. "Especially these damn pizza rolls. I could eat them every day."

"You'd get sick of them after a while," Brody interjects. "Right, Rhonan?"

I'm so immersed in my computer that I wasn't really paying attention to their conversation. Glancing up from my monitor, I make eye contact with Brody. "What?"

"Dude...you all right? You've had your head buried in your computer for hours."

Shaking off the hypnosis I feel like I've been under, I lean back in my desk chair and drag my hand down my face. "Yeah, just...got a lot on my mind." My phone vibrates next to me, so I pick it up from my desk and see my sister is calling me. "Sorry, guys. I've got to take this." I stand from my desk as I answer. "Hey. Aren't you supposed to be leaving for your honeymoon right about now?"

"Yes. We're on our way to the airport as we speak, but we just tried video calling with Vienna so we could ask Ellis what she wants from Bora Bora and she didn't answer."

"Okay, well, try calling again."

"I did, Rhonan." Laney clears her throat. "The first time it kept ringing, but then the second time it went straight to her voicemail, like she turned her phone off or something."

Awareness crawls up my spine. "She never turns her phone off... Maybe it died."

"That's what I was thinking. I—I don't want to worry you, but I just wanted to let you know. Maybe she'll answer if you call, but..."

"I'm sure everything is fine," I say, more to convince my sister than myself because my mind is spinning at the moment. "I'll try calling her and let her know that you want to talk to them, all right?"

"Okay. I love you."

"Love you too. Have a great time."

After Laney ends the call, I immediately bring up Vienna's number to call her, but unfortunately, I'm met with her voicemail.

A bad feeling races through me. "Fuck. Something's wrong."

Brody stops chewing as he watches me slide right back up to my computer. "What do you mean?"

"Vienna isn't answering her phone. That's not like her."

He wipes his mouth with his sleeve. "Okay..."

"Hart!" Chief Banks enters the room, a worried look on his brow. "Yeah?"

"You...you need to come back here with me."

I follow him into his office and shut the door. "Chief?"

He blows out a breath. "I finally got an ID on that man that Mrs. Higgins was complaining about."

"All right. That's great, but why are you just telling me and not the other guys?"

Our eyes lock. "He'd been walking everywhere until this morning, when she saw him driving a black SUV. And then one of the office ladies at the school reported that the car was parked in front of the school virtually all day."

Sweat forms on my brow the longer he talks. "Get to the point, Chief. Please."

"Have you spoken to Vienna today?"

"Earlier."

"What about now?"

"Respectfully, sir. What the fuck are you trying to tell me?"

He inhales deeply and says, "Your girlfriend isn't exactly who she seems, and the man who's been hanging around town might have something to do with her."

***

By the time Chief Banks finishes telling me about Vienna's husband and how the guy snooping around town is a private investigator, my stomach is churning so hard I can barely stand up straight.

"Well, I knew about her husband, but the rest? How do we know this guy was here for Vienna?"

"He's from the D.C. area. I called a few of my contacts out there and showed his picture once I had a decent one from Mrs. Higgins. Then when I started to look at where he spent the most time, several of the office ladies and teachers at the school recognized him, and I started to put two and two together."

"Wait. He's been at the school?"

"Yes. That's what really startled me, especially after what happened to Hailey Zachmann." Shaking his head, he says, "I don't ever want to relive something like that again."

I pull out my phone and try calling Vienna again with no luck. "Chief, Vienna isn't answering her phone."

His face grows pale. "Please tell me you're joking."

"No. And she's at home with Ellis. I need—"

"Don't say another word. Go. I'll send Brody as back-up just in case."

"Thank you."

Brody and I race out to our cruisers as fast as we can after I tell him that his assistance is urgent, and then we flip on the sirens and speed across town.

I know I joked with Vienna about how getting to put on the sirens in my cruiser has always been something that brings me joy, but right now? I feel nothing but dread as I close in on my house.

I'm trying to convince myself that my paranoia is just rearing its ugly head, but deep down, I know something is very wrong, and I'm not going to believe it for myself until I see with my own two eyes that my daughter and the woman I love are okay.

Every cell in my body is vibrating. My palms are sweaty and my chest is so tight that breathing is difficult.

Fuck. I can't lose them too.

I spin my cruiser into my driveway and barely park before I leap from the vehicle and barge inside, finding the front door unlocked but the house silent. "Vienna? Ellis?" With no sign of them anywhere, I reach for my gun on my hip, lift it into position, and slowly walk down the hallway, uneasy about what I might find.

But I find nothing.

They're not in my room or Ellis's.

They're not in the backyard.

Maybe they went to Vienna's house?

When I exit my house, I find Brody standing watch in the front yard. "Anything?"

"No. I'm going to Vienna's house to see if they're there."

When I arrive at her door, I don't bother knocking, entering the house with my gun poised just in case. But the silence is deafening, eerie even.

Then Roscoe scratches at the back door, begging to be let in. I head for the sliding door as I return my gun to my hip and let him inside. "Hey, buddy. Where's your mom?"

He runs to the front door, scratching to go out there.

This dog and I haven't exactly seen eye-to-eye since I've met him, but I know he might be my only shot at figuring out what happened to Vienna and my daughter at this moment.

"All right, let's go for a walk."

I grab his leash from the hook by the door, attach it to his collar, and open the front door.

"We're walking the dog right now?" Brody calls out to me.

"He loves the girls. I'm hoping he might be able to pick up their scent, or something."

Roscoe starts sniffing away from the house and down the sidewalk. He doesn't stop to pee or doddle, though. No. He's got something on his nose and he's following it with a passion. We walk for a few blocks before he stops completely, fixated on something on the sidewalk.

"What did you find, buddy?"

But when I lean down and pick up the rainbow charm that's on the ground—the same one that I know is from my daughter's new shoes I bought her a few weeks ago—panic washes over me.

And when my eyes land on the smashed cell phone on the street right near it, I have to fight not to collapse onto the ground.

Instead, I lift my radio from my chest and immediately call into it.

"AMBER alert. Missing child. Ellis Hart, age five, last seen with Vienna Lewis, age twenty-eight, also a missing person."

Chapter 28

Vienna

Temper Tantrums & A Lucky Rock

"You're a bad man." Ellis is sitting next to me on the couch, holding my hand but beyond irritated as Cole paces the room in front of us.

The man who was driving the SUV is outside of the cabin keeping watch, and all I've been able to think about is how long it might be before someone realizes we're missing.

Cole's minion took my phone and smashed it to the ground before he sped down the street and toward the mountains that surround Blossom Peak.

For a couple of months, those mountains felt like a safety net, but right now, they feel like a death trap.

Don't think like that, Vienna. Cole may have a gun, but he probably doesn't know how to use it. Lord knows you've never seen him fire one.

Not sure if that's a good or bad thing at this moment.

Cole leans closer to Ellis, glaring at her. "Yeah, well you're probably a rotten child."

"Don't talk to her like that!"

White light fills my vision as the butt of Cole's gun slams into my temple. "Don't fucking talk at all, you whore!"

It takes me a few seconds to process what happened, and when I do, I'm looking up at Cole from the floor.

"Keep your hands to yourself!" Ellis yells at him.

"Shut the fuck up!"

My hand lands on the knot forming on the side of my head, but I try to refocus and keep my eyes on Ellis. I swear, if anything happens to her, I'll never forgive myself—and I know that Rhonan will never forgive me either.

This is my fault.

I had a feeling Cole wouldn't take being served the divorce papers well. I just never imagined he was capable of something like this.

Yeah, well, I think we've established you didn't know your husband very well already, haven't we, Vienna?

Ellis drops to the ground beside me. "Ms. Vienna..."

"I'm okay, sweetie," I manage to croak out as my eyes continue to water. But then I look up at Cole. "So what's your plan here, Cole? Just hit me since you never got the chance to while we were married?"

He pulls me up from the floor by my hair, making me shriek. "Did you honestly think that I would let you leave me? That I wouldn't have you followed? You left your phone at home, but I have money and connections, Vienna. I've known where you were for a while. I have to hand it to you though...the new identity was a nice touch." He yanks on my head. "I always wondered what you'd look like as a blonde."

"Fuck you." I spit in his face.

He tosses me back onto the couch as Ellis climbs up beside me. Pain is radiating all over my head, but I have to stay strong for her. Plus, I have no idea how much longer Cole's temper tantrum might last, and I need to save my strength in case we get the chance to run.

This poor girl will never forget this, but I want her to remember that I was strong—for both of us.

Cole laughs. "Seems you were too busy fucking some other guy to worry about my needs."

"I told you I was done. We don't belong together."

He reaches forward and grips my chin hard. "No, Vienna. *You* will always belong to *me*. You promised me til death do us part, and that's what you'll get." When he pushes me back, he presses the gun to the center of my forehead.

Ellis screams. "No!"

"Shut up, kid!"

"My daddy has a gun. He'll shoot you!"

"Yeah, well, your daddy isn't here, now is he?" Cole cocks the gun and then leans down slightly so our eyes meet. "You went and got yourself a family here, didn't you, Vienna? Just like you fucking wanted but wouldn't give me."

I want to scream at him that he's not necessarily demonstrating his fatherly abilities right now, but I refrain. He has a gun resting against my head. The last thing I should be doing is making him angrier. "This isn't going to fix anything, Cole," I grate out instead.

"I'm Cole Cassidy. You thinking you could leave me is laughable, but at least you got to whore it around for a while before I take you back where you belong."

"Let Ellis go and I'll go home with you," I say through gritted teeth. "She doesn't deserve this. She's five, Cole."

"I don't give a shit how old she is. What am I gonna do? Release her into the fucking woods?"

"Have your minion take her back to her house. As long as she's safe, I don't care what you do with me."

Noise outside pulls his attention to the window, and for one split second, I debate reaching for the gun and attempting to take it from him, but I also don't want to risk him firing a shot and hurting the little girl that I love more than life itself.

Cole turns back to me, his eyes wide, yet dilated. "Stay put! Both of you. One wrong move, and I'll shoot you both." He heads toward the front door and steps outside, and as soon as the gun isn't pointing at me anymore, I let out the breath I was holding.

"It's okay, Ellis." I pull her into my side. "It's going to be okay."

"I want my daddy." Tears fall from her eyes as she squeezes me.

"I know. You'll be back with him soon, okay?"

There's a soft creak behind us and then the sound of a pebble bouncing across the floor draws our attention to the side.

But it's not just any pebble—it's a rock, one that Ellis and I both recognize instantly.

Ellis leaps from the couch to grab it. "It's Daddy's lucky rock!"

"What the fuck?" Cole calls out from the front of the house as he walks back through the front door far too quickly.

I turn my eyes back to him just in time to see him raise the gun and point it in Ellis's direction.

And I don't even think as I jump from the couch and leap in front of her.

Shots ring out, but I don't care.

Pain slices through my shoulder, screams echo around me, and I land on the floor with a thud before everything goes black.

And then, I see a rainbow.

Chapter 29

Rhonan

Pleas and Surprises

"Fuck!" I race over to Vienna and Ellis as blood pools on the hardwood floor beneath them. "Girls! Girls!"

"Daddy!" Ellis scrambles up from the floor and launches herself into my arms.

"Ellis, are you okay?" Pushing her back, my eyes roam over her, searching for any sign that she's been hurt.

"I'm scared, Daddy."

"I know, sweet girl. I know."

"I've got EMTs on the way," Brody announces as he puts handcuffs on Cole by the front door. "Chief has the guy out front in cuffs..."

That's when my eyes land on Vienna, lying flat on the floor, not moving.

"Brody, call Jake in here to take Ellis."

"No, Daddy!"

I take my daughter's face in my hands, shielding her from the blood all over the floor. "Ellis, I need to help Vienna, okay? She is hurt, and I need to make sure that she's okay."

"Come on, Ellis. Come with me," Jake says from behind me, pulling Ellis by her hand as she fights him.

Her tiny voice rings out as I watch her leave. "Daddy!" My eyes lock on hers as Jake lifts her from the ground, her legs kicking and her screams growing louder as he carries her away.

"It's okay, Ellis. I need to help Vienna right now, okay?"

"No, Daddy!"

"I love you!" I yell out to her, keeping the image of her alive and safe in my head before focusing on saving the other girl I love.

Reality clicks back on. "Shit, Vienna! Vienna!" Blood is pouring from her upper chest, right below her collarbone. "Vienna..." I rip off my shirt, so I can apply pressure to help stop the bleeding. "Vienna, baby. Please say something."

But as my hands make fast work of pressing my shirt around her upper body, her skin goes white, her mouth falls open, and I fear that the universe would be so cruel to test my strength yet again by taking a third woman that I love away from me.

Luckily, a groan escapes her lips, and then the paramedics are rushing through the front door. Two of them approach Cole on the other side of the room, who's also been shot. Luckily for him, I aimed for his leg. But honestly? I don't give a fuck about him. He deserves whatever happens to him.

He fucking kidnapped my kid and the woman I love.

He doesn't deserve to live as far as I'm concerned, and he sure as fuck never deserved Vienna.

When the other two arrive near me and Vienna, they push me aside. "Let us take care of her, Rhonan." Billie, one of the paramedics I've worked with for years, says to me. "We've got it from here."

And even though I know that she's in good hands now, there is only one thing on my mind that I keep repeating over and over as I watch them load her onto a stretcher, into an ambulance, and take her to the hospital.

Please God—please, save her. I can't lose her too.

***

It's been five years since I've been in this hospital, and yet the sounds of machines beeping and people running down halls is way too fucking familiar for my comfort.

The last time I was here was supposed to be one of the best days of my life, but it was also the worst—and now, I'm scared as hell of how this day will end.

My hand hasn't left Vienna's since they put her in this room after her surgery. The bullet that Cole fired at her—the one that she dove in front of my daughter to take—lodged itself in her shoulder blade. But by the grace of God, it missed her heart by an inch. She also has a concussion and bruising on her head from where that asshole hit her with his gun.

She lost a lot of blood and has a hard road of recovery ahead of her, but she's alive.

She's still fucking here.

And all I want is for her to wake up so that I can tell her how much I love her.

I should have told her the night of the wedding, but I didn't want to scare her. Truth be told, my feelings for this woman have developed so suddenly and strongly that I still needed a minute to wrap my head around the fact that I wanted to start over with someone new too.

Looking at her now, though—so fragile in this hospital bed, beaten and bruised and fighting for her life—it makes me wonder how I could ever have doubted what this woman makes me feel.

"How's she doing?" My sister's voice startles me as she enters the room behind me.

I peer over my shoulder as I sigh. "The same. Doctor said it could be a while before she wakes up, but..."

Her hand lands on my shoulder. "She will. Give her time, Rhonan."

My eyes travel right back to Vienna's face. The early morning sunlight is peaking through the blinds as the sun starts to rise in the distance. So much time has passed since we arrived here last night, and yet? It also feels that time is passing way too fucking slowly right now.

"Time hasn't been very kind to me lately, Laney."

"I actually think it has."

"How do you figure?"

"Well, a little over two months ago you were grumpy and making it everyone else's problem. But now you're in love." She smirks down at me. "A lot can change in a short amount of time."

My shoulders fall. "I'm sorry that your honeymoon was ruined."

"You did *not* ruin my honeymoon. There is no place Fletcher and I would rather be right now."

"How's Ellis?"

"She's shaken up, but she's powering through and trying to be tough. She really wants to see Vienna though."

I shake my head. "I don't want her to see her like this. She already saw her after she was shot, but..."

"I get it. Maybe once Vienna wakes up, then Ellis can really see that she's okay…"

"That's what I'm thinking." My eyes begin to sting as I press a kiss to the top of Vienna's hand. "She took a bullet for my kid, Laney."

"I know." My sister squeezes my shoulder. "She loves her."

"I can't lose her," I croak out.

"You're not going to, Rhonan. This was all just a test, and I think you both passed with flying colors." Leaning down, she presses a kiss to the top of my head. "Do you want some food, or…"

"No, I'm good."

"You sure? You need to eat something…"

I shake my head. "I'm okay."

"All right. I'll come back later with some breakfast. Keep me posted in the meantime. Dad is gonna take Ellis today for a bit. He thought taking her to the winery and letting her boss people around might get her spirits back up."

I manage to chuckle, which makes my chest feel lighter for the first time in days. "She'll like that."

"That's what I said." Laney winks at me over her shoulder. "I love you, Rhonan. Everything is going to work out, okay?"

"Love you too, Laney."

When she shuts the door, I hang my head and rest it on top of Vienna's arm, leaning forward in this chair that is making my back ache the longer I sit here. But I welcome the pain. I'm not fucking leaving until I hear this woman's voice again.

I'm not sure how much time passes between me resting my head on the bed and a voice startling me awake, but when I hear and feel Vienna start to stir, my entire body comes alive.

"Rhonan?"

My head pops up as my eyes land on Vienna, her eyes still closed but there's a pinch in her brow that wasn't there before. "Vienna, baby?"

Her eyes start to flutter open and when they land on mine, I nearly choke on the lump in my throat. "Rhonan...Is Ellis?"

"She's fine, baby. You—you saved her."

Her lips curl up as she starts to cry. "I—"

I stand from the chair so fast and press my lips to hers, cutting her off. The warmth of her mouth comforts me, reminding me that she's still here. "Fuck, Vienna. You have no idea how fucking terrified I was when I realized that you two were gone."

"I'm sorry..." she croaks out, clearing her throat as she groans from her movements. Her arm is in a sling and her head must be pounding.

I reach behind me to the side table and pick up the cup of water with a straw, letting her take a few sips. "Easy does it. Not too much."

Once she's satisfied, I set the cup back down and scoot my chair closer to her bed, taking my seat again but keeping her hand in mine, right next to my lips. "I'm so fucking happy that you're awake."

"Was I..."

"Cole shot you. Well, he was aiming for Ellis but you freaking jumped in front of her."

"He never would have been here if it weren't for me, Rhonan. I'm so sorry."

I reach up and brush her hair from her face. "You have nothing to be sorry for. He is the one who spun out of control."

"Is he..."

"I shot him in the leg at the same time he fired at you. He's stable, but he'll be going to prison for a long time, Vienna. You won't have to worry about him ever again."

Tears flow down her face. "God, I've made so many mistakes, Rhonan, but I think I've finally learned something too." She reaches up to wipe her tears away. "Jealousy feels a lot like love, until you experience trust. Lydia said that to me once when she was trying to convince me to leave Cole, and I didn't want to listen at the time. But she's right. I've never felt trust and safety with anyone like I do with you. You trusted me with Ellis, and I didn't want to let you down."

"You didn't. You took a fucking bullet for my daughter, Vienna. You saved her."

"I love that little girl."

"She loves you too." I take a deep breath and then on an exhale admit, "And so do I. Fuck." I choke down the sob that's threatening to leave my throat as I hang my head. "I should have told you a million times before. I just didn't want to rush this—"

"I love you too," she says, cutting me off. My head lifts and our eyes connect, both full of tears. "I think I have since that first night."

"I love you so fucking much, Vienna Lewis."

"Well, it's actually Cassidy..."

I shake my head. "You'll never be that man's wife to me, and someday, your last name will be Hart."

Her lips curl up slightly. "Is that so?"

"Yes." I bring her hand to my mouth again. "But no more secrets, okay?"

"I promise."

"You should have told me about the guy that was following you."

"I know, but I thought it was just my paranoia."

"Well, thank God other people around town picked up on it because Chief was already watching this man. He's the one who made the connection between you and him. The day you were kidnapped is when all of the pieces started coming together. And thank God I put that tracker in Ellis's bracelet..."

"Wait, what?"

I rub the back of my neck. "When Ellis went missing that day at your house, it freaked me out so bad that I researched ways to keep track of your kids. Some people suggested using bracelets with location trackers, so that's why I bought Ellis the *Frozen* bracelet to match her *Frozen* Crocs. There's a tracking device in the snowflake charm in the center of her bracelet. I knew she'd never take it off, so it made me feel more confident that heaven forbid anything were to happen to her, I'd be able to find her." I blow out a breath. "That's why I was able to find you guys so quickly, and thank God for that."

"I'm sorry, Rhonan. I never thought Cole would snap like he did." She takes a deep breath. "I've been trying to keep my old life out of my new one. Then I met you and everything changed, and…"

I cut off her words as I lean down and press my mouth to hers. Our tongues touch and the nerves that have been humming in my chest since she was missing finally start to melt away.

Vienna clings to me with her good arm, savoring this kiss, and showing me that everything is going to be okay.

A throat clearing behind us forces us to part. When I look over my shoulder, I see the doctor standing there with a smirk on her face. "Sorry to interrupt, but the monitors were going off, so I assumed our patient was awake."

I take my seat back in my chair, bringing her hand to my mouth again. "She is. Sorry, I just needed a moment with her alone."

"I understand." The doctor walks further into the room with a nurse accompanying her. "Well, I'm Dr. Adler. How are you feeling, Vienna?"

Vienna winces as she tries to sit up higher in the bed, but I leap from my chair and help her instead. With her arm strapped to her body, she can't push herself up. "Not gonna lie, I'm in pain."

"Well, that's to be expected. With your condition, we are more limited in pain management options, but—"

Vienna clears her throat. "What condition?"

The doctor glances at me. "Are you okay if I discuss this in front of Mr. Hart?"

My eyes meet hers before she looks back at the doctor. "Yes, of course."

"You're pregnant, Ms Lewis, which is why we could give you more for the pain..."

Vienna gasps. "Wait. What? I'm—I'm pregnant?"

The doctor glances between the two of us. "Yes. Around five weeks, but I'm sorry." She clears her throat. "I wasn't aware that you didn't know. It is really early..."

Vienna and I lock eyes at the same time, and my heart is thumping so wildly that it takes me a minute to process everything. But when I see Vienna's tears slide down her face and her smile form, the same excitement she feels slams into me at the same time. "Oh my God," she whispers. "Rhonan, I..."

"You're pregnant."

She shakes her head. "I had no clue. Oh my God, this is crazy..."

I rest my forehead on hers, breathing her in as excitement and fear rush through me. "Fuck, I love you."

"It hadn't even occurred to me that I missed my period last week..."

"Well, I want you to know that we monitored the baby during the surgery and everything looks good," the doctor interjects. "The development is right on track as well for how far along you are, and in a few, I can have the doctor from the OBGYN department that monitored you come in and speak with you about your next steps. Luckily, the gunshot wound and surgery wasn't too stressful on the baby, so in my opinion, your pregnancy should proceed without any complications, but the OBGYN will be able to go into more detail for you."

Vienna is crying and shaking her head. "I'm sorry. I'm still wrapping my head around the fact that I'm pregnant."

The doctor laughs. "I understand. Let Nurse Amy take your vitals, I'm going to assess you as well, and then we'll leave you two alone to discuss this privately. But congratulations."

After the doctor and nurse leave, I sit on the edge of Vienna's bed, staring down at her and toying with her bottom lip. "You're pregnant."

"I am."

"Your worst fear was not being able to have kids."

"You remember that?"

"I remember everything about you, baby." My hand finds her stomach, pressing over it lightly. "Ellis is gonna be a big sister."

Vienna smiles. "She is."

"I love you, Vienna."

Her eyes lift to mine. "I love you too, Rhonan."

"I promise, I will do everything in my power to keep you safe."

"I know you will."

"And our child."

"I know that too."

"There's so much to figure out, but right now, I want a minute with just the two of us." I press a kiss to her forehead. "To remind myself that this is real. That you're alive." My heart is thrashing violently in my ribcage, my breathing strong, just like my grip on Vienna. "Is that okay?"

She nods as I lean down on the bed next to her and guide her to rest her head on my chest. "That sounds perfect."

And that's where we stay for so long that Vienna drifts off to sleep. But I keep holding her, thanking God that I didn't lose this woman too. Instead, I'm being given a second chance at a family, and this time, I'm going to search for and hold onto the feeling that it's going to all work out.

Chapter 30

Vienna

Coming Home

"You guys really didn't need to go to all of this trouble." Walking into Rhonan's house with him by my side after five days in the hospital, I'm greeted by his entire friend group, his father, and Joanne, who has tears in her eyes. There's a banner hung above the mantel that says *Welcome Home* and get-well-soon balloons are stacked in the corner of the living room by the TV.

Then my eyes land on the tower of onion rings from Blossom Brews on the table, and I nearly start crying right there on the spot.

Laney approaches me and pulls me in for a hug, being careful not to squeeze my arm in the sling too hard. "Are you kidding? You took a bullet for my niece. It's the least we could do."

"Vienna is my hero!" Ellis announces to the room, her outburst met with emotional laughter. She runs up to me and then stops herself before she collides with my legs. Rhonan explained that I was going to be recovering from my injuries for a while, so she's been really sweet about wanting to be gentle with me and help me do whatever she can.

I seriously love this little girl and can't wait to see how she's going to act with her little brother or sister.

Rhonan and I haven't told anyone about the baby yet because naturally, I'm terrified that something might happen and I lose it. In my eyes, it's a miracle that I'm even pregnant. I'll never know the true reason why I wasn't able to conceive up until this point, but I just want to celebrate that it's real instead of worrying about everything that could go wrong.

Rhonan respected my request to keep it to ourselves, even though he's done nothing but hover over my stomach for the past five days in the hospital, talking to our unborn child and making me fall in love with him even more.

He's being the man I always wanted Cole to be, but now I know that Cole was never going to be that man—and I'm so grateful things worked out this way.

The sheriff's department and the FBI came to the hospital to drill me about Cole and what transpired, and I was assured that Cole Cassidy would be staring at the inside of a prison cell for the rest of his life.

That night, I think I slept better than I have in the six years that I was married to him. Cole begrudgingly signed the divorce papers in the hospital before he was transported back to D.C. to the prison where he will await his sentencing. I declined the opportunity to appear.

I don't want to be involved in that man's life anymore.

I'm ready to close that chapter and start this new one with Rhonan Hart—my protector, my lover, and my best friend.

Lydia would have loved him so much, but I think she had a hand in bringing us together anyway.

When I woke up in the hospital after passing out on Rhonan's chest, the first thing I saw outside through the window was a rainbow—and that's how I knew that she was with me.

I'm finally getting the life I've always wanted and deserve—something I know is going to take me a while to accept, but I'm going to continue to fight hard for that.

Because when you have people in your life who bring out the best in you and make you feel alive, you do everything in your power to hang on to them.

I've been going through the motions for far too long, and now it's time for me to embrace the joy, something that Rhonan and I are going to work on together. One of the first things he suggested when I woke up was that me, him, and Ellis go to therapy to help process what we all experienced, but also so that he can be the best version of himself for me.

And I know that my past relationship is going to haunt me too if I don't do something to move past it. So, the idea was a no-brainer to agree to.

"Hell yeah, she's your hero!" Dilynne shouts, lifting her glass of champagne in the air. "Cheers to that." She reaches for a half-full glass and then hands it to me. "Want a glass to celebrate you busting out of the hospital finally?"

Rhonan and I lock eyes at the same time. "No, I'm okay."

Dilynne rolls her eyes. "Jesus, what's wrong with everyone today. We should be celebrating that Vienna's alive and freaking took a bullet for Ellis. But nooo... Laney won't even take a drink and my brother said it's too early for champagne. Fletcher doesn't drink, Elliot all of a sudden doesn't want alcohol, but at least Elodie knows that there's no limitation to when champagne is acceptable." She clinks her glass with

Elodie's and then shakes her head as my sight goes straight to Laney who's folding in her lips to keep from talking.

I arch a brow at her and then she does the same thing back to me.

Rhonan blows out a breath, but there's a smile on his lips. "No way."

Fletcher and Laney lock eyes and then he pulls her into his chest. "We were gonna wait until she was further along, but..."

Elodie slaps the counter. "Oh my God. Are you pregnant?"

Laney nods as a tear slips down her cheek. "Yes! I found out the morning we were supposed to leave for our honeymoon." Her eyes meet mine. "But then..."

"I'm so sorry you didn't get to leave," I interject, feeling even more guilty how this whole thing with Cole interrupted everyone's lives.

She reaches for my hand. "Nonsense. There's nowhere else we would have rather been. We're just glad you two are safe."

George Hart steps forward, tears in his eyes. "My baby is having a baby?" he says to Laney.

"Yes, Dad. You're going to be a grandpa again."

Everyone fights with their emotions as we celebrate Fletcher and Laney's news, but then Elliot steps toward me, his voice low. "Vienna, I..."

I reach out to hug him, whispering in his ear. "Thank you."

"Why are you thanking me? Me sending the papers is what brought your psycho ex to town."

I lean back and meet his gaze. "Yes, but I told you to. You just did what I asked of you because without your help, I wouldn't have been free from him. What happened is not your fault, okay?"

"It's not," Dilynne adds, holding her champagne flute out to him. "We talked about this, remember?"

Henley's brows draw together. "Wait. You two talked and there were no threats involved?"

Dilynne arches a brow at him as she takes a sip of her champagne. "I didn't say that."

Elliot releases me and flips Dilynne off, but I'm not going to lie. I'm intrigued about their conversation. If there's one thing that's been highly evident since I met this group, it's that those two barely tolerate each other.

Elliot places his hand on my shoulder. "Still, I'm glad that you're okay, Vienna. Not sure I could have gone through watching my friend lose another person that he loves."

"That means a lot, Elliot. Thank you."

Rhonan pulls me back into his arms. "And that's enough hugging."

Elliot rolls his eyes as everyone snickers. "Jesus, calm down. I'm not trying to steal your girl. Trust me, I have enough girl problems of my own at the moment."

"What do you mean?" Laney asks, but Elliot doesn't get a chance to respond before Ellis inserts herself back into the conversation.

"Ms. Vienna?"

"Yes, sweetie."

"Can I show you the drawing that I made for you now? It's in Daddy's room."

A yawn escapes my lips as I nod. "I would love that."

Rhonan clears his throat. "Actually, I think it's time that everyone takes off. Vienna needs to rest and…"

Laney holds her hand up. "Don't say another word. We are on our way out."

I pull Laney in for a hug before she gets too far. "Congratulations on the baby. And thank you."

"For?"

I lean back and meet her eyes. "For your friendship, for your support, and for bringing me and your brother closer. I—I sort of feel like Lydia brought me *you* too."

Laney instantly starts to cry. "Sorry, these damn hormones." She lunges for me again. "I'm so happy that you and Rhonan found each other, Vienna."

"Me too."

She lowers her voice to a whisper now. "And thank you for showing him that it is okay to love again."

"He's shown me the same thing. Now enjoy your trip tomorrow. Please."

"I'm ready. A little bummed I can't drink and celebrate my new husband," she says with a wink in Fletcher's direction. "But totally worth it."

When we part, I spend a few more minutes saying goodbye to our friends—because these people have become so very important to me as well—and then Rhonan and Ellis lead me back to Rhonan's room and help situate me in bed. Joanne stands in the doorway, watching our interaction.

"Can I show you my drawing now?" Ellis asks, reaching for a gold frame on the nightstand next to the bed and hiding it against her stomach.

Rhonan sits on the bed beside me, smiling at his daughter.

"Yes, I would love that."

"Okay." Ellis flips the picture around and I gasp as I see it.

"Oh my gosh, Ellis. This..."

Ellis looks at her dad, and he nods, as if she was seeking his encouragement. But instead of speaking, she tosses the picture at him and lunges for me, wrapping her arms around my waist as far as she can. "I love you," she whispers against my stomach, making me instantly cry.

"I love you too, Ellis." Rhonan swipes under his eyes too.

"I'm really happy that you're okay."

"Me too, sweetie."

Her head pops up and our eyes meet. "Will you be my mommy, please?"

"I would love to be your mommy, Ellis."

"Good. You're the best mommy on earth I could ever ask for."

Tears are streaming down my face as I make eye contact with Rhonan. "Just in case it's not clear, I'm gonna marry you someday soon, Vienna Lewis."

Ellis's head pops up. "Does that mean I get to wear a princess dress?"

Rhonan and I both laugh. "Yes, sweetie."

Ellis fist pumps the air. "Yes!" Then she reaches for the picture and holds it out to me again. "I drew you wearing a princess dress."

"I can see that." I've seen many of Ellis's drawings at this point, but I'm having trouble deciphering everything that's going on in this picture. "And what am I holding?"

"That's your rainbow trophy for saving me," she explains so matter-of-factly. "And Daddy is holding the cupcakes we made for you, and there's a rainbow in the sky."

"And what are you holding?"

"My baby sister," she says, making me gasp.

"Really?"

Rhonan shakes his head at me, which I'm guessing means he didn't tell her or doesn't want to tell her about the baby just yet.

"Yes, because I need a baby sister."

I cup the side of her face. "Is that so?"

"Yes."

"Okay then..."

"And these are all of the rocks we've painted," she goes on to explain, pointing to the circles of various colors she drew on the bottom of the paper. "But we need to paint more because I love painting rocks."

"I love that too." Another yawn leaves my lips as Joanne clears her throat from the door.

"Vienna needs some rest, sweetie," Joanne says to Ellis. "Maybe we can start making some cupcakes while she's sleeping and then decorate them together when she wakes up?"

Ellis nods enthusiastically. "Yes! We bought new rainbow sprinkles, Ms. Vienna."

"I can't wait to see them."

Ellis gives me one more hug. "Sleep tight."

"I will, sweet girl. Thank you."

Ellis runs out of the room just as Joanne walks in further. "I know you need to rest, but I want to bring something up to you two sooner rather than later."

"Everything okay?" Rhonan asks her.

Joanne has tears in her eyes. "Everything is perfect, Rhonan, because you've finally found someone to build a life with again, which means it's time for me to move on with mine too."

"Fuck, Joanne...really?"

"You can handle this now. You have Vienna. She'll be healed in no time, and with the new baby coming along, you're going to want your space to build your new family and new normal..."

I glance over at him. "You told her?"

"Yes. I had to tell someone, and she was going to find out sooner or later having you here," he explains before directing his gaze back to Joanne. "But I need you..."

"No, you don't. You and Vienna have a lot to figure out, and I'm not going anywhere until Vienna is back on her feet and you two have decided on your next steps, okay? But it's time that you build your family together. Besides, my family is in Charlotte and I'm ready to be a grandma." She smiles wide. "I just found out that my son is expecting his first child, and I want to be closer to them."

Rhonan stands from the bed and pulls Joanne into his chest, towering over her and enveloping her in his arms. "You have no idea how much I appreciate all that you've done for me."

Tears fill my eyes as I watch them.

"I do know that, Rhonan Hart. And you've given me purpose for the past five years. Me leaving doesn't mean that I won't still keep tabs on you and your family, but it's time everyone moves on, including me." When they part, none of us have dry eyes. "Like I said, I'm not going anytime soon, but I wanted to let you know so you can factor that in as you discuss what comes next."

Rhonan nods. "Thank you."

Joanne leaves the room and then he returns to his spot on the bed beside me. "Fuck, this is a lot to take in."

"She means a lot to you."

"I wouldn't have survived the past five years without her."

"But what about when we have this baby...*if* we have this baby..." My fear is ever present, even though I truly feel like things are all going to work out for us.

He presses a finger to my lips, silencing me. "Don't talk like that. This baby *will* be here in a little less than nine months and we can figure out what that's going to look like after you're healed, okay? We also need to decide if you want to stay home with the baby or fill in one of the vacancies at the school next year." Naturally, I told Rhonan about the possibility of me having a full time job at Blossom Peak

Elementary next year while I was lying in that hospital bed and we were discussing the future. Yet I'm still very much undecided.

I can feel my eyes growing heavy. "Okay. I can't believe that your sister is pregnant too though."

"It was taking all of my restraint not to blurt it out loud to everyone that you're pregnant as well."

"Maybe we should tell everyone then?"

"That's up to you."

I rub my stomach, staring down at it. "It might make me feel better to know someone else is going through the same thing."

"Then we'll tell them when Laney and Fletcher get back from their trip." Rhonan leans forward to kiss me. "I love you, Vienna. You are my future, and that's all I want to focus on now, all right?"

"I don't want a future if it doesn't involve you and Ellis."

"Same, baby. Get some rest. We have the rest of our lives to look forward to now."

Those words are the last thing I hear as I drift off into a deep sleep, thanking the universe for everything that I've gone through to get to this moment because this man is the type of man that Lydia told me I deserved—and now that I found him, I'm going to do everything I can to keep him and love him until my very last breath.

Chapter 31

Rhonan

A Plan None of Us Saw Coming

"Where the fuck is Elliot?" Henley asks, checking his phone again for the tenth time. "He's never this late."

Fletcher shrugs from his seat at the blackjack table. "Did anyone try to call him?"

Henley nods. "I did about ten minutes ago, and it just went straight to his voicemail, but then he sent me a text saying he was on his way." He glances back at the front door of my house. "But his office isn't that fucking far from your house, Rhonan."

"I'm sure he'll be here any minute," Fletcher says as he shuffles the cards on the table in front of him.

He and my sister got back from their honeymoon just a few days ago, and since it's been nearly three weeks since their wedding and longer than that since we've played blackjack, I invited the boys over to my place for a game tonight. Even though I knew that Joanne would be here with Ellis and Vienna, I didn't want to be too far away. I only just went back to work last week and I'm finding myself struggling when I'm away from the two of them, more than I care to admit.

I know time and talking it through with my therapist is the only way that anxiety will dissipate, but I've only had one session with my therapist so far, so I'm not exactly a straight A student yet in that capacity.

So, while the boys and I are playing blackjack, the girls, including my sister, are over at Vienna's house hanging out. Her lease is good for another three months, so we decided to keep her house for extra space and a place for us to hide to be alone once she's fully recovered, if you catch my drift. Once her lease is up though, she will be moving in with me and Ellis and then I'm gonna try to convince her to marry me before this baby is born once her divorce is finalized.

I want to make this woman my wife and I'm not going to waste any more time contemplating a timeline for that.

"Do you think the girls are going to be able to stay awake for the movie?" Fletcher asks me from across the table.

I chuckle. "Doubt it. Vienna will just fall asleep at random times right now. Between recovery and the baby, she doesn't have much energy at all."

Henley shakes his head. "I still can't believe that the two of you are going to have kids within a few weeks of each other."

As Vienna and I discussed after she got home, we decided to go ahead and tell everyone about our baby too. To say the reactions were a mix of shock and elation would be an understatement.

I think the person that was the most elated was my dad, though.

It's been a long time since I've seen him cry that hard but knowing he was going to get not only one, but two new grandbabies sent him reeling. The smile on his face has been permanent ever since he heard mine and Vienna's news as well, and he even told us that he's thought about trying to date lately.

"Seeing you take another chance on love has made me realize perhaps I should do the same."

Hearing those words from him is something that I'll never forget. For the longest time, he's been the person I've looked up to, admired, and respected so much. But in that moment, he told me that I was that person for him.

The past three months have taught me more about myself than years before have, and I'm soaking up each nugget of wisdom. I thought that at this point in my life, there wouldn't be much more for me to learn. I've gone through some of the toughest moments a man should have to, but like my dad said, suffering brings gratitude—and now, that is the promise I'm making to myself for this next phase of my life—to be grateful for the lessons, the blessings, and everything in between.

"Don't you want another kid?" Fletcher asks Henley as I reach for the bowl of pretzels in the center of the table.

"Hell yeah, I do. But I've got to put a ring on Elodie's finger first."

"Any ideas on when that might happen? You know, just so I don't steal your thunder," I tease.

He lifts a brow at me. "Already thinking about popping the question to Vienna?"

"She's having my child and sacrificed her life to save my other child. I think I'd be a fool if I didn't marry her."

Fletcher and Henley laugh. "Well, I do know the date of when I'm going to ask her to marry me," Henley continues just as the front door of my house opens, and Elliot comes barreling through, slamming it shut behind him.

"Fucking great. We're talking about marriage already?" Elliot yanks at his tie as he walks into the room and then darts to the kitchen, grabbing a beer from the fridge.

"Are you okay?" Fletcher asks. "You seem agitated."

"No shit." Elliot pops the top from the bottle and then drains the entire beer in one drink. He returns to the fridge for another and then empties half of that one before finally taking a seat at the table and groaning. "Motherfucker."

Henley taps the table. "I'm gonna go out on a limb and assume something is bothering you."

Elliot glares at Henley while Fletcher and I try to fight our laughter.

"You have no idea the hell that I've been in for the past two days."

Fletcher drops the cards on the table. "Start talking."

Henley nods as he drops the playful smile and leans forward. "Dude, we're here for you. You fucking know that."

I jostle his shoulder. "No more holding shit in, remember?"

His eyes bounce back and forth between us before he takes another sip of his beer. "Tori is back in town."

The three of us freeze as silence descends upon the room. "I...uh...Are you fucking serious?" I ask once I can finally form words.

Elliot huffs out a laugh. "Trust me, I wish I were joking."

Fletcher pushes a hand through his hair. "Fuck. I didn't see that one coming."

Elliot takes another drink. "Me neither, especially since now she's working at my parents' law firm."

Henley's jaw falls to the floor. "You're fucking joking. Please tell me you're fucking joking."

Elliot narrows his eyes at him again. "Do I look like I'm joking?"

Fletcher clears his throat. "What the actual fuck, man? Your dad hired her?"

"Yup."

"Why?"

Elliot blows out a breath. "I haven't fucking figured that out yet, but trust me, he got an earful from me yesterday. And then today, he returned the favor when..."

I tilt my head in his direction. "What happened today?"

Elliot sets his beer bottle on the table and then hangs his head in his hands. "I've sort of agreed to a fake relationship."

"With who?"

"I'm afraid you wouldn't believe me if I told you," he mumbles just loud enough for us to hear him.

Henley narrows his eyes at him. "Are you fucking serious?"

Fletcher and I share a look, clearly not up to speed.

Elliot lifts his head and locks eyes with Henley. "Don't hate me."

"I don't hate you, but my sister sure does."

"Well, if it makes you feel any better, it was her idea."

Fletcher's mouth falls open. "Wait..."

"No fucking way," I add.

Elliot blows out a breath. "Trust me, if I thought there was any other way to make Tori believe that there is no second chance for us, I would consider it. But I'm afraid this is the only option."

"You're going to pretend that *my* sister, Dilynne Clark, is *your* fake girlfriend?" Henley clarifies.

And then Elliot shocks us all even further. "Not just my girlfriend. My fiancé."

THE END

***

Do you want a glimpse at Rhonan and Vienna's future? Click here for an exclusive bonus epilogue!

Scan Here for the Bonus Epilogue

***

Ready for Elliot and Dilynne's story? It's About Time is coming July 10th!

Also By Harlow James

Somehow You Knew (Gage and Hazel)

***

The Ladies Who Brunch (rom-coms with a ton of spice)
Never Say Never (Charlotte and Damien)
No One Else (Amelia and Ethan)
Now's The Time (Penelope and Maddox)
Not As Planned (Noelle and Grant)
Nice Guys Still Finish (Jeffrey and Ariel)

***

The Newberry Springs (Gibson Brothers) Series
Everything to Lose (Wyatt & Kelsea)
Everything He Couldn't (Walker & Evelyn)
Everything But You (Forrest & Shauna)

***

The California Billionaires Series (rom coms with heart and heat)
My Unexpected Serenity (Wes and Shayla)
My Unexpected Vow (Hayes and Waverly)
My Unexpected Family (Silas and Chloe)

***

<u>The Emerson Falls Series (smalltown romance with a found family friend group)</u>
<u>Tangled (Kane & Olivia)</u>
<u>Enticed (Cooper & Clara)</u>
<u>Captivated (Cash and Piper)</u>
<u>Revived (Luke and Rachel)</u>
<u>Devoted (Brooks and Jess)</u>

***

<u>Lost and Found in Copper Ridge</u>

A holiday romance in which two people book a stay in a cabin for the same amount of time thanks to a serendipitous $5 bill.

<u>Guilty as Charged</u>

An intense opposites attract standalone that will melt your kindle. He's an ex-con construction worker. She's a lawyer looking for passion.

<u>McKenzie's Turn to Fall</u>

A holiday romance where a romance author falls for her neighborhood butcher.

Acknowledgements

It feels AMAZING to finally have this book out in the world, especially after the trouble it caused me.

The first draft of this book was NOT what you just read. LOL But I am beyond thrilled with the final result AND this series. It's fresh, emotional, and steamy. These men are down bad for their girls, and are willing to put in the work to keep them.

With each new series, I pinch myself that I get to write love stories and people read them. It is truly is an honor, and I hope to keep doing this for many years to come.

To my husband: Thank you for believing in me and cheering me on every step of the way. Thank you for traveling with me, investing in my success, and being my person, my best friend, the man that inspires all of my book boyfriends, and my official Book Bitch. I love you.

To my beta readers: Emily, Keely, Carolina, and Kelly: you four are the best voices I have in my corner. Each of you gives me the advice, feedback, and support that I need in your own way. I'm so grateful to have the four of you on my team still after all this time. I love you all and appreciate you more than you'll ever know.

To Kait, my P.A.: Hiring you has been one of the best decisions I've ever made. Your friendship and professional support have helped me so much this year. Thank you for being my newest cheerleader!

To Jess, my social media manager: You have single-handedly made my life better! I have so much more time to focus on writing and other aspects of my business thanks to you. Your time and creativity is appreciated SO much. Thank you from the bottom of my heart for doing what you do for me.

To Kari, my content team leader: I'm SO honored that you agreed to help me with this new aspect of my team! You are such an incredible support and I'm looking forward to how much we can grow this team together.

And to my readers: thank you for supporting me, whether you've been here since the beginning, or you're brand new. I LOVE this hobby turned business of mine. It's an amazing feeling to be able to create art for someone to enjoy and forming a relationship from that. I never take my readers for granted and know that there would be no Harlow James without you.

So thank you for supporting a wife and mom who found a hobby that she loves.
And a future career that I'm working toward with each passing day.

About the author

Harlow James is a wife and mother who fell in love with romance novels, so she decided to write her own.

Her books are the perfect blend of heartwarming, addictive, and steamy romance. If you love stories with a guaranteed Happily Ever After, then Harlow is your new best friend.

When she's not writing, she can be found working her day job, reading every romance novel she can find time for, laughing with her husband and kids, watching re-runs of FRIENDS, and spending time cooking for her family and friends while drinking margaritas.

Connect with Harlow James

Follow me on Amazon

Follow me on Instagram

Follow me on Facebook

Join my Facebook Group: https://www.facebook.com/groups/494991441142710/

Follow me on Goodreads

Follow me on Book Bub

Subscribe to my Newsletter for Updates on New Releases and Giveaways

Website

www.ingramcontent.com/pod-product-compliance
Lightning Source LLC
Chambersburg PA
CBHW031110160726
47991CB00004B/1314